A Wish for Christmas

A Wish for Christmas

A Cape Light Novel

THOMAS KINKADE

& KATHERINE SPENCER

JOVE BOOKS, NEW YORK
A Parachute Press Book

THE BERKLEY PUBLISHING GROUP
Published by the Penguin Group
Penguin Group (USA) Inc.
375 Hudson Street, New York, New York 10014, USA
Penguin Group (Canada), 90 Eglinton Avenue East, Suite 700, Toronto, Ontario M4P 2Y3, Canada
(a division of Pearson Penguin Canada Inc.)
Penguin Books Ltd., 80 Strand, London WC2R 0RL, England
Penguin Group Ireland, 25 St. Stephen's Green, Dublin 2, Ireland (a division of Penguin Books Ltd.)
Penguin Group (Australia), 250 Camberwell Road, Camberwell, Victoria 3124, Australia
(a division of Pearson Australia Group Pty. Ltd.)
Penguin Books India Pvt. Ltd., 11 Community Centre, Panchsheel Park, New Delhi—110 017, India
Penguin Group (NZ), 67 Apollo Drive, Rosedale, Auckland 0632, New Zealand
(a division of Pearson New Zealand Ltd.)
Penguin Books (South Africa) (Pty.) Ltd., 24 Sturdee Avenue, Rosebank, Johannesburg 2196,
South Africa

Penguin Books Ltd., Registered Offices: 80 Strand, London WC2R 0RL, England

A WISH FOR CHRISTMAS

A Jove Book / published by arrangement with Parachute Publishing, LLC

PRINTING HISTORY
Berkley hardcover edition / November 2009
Berkley trade paperback edition / November 2010
Jove mass-market edition / November 2011

Copyright © 2009 by The Thomas Kinkade Company and Parachute Publishing, LLC.
Cover design by Lesley Worrell.
Cover image of *Moonlit Sleigh Ride* by Thomas Kinkade. Copyright © 1992 by Thomas Kinkade.

ISBN: 978-0-515-15009-4

JOVE®
Jove Books are published by The Berkley Publishing Group,
a division of Penguin Group (USA) Inc.,
375 Hudson Street, New York, New York 10014.
JOVE® is a registered trademark of Penguin Group (USA) Inc.
The "J" design is a trademark of Penguin Group (USA) Inc.

PRINTED IN THE UNITED STATES OF AMERICA

10 9 8 7 6 5 4

This book is dedicated to the men and women in the U.S. military and to their families. With humble thanks for their great service and sacrifices.
—Katherine Spencer

CHAPTER ONE

$\smallfrown$

$\mathcal{L}$ILLIAN WARWICK HAD INVITED HER ENTIRE FAMILY to celebrate Thanksgiving at her house this year. In fact, she had insisted upon it.

This was despite the fact that Lillian was many years beyond entertaining and could no longer shop, clean, or cook. Or even arrange the table with her treasured set of heirloom china, her sterling silver flatware, and the lace-trimmed table linens that she had bargained for in the streets of Florence on her honeymoon, decades ago.

The truth was, Lillian had never expended much energy or interest in such homely tasks. For the better part of the matriarch's long life, there had been dutiful servants to carry out these mundane chores. Though Lillian had always been quite enthusiastic in directing exactly *how* things should be done.

And still was, her oldest daughter, Emily, knew well.

When Lillian had extended the invitation—more like a decree—to her two daughters, their husbands, and all her grandchildren, Emily knew that her own daughter Sara would be shouldering the lion's share of the work. Sara and her husband, Luke, had been living with Lillian in the looming, mansard-roofed Victorian on Providence Street for the past three years. The grand old house was certainly large enough to afford everyone their privacy, though Emily knew that her mother was so nosy and opinionated, it probably felt like very close quarters to Sara and Luke.

But this was the last holiday that Sara and Luke would spend as part of Lillian's household. They were moving to Boston the Saturday after Thanksgiving. Sara had found a new job, as a reporter for the *Boston Globe*, and they had signed a lease on a charming apartment in Cambridge.

Sara had broken the news to her grandmother in early November. As everyone had expected, Lillian had not taken it well. She had pouted and sulked ever since, making Sara feel very guilty. As if her granddaughter were abandoning a sinking ship.

Surely, Emily thought, her mother realized the young couple could not live there forever. The arrangement was originally meant to be temporary, some family help while Lillian recovered from a fall, but it had somehow solidified and dragged on.

"Your grandmother will have to make some adjustments. It's well past time," Emily had told her daughter. "I know you love her, but she's not your responsibility. She's mine. Mine and your aunt Jessica's, of course. Don't worry, we'll figure it out."

Emily had hoped her words had eased Sara's guilt and concern, or at least been a buffer to Lillian's dark looks and sulky silences.

The truth was, this Thanksgiving could be everyone's last holiday in the big house. Who knew what would happen once Sara and Luke left? Emily and her sister had been mulling over the possibilities for a long time. It definitely seemed time for their mother to downsize, which was a pleasant way of saying Lillian had to sell the place, move to some senior community, or move in with one of her daughters. But none of that had been discussed yet.

As her husband, Dan, drove up to the house and parked in the driveway, Emily could see they were the first to arrive. Carrying covered dishes and trays, they walked up the path to the side door, which led into the kitchen. Her mother hated it when guests came in through the kitchen.

"Dinner guests enter through the front door. Not the back, like servants or a delivery service."

But the etiquette faux pas could not be avoided. There was too much to carry. Sara was a wonderful cook, but Emily wanted to contribute something to the meal and had ended up assigned the salad and hors d'oeuvres.

Her younger daughter, Jane, who was only four, carefully carried a bowl of artichoke dip, which Emily hoped would make it to the kitchen intact. "Try to hold it straight, Janie," Emily told her.

Nearing the house, they found Sara outside, snipping sprigs of rosemary from a large bush near the kitchen door.

Emily kissed her cheek. "Hi, sweetheart. How's it going?"

"Grandma's driving me crazy. Luke and I have been cooking for two days, and nothing is right, of course."

Emily had expected as much. "Let me handle her. You did your part."

"And more, I'm sure," Dan added. He grinned at Sara, balanced a tray of stuffed mushrooms with one arm, and swung open the side door with the other. "Here we go, ladies. Ready or not."

Emily led the way into the house and soon found her mother in the kitchen. Lillian stood at the sink, holding a crystal wine goblet up to the light.

"Happy Thanksgiving, Mother." Emily placed her foil-covered dishes and trays on the table. "Wow, it smells delicious in here. What did you cook? Let me see . . ." Emily glanced at Sara with a proud, approving smile as she walked over to the stove where pots and pans covered every burner.

"Happy Thanksgiving," Lillian said absently, still turning the glass. "Or it would be if the table was set properly." She looked over at Emily. "These glasses are dirty. Spotty stemware ruins the whole table setting. You have to be more careful, Sara."

Before her exhausted daughter could reply, Emily stepped between them. "Here, let me see." Emily took the offending goblet in hand. She could not see a spot and doubted she would be able to find one even with a magnifying glass. But she made a good show of rinsing the wineglass under warm water. Before she could dry it, her mother snatched it away.

"I'll do it. The *right* way," Lillian insisted, wiping the glass carefully with a paper towel.

That was her mother for you. She not only saw the glass half empty, it was marred by a hideous spot.

"You had better check the rest, Sara," Lillian said. "Bring the dirty glasses in here to me. Hurry, the others will be here soon."

"I'll go," Emily offered. She walked into the dining room. "Oh, look at the table," Emily called back to Sara and her mother. "It's so beautiful, like something out of a magazine."

It was no exaggeration. The table really did look splendid. It must have taken Sara hours—polishing the silver; rinsing off the Wedgwood china dishes that were hardly ever used; ironing the cloth napkins, which had been folded into fan shapes; and even making the centerpiece, a combination of autumn-colored flowers and leaves and swirling vines.

Sara had even bought a chocolate turkey for each of the children, which she set next to their place cards. Emily expected Janie would want to eat hers before dinner; her grandmother would certainly have something to say about that.

Emily heard the chimes in the foyer sound and Luke calling out that he would get it.

Then she heard the door open and the voices of her sister Jessica, her brother-in-law Sam, and their two boys, Darrell and Tyler, all talking at once as they came in. Emily picked up two wineglasses and went back into the kitchen.

"They're here. It's about time." Her mother sighed, looking as if she were preparing herself to face some irksome but unavoidable duty. Hardly the doting grandmother, cheerfully greeting her offspring on a holiday.

Lillian smoothed the white satin cuffs on her gray wool dress and adjusted a cameo that hung from a gold chain.

"We had better get out there before the barbarians storm the kitchen," Lillian warned. "Children aren't taught any manners these days."

"Oh, Mother," Emily said with a laugh. "This isn't a state dinner at the White House. It's Thanksgiving."

"Do you need your cane, Grandma?" Sara asked.

Lillian shook her head, then held out her arm. "Just take me in. You know how I hate that walking stick. It makes me look like an old crone."

It really didn't, Emily thought. Her mother always dressed well and carried herself with great dignity. But Lillian would soon enough miss an arm to lean on, figuratively and literally. Emily looked on with mixed emotions as Sara dutifully stepped beside her grandmother, clasped her arm, and led her out to greet the family.

Her mother's big house sometimes seemed to Emily like a museum or the carefully preserved residence of some notable person—one with very limited hours open to the public. But today, filled with family, the house felt warm and full of life as rambling conversations and even laughter echoed through the long hallways and high-ceilinged rooms.

While Lillian greeted her guests in the large front parlor, Emily helped Sara and Jessica put the finishing touches on dinner. Emily smiled as she heard the sounds of a football game on TV. Normally, her mother did not permit TV viewing during family gatherings. Obviously, she had been overruled.

Of course, Dr. Elliot had been invited to join them. He had a gift for engaging Lillian in conversation and keeping her out of everyone else's hair. He had probably handled the delicate TV negotiations, Emily guessed. Ezra and Lillian had known each other since they were young, and it often seemed he was the only one who had any influence with her.

Of course at some point, her mother was bound to return to the kitchen to supervise.

"Isn't the meal ready yet? I'm about to faint away from low blood sugar." Standing in the doorway to the kitchen, Lillian surveyed the scene with a critical eye. "What's that you're adding to the gravy, Jessica? Light on the seasoning and the salt, please. I wake up parched in the middle of the night."

"Don't worry, Mother. It will be just right," Emily's younger sister, Jessica, promised. She turned to face Emily and rolled her eyes. They both knew that if it were left up to Lillian, the food would taste bland as cardboard.

Before her mother was able to take too many steps past the doorway, Emily stepped over and headed her off.

"We're just about to carve the turkey. Why don't you ask everyone to sit down at the table, Mother? You're the hostess, after all."

"Very well," Lillian agreed reluctantly. "And please don't serve until they're all settled in their seats. I don't want to go through all this trouble and eat cold food."

"Good point," Sara agreed.

Lillian nodded curtly and disappeared.

The three women stared at one another, then burst out laughing.

"Mother doesn't change, does she?" Jessica added a pinch of salt and a touch of fresh rosemary to the gravy.

"No, she doesn't." Emily glanced at Sara. "But I know it means a lot to her to have us all here. Let's just try to relax and enjoy it."

The family was finally seated and, with Dan and Luke's help, all the platters and bowls were brought in, and everyone began passing food around the table. When all the plates were full, Lillian bowed her head and led the family in a blessing.

"Dear Father, we offer our thanks for this bountiful table and the well-being of everyone seated here today. We ask for your continued blessings and guidance. On this Thanksgiving Day, please look into our hearts and help us understand the true meaning of . . . *gratitude*."

Emily saw her mother lift her head and catch Sara's eye. Her mother was sending her a silent message, even now, across the dinner table. Trying her best to make Sara feel guilty over her plans to move. As if she and Luke were horribly ungrateful grandchildren to abandon her this way. As if, at the very last minute, the young couple would suddenly see the error of their ways and change their plans.

Though these looks were blood-chilling, no sudden change of heart was likely, Emily knew. She wished her mother would give up and let Sara enjoy the day.

"Everything is perfect. I think we should make a toast to the cook," Emily proposed, raising her glass. "And to Luke, too."

Everyone raised their glasses. Even Lillian stuck her hand out and fiddled with her wineglass, though she didn't quite lift it.

"To Sara and Luke. Thank you for cooking this absolutely wonderful meal," Emily said. "And to my mother, for inviting us all here to share it."

"Thank you for the footnote, Emily," Lillian said huffily. "How kind of you."

"Cheers, everyone," said Dan.

Lillian seemed about to make some other disparaging

remark, but Dr. Elliot quickly leaned over and clinked glasses with her. "Lift your glass, Lily," he urged her. "You remember how to make a proper toast, don't you?"

"Don't be ridiculous. Of course I do." Lillian finally grudgingly lifted her glass all the way. "If the political speeches are concluded, I'd like to eat. Before my food is intolerable," she said, glaring at Emily. "If it isn't already."

"Try some hot gravy," Dr. Elliot said, passing the china gravy boat. "Does wonders."

"A doctor pushing gravy? There's something wrong with that picture, wouldn't you say?" Lillian shook her head but took the china boat from him anyway and ladled a minute amount over her plate.

"It's a holiday," Dr. Elliot told her. "We won't worry about our diets again until tomorrow."

The conversation jumped from cholesterol to current affairs. From gossip around town to the progress of Jessica's pregnancy.

"When are you due, dear? No, let me guess." Dr. Elliot squinted at her and rubbed his chin. "January . . . twenty-third?"

Sam put his arm around his wife's shoulders. "That's amazing. You hit it right on the nose, Ezra."

Dr. Elliot laughed. "I've brought a few babies into the world in my day."

"Or I mentioned the date and you remembered. It's marked right on my kitchen calendar," Lillian chided him.

Ezra shrugged and winked at Jessica. "That's possible, too," he admitted.

"Two months, I can't believe it. It's going to pass so quickly," Emily said.

"Not fast enough for me." Jessica sighed and pushed back from the table. "The last few weeks are the hardest part."

"I'm sorry we won't be here when the baby is born, Aunt Jess," Sara said. "But we'll come up as soon as we hear."

"Sara, how sweet. Don't worry about it. You'll see the baby when you can," Jessica said. "We're having Christmas Eve at our house. I hope you guys can make it."

Lillian sat back and sniffed. "She's moving to Boston, not the moon. Of course, she'll return for Christmas. That's a full month away. I expect she'll come back even sooner."

Emily understood what her mother was hinting at. Sara might stay in Boston with Luke's family for Christmas. Or go down to Maryland to her adoptive parents.

"We'll see, Mother," she said, running interference for her daughter. "They haven't even moved yet. I'm sure they don't know where they plan to be for the holidays."

"A lot will depend on how much time we get off at our new jobs," Sara explained. "I might have to work over Christmas, being low man on the totem pole and all."

"I don't see why a person would bother making a big move for a new job if they weren't going to get some preferential treatment," Lillian mused aloud. "It makes little sense to me. But that's none of my business, I suppose."

"It's the *Boston Globe*, Mother. It's a great opportunity for Sara." Emily knew she was stating the obvious. "Of course she'll pay her dues for a while. That's only fair."

At least Sara knew she understood. Emily had been ecstatic about Sara's new job and totally supportive of the move. Much as she wanted her to be here, she would never insist that Sara come back for Christmas. Emily knew that decision was Sara's. She also knew she had to share her daughter with Luke's family and with Sara's adoptive parents in Maryland.

Emily, her birth mother, had given Sara up when she was just a few days old. Emily had been barely nineteen when her husband, a commercial fisherman only a few years older, had died in a car accident just days before Sara was born. Emily's parents never approved of the match, and so she had eloped, leaving Cape Light.

After the accident, her mother appeared at her bedside

to help her recuperate and take her home. It was Lillian's idea to put the child up for adoption, and Emily finally agreed, believing she was making the best decision for her baby. But she had never gotten over the loss. She hadn't remarried or had another child. Her heart remained frozen in grief.

Until Sara came to Cape Light and found her. And Emily's life began again.

Of everyone at this table, Emily knew she would miss Sara the most. But the real question was not how often Sara and Luke would be back to visit. The real question was, what would happen to her mother once they were gone? How would she manage alone in this big mausoleum of a house? That's what everyone at the table should have been discussing, Emily thought. Instead, it seemed as though they had all made a silent pact not to talk about it, especially on the holiday.

As if honoring the pact, Jessica got to her feet and picked up a few plates. "Why don't we clear the dishes and bring out dessert? I made some beautiful pies."

"Yes, one for each of us," Lillian grumbled. "It's a regular smorgasbord. Though I did suggest that one or two would be plenty."

Ezra sighed wistfully and adjusted his bow tie. "Bring it on, young lady. Real whipped cream on top, I hope?"

Jessica smiled. "Yes, real cream, Ezra. As soon as we whip it up. We'll be right back."

Sara, Emily, and Jessica convened in the kitchen, cleaning up and putting food away while Dan and Luke carried in all the plates and glassware. Sam took the children outside so they could burn off some energy before the last lap at their grandmother's table. Emily could see them through the kitchen window, playing in the backyard with a Frisbee. Jane raced between her older cousins, unable to catch them and, occasionally, flopping on the ground like a rag doll, though she was always laughing.

"Those tights will go straight into the trash tonight," Emily said, turning away from the window. "But they really needed a little fresh air."

"They deserve a break from the grown-ups," Sara agreed.

The children had all been surprisingly well behaved during dinner—no chairs or water glasses overturned, no fights or whining.

"Sara, I hope your grandmother didn't make you feel pressured about Christmas," Jessica said as she stacked dishes in the dishwasher. "Of course we'd love to have you back, but whatever you decide is fine."

"Thanks, Aunt Jess. We'll figure it out . . . but I am concerned about something," Sara confessed. "It's Lillian. What's going to happen to her once Luke and I leave? I don't think she can live here on her own anymore, not without help. She acts very independent, but I'm not sure you both realize how much we do for her, how much she relies on us . . ."

Emily touched her arm. "We know, dear. We know how much you've been doing. It's been terrific of you to stay here and help her, Sara, honestly. I also know she's been trying to make you feel guilty about leaving, and that's not right."

"I know . . . but I just hate leaving everyone in the lurch. I mean, what's going to happen to her now? What's going to happen to this house?"

Emily and Jessica glanced at each other. "Don't worry. We'll take care of her," Emily promised. "We've always known that these questions would have to be faced, sooner or later."

"At least Mother is relatively healthy, and it's not an emergency," Jessica said.

"Well, not yet," Emily replied. "We'll have to figure it out quickly, though. You never know with someone her age. The situation can change overnight."

"Yes, it might," Sara agreed, sounding worried.

"We'll be looking in on her every day," Jessica reminded her. "Until we find a better solution."

Emily spooned leftover stuffing into a plastic container. "It would be nice if she would let us hire someone, just to keep her company. But you know how she is about strangers in the house."

Sara gave a helpless little shrug. "Maybe once we leave, she'll feel lonely and give in."

"Yes, maybe." Emily put an arm around her daughter's shoulders. "Sara, please don't worry. We'll sort it out. Your grandmother knows you love her and she loves you, no matter how she's acting right now. Once your byline shows up in the *Globe*, she'll be the first one bragging about you all over town."

"That's probably true," Sara said. "Remember when I first started working at the *Messenger*? Grandma and I weren't even close then, and she saved all my articles and put them in a scrapbook."

"Mother has always valued achievement," Jessica said. "I'm sure she's already proud of your new job."

"Though she'd rather die than admit it," Emily added. "She never has been easy—about anything."

"Can I be of help?" Ezra poked his head through the half-opened door. "A man can operate a sponge or even a hand mixer, you know. It's been scientifically proven."

Emily smiled at him. "Ezra, we'd be delighted to have you prove that theory. So far, I've never witnessed the phenomenon."

"Neither have I. Though Sam can make hot wings and pizza," Jessica added.

"Step aside. I'll show you how it's done." Ezra slipped off his jacket and hung it neatly on the back of a chair. "You realize I'm just trying to speed up the appearance of the pies."

"I do," Emily said with a laugh. "But it's nice of you to

admit it." She handed him an apron, a bowl, and the hand mixer, and he quickly set up shop.

"Don't ever underestimate seniors, my dear. We can be rather resourceful."

"I wouldn't dare, Ezra," Emily promised. She already knew a bit about how crafty seniors could be. And in the days to come, Emily had a feeling, she would be learning entirely new chapters on the subject.

IN ORDER TO MAKE ABSOLUTELY SURE THAT THEIR DINNER would not be interrupted, Jack Sawyer had nailed a sign to the fence of the Christmas tree farm:

CLOSED FOR THANKSGIVING—SEE YOU TOMORROW

Then, for good measure, he removed the clapper from the brass bell that customers used to call him from his house and carried it inside like a prize.

David had never seen his father do that, not in all the years he had grown up here. But things were different now that his father had married Julie. Everything was different.

"There." Jack dropped the brass bell piece on the kitchen table. "Just in case some crazies decide they have to pick out their Christmas tree today."

Julie stood at the stove cooking, where she had been stationed since the morning. She glanced at him over her shoulder and laughed. "Good move, Jack. That will do it."

"Thank you, dear. I thought so."

Julie and Jack had been married about eight months, but they seemed so in tune with each other, David thought it could have been years.

"I hope you can put that bell back together," she added. "We're going to need it."

"Don't worry. I can fix it." Jack walked up behind her and brushed her cheek with a quick kiss.

David sat in the living room reading the paper but could see and hear them clearly. When his father glanced his way, suddenly aware that someone else was there, David stared intently at the sports section.

"Hey, Dave. Doing okay?" David looked up from the paper and nodded. "Need anything?"

"I'm fine." They both knew it was better for David to get up on his own if he needed something. But ever since he had come home, his father was ever watchful, ready to bring him a cold drink, a cup of hot tea, a beer, the newspaper, the TV remote. Anything to spare David an extra step, an extra moment of pain.

Maybe at one point in his life David would have enjoyed, even encouraged, that kind of attention. But the army had effectively weeded out such lazy, immature tendencies. David knew his father meant well, but sometimes it was hard to fend him off politely.

"Julie says dinner is going to be a while longer. I think there's a game on, college ball. Should I try to find it?" His father picked up the remote and aimed it at the TV.

"I don't care. You can watch if you want."

"It's okay. I'd rather watch the pros." His father clicked off the TV set again and sat down next to David on the couch. "Feel like a game of chess . . . or some cards?"

David considered the offer. His head was pounding and his hip ached. He wasn't sure what was worse—taking the pain medication and feeling foggy and out of touch, or enduring the pain and being out of sorts and unable to focus.

"Maybe later. I think I might lie down awhile. I didn't sleep much last night."

His father knew all about that. The night before, David had woken up screaming from one of his nightmares, and Jack had run down to help him before he could stumble out of bed and injure himself.

"Oh . . . sure. Good idea." Jack jumped up and grabbed David's walker and then brought it around to the side of the couch so David could pull himself up.

David focused on balancing himself and shifting his weight, good side to bad, the foot that had feeling to the one that had gone numb. Step-by-step, he managed to make it out of the room and into the kitchen.

Behind him, he could hear his father let out a long sigh. David could almost feel Jack itching to help him but holding himself back. Which made David feel even more frustrated.

David knew his father felt bad for him, watching him on the walker. David felt worse. He hated having to drag himself around on the metal support like a decrepit old person. But that's where he was right now. He only hoped he would get rid of it someday.

When that day came, he was going to put this darn hunk of metal in the middle of a road somewhere and run it over. Then turn the vehicle around and do it again.

As he passed the doorway to the kitchen he saw Julie and her daughter, Kate, setting the kitchen table for dinner. The house didn't have a dining room so all their meals, holidays or not, were eaten in the kitchen. That was the way it had been all through David's childhood, and it was good to see that tradition hadn't changed.

"Hey, David. We're making everyone a surprise," Kate called out. "I'm making one for you, and Mommy is making one for Jack."

David couldn't help smiling at his stepsister. She was like a walking, talking flower, he thought. She had stolen his heart the first minute they met. The feeling seemed mutual, too. Kate followed him around like a puppy. He hardly ever minded. He had time on his hands and plenty extra to give her attention.

"Want to see your surprise?" Kate asked him eagerly.

David could already tell from the cutout shapes of colored paper that his surprise was going to be something in the turkey family. But he didn't want to ruin it for her.

"Sure I want to see it. But then it won't be a surprise, silly."

She leaned back in her seat. "Oh . . . right. I forgot."

"David will see it later, honey, when we have dinner. I think he wants to go into his room now, for a rest." Julie looked up and smiled at him. "Dinner will be ready in about half an hour. I shouldn't have bought such a big turkey. It's taking forever. Do you need anything?"

"I'm okay." David forced a smile then turned away. He gritted his teeth and pushed on with the walker. His hip was hurting something awful, and he hoped lying flat would ease the pain.

When he got into his room, he swung the door shut, ambled to his bed, and dropped down. Then he stretched out and let out a long breath, waiting for a wave of pain to pass. His father and Julie meant well. They were only trying to help. He knew that. But it was hard. He felt as if they were watching him every minute. As if he were a creature, the kind he used to collect out in the woods and keep captive in a glass tank in his room.

Julie was all right. It would have been even harder being here alone with his father, that was for sure. Something about Julie's even temperament balanced out the house and made everyone calmer.

From the minute that he met Julie, almost a year ago, David could tell she was perfect for Jack. Just as calm and patient as his mother, Claire, had been. Just as sweet and kind. Just what Jack needed. His father nearly let Julie slip away, but David had told him to take a chance and chase after her. It was the only advice he had ever given Jack, and it changed his father's entire life.

After David's mother died when he was eighteen and David left Cape Light, his father had been lost, buried alive in his grief, but Julie and her daughter, Kate, had brought

Jack back to life again. His father's nursery and landscaping business was booming now, and the Christmas tree farm had never looked better. David could see that Julie helped Jack a lot with the business, even though she had taken a job as an art teacher at a school in town. David was truly happy for his father, happy for them both.

Still, it was hard to come back to the place he had always known as home; it felt so different now. Not just because of Julie and Kate. Because of what he had been through, what he had seen. Because he had been living on an army base in the middle of the desert, feeling he had been dropped on another planet. And now that distant place seemed like reality and here at home, in the place that should be familiar, he felt like a stranger in a strange land.

Sometimes David thought that spending most of the first two months after his tour in the hospital had been a good thing. The hospital wards had been a spare, controlled environment where he didn't have to deal directly with the shock of leaving army life and the jolt of returning to the States.

Those weeks were a blur, the operations and days on pain medication melting one into the next. He could barely remember any of it now, though at times the pain in his bad leg was still fearsome, almost enough to make him cry.

He was not fully recovered, physically or emotionally. But he was home, back in a world that was at once so familiar and so foreign.

He had been home four weeks and he still wasn't used to it. At times he felt worse instead of better. Though he hated to let on to his father or Julie when he was having a rough time, he was sure they could tell. He wasn't exactly Mr. Easy to Be Around. But they had a lot of patience, too much maybe. They had both been making such a fuss over him. Especially his dad.

When Jack came to see him at the hospital in Germany, where David had been transported from Iraq for surgery,

Jack could not stop crying. Tears ran down his father's face; he didn't even try to hide them or hold them in. David had never seen his father like that, not even at his mother's funeral.

"Thank God you're alive." David remembered how Jack choked out the words through his tears. "You'll get through this, son. Whatever it takes, you'll get through it. You're alive, that's all that matters. You're a lucky one, David. An angel was watching over you."

At the time, David felt the same. Why had he been chosen to survive the attack when the soldier sitting right next to him had not? He had seen guys get hurt over there plenty of times. Lots of them left in much worse shape. At least he had come out of it with both arms and legs. He hadn't been burned or crushed by the exploding metal. He hadn't bled to death in the wreckage.

His left leg was healing pretty well. It had been badly fractured and had pins and a metal piece holding it together now. But his right hip and leg were so screwed up, he might not walk again without a walker. But he had to be grateful, didn't he? That's what everyone told him. He was lucky, very lucky.

He had to be thankful, David reminded himself. Today, of all days, he couldn't let himself sink into a swamp of the blues and bitter self-pity. He couldn't focus on what he had lost, the pain that was almost continuous, the broken places that would never heal. Picking over the plans and hopes that had been taken from him. Or the fear of what would be.

What if he never walked normally again? He wasn't even twenty-three years old. How could he live like this? What kind of work would he find? What kind of woman would want to be with him?

Not Christine. She was engaged. It was no use even thinking about her. It had helped while he was in Iraq to think of her, to imagine he would come back and persuade her to be with him again. That was just a soothing daydream to help him get through the worst of it. He could see that now.

She had called the house a few times since his return, but he didn't want to see her. He kept telling his father to make excuses. Pretty soon she would get the hint and give up. Maybe she had given up already. They went back a long way, and she just felt sorry for him; he knew that.

Thinking about Christine was just another kind of pain. David had learned the full A-to-Z list this past year. If they gave out college degrees for such matters, he would be a PhD by now.

DAVID WASN'T SURE HOW LONG HE HAD BEEN ASLEEP. THE room was dark when he opened his eyes, and his father was standing in the doorway, calling to him. "David? Can you get up? Time for Thanksgiving dinner."

David shook his head. "I'll be there in a minute," he promised, though he knew it would take much longer to maneuver himself out of bed and make the short trip from his room into the kitchen.

He lay in bed, wondering if he could somehow avoid joining the family. He could say he had too much pain to get out of bed, or he felt too tired. It suddenly felt as if he were facing some sort of ordeal, just going out there and having to make small talk with all of them.

But a few moments later, he gathered his energy and pushed himself up and off the bed. He had to at least try. Julie had been cooking all day, and his father had been making such a big deal of this holiday. If it felt like too much, he could always excuse himself.

When he finally arrived in the kitchen, the family was already seated around the table, waiting for him. He awkwardly shifted from the walker into a chair. His father made a quick move to help him, but David stopped him. "I'm all right, Dad."

His father nodded and sat back down again. David noticed Julie glance across the table and meet Jack's gaze, but she didn't say anything.

"So, do you like your surprise?" Kate asked him, breaking the tense silence.

David felt as if someone had shaken him awake from a dream. He stared around and finally realized what his little stepsister was talking about. A colorful object, made from construction paper, sat on top of his dinner plate. He guessed it was a turkey, though it was unlike any bird he had ever seen. He picked it up and looked it over with interest, noticing his name spelled out on the tail, one letter on each feather.

"Wow, look at that. My own personal turkey! Did you make this for me?"

Kate nodded quickly, obviously pleased by his reaction. "I did."

"That is something else. Thanks, Kate. I love it."

Julie smiled at him. He saw Jack trying to hide a grin, too.

"Nice touch." Jack held up his own construction-paper turkey then put it aside. "Thank you, ladies. But I'm starved and ready to pounce on the real one. What do you say, everybody?"

"I say, how about a little blessing over the meal before we begin?" Julie reminded him.

"Oh . . . right. How could I forget, on Thanksgiving no less? When we have so much to be thankful for this year," Jack added, looking over at David.

David didn't know what to say. His father was thankful enough for his return for both of them. For all of them.

Jack bowed his head. "Dear Father above, we humbly thank You today for the many blessings You've given our family. For our good health and well-being. For the bounty of food on this table. For all that You provide in our lives, every day of the year. We are most thankful for the well-being of our family and for the safe return of our beloved

David. Help us to remember the important things in life and to cherish those near and dear."

David had heard his father say grace countless times at a holiday meal. But had never known Jack—who was normally not the most eloquent guy in the world—to deliver such heartfelt words.

"Amen," Julie said. She lifted her head and smiled at her husband. "I'll bring the turkey over, and while you carve, Jack, I'll get the side dishes."

"Good plan. Just swing that bird my way. I'll have it carved in a jiffy." Jack stood up, wielding his carving knife and long fork, and began slicing. "Who wants a drumstick?" he asked.

Kate raised her hand, as if she were in school. "I do!"

Jack gazed around, pretending he didn't hear her. "Nobody wants a drumstick? Hey, guys, that's the best part."

"Me! I want a drumstick, Jack." Kate kneeled on her seat, trying to get his attention.

Jack cupped his ear. "Do you hear something?" He gazed around and looked at David. "Do you hear like . . . a little mouse or something . . . saying she wants a drumstick?"

David shook his head. "I don't hear a thing. A mouse, you said? Like, a little squeaking sound?"

Kate sat back, giggling, finally figuring out the joke. David laughed, too. His father had pulled the same stunt on him when he was Kate's age.

Jack put the precious drumstick on Kate's dish just as Julie returned to the table. "Jack, you two. Now she's all giggling and practically falling out of her seat."

It was true, Kate was a silly little mess. Jack had gotten her going.

"Oh come on now, it's a holiday. And we have plenty to celebrate." Jack glanced at David then delivered the second drumstick without even asking.

"That is so true." Julie sat down and began passing around

the many side dishes—sweet potatoes, stuffing, mushrooms, fresh cranberry sauce, string beans, and red cabbage.

"Wow, this food looks awesome," David said. "I haven't had a meal like this in ages."

His words were not an exaggeration. This was the first time since leaving home almost four years ago, right after his mother died, that David had shared a family holiday dinner. Most of that time when he was away, he had been working—at a gas station or in a restaurant kitchen, or at some other drudge job where the staff worked while the rest of the country celebrated.

"You enjoy it, David," Julie said. "The best part is having you here to share it with us."

"Amen to that," Jack agreed between mouthfuls.

David didn't know what to say. Their gratitude over his safe return was sometimes overwhelming.

It made him feel a bit small, being so focused on his own problems that he had to force himself to come out here a few minutes ago. He resolved to pull himself together, at least long enough to get through dinner, and not spoil everyone's day.

CHAPTER TWO

~~~

THE SUITCASE WAS BACK HERE SOMEWHERE. GRACE was sure of it. Why, she had seen it just a few weeks ago when she pulled out that brass torchère lamp. The bag with the straw weaving and thick leather straps. The handle was frayed, Grace recalled, but she could probably fix it.

If she could find it. Grace had to open the shop in a little while, and she was prepared for a busy Saturday, the first after Thanksgiving, bringing a wave of Christmas shoppers.

She did want to open on time and made a final effort to find the case. She peered into the pile of antiques, near antiques, and just plain junk haphazardly stacked all around the loft. The bare bulb hanging from the rafters did not provide much light, but she had thought ahead and brought along a flashlight.

Its thin, sharp beam darted around the collection like a firefly, bouncing off the wood beams, decorated with cobwebs like crepe paper left over from some long-forgotten celebration. The light fell here and there, randomly illuminating a broken rocking chair, a large hall mirror with a gilt-edge frame, a tattered wedding veil with a pearl tiara, a coat tree draped with dusty hats, and large black umbrellas.

One of these days, when she had the time and energy, she would sort things out up here, get it in some kind of order. Grace made that promise every time she came up. But her business, the Bramble Antique Shop, and her responsibilities caring for her father, kept her busy.

Luckily, her life was pretty much condensed into a small space, with the shop on the first floor of their Victorian house and their apartment taking up the two upper stories. The efficient arrangement suited her. Half the big barn in back held stock. The other side was rented out to Sam Morgan for his woodworking business. Grace could hear him in there now, making a racket with an electric saw.

Now Christmas was coming. Grace braced herself, though she doubted the trade would be overwhelming this year, with the bad economy. It was the kind of year when people were giving needful things, not china teapots and cloisonné figurines. That's why when a special request came in from one of those fancy decorators, it was best to hop to it. You got a good reputation that way. One would tell another and before long, you had a nice clientele of those folks, professional shoppers for rich people. They hardly cared how much they spent. After all, it was someone else's money.

Enough of those decorators coming around and you wouldn't have to worry so much about the regular shoppers, the perennial browsers, looking and looking and hardly buying a thing. Especially the ones who always offered less at the register, even when they could see the price marked on each item, clear as day.

People thought her business was easy. Well, it was not.

She stepped back and sighed, about to give up on her quest. The dust was getting to her. She took out a tissue and dabbed her eyes and nose. She must have imagined the suitcase. She could have sworn there were two, and she had sold the other last summer. Maybe there had only been one? Was she getting old and confused now like her dad? Lord help them both if that was true.

Then, the moment she pocketed the flashlight, she saw it. Down at the bottom of a pile, but thankfully, not under too much paraphernalia. She crouched down, moved some boxes and a small ballroom chair with a torn velvet seat cover, then carefully shimmied it loose.

Eureka. Just what the decorator asked for.

Grace examined the suitcase. The brass latches and hardware on the leather belts would look fine with a little polishing. The straw was worn in some places, but that added to its charm. So did the stamped gold monogram near the handle, *P.G.H.*

She took hold of the leather handle, about to carry it down, then paused. It seemed awfully heavy. She didn't want to kill herself climbing down the ladder with that load.

Of course, there must be something in it making it so heavy. Clothes or books, old shoes or some such. Everything was such a muddle up here, you never knew what you might find.

Grace set the case down flat and flipped open the latches. She hoped it wasn't locked. Where would she ever find the key?

The first latch opened easily. The other side was stuck. She found a metal doorstop shaped like a squirrel and gently tapped the latch. Finally, it sprang open.

Grace leaned forward and slowly lifted the top of the suitcase. It did feel like there was something bulky inside.

She saw an old sweater, the fisherman-knit type. Dark gray, full of moth holes and not very pleasant smelling, either. It had to be her father's. She pushed it aside, expecting more useless old garments. But that's not what she found. Not at all.

Grace looked down into a suitcase full of money. Bills and more bills, neatly stacked and secured by thick rubber bands.

Her breath caught in her throat, and she thought her heart missed a full beat. What in the world?

She picked up a wad of money and examined it. Was this some sort of joke?

She pulled out the flashlight then pulled off the rubber band. The bills scattered and floated down into the case, covering the sweater. Grace dug her hands into it and felt the paper.

For mercy's sake . . . the money was real. Big bills, mostly hundreds and fifties. She pressed a few to her nose. On those detective shows she and her dad watched on TV, the investigators always said you can tell fake money by the odor. This money smelled real to her. It had a vaguely fishy scent, no doubt from being imprisoned with that sweater for who knew how long. But it definitely looked, felt, and smelled like real money.

And if it wasn't, why would she find a suitcase full of fake money up here? Under her father's old fishing sweater? Well, that would make even less sense, she reasoned.

Her father. He was the one to ask about this treasure chest.

Grace put the bills back inside then closed the case. It took some ingenuity, but Grace got the suitcase down from the loft with the use of a length of clothesline. She watched it land on the floor below, then quickly followed.

Grace entered the building by the back door, then lugged the suitcase up the back stairway to their apartment. She soon found Digger in the kitchen, fixing himself breakfast.

"Found that old suitcase you were looking for? Good for you," he said mildly. "You already made one good sale today, Gracie, and you ain't even opened the shop yet."

Grace stared at him a moment. Over the last few years,

her father's memory had grown foggier and so had his powers of reasoning. It was impossible to tell if he really had no connection to what was inside the case—or if he just didn't remember.

"Dad," Grace began calmly, "don't you recognize this case? I think it's yours. See the monogram? Your initials."

As she pointed out the gold stamp to him, Digger glanced down, barely missing a beat as he slathered a slice of pumpernickel toast with strawberry preserves made with the berries from Grace's garden.

"So it is. Nice-looking piece. They don't make them like that anymore. But you can have it. It's probably too heavy for me to haul around these days anyways. Inconvenient, and I sure ain't going anywhere real soon."

"It is heavy," she admitted.

She didn't want to shock him, not in his frail condition. But it was hard to work her way around to the fact that the case was full of money. Full to the brim.

Digger was just about to bite into his toast. Grace rested her hand on his arm. "Dad, wait a second. I need to show you something."

He stared at her, obviously confused. "What is it, Gracie? Something wrong?"

"I hope not," she said carefully. "I found something in the case. It must be yours. It's really quite . . . quite a shock when you see it. Prepare yourself."

She set the case down on the floor and crouched down to open it again. Her father was watching but still didn't seem to remember anything special about the old suitcase.

She popped the latches, lifted the top, and then stood up. "There, see what I mean. Look at all that money. Can you believe it?"

She heard Digger draw in a quick breath. He leaned over to take a closer look. "Well, I'll be . . . That's a pile of greens, all right." He looked at Grace. "You say you found it just now? Sitting right in there?" He pointed toward the barn. "I'll be a monkey's uncle."

Grace sighed. He didn't remember anything about it, did he?

"Yes, Dad. I just found it. I think it's real, too. See?" She picked up some bills and let him handle them.

Digger examined the money and nodded his head. "Seems real to me, though I guess you need to take it to a banker to tell for sure."

"Probably," she agreed. "I'm just wondering how it got there. Any ideas coming to you? I found this old sweater on top of it, sort of covering it. Looks like yours."

She pulled the sweater from a plastic bag and showed it to him. Her father's face lit up, looking much more excited and pleased by the sight of the old ragged sweater than what Grace guessed had to be thousands of dollars.

"My sweater! Well, what do you know? Where did you find this?"

"In the suitcase, sitting right on top of the money," Grace repeated patiently.

Digger lifted the beloved sweater up to feel the rough wool on his cheek and inhaled the smell. Then he gently laid it in his lap, stroking it as if it were a living thing, a little pet cat, perhaps. "Your mother made me this sweater. Gave it to me one Christmas, not too long before she died. Remember?"

Grace shook her head. "No, Dad. I'm sorry, I don't remember that."

"Oh well, she did." Grace believed him. His memory for distant events was still quite accurate. "After she died, when I sold the house on Clover Street, I didn't want much inside. I let you and your sisters take the lot of it."

"Yes, I remember," Grace said. His mind was wandering again. He didn't even seem to notice the money anymore. Why was he talking about the old Clover Street house? The sweater must have reminded him.

Grace lost hope of him offering any explanation for the

suitcase, at least right now. "You just took your clothes and books and maps. You told us to split up the rest."

"Yes, I did." Digger nodded. "I took this sweater. And some other stuff. I gave you girls all the money, too. Most of it, anyways. Set some aside for my old age . . . and then another little chunk, just in case." He looked down at the case and poked it with his toe. "I expect that's what this here is. That little chunk I squirreled away. Sort of like an inheritance for you, Grace. A gift for taking care of your old man all these years. You were supposed to find it after I passed on."

So, he did remember. Grace stared at him. His intentions were touching, but Grace couldn't help but find fault with his plan. "After you passed on? How was that supposed to happen? Did you leave a note about it somewhere for me?"

"Not that I recall . . ." He shook his head, as if the effort of all this thinking was wearing him out. "But what are you complaining about, Grace? You found it, didn't you? And I'm not even dead."

Grace was momentarily stumped by this logic. She could see it was useless to argue the point any further.

She looked down at the suitcase again. "I guess I'll have to bring that to a bank. Bet I get some good service when they see that deposit."

"A bank?" Her father nearly choked. Looking the most animated she had seen him during this entire conversation, he shook his head. "No, ma'am. No banks."

"Dad, what are you talking about? Of course we have to put it in a bank. Why in the world not?"

"Don't trust them, that's why. Open your eyes, Gracie. Bankers are . . . Why, they're shifty-type people. I'm not letting them get their grubby fingers on a dollar of mine. I saved that money all these years. For you. I'm not letting it out of this house."

Grace let out a long, exasperated sigh. "Do you think it's safer in an old suitcase, stuck up in the rafters of the barn, than in a big, solid bank?"

He didn't answer, just frowned and started eating again.

"Anything could have happened to it by now, Dad. A leak in the roof . . . a fire . . . a robbery . . ."

The more calamities she listed, the less he seemed to be listening. "How about a safe-deposit box?" she asked. "It's solid metal, and they give you your own key. It would still be hidden, and it's very secure, Dad. Honestly."

Digger picked up a bit of toast crust and popped it into his open mouth. "Oh, heck. The money's yours now. Do what you like with it."

"That's not true, Dad. I don't want to do anything with it that upsets you. I'm not going to make any decisions without your say-so," she promised him. "I just want to be . . . reasonable about this. There's a lot of money in there. It's not safe sitting here in the middle of everything."

"How much would you say is there, Grace? Just ballpark."

"Oh, I don't know." Grace leaned over and looked into the case again, studying the neat, thick piles of green bills. "At least thirty thousand. Maybe more."

"A tidy sum." Digger finished his toast and began cutting up an apple with his pocketknife. He offered Grace a slice on the blade, the way he always had when she was a girl.

"Yes, very tidy." She bit down on her apple slice and chewed.

"It's funny but I can't think of anything I want to buy. Can you?" Digger asked her.

Grace thought for a moment. "No, I really can't. We have all we need, thank heaven. We are very blessed, Dad."

"Yes, we are, Grace, blessed indeed. I'm just thinking that maybe we could use some of that money to help some folks who don't have so much as us. Being it's Christmas coming and everything."

Grace lifted her head and looked at him. "That's a nice idea. It's just found money. Really found money," she added with a short laugh at her unintended pun. "We should give some to charity."

"Yeah, sure. Charities are okay. But I was thinking more of folks we know, right here in town. Families are hurting. This one's lost a job. That one's got medical problems or the furnace broke down. You don't have to look too far these days to find folks in need. I'm figuring a few handfuls of that money, sprinkled around the village, will go a long way to giving some folks a happy Christmas."

Grace was surprised at her father's proposal. She'd never even thought of it. It wasn't that she didn't like to help people. She did, if she could. She always volunteered at church and gave to the special causes, emergency relief for an earthquake or famine in some far-off corner of the world. She slipped donations into the mail for all kinds of charities—from cancer research to protecting polar bears. It was important to do that, Grace thought. If everyone helped just a little, the world would truly be a different place.

But easing the burdens of people they knew, that was another thing altogether. She would never be known about town for showing her feelings openly to others. That just wasn't her way, had never been and never would be.

Grace knew very well some people thought she was cold and unfeeling. Just because she was uncomfortable calling attention to herself, it didn't mean she didn't notice or lacked sympathy.

She had certainly had her share of problems in life. They had not been big earners, she and her father. But they had been careful savers and made good investments. She now had plenty to retire on when the time came and enough to take care of her dad for as long as he lived.

It seemed that so many now were falling on hard times. Just the other day she heard two women talking while they browsed in her shop. One said that her husband had been sick and lost his job, and now they were buried under a pile of medical bills. The couple was thinking of selling their house, but maybe even that desperate move wouldn't solve the problem.

Grace had felt so sorry for her. When the woman asked the price of a bone china teacup she had been admiring, Grace insisted that the price tag said two dollars, when she knew very well it said twenty. When the woman seemed confused, Grace pointed out an imaginary chip and claimed she had to mark it down. It was a small gesture. But she hoped the pretty piece would bring the woman some plea-sure.

What her father was proposing would be a real help to people. An answer to their prayers.

"So, what do you think, Gracie?" Digger prodded her. "Should we do it?"

Grace nodded quickly, a lump in her throat. "I think we should, Dad. I think it's a fine idea. I'd like for us to be anonymous, though. I don't want any attention for this. You know this town. All you have to do is offer someone a tissue, and your picture winds up on the front page of the newspaper. That doesn't seem right."

Digger laughed. "That's the same way I feel about it. I don't want anyone to know. I don't want anybody to feel beholden to us. That's the way it ought to be, giving for giving's sake."

"Right." Grace nodded, then shut the suitcase. "That settles it then. We have some figuring out to do, I guess."

"Yes, we do. What do you plan to do with the money in the meanwhile?"

Grace thought a moment. It would be best, under the circumstances, she thought, to keep the money handy.

She walked over to the cupboard and took out a roll of foil and a box of Ziploc bags. "I'm going to wrap it up and put it down in the deep freeze. It will be safe there. God forbid we have a fire. No one will find it under all that fish, that's for sure."

Her father had been a commercial fisherman all his life, the fastest, most successful clammer in the area. Some-times he claimed he could hear the clams under the sand, trying to hide from him. Sometimes Grace believed that, too. But her father had been no stranger to fishing boats either—out in every season, in all kinds of weather, casting his nets on the choppy waters.

In his retirement, Digger fished for pleasure and not even much of that anymore, though his friends Harry Reilly and Sam Morgan would take him out from time to time in the summer. Her father always brought home such a large catch that Grace suspected Sam and Harry were contributing, filling their deep freeze with enough fish to last all winter long.

Her father nodded approvingly as she began wrapping stacks of bills in foil. "Good thinking, Grace. I like that idea better than some old bank. Maybe you could bring up some scrod while you're down there and cook it up for dinner?"

"Yes, Dad. That's the least I can do, seeing how you're making such a grand gesture with your windfall."

Digger laughed. "I always liked dressing up as Santa when you and your sisters were little. That's why I kept this long beard."

"All you need now is a red hat and a sleigh."

It was good to see her father so happy and animated, his mind engaged in such a worthwhile endeavor. Grace knew in her heart, her father wasn't going to be around forever. But this was going to be a special Christmas. One she would always remember.

As Emily drove to her mother's house on Saturday morning, she reminded herself that she knew this day was bound to come. Well, here it was. No avoiding it. Sara was moving.

Why did it feel like such a shock? Emily had known for weeks now. Actually, she had always known it would happen, the possibility hovering just around the corner, ever since Sara had appeared in her life, an amazing, second-chance miracle.

They'd had six years together now. It had been a challenge in many ways to suddenly jump into the role of mother to a grown daughter. Sara had been angry with her at first, rightfully so. And there had been some tension with Sara's adoptive family, who couldn't understand Sara's need to remain in Cape Light.

Sara's adoptive parents thought Emily had pressured Sara to stay in town and work on the newspaper. But that had been all Sara's idea. Emily had rejoiced, of course. And after Sara and Luke were married, Emily secretly wished the couple would find their own home in town and put down real roots. Maybe even start a family?

But in her heart, she knew Sara too well to ever believe it would be so simple. Her daughter was born to be a newspaper reporter. She thrived on the pace and pressure of deadlines, loved digging up the story, seeing her words in print, then rushing to write the next story.

The truth was, it was amazing Sara had stayed so long, reporting for the *Cape Light Messenger*. As Emily's husband, Dan, had pointed out, "The question has never been 'Will Sara leave for a better job on a bigger paper?' It's always been 'When?' "

Since Sara had found her, every day had been a gift, and one Emily believed she never took for granted. She would not have traded one single hour of her time with Sara for anything. Today, of all days, she had to be grateful for what she'd been given, even though she had a sudden, uncontrollable urge to cling to her daughter.

Now Emily pulled up to her mother's house to find her brother-in-law Sam's truck parked in front, packed with Sara and Luke's belongings—a few pieces of furniture, a few lamps, boxes, and suitcases. Sam would be driving to Boston to help them move in, but Jessica, who was too pregnant to be loading and lifting, was staying behind. Besides, she had the boys to look after. Emily saw her nephews playing on the front lawn with Sam, tossing a football back and forth, making too much noise for their grandmother, she was sure.

She waved to Sam and walked up the driveway where Luke's SUV was parked, tailgate open and full of boxes. Sara came out the side door, carrying a big carton.

"Here, let me help you," Emily offered.

"That's okay. I've got it." Sara heaved the carton into the truck with a grunt. "Luke said he should have known better than to marry a brainy woman. He's going to be hauling boxes of books around his whole life."

"I think he's still got the better end of the deal," Emily said, leaning over and hugging her. "Oh, boy, I'm going to miss you."

She was trying not to cry but it wasn't easy.

"I'll miss you, too." Sara hugged her back. "But we're not moving far. I'll be back all the time, and you'll come into the city to visit whenever you want."

"Yes, of course we will," Emily agreed, though she knew it wasn't true. Once Sara and Luke became entrenched in their new jobs and new life, they wouldn't come back to Cape Light very often. Nor would she be running into Boston, with her demanding job as mayor and Jane to care for.

But she didn't say any of this. She hugged her daughter fiercely and quickly pulled away. If they'd had a normal parent-child relationship, she would have been through this before—Sara going away to summer camps and on trips, then off to college. She would have gotten the hang of it by now, Emily told herself.

But when she stood back and looked into her daughter's lovely face, Emily knew parting with Sara would have never become easy or routine.

She forced a smile. "So . . . anything else to bring out?"

"I guess there are a few more boxes," Sara said.

"How is your grandmother doing?" Emily asked as they walked into the kitchen. The truth was, Emily had been so wrapped up in her own feelings this morning, she had barely given her mother a thought. For once.

"Grandma is very . . . quiet. She's acting as if there's nothing unusual going on. I think she's still mad at me."

"She has nothing to be mad at you for," Emily insisted.

"I know. But—" Sara shrugged. Emily could tell that Sara understood Lillian's reaction but still felt hurt.

"She'll get over it. Don't worry."

"I just hope she's okay here on her own. It would break her heart to leave this house."

"I know. We'll just have to see what happens, honey."

They both looked up as Jessica walked into the kitchen, carrying a laundry basket of miscellaneous items. "This looks heavy but it's very light," she quickly explained. "But we need to cover it before you can put it in the truck. Luke said everything else is packed and he's ready to go."

So soon? Emily had hoped for a few more minutes with Sara before they took off. "A big trash bag should do it, right?" she asked.

She went to the pantry and found a bag then helped Sara and Jessica cover the basket. Jessica, with her very pregnant stomach getting in the way, was not much help and finally stepped back, laughing at her awkwardness.

Emily laughed, too. She couldn't help it. Despite the fact that her heart was breaking in two.

They finally had the basket covered. Sara was about to carry it out when Lillian walked in.

"I thought you'd at least say good-bye to me, Sara."

"Of course she's going to say good-bye," Emily said quickly. "She's carrying something out to the car. She'll be right back."

"And how would I know that? Nobody's spoken a word to me all morning. I have no idea of their plans."

Emily sincerely doubted that was true. It was probably more that Lillian had given Sara and Luke the cold shoulder for the last few days, and they were afraid to talk to her.

Luke walked in from the side door. "I think that's it. We can always come back if we forgot anything, right Lillian?"

"I suppose. Though I will change the locks. I don't want my front door keys floating all over Boston."

Before Emily could point out that this precaution was totally preposterous, Sara stepped forward. "Of course not, Grandma. Good idea."

"You can't be too careful, *living alone at my age*," Lillian replied quickly.

Emily and Jessica exchanged a look. It had already started, and Sara and Luke weren't even out the door.

"Well, time to go." Luke stepped toward Lillian, looking a little awkward.

Emily could tell he wasn't sure what to do next. Offering Lillian his hand seemed too formal. But Lillian stood stiffly, daring him to make any gesture even slightly more affectionate.

Finally, Luke leaned his body toward hers and gently patted her bony shoulder. "Good-bye now, Lillian. Take care. We'll come back and see you soon," he promised.

"No need to speak to me as if I were a child. I'll be fine," Lillian replied sharply. "You need to concentrate on finding a job, young man. Don't leave it all to my granddaughter."

Someone else might have taken offense at this. Fortunately, Luke was used to Lillian and just laughed.

Emily was not sure if Lillian would ever think the ex-cop-turned-youth-counselor would ever be good enough for Sara. But no one could ever doubt how much he loved Sara and how hard he tried to make her happy.

Case in point, he'd agreed to live in Lillian's house for the past three years because Sara was so worried about her grandmother's well-being. If that wasn't an act of sheer devotion, Emily did not know what was.

When the *Globe* offered Sara a job, Luke had no hesitation about moving, although it meant leaving his job as director of New Horizons, the retreat and school that helped kids in trouble, a center that he had founded in Cape Light years ago.

Luckily, Luke had just heard that the New Horizons Foundation might have an opening for him in their Boston office. He was interviewing next week for a position that would involve starting up centers around the country.

"Don't worry, Lillian. I won't turn into a deadbeat," he promised. "Though Sara is getting such a big bump up in her salary now, I'm tempted."

Lillian frowned at him. "You jest, but I would not be surprised."

"Grandma, please. Can't we leave on a good note?" Sara stepped forward and gave Lillian a hug. The old woman resisted at first, then Emily saw her mother close her eyes briefly and pat Sara's long, dark hair.

When they broke apart, Lillian lifted her chin, her pale blue eyes glassy. "I know you're an eager beaver on the totem pole and all that," she said sharply, "but you mustn't work too hard and wear yourself down. Save your powder. And when you get home, let him do the housework," she added, pointing at Luke with her cane.

Her mother, mixing metaphors? Emily felt a little jolt. Her mother really *was* upset.

"Yes, Grandma, I'll remember," Sara promised. She was still holding Lillian's hand. She patted it once and then let go.

"Well, I guess we're off." Sara looked around, forcing a smile.

Luke put his hand on her shoulder but didn't say anything.

"So long, Sara. Call me once you get settled in." Jessica gave Sara and Luke each a quick hug. "Why don't you walk them out, Emily? I'll stay here with Mother."

Emily nodded but didn't speak. She felt a lump in her throat the size of a softball and didn't want to burst into tears. Not before they had at least turned the corner.

Once they were outside, their parting went very quickly.

Emily hugged Luke and Sara in turn, bid them a safe trip, and then watched as they climbed inside their SUV. She stood on the lawn with her nephews as Sam drove off and then Luke followed. Sara waved from the window, and Emily and the boys waved back.

The boys quickly returned to their game of passing a football and tackling each other. Emily remained on the lawn, watching Luke's vehicle disappear from view. It was chilly and damp outside. She hadn't noticed that before. She was wearing just a heavy sweater and jeans and suddenly felt very cold. She took a few deep breaths, then turned to go inside.

She found her sister and mother still in the kitchen. Jessica stood by the stove, pouring hot water into a teapot.

"Don't make it too strong, Jessica. If I want to drink mud, I'll take coffee."

"Don't worry, Mother. I'll make it just the way you like." Jessica looked up as Emily walked in. "Want a cup of tea, Em?"

"Yes, please." Emily sat at the table across from her mother. "Well, they're gone."

"So I've heard. I hate long good-byes," Lillian said. "They're so tiresome."

Emily wasn't surprised by this. Her mother had never been one for emotional displays.

Jessica set down a cup of tea in front of Lillian and another in front of Emily. Then she sat down at the head of the table with her own cup.

"How are you feeling, Jess?" Emily asked her.

"I'm okay. But I'm getting bigger every day."

Lillian rolled her eyes. "I think that doctor has miscalculated. I think that baby is coming sooner than he says. Just don't go into labor in the middle of my kitchen, if you please. I don't need the excitement."

"I'll make a note of that, Mother," Jessica said, biting back a smile.

The baby was coming soon, early or not, Emily thought. Jessica would have her hands full with an infant and her two boys to look after. She wouldn't have much time to run over here, to take care of Lillian. They'd both had it so easy with Sara living here. They had been spoiled, and now it was time to deal with some realities, some harsh realities.

· "Mother, now that Sara and Luke are gone, we really need to talk about how you're going to manage in this house," Emily began.

"Manage? How do you think I'll manage? The same way I've been doing it since your father died, I expect."

"Not quite the same, Mother," Jessica said. "That was nearly thirty years ago."

"Just about. I was only forty-nine, a very young widow. You girls forget. You've always thought of me as an old woman, but I was quite young to be left alone. I just felt old," she admitted. "I've made it this far on my own. I fail to see the problem."

"The problem," Emily said, "is that for the past three years, you've had live-in help here, Mother. Whether you want to admit it or not, Sara and Luke looked after you. After that fall on the attic stairs, you couldn't have remained here without them."

Lillian sat back and waved her hand airily. "Rubbish. Of course I could have. I was perfectly able, once my bones mended and I got out of that wheelchair. They didn't have to stay. They wanted to."

The back door burst open and for a moment, Emily thought it was Sara and Luke, returning because they had forgotten something. Or they'd had a sudden, astounding change of heart and couldn't stand the idea of leaving, after all.

Wishful thinking, she quickly realized and smiled to herself as her nephews clomped into the room in their big sneakers and baggy jackets that flapped open.

"Hey, Mom. We're hungry. Can we have some lunch?"

Darrell walked up to Jess and put his arm on her shoulder. He was fifteen and getting so tall; his face and voice were changing, too. He was a big help to Jessica now, watching his younger brother and helping in the house. Tyler was only five but pretty independent for his age. Emily wondered how he would react once the baby came.

"Lunch, right." Jessica nodded. Emily could tell what she was thinking. It would be hard if not impossible to feed the kids here. She doubted her mother had anything suitable in the house, the cabinets full of potato soup, Saltine crackers, and tuna fish in water, which Lillian ate with a squirt of lemon.

Never mind the fuss Lillian would make over the mess—or the imagined mess.

Jessica rose slowly and picked up her jacket. "Well, in that case, I guess we'd better go. We'll pick up something on the way home, Darrell. Some pizza or burgers."

"Sweet." Darrell was pleased by that announcement.

"I want pizza," Tyler said, tugging on Jess's jacket.

Lillian made a snorting sound. "Junk food. You need to give these children nutritious meals, Jessica. With fruit and vegetables."

Not that she stocked any in the house for their visits, mind you, Emily wanted to point out.

"I usually do, Mother. But I'm too tired right now to go food shopping, and they're too hungry to wait."

Emily nodded and touched her arm. "You get going. I'll just stay a minute and finish my tea."

Lillian pursed her lips and stared hard at her older daughter. "You'd better be moving along, too, Emily. I'm going out."

Emily was instantly suspicious that this was just a trick to get rid of her. Lillian, feeling cornered, was trying to cleverly wriggle out of her grasp and escape a discussion of the unthinkable—hiring help to come into this house.

"Where are you going, Mother? You never leave the house on Saturdays." *Unless one of us takes you out on errands,* she added silently.

"Not that you would know it, but perhaps I have a social life beyond the rounds of doctor visits and supermarkets, where you and sister escort me."

Not much beyond that, Emily wanted to correct her. The tactic was clear. Her mother was suddenly trying to portray the image of an active, independent person. Which they all knew was not the reality.

Lillian rose and carried her teacup to the sink, which wasn't easy, walking with a cane. "Ezra's bridge club is short a hand, and he invited me to join them. They meet in a very nice club room at some senior living community . . . Happy Valley or some such? All those senior villages sound the same to me."

Happy Valley? Emily nearly laughed out loud. That said it all, though she doubted it was really the name of the place. "Sounds very nice," Jessica said, helping Tyler with the zipper on his jacket.

"They serve a decent buffet," Lillian noted. "I'm just going as a favor to Ezra. There are some wretched card players in that bunch. I hope we don't get a bad table."

Well, at least she would be with Ezra today. That was a comfort.

"I'm sure Ezra appreciates your help," Emily said. She picked up her purse and kissed her mother's cheek. "Call me when you get back, okay?"

"Do I have a curfew? Have I suddenly regressed to my teenage years?"

"Mother, we just want to know that you got in okay," Jessica explained. "Humor us, please?"

"Yes, humor us," Emily echoed, but in a much firmer tone.

Lillian sighed. "I will call. And I'll speak to a machine, I expect, since neither of you ever deigns to pick up the phone."

"Good-bye, Mother," Emily said, heading for the door. "I'll pick you up for church tomorrow at the usual time."

"Of course. Whenever that turns out to be," Lillian grumbled.

"Yes, see you tomorrow, Mother." Jessica kissed her mother and gave her boys a look. Getting the hint, they politely said good-bye to Lillian. They were more than a little afraid of their grandmother. Lillian liked it that way, considering their apprehension a form of respect.

Once they were outside, Emily stood at Jessica's car for a few private words. "Well, what do you think? We didn't get very far."

Jessica leaned into the backseat to make sure Tyler's seat belt was secure. "I didn't think we would, not on the first try."

"I know, but now that they're really gone, it's suddenly hitting me. She's all alone in there. It's just not safe, Jess. How can she argue with us about it?"

"I'm worried, too. We definitely have to do something. But it will be easier for us, and for her, if we can get her to agree to some plan. Otherwise—"

"Yes, I know. No point without her signing on."

Emily looked up to see her mother watching from the front parlor window. She waved, and the curtain quickly snapped back. Emily laughed. "We're being spied on."

"She's suiting up for a royal battle, that's for sure." Jessica slipped into the driver's seat and shut the door. "You've had a hard day, Em. Don't worry about any of this right now. We can't solve it in one conversation with her. It will all work out—one way or the other. Let me know when Mother calls you later, okay?"

"Yes, I will," Emily promised, stepping back from the car.

Jessica drove off and Emily headed for her Jeep. She and her sister were already working hard to manage their mother, and it had barely been an hour since Sara and Luke had left town.

That was not a good sign. Not at all.

CHAPTER THREE

$\sim$

$\mathcal{D}$AVID KNEW THEY WEREN'T MAKING NOISE ON purpose. They weren't intentionally trying to drive him crazy. But how long did it take for three people to eat breakfast and leave the house, for goodness' sake?

He lifted his head and peered at the clock on the nightstand. Half-past eight. If he were still in the army, that would be . . . the middle of the afternoon.

But he wasn't a soldier anymore. He wasn't running on the army's schedule. He wasn't on any schedule. All he wanted to do was sleep, to sink into blessed, unconscious oblivion.

Was that so much to ask?

Obviously it was, he realized as the door opened a crack, and his father stuck his head inside.

"Oh, you're awake. I thought you were still sleeping."

"I want to be," David mumbled.

"Sorry. I just wanted to see if you needed anything

before we leave for church. There's some coffee left. Want a cup?"

"I can get it for myself later, Dad. Thanks."

His father paused and glanced at his watch. "The service doesn't start till ten. Want to come? We can wait for you."

David shook his head. "No thanks. I'm just going to hang out here."

"Okay, sure. See you later." Jack nodded and closed the door.

David sank back into the pillows. A few minutes later he heard the sounds of the front door closing and his dad's pickup driving away.

He was glad his father hadn't tried to persuade him. It was funny how fighting in a war zone had made him more inclined to think about spiritual things, to even say a prayer from time to time. But less inclined to go to church. Maybe it was because he just didn't like the idea of struggling with the walker, everyone turning to look at him.

He wasn't ready for that.

The house was so quiet. He could hear squirrels running around on the flat roof above his room, and water dripping into the kitchen sink.

He didn't think he would fall asleep again, but he did. Then suddenly, he woke up.

Someone down at the tree farm was ringing the bell for service. It had been ringing a lot this weekend, ever since his father put it back together the day after Thanksgiving.

David checked the clock. Ten thirty. The family wouldn't be back until at least noon. The customers would have to wait until then. He sure couldn't run out there to sell Christmas trees.

The bell stopped. Then started again. David pulled a pillow over his head, but it was impossible to block out the noise. Finally, he gave up. The ringing had stopped but it was too late; he couldn't sleep anymore.

He sat up and flipped off the covers, feeling a sharp pain in his hip that radiated down his entire leg. He took a deep breath, then leaned over and grabbed the support he always had to wear now on his right leg due to the numbness in his foot. He strapped it on grudgingly. He knew it helped some, but he hated it, a daily reminder first thing in the morning that his body was damaged—probably irreparably.

The custom-fit device was state-of-the-art, made of two thin, light plastic pieces that fit the front and back of his foot and lower leg, secured with Velcro straps. A thin layer of plastic covered the bottom of his foot, holding it at the proper angle. Since the nerves in that foot had gone numb after his last hip surgery, his body was no longer able to do this. So if, and when, muscle control in that area came back, his foot would not be damaged by dragging it.

The house felt chilly. He pulled sweats over his boxers and T-shirt, then peered at his face in the bathroom mirror. He needed a shave but didn't feel like bothering. He splashed his face with cold water and brushed his teeth. His army buzz cut had grown out, and his thick, dirty blond hair needed a real haircut, but he hadn't made it yet to the barber.

Out in the kitchen, he found the coffee and fixed a bowl of cold cereal. Katie's brand. So sweet it made his teeth ache, but the box and bowl were right on the table. Proximity was all these days.

He picked up a few sections of the newspaper, balanced them on the walker, and ambled into the living room.

He was just about to sit down when a knock sounded on the front door. These people wanted their Christmas trees. They didn't care how rude they were.

David decided to just ignore it. They would go away eventually, like the bell ringers. Still, curiosity made him peer out the window to get a look. He tried to step back quickly but it was too late.

She had seen him.

Christine. She was at the door.

What was she doing here?

She knocked again, harder this time. Then she called out to him. "David? Are you there? It's just me, Christine."

Just Christine? The two words were totally contradictory. At least, by his definitions.

He let out a long breath and stood up straight. Would she go away if he said he wasn't feeling well? Doing that meant he would have to talk to her, through the door. That seemed childish, weak. He didn't want her to think he had turned into a complete invalid.

At least he was dressed, sort of. He looked down at his bare feet and wished he had put on shoes. Too late now.

He had to face her sooner or later. It was probably better to get this over with. Like yanking off a bandage. He looked like a slob, but maybe that was better, too.

"Just a minute. Be right there," he called back.

He smoothed his hair down with his hand and headed for the door. He had been to war, for Christmas' sake. He had fought in battles with bullets whizzing by his head and mortar explosions. But he suddenly felt he would rather face enemy gunfire again than open that door and face her.

You can do this, he coached himself. It's *just* . . . Christine.

David settled the walker to one side of the door, then pulled it open. She stood in the doorway a minute and stared, taking him in from head to toe.

It was just for an instant—a heartbeat, really—before her features relaxed into a smile. But that single, swift look spoke volumes. His appearance had shocked her. He looked worse than he thought, her reaction said. Much worse.

He suddenly felt embarrassed. Why had he opened the door for her? He couldn't remember now.

"Hey, David. I hope you don't mind me dropping by like this. I was on my way to town and I wanted to say hello. I called a few times, but I kept missing you."

"Yeah . . . I know. Sorry about that." David didn't know what to say. If she suspected that his father had been making excuses for him, she hid it well.

"You're up and around, I see," she said cheerfully. "That's good, right?"

"I'm pretty mobile with this thing." He slapped the side of the walker, which felt like a metal cage about then.

"How do you feel?" she asked, her voice low and sincere.

"Oh . . . coming along. I had a few operations. On my legs mostly." He wanted to slap himself for going into that. She didn't need to hear his medical history. He was starting to sound like an old man.

"Yes, your father told me. At a hospital in Germany, right?"

"That's right. I was airlifted there after . . . after the army medical unit in Iraq." He felt suddenly awkward, unsure of what to say or do next or how much to tell her. It had been a long time since he had been in the company of a girl.

He looked up and forced a smile. "You look great," he said sincerely. She did, too. She hadn't changed a bit. Tall and slim with long blond hair, pulled back today in a ponytail. She had the best smile. He'd always thought so anyway.

"How's school going?" he asked her. A good topic to get into, instead of his ailments, he thought.

"School is great. I'm just finishing my course work. Next semester, I'll be student teaching. Then I'll graduate."

She smiled at him, and he felt as if his heart stopped beating.

Or maybe it was just that feeling he got, staring into her very blue eyes. As if time just stopped.

She was prettier than he remembered. Beautiful, truly. Hard to believe now that back in high school, she had been his steady girlfriend. She only wanted to be with him, nobody else, though a lot of other guys had been after her. How had he been so lucky to have won her? What had she seen in him way back when? He had never been able to figure that one out.

"Sounds great," he said finally. He nodded and took a breath. "Sounds like you found something you really like to do."

"Yes, I did. I love teaching."

"You always liked babysitting. I used to come visit and help you, remember?"

Christine laughed. "Yeah, I do. You'd get me into trouble with the parents, usually. It's not quite the same thing, David. But I've always loved kids. I wasn't sure when I first started college what I wanted to do. Somehow, though, it all fell into place. Now all I have to do is find a job once I graduate."

She hadn't mentioned anything about getting married this summer, he noticed. She had told him about her fiancé when he saw her last Christmas. He pushed that thought aside, unable to ask about those plans.

"So, four years," he said. "That went fast."

"It did, didn't it?" She sounded wistful.

He wondered if she was thinking the same thing he was. Thinking back to their senior year in high school, the year his mother died and he ran away from home right after school ended. He had been at odds with his father all through high school, all through his mother's long battle with cancer. Then one day, they'd had the usual argument—he couldn't even remember now what they'd been shouting about—and he just up and left. Stopped at the bank in town, withdrew the pathetic amount in his account, and hitched a ride out of town with just the clothes on his back.

"*Some* of it went fast," he corrected himself. "The last year or so in the army . . . that didn't exactly fly by for me."

Her expression grew suddenly serious. "I'm sure it didn't. You were very brave, David, to enlist and go over there."

David felt the blood rush to his cheeks. Was he blushing, like a girl, from her compliment?

"Brave? More like plain ignorant. I wanted to do some good, I guess. I didn't know what I was getting into. Nobody does. You have some idea of what it's like, what you're going to do, and what you're going to feel. The training is supposed to prepare you. But when you get out there, it's a whole different ball game. It's nothing like you see in the movies—or even on the news. There's just no way to imagine it. . . ."

He took a breath, realizing he was going off on a tangent.

"I don't think I could imagine it." Christine's voice was soft, understanding, the way it always had been.

He didn't know what to say. He met her warm eyes and looked away.

This was too hard. He didn't want to see her. Not like this. She only came because she felt sorry for him. She was so good-hearted. That was one of the things he had loved about her.

"Listen, you must be tired." She leaned over and briefly touched his arm. "I just wanted to say hello."

David nodded, staring down at the place where she'd touched him. He felt it deep inside, that brief connection. It made him realize suddenly how much he had lost.

"I am tired. It's hard to stand for a long time like this, talking. I think you'd better go," he said harshly.

He felt startled at the sound of his voice, the cold tone he had suddenly taken with her. What had come over him? He couldn't control his anger sometimes; it just burst out. Like a gunshot.

Maybe she didn't mean to react, but he saw her move back, her expression frozen. Oh, for crying out loud. Now he had scared her. She was going to think he'd gone nuts or something.

"Thanks for stopping by. It was good to see you. Really," he added in a quieter voice.

"It's good to see you, David. I'm glad you decided to answer the door."

"I'm glad I did, too." He sighed and looked at her. He wasn't entirely. Half of him was glad. The other half felt like a dagger was plunged into his head. She was so pretty, it almost hurt to look at her.

She seemed about to go. He didn't want her to. There were things he wanted to say to her. Things he had thought about for months, imagining a day when he would be with her again. Alone, just talking together, the way they were right now.

"Listen," he said quickly. "I wanted to tell you something if I ever got the chance. . . . I really liked those letters you wrote to me. They were really good. I mean, it helped a lot, hearing from someone at home."

He stopped, unable to say what he really meant. That he had lived for her letters. That he read them over and over again and carried them in the pocket of his flak jacket. Right over his heart.

Christine didn't answer, just smiled at him, a soft look coming over her eyes. "That's okay. I wanted to stay in touch. I said I would write, remember?"

She had promised when they had seen each other last year, but he hadn't been sure she would. Maybe her fiancé wouldn't like the idea of it, David had thought, or maybe she would just forget after a while. But she did write. Very faithfully, too.

"Of course, I remember. It's just that . . . well, you didn't have to. I mean, we hadn't been in touch for years, and I just came to see you out of the blue last winter and said, 'Guess what, I'm shipping out to Iraq next week,'" he tried to make a joke out of it, but he could tell it wasn't coming out right. "Someone else would have said, 'Well, good-bye and good luck, pal.' They wouldn't have gone to all that trouble."

She didn't answer for a minute. He thought she looked a little embarrassed. Had something he'd said upset her?

"I liked reading your letters, too," she said finally. "They were very descriptive. Lots of good stories. It helped me understand a little of what you were going through."

She glanced at him but he didn't answer. He had wanted her to know what he was going through, what he saw and how he felt over there. He had poured out his heart to her, as well as he could. He'd never been a great student or very good with words.

He watched as she lifted her hand to check her watch. The diamond solitaire on her finger sparkled. It wasn't very large, David noticed, but big enough to catch his eye.

"I'd better get going. See you around."

"Right. See you," he said, though he knew there was little chance of them running into each other in town, even though Cape Light was certainly small enough. He only left the house these days to go down to the Veteran's Administration Medical Center, with his father driving him both ways.

She stepped out the door and he closed it behind her. He heaved a great sigh of relief. And regret.

At least that was over with. He didn't have to think about it anymore, dreading the first time he would see her again, imagining what it would be like. It had happened, and he had been totally unprepared, looking like a wreck with his hair barely combed and his face unshaven.

What the heck. If she'd had any ideas at all about him, any feelings starting up again while he was away, this get-together should have changed her mind pretty quickly. Like waking someone up with a dash of cold water to the face.

He'd had some ideas, too, some hopeful daydreams about her.

He had pictured himself coming home fit and full of energy. Full of confidence. The way he had been when he last saw her, feeling very proud of himself in his uniform. He had imagined finding work in law enforcement, or maybe with the fire department. He would have good prospects, something to offer her. He would slowly but surely win her over again. Show her he could be trusted this time. Show her that he had changed from the screwed-up guy she knew in high school.

But nothing had turned out the way he'd planned. The way he'd imagined it.

David pushed himself along on the walker, back into the kitchen. He poured himself a cold drink of water and gulped it down quickly.

He felt like he wanted to scream. Or cry. Or do both at the same time. If his legs were working like a normal person's, he would have done something physical. Run a few miles out in the cold or chop a pile of wood, swinging the ax until he felt ready to collapse.

Instead, he was stuck here with all these feelings in his head, whipping around like a tornado. He felt like just letting loose and busting something up.

Christine . . . She would never know what she meant to him. He would never be able to find the words. Or the guts.

It was just as well. She wouldn't want him the way he was now. He wouldn't want to ruin things for her. She had everything worked out just right, didn't she? No, he wasn't for her. He was the messed-up type and always would be. The army hadn't changed that about him. He had thought so once. But now it seemed his days as a soldier had only made it worse.

At least he had thanked her for the letters. At least he'd said that much. David took a deep breath and then another, the way the nurse at the hospital in Bonn had taught him, to help control the pain and his roller-coaster emotions.

It was funny how Christine had been his link to home twice now, he suddenly realized. While he was fighting in Iraq and even before that, after he ran away from Cape Light.

Christine was the only person he called or sometimes

wrote. She was the only person who ever knew where he was. He had made her promise not to tell his father. She kept her word, too.

Even then, their phone calls had been sporadic, mostly whenever he felt lonely. He had tried to persuade her to join him, to leave home and bang around the country with him. Once or twice, he thought maybe he had talked her into it. Then one day he realized she was never going to leave this town. Not for him. She had plans to start college, and she wasn't going to let him talk her out of it.

He had been so angry at her. He'd felt betrayed and abandoned. But eventually he realized that she had been strong and smart to refuse him. It had been wrong of him to try to drag her into his self-imposed exile and family drama. He was glad now she hadn't come to meet him. He would have messed up everything for her.

Now, here she was, with everything in order. She was graduating college, about to be a teacher. About to get married to some smart, on-the-right-track guy. Everything on schedule. Everything the way it should be for a girl like her.

It was no coincidence, David thought, that Christine's life was picture-book perfect now, and he was no part of it. He would be doing her a big favor by keeping it that way. By staying away from her, no matter how nice she was to him. Or how sad she felt for him. That wasn't the way he wanted things between them anyway.

BY THE TIME HIS FAMILY RETURNED FROM CHURCH, DAVID had showered, shaved, and dressed in jeans and a sweater.

While Julie and Kate ran upstairs to change out of their church clothes, his father stayed in the living room, picking up some stray pieces from one of Katie's games.

"Hey, Dave. How are you feeling today?" He kept his voice casual, but David could see that he was pleased to see him up and around. "Guess you didn't sleep in too late."

"Some eager customers couldn't stop ringing that stupid bell. You'd think they'd realize no one was home."

"Oh, right. I should have put up the sign about opening at noon today. Sorry."

"That's okay. I survived." David shrugged. He wanted to tell Jack that Christine had visited, but the words wouldn't come out. He knew his father would be interested to hear that she had dropped by. Maybe too interested.

Julie came downstairs dressed in her work clothes, a heavy fleece pullover, jeans, and hiking boots. It was time to get out to the tree stand. Past time, David thought, judging from the cars that were starting to pull up.

Julie pulled a Red Sox cap over her long hair, and slipped on heavy gloves. "Why don't you stay inside awhile and keep David company? I can take care of things out there for now."

"Oh, okay." David could see his father was surprised by the suggestion. "I'll be out in a little while then."

"Take your time. Kate wants to watch her video. She's going to stay inside with you for now." Julie gave Jack a quick kiss on his cheek then left through the front door.

While David welcomed the company after being alone for most of the morning, he felt guilty keeping his father indoors. Especially today, a prime day for tree shopping.

Jack stood in the middle of the living room, his hands stuck in his front pockets as he gazed out the window. Counting the cars in the parking lot, David knew.

"You can go outside, Dad. It's okay. You don't need to babysit me. I'll watch Kate for you."

"Babysit you? What are you talking about?" His father suddenly looked away from the window. "Julie will have a turn now, then I'll go out later, when it gets cold."

"And she comes in to make dinner," David teased his father.

"Well, she might do that. But I cook. Sometimes. I try at least."

David knew his father did try. He wasn't a terrible cook and could make some simple dishes. But he clearly didn't like cooking. Not like David did. While roaming around the country, he had done a lot of grunt work in restaurant kitchens and had learned a few things, too.

"You want some lunch?" Jack offered. "I can make you a sandwich."

David laughed. "Sure. I'll take a sandwich."

"Coming right up. How about grilled cheese with tomato?"

David had to smile at the suggestion, one of his childhood favorites. "Sounds good."

"You got it. Katie likes that, too. Why don't you call her down?"

A short time later, David sat at the kitchen table with his father, both eating their sandwiches. Katie had taken hers into the family room, eager to watch one of her videos, some Christmas story she had already seen a hundred times.

David wasn't sure why, but he felt down again. As if his father really wanted to be outside working with Julie, the way they had been all weekend long. There had been a lot of early tree shoppers this year, and even Kate had gone outside to help them. David had been left inside to watch from the window or hang out alone in his room, feeling useless and out of the loop.

His father was making an effort to keep David company today, but that didn't seem to satisfy him either. David wasn't sure what he wanted from his father. What he wanted from anybody.

"Is your sandwich okay? I didn't burn the bottom, did I?" Jack asked.

"It's fine, Dad, thanks," David said quickly. "You can go outside now. You don't have to hang around in here with me."

Jack looked surprised, then annoyed. Then suddenly he

laughed. "Whoa, there. . . . Can I finish my lunch at least? I didn't eat my pickle yet."

David took a breath. "I can tell you want to get to work, that's all."

Jack waved his hand. "Those trees aren't going anywhere. I'll be hauling them around for the next month— until I'm sick of looking at them."

"Maybe. But you're always excited the first weekend you open up," David reminded him.

Jack laughed. "Yeah, that's true. Remember what we used to do out there when you were a kid? The horse-drawn sleigh and the hot cider, the Christmas village. What a show we put on. That was all your mother's idea."

"Yeah, I remember," David said quietly. Those were good memories, but it was hard looking back. When he was old enough, he had worked out there with his parents. They'd had a lot of fun together, and he had liked the feeling of working in the family business, being grown-up enough to contribute to something so important.

"Those are nice memories," Jack said wistfully. "But you can't get stuck in the past. You have to look forward, always forward. I figured that out. Finally."

"Good for you," David said.

His father looked up, sensitive to David's sharp tone, but he didn't say anything. Just looked back at his plate again and kept eating.

David could see his father had found happiness with Julie and Kate and the new life they had built together. David was honestly happy for him. But it was still hard to be around his father at times. Sometimes David wished his Dad was still depressed and distant, like in the good old days. He could deal with that a lot better.

They sat for a few moments without saying anything. Jack looked relaxed, lost in his thoughts. David felt edgy and tense.

"Christine dropped by. While you were all at church."
David hadn't meant to tell his father; it just popped out.

"She did?" Jack sat up and put down his sandwich. "How
did it go?"

David shrugged. "All right, I guess. She didn't stay long.
We just talked for a few minutes. She seems happy. She
sounds like she has life all figured out. She's graduating
college in the spring. She's going to be a teacher."

"Right. I remember that."

"And she's getting married in the summer, she said.
To some guy . . . She didn't say much about him," David
added.

It was funny how she had never said a word about her
fiancé. But David realized he hadn't asked her any questions about him. As long as the guy remained a big blank,
he didn't quite exist.

"She's a nice girl. I wish her all the luck in the world."
Jack took a final bite and tossed the crust on his plate. "So,
how did you leave it with her?"

"What do you mean?"

Jack rose and brought his plate to the sink. "Do you
think you'll see her again?"

"One of these days, I guess. It's a small town. We're
bound to run into each other." It was hard to hide the bitter
note in his tone.

"I see." David thought Jack was going to grab his coat
and go outside to help Julie, but he poured himself a mug of
coffee and sat at the table again. "I'm sorry, Dave. I know
you still care for her."

David didn't even glance at his father. He knew if he
did, he might start crying like a little boy.

"It's okay, Dad," he managed. "She's all on track with
her life. I'd just be messing her up. I know that."

Jack stirred a spoonful of sugar into his coffee. "All
right. Whatever you say. But it's hard to let go of something
like that, Dave. You've known each other a long time."

"Since grade school. Maybe that's why she wrote to me while I was away—because we grew up together." *Not because she has feelings for me. The kind I have for her.*

"At least she kept in touch. I know it meant a lot to you."

David shot his father a quick look, then glanced away. His father knew how he felt. David didn't need to say more.

"This is the hardest part of being a parent, David. Maybe you'll remember I said that when you have your own kids."

Not much chance of that happening now, David wanted to reply. "What's the hardest part?" he asked instead.

"Having to stand by and watch you get hurt and disappointed. And not being able to do anything for you. Even your physical pain—if I could take it away from you, and feel it myself, I would. I just don't know what to do for you," Jack admitted quietly.

David was surprised by his father's honesty. They had never talked much when he was a teenager, living at home. Argued a lot? Yes, indeed. But never really talked, not like this.

"There's nothing you can do, Dad," David said. "But . . . thanks for saying that."

"I wish I could just speed up time, flip the calendar ahead to a day when you'll feel better. I know you will, too—someday. Day by day, things will get better for you, David. I know it seems overwhelming right now. Like when I lost your mother. But you'll get through all this." Jack paused. David could tell he was searching for the right thing to say. "Coming off a battlefield, leaving army life, that's a heck of a lot to handle. Especially after what you've been through. The important thing is that you came back. You're alive. You have your whole life ahead of you. Don't get lost in your pain. Don't give up on yourself."

David didn't know what to say. He knew his father meant well and was trying to help. But he'd heard this all before. It was impossible to look ahead to some sunny someday, when his future stretched ahead long and dark and frightening.

Now it was clear that he didn't even have Christine to hope for anymore. That was a blow. His physical injuries had wiped out all his plans, everything he had wanted. What would he do with his life now? He had no idea.

David looked across the table at his father. *He has good intentions,* he realized, *but he really doesn't have a clue about what I'm dealing with.*

"Dad, I know you believe I'm going to make a full recovery and be just the way I was when I left. But not one single doctor so far has told me that's what will happen. Every day that I wake up dragging around this dead foot makes it seem more and more unlikely," David said bluntly. "I'm going to be this way the rest of my life. I have to face it."

"David, David." His father shook his head, as if he really didn't want to hear the truth so plainly spoken. "You don't know that for sure. You could get the feeling back anytime. That's what I heard them say. The nerves aren't damaged, they're just in shock or something—from all the operations. Let's try to think positively, okay?"

David felt a lump of emotion well up in his throat but swallowed it back. He nodded, saying nothing, trying hard not to have an angry outburst at his father for all this . . . this "happy talk." As if he wasn't walking right due to some weakness of will, or because his thinking was too negative. Because he was being too honest with himself about the hopelessness of the situation.

"Maybe the physical therapy will spark up something in your muscles, get things working again," his father added. "The last doctor you saw thought it might."

David was scheduled to start physical therapy tomorrow, with a new therapist at the VA Center in Beverly. He had already had some PT and unlike his father, didn't expect any miracles.

"A small chance, he said," David clarified. "But I need the therapy anyway. I just want to get rid of this damn walker."

Jack nodded, looking encouraged. "That's a goal, a good one. Start there. That's all it takes."

David rubbed his chin. He thought about Christine again, even though he didn't want to. The expression on her face when she had first walked into the house. The way she had looked at him. It might have all gone differently if he hadn't been standing behind the walker and had faced her on his own two feet.

"All right. Fair enough," David said quietly.

"Maybe by Christmas?" his father asked.

Now he was setting a deadline? Putting the pressure on? "Yeah, maybe . . . What's the difference?"

Jack shrugged. "It's good to set a date. Even if you don't make it. Which reminds me of something . . ." Jack suddenly jumped up from his chair. "Wait right here. I have something for you."

Where would I go? David wanted to ask him. But he held his tongue.

Jack ran into the little room off the kitchen that served as his office and quickly returned with a brown shopping bag. "Here, this is for you. An early Christmas present."

David took the bag and took out a box that was inside. He could see what it was from the label. "A laptop? Dad . . . you didn't have to buy me this. It's too expensive."

Jack ignored him. David could tell his father was excited about the gift. "It's wireless, see? You can use it anywhere. More convenient for you."

Jack had a desktop computer in his office that David sometimes used to keep up with friends or search information on the Internet. But it was in an uncomfortable spot for him, and Jack often needed to use the computer at the same time for work.

"I know you want to stay in touch with your friends, and it's better than watching TV," Jack said.

Better than lying on my bed, staring at the ceiling, David silently added, which is how he passed most hours lately.

David looked down at the box again and started to open it. "This is a really good one. It was a great idea, Dad, but I'm going to pay you back. I can afford it."

"Yeah, I know you're a rich man now with all that back pay. But this is a gift, from me and Julie, okay? Now, just use it and enjoy it. I don't want to argue about it anymore."

David had to grin at his father's sudden change in tone. It had been a while since he had heard that line around here.

"Okay, sir. Will do. Thank you very much."

Jack stood up and roughly patted David's shoulder. He didn't answer for a moment.

"Thank you for coming home, David," he said finally. "That's all you ever have to do for me."

David thought his father was about to cry, but Jack turned away before he could tell for sure.

CHAPTER FOUR

❧

$\mathscr{E}$MILY, I NEED YOU. IT'S AN EMERGENCY."

"What's going on, Mother?" Emily asked quickly. "Should I call the fire department?"

Emily thought her mother's voice sounded very calm and controlled for someone in the midst of a crisis. But her mother could sound that way even if the roof was caving in.

"I can't find my medications. I've looked everywhere. I think my pill case has been stolen."

"Is that all?" Emily sighed with relief and smiled over at her secretary, Helen, who was sitting nearby, ready to start their regular Monday lunch meeting.

"Well, it may be a small matter to you," Lillian snapped, "but it's an emergency to me. Someone's stolen them, I'm sure. I can't see how my pill case would have disappeared from this house otherwise."

"Who in the world would steal your pills, Mother? You haven't had any strangers in your house for weeks."

That was one of her mother's pet fears, suspecting that

anyone who came into the house to repair an appliance or read a water meter was really there to rob her.

"I had my pills with me at the bridge party. Maybe some senile senior stole them out of my purse. Or one of the servers?"

Emily waited a moment before replying. If she didn't watch it, she was either going to laugh out loud or totally lose her patience. She tried her best for a reassuring tone.

"The pill case must be in the house somewhere, Mother. I'll stop by after work and help you look."

"Tonight, you mean? Well, by then I'll probably be dead from a stroke or a heart attack," Lillian predicted airily. "Why don't you come tomorrow? Or the day after? Just to be sure. I'm already feeling a bit unsteady."

"No need to be sarcastic. I get your point."

"No you don't. You obviously don't understand, Emily. I need to take those medications at the same time each day. Or else. That's what the doctor told me."

Before Emily could answer her mother gave out a long exasperated sigh. "Don't trouble yourself. I'll deal with it. Though it's very difficult for me to look behind the furniture and in all the nooks and crannies. Bending over and moving the sofa and such makes me very dizzy. . . ."

"All right, Mother. Just stay put. But I can't visit for very long, I have a meeting at two thirty."

"That goes without saying. You are so important. But I do appreciate you taking a few minutes from your busy schedule."

Emily rolled her eyes at her mother's mocking tone. "Not a problem. I'll be right there."

Emily quickly left her office at the village hall and drove the short distance to her mother's house. She let herself in with her own key and called out from the foyer, "Mother? I'm here. It's me, Emily."

"Finally," Lillian called back.

Emily followed the sound of her voice to the kitchen where she found her mother at the table, calmly eating a bowl of soup and working on a crossword puzzle.

It took a moment for Lillian to look up at her, over the edge of her reading glasses. "What took you so long?"

"I came as fast as I could." Emily slipped off her silk scarf and wool jacket and draped them over the chair. "Where have you looked for the pills? Did you check upstairs yet? Maybe the case was on the night table and it fell under the bed."

Lillian squinted and held up her hand, a sharp yellow pencil poised to fill a word on the puzzle. "Just a moment. . . . Can you keep quiet please while I think?" Then her eyes opened and her expression looked very pleased. "Zeitgeist . . ." She quickly counted the letters in the word on her fingers then nodded with satisfaction. "What took me so long? So obvious," she scolded herself as she filled in the spaces on the page.

Emily sighed out loud, wondering if other mothers were this exasperating. Somehow she suspected Lillian took the prize.

"Would you like some soup?" Lillian asked, frowning at the puzzle. "There's more in the pot, chicken noodle. It isn't very good. Your sister didn't buy the brand I prefer."

"Thank you. I just had lunch." Sort of, she silently amended. She had dashed out before eating even half of her salad. "So . . . the pills? I thought finding your medications was a dire emergency."

Emily wanted to add that she had fully expected to find her mother in the middle of a fainting spell, at the very least. But Emily knew better than to call Lillian on her wild exaggerations.

Lillian suddenly looked up. "Actually, I found the pills. A short time after we spoke. It was the oddest thing. I thought I would work on my embroidery while I waited for you, to calm my nerves. And there it was, the pill case, in the bottom of my sewing tote. I can't imagine how it got in there," she added with a shrug.

"Neither can I."

Lillian shook her head and lifted a spoonful of soup to her lips. "Perhaps the case fell off the side table while I was sewing last night. That's the only explanation I can think of."

"That's probably how it happened, Mother." Feeling thoroughly frustrated, Emily sat down at the table and picked up a cracker.

Crackers in this house always tasted stale, and Emily was on a low-carb diet and knew she shouldn't be eating any kind of cracker, stale or otherwise. But she didn't care. It was either busy her mouth chewing something or chew out her mother for making her run over here as if the house were on fire.

Her mother glanced back at the puzzle again. "Can you think of a word that means both apparition and a cool dark place? Five letters, starts with *S*."

"I have no idea. I really don't like crossword puzzles. I'm terrible at them."

"I don't know why that should be. You have a good vocabulary. I think it's more that you just don't apply yourself."

Emily had to smile at the half-baked compliment. "Thanks, Mother. I think. But I didn't run over here to do a crossword puzzle with you."

"Of course not. It's the middle of the day, and you're a very busy woman. . . . Oh, I've got it," Lillian said, staring down at her puzzle. "It's shade. How simple. Why didn't I see that?"

"You know what I mean." Emily cleared her throat, getting ready to make another pitch for home help. It would have been much easier if her mother could just stop doing the puzzle and listen to her. But that would be asking too much.

"This is just what Jessica and I were trying to tell you on Saturday, Mother. You need someone in the house, to help you. Someone to keep things in order or find things that are misplaced, to help you with a crossword puzzle, if that's the only problem."

"Oh, I rarely misplace anything. There's a place for everything, and everything in its place. And I certainly don't need a partner for my puzzles. What would be the point of that? I'm trying to exercise the gray matter. Very necessary at my age." She tapped her temple with the yellow pencil.

Emily dipped her head in order to catch her mother's eye. "And the pills getting lost? How did that happen?"

"That was an accident, a total fluke. You know I never lose things. Why would you even ask such a thing?"

It was true. Her mother was not one to misplace her possessions. She was just the opposite, clinging fiercely to every belonging, constantly taking inventory, and quite unnerved if every object was not in its designated spot, as it had been for years and years. Emily sometimes wondered if the vases and figurines had little numbers on the bottom to match specific spots on the end tables and mantel.

Now Emily wondered if the pill case had really been lost, or if her mother had felt lonely and wanted some company this afternoon.

"So," Emily said, "you found the pills and you took all the medicine you needed?"

Lillian nodded, patting her mouth with a paper napkin. "Yes, I did. There are a few more pills I have to take at night."

"And how was your lunch? Can I get you anything else? Some fruit maybe?"

"Fruit would be nice." Lillian looked surprised but pleased by the offer. "There's a pear on the windowsill. It should be ripe by now."

Emily rose and found a fine-looking yellow pear. It was perfectly ripe, as her mother had predicted. She washed it, then cut it into thin slices and arranged them on a china dish, the way her mother liked it.

"How nice," Lillian said, taking the dish. "Thank you."

"It's nice to have some company during lunch," Emily said, sitting across from her. "I ate at my desk today, but my secretary came in and we ate together. We do that every Monday, go over the week's schedule."

Lillian nodded. "Very efficient."

"We get organized," Emily agreed. "But it's nice to just chat and have a visit. The office gets busy. We don't have much time to talk about personal things."

Lillian's eyes narrowed as she picked up a slice of pear and took a small bite. She was wondering where this conversation was going, Emily could see. Lillian wanted to prepare herself, get one step ahead of her daughter.

"Mother, did you really call me over here today for those pills? Or was it because you felt lonely and wanted some company? You can tell me. It's a perfectly reasonable way to feel."

Lillian sat up straight in her chair. "What a ridiculous suggestion. I called because the medicine was lost. Fortunately, I found it."

Emily should have known. Her mother would think any admission of loneliness or needing other people was proof of some great deficit in character.

"Yes, that was lucky," Emily agreed. "Have you given any more thought to what we talked about on Saturday? Having someone come in here, a live-in housekeeper or even someone who comes for a few hours a day, to help you?"

Lillian shrugged and took a small bite from the pear slice she was holding. "No, I did not. In fact, I didn't give it a single thought. I'm sure I made my feelings perfectly clear to you and your sister."

"Yes, you did. But we really wish you would consider our feelings, too. We're both worried about you now that Sara and Luke are gone. Maybe you don't think you need anyone coming in to help you. Maybe that's true," Emily conceded, though she certainly didn't think so. "But it would make us feel better—much better—to know someone was here, helping you. Looking after you a bit, doing whatever needs to be done when we aren't available."

Lillian shook her head. "That's all a very nice way of saying I need a babysitter, Emily. And I won't have it. Some smug, overpaid, untrained stranger coming in here . . . touching everything, pestering me with their endless questions. It's simply an unnecessary and unwanted intrusion, not to mention a waste of money—my money, it goes without saying. And those people are quite expensive. . . ."

Emily's cell phone rang and she checked the number. "Excuse me, I need to take this," she said to her mother.

It was her secretary, Helen. "Emily? Mr. Cummings, from the Parks Department, is here. He was in the building for another meeting and wants to know if you can see him earlier than you had planned."

"Oh, let me see." Emily glanced at her watch. *Was it a quarter to two already? Time sure flies arguing with my mother.* "I guess I can be back in a few minutes. By two o'clock. Will that be all right for him?"

"Hold on, I'll ask." A moment later, Helen came back on the line. "That's fine. He'll be waiting for you."

"Great. I'm on my way." Emily didn't like running out on her mother like this, in the middle of such a conversation. But she wasn't making any headway, and she didn't want to miss Mr. Cummings or risk getting on his bad side when she knew he could help the town.

"Sorry, Mother. I have to get back to work." Emily rose and grabbed her jacket and purse. "I'll stop by tonight. Do you need anything from the store?"

Lillian seemed upset by the abrupt departure. "Don't bother. I have everything I need. Stores deliver these days, you know."

Emily knew her mother much preferred to have someone shopping for her and complained endlessly about deliveries, soggy vegetables, or the wrong brands or sizes.

"Well, call me if you need anything," Emily said. She kissed her mother on the cheek and left by the side door.

Score one more for Mother, Emily thought, heading for her car. She would have to call Jessica later and report this latest conversation. They definitely needed to strategize.

It seemed their mother was easily winning this match. So far, at least.

MOST OF THE BUILDINGS AT THE VA HOSPITAL IN Beverly were drab brick buildings, built sometime around World War II, David guessed. It looked more like an old military base to David than a place that would help him recover.

But when they finally found the building that housed the Physical Therapy Department, David was relieved to see it was newly built and not so ominous looking. Once Jack helped him find the wing where the new therapist was located, David urged him to go.

Jack seemed about to argue with him, then agreed. "All right, I have some errands to do. I'll come back in about an hour. Meet you here, okay?"

David nodded and watched as his father walked off down the long corridor. Why did he feel like he was being left at his first day of school?

Maybe because he had set that deadline with his father, shedding the walker by Christmas. He'd had some physical therapy before, but now there was pressure.

He hoped this therapist was good. He hoped the guy knew some magic the others had not. David picked up a magazine, *Auto World*, and paged through the pictures of new cars. Man, would he ever love to get behind the wheel of a new car. That would be an instant mood booster. He could afford a new car, right out of the showroom, but driving wasn't very likely right now. Not until he either got the feeling back in his foot or learned how to control it better.

A door near the reception area opened, and a man in a medical uniform walked out. He was quite tall with broad shoulders and an impressive, muscular build. His pale blue uniform made a stark contrast with his brown skin.

He glanced down at the file in his hand. "David Sawyer?"

"Right here." David raised his hand then lifted himself up on his walker.

The man smiled and waited by the door, holding it open while David made his way over. "Hello, David. How are you doing today?"

"Okay, I guess." David hated it when these medical people asked that question, as if they were reading from a script. David knew this guy saw a hundred patients a day and doubted he cared one way or the other.

"I'm George Henson. Just follow me, and we'll get you started with your appointment."

"Sure. No problem." David was eager to ask the new therapist a few questions, but he was having enough trouble keeping up with the walker.

Finally, they reached a large, open space where David saw several leather-covered tables, separated by curtains, lined up against each wall. The middle of the room was filled with exercise stations—bikes, treadmills, weights, traction devices, and a padded walking track with a railing on either side. In another corner, David saw a Jacuzzi tub.

Several patients were working with therapists. One guy, working on a weight machine, was missing an arm. But David noticed he had pretty impressive biceps on his other arm and a large tattoo.

George led him to one of the leather tables and pulled the curtain to one side. "I'd like you to sit up here," he said. "Need some help?"

David thought he did need help but didn't want to admit it. "I'm okay," he said. With a mighty push on his arms, he managed to hoist himself up, though the effort hurt his hip.

"So you've had some operations? Two on your right hip?" George asked.

"Right. The first didn't work out that well. They had to go in again."

"I see. Have you had any PT yet?"

David nodded. "For a few weeks after my first surgery, back in September. But none after the second."

George nodded and made a note on a chart. "Okay. Gena will be right with you. She's just finishing with another patient."

"Gena? Who's Gena?"

"Your therapist, Gena Reyes."

"I thought you were my therapist."

George smiled and shook his head. "I'm a nurse here. You've been assigned to Gena for your therapy. I work with her. Didn't someone at reception give you her name?"

David shrugged. "I don't think so."

The receptionist might have given him a name when he checked in. David had not been paying attention. He didn't listen to half of what people said to him these days, just sort of zoned out.

David glanced at George, who was looking through his medical history folder. He felt foolish for automatically assuming that a man would be a doctor or therapist and a woman would be a nurse.

Okay, his therapist was female. He could handle that. It might even be fun on some level. If anything about this deal could be pleasant.

While he considered this unexpected twist, a small, dark-haired woman whisked the curtain aside and looked straight at him. She had large brown eyes and long hair, pulled back in a tight ponytail. Her smooth skin and fine features were bare of makeup, and the only jewelry she wore was a pair of tiny gold earrings. She was in her early thirties, David guessed.

Not bad, he thought, even in her baggy medical uniform. But how was this little woman going to lift him, move him, help him exercise? He didn't mean to be a chauvinist, but he doubted she was strong enough. Maybe that's where George came in.

"Hello, Mr. Sawyer. I'm Gena Reyes, your new therapist." She extended her hand and he shook it. Her grip was firm and strong. "May I call you David?" she asked politely.

"Sure."

"Please call me Gena," she replied. Despite the offer to go with first names, her demeanor was serious, totally professional.

George handed her the file, and she began skimming David's records. "So you haven't been to therapy since October. Is that correct?"

"I needed a second operation on my hip. And I didn't start up again after that one. I've lost feeling in my right foot. I need to wear this support." He pulled up his pants leg to show her the prosthesis. "And I can't really get around without the walker."

"Have you experienced any return of feeling in your foot lately? Any tingling or even a pins-and-needles sensation?"

"No, nothing like that."

She made a note on the file. "Do you perform any exercises at home? Any stretching or the exercises you were shown?"

"Not really."

She lifted her head and looked at him. Her expression showed nothing, but David did notice a spark in her dark eyes. "What's 'not really'? Can you be a little more specific, please? Not at all? Or did you try, and feel too much discomfort to continue?"

"I did try once or twice," David replied, put on the spot. In truth, he really hadn't tried at all. "I thought I wasn't doing it correctly. I didn't want to hurt myself or throw the hip out of whack."

She didn't say anything. Just looked at him briefly then made another note on the chart.

She would sure look a lot better if she lost that deadpan expression. It was just physical therapy for goodness' sake, not brain surgery.

"All right. I need to evaluate your condition, and then we can talk about a plan for therapy. Can you get down on your own?"

"No problem," David replied, though he knew he had to be careful to land on his good foot or he might fall over.

However, in his eagerness to show Gena Reyes he was not a total mess, he miscalculated and his numb foot slipped out from under him. David would have hit the floor if not for George, who swiftly stepped forward and caught him. "Whoa there, buddy," George said with a grin.

David felt like an idiot. A lame idiot. He managed to smile back at the big man. "Thanks. I'm okay."

With both feet on the ground, not even bothering to look at Gena, he took hold of his walker again.

Gena watched him fumble a bit, which made him feel even more self-conscious and clumsy. "Okay, come with me," she said, making no move to help him. "Out to the exercise area. Let's get a better idea of what we're dealing with."

"Yes, let's," David replied tartly.

He would have liked to watch Gena the way she was watching him, which he couldn't do, of course, without falling on his face. He couldn't get a read on her. She wasn't exactly the warm and nurturing type. In fact, he had known a few drill sergeants who exuded more charm.

Out in the exercise area, David did the best he could as Gena asked him to execute certain movements—travel across the room and back with the walker, pick up an object from the table and then from the floor. Sit and rise from a chair. Attempt sit-ups, modified push-ups, and leg raises. Stretch to touch his toes. He knew this was a necessary part of the process . . . so why did he feel as if she was purposely making it hard for him? Why did he feel like some sort of trained animal being put through its paces? This didn't bode well for the future, he thought grimly. If Gena was such a taskmaster during a basic evaluation, what was she like during the real therapy?

"Is that as far as you can stretch, David? Are you sure?"

"Yeah, that's it," David grunted. He sat up straight, feeling beads of sweat break out on his forehead. Man, was he out of shape. And when was the last time he had broken a sweat like this? He couldn't remember.

"I'd like you to try walking without the walker, using the handrails over here." Gena directed him to an exercise station where two parallel handrails were set up about waist high, a lane of matted flooring between them.

David parked his walker and positioned himself between the rails, then tried to take a few steps, mainly supporting himself with his arms. It was hard work to maneuver his bad leg. He could hardly make it down the lane. About halfway through, he had to stop, taking deep breaths to try to ease the pain.

"Okay, that's enough. George will help you now."

David was about to insist he could reach the end but found he didn't have the energy to argue. Feeling beat down and embarrassed, he allowed George to help him off the rails and get back in the walker.

"You can rest up on the table," Gena told him. "Do you want some help?"

"I can do it, thanks," David insisted. He slowly made his way back to the table, exhausted and hanging on to his walker like a life preserver. He didn't want to admit that he needed help but realized if someone didn't give him a hand, he might end up on the floor. For real this time.

As he reached the table he looked toward George, but Gena stepped up and before he knew what was happening, she wrapped his arm around her shoulder, put her arm around his waist, and easily lifted him up so he was sitting on the table.

Man, she was strong. He had about an entire foot of height and sixty or even seventy pounds on her. How had she done it? It was like a magic trick.

When he looked down at her, the corner of her mouth had edged up just a tiny bit. It wasn't what you would call a smile, not even close. But David could tell his shock had amused her.

"What's the matter, David? Do you feel all right?"

He nodded and quickly looked down at his sneakers, realizing he had been staring at her. "I'm fine."

"Would you like some water?"

"Yes, I would. Thanks."

She took a frosty water bottle off the side table and handed it to him, then continued to write on his chart as he drank.

He had to say one thing for this routine. He wasn't staring out a window, lost in a fog. He felt more alert and focused than he had for weeks.

When Gena finally looked back at him, he expected her to give him an assessment of his condition. Instead, she started asking more questions—questions about his injuries, his operations, and how long it took to recover from each.

"Let's see, I'll start from the top and go down," he began. He had been asked these same questions so many times, he felt like a recorded announcement. Was she too lazy to just read the chart? "I had a fractured skull and a concussion, dislocated shoulder, broken collarbone and arm . . ."

"Right arm?" she said, her eyes scanning his file.

"That's correct. It was fractured. I needed a plate in there. A few broken ribs, punctured lung. All that wasn't so bad. The legs, that was the worst of it," he said. "Both of them got smashed when the Humvee turned over."

"You were fired on?" she asked.

"Yeah. I was in the motor pool, a mechanic. My team was sent to service a vehicle not too far from the base." But any time you left base, there was danger of an attack, even on well-patrolled roads. "The Humvee we were traveling in was fired on." David paused. It was still hard to recount the story without getting emotional. "We were hit, and it turned over."

Gena cast him a rare, sympathetic look. "You were lucky you got out alive."

"Yes, I was. My sergeant pulled me out before the whole thing exploded. He was a real hero."

Not me, David thought. *I didn't do very much. Just managed to come back in one piece. Sort of.* It made him uncomfortable when people praised his service, as if he had been incredibly brave over there. He knew what real courage was. What real sacrifice was. He didn't feel he deserved to be called anything like that, not next to a man like Nolan.

Gena held him in her dark, steady gaze. "So you sustained substantial injury to both legs. And on the right, the hip as well."

"Correct. The right leg seems the worst of it. Even though the left one's still pretty messed up."

Not a very precise medical description, he knew, but it about covered his condition.

"How did you feel after the hip replacement surgery?"

"The first or the second?" he asked. "They screwed something up the first time. The wrong size ball joint or something. They had to take a do-over."

"Right. A second surgery. How did you feel after that one?"

"I was in pain. I still am," he added. "And no feeling at all in my foot. But you know that already, right?"

She ignored his question. "I see you're taking medication. What about your diet? Are you eating well—a balanced diet, nutritious foods?"

"If it was up to my father and stepmother, I'd be eating ten meals a day. I'd be big as a barn." He looked down at his body, which was not only thinner but much less muscular than it had been months ago when he shipped out of Fort Bragg.

Gena's mouth twisted in a half smile. "What's your social life been like since you've come back?"

"Social life? What's that?"

Her eyebrows went up a notch. "Do you see any friends? Do you have a girlfriend?"

"No . . . nothing going on like that right now. I lost touch with the guys I went to high school with. Most of them have moved away. I wouldn't have much to say to them now anyway."

He thought of Christine. She was a friend. But seeing her that one time wasn't what Gena meant, and David was sure he wouldn't be seeing Christine again anytime soon.

"Friends from the army?"

"Once in a while there's an e-mail. My life is pretty dull. I don't have too much to say. Most of the guys I was tight with in my squad are still over there . . . except our sergeant. He died that night we got hit."

"I'm sorry," she said sincerely. "I'm sorry you lost your friend."

David shrugged. He didn't know what else to tell her. He hadn't known those guys too long. But they had grown tight, especially the nine guys in his squad. They had depended on each other for their very survival. Training together, sleeping together, eating together, going through life-threatening experiences together—he felt a bond with them that he had never felt with anyone before. And never expected to feel again.

It had been pure, blind chance he had not died when the Humvee was hit and later, when it exploded. He knew that there was nothing he could have done to save Sergeant Nolan. To change the flip of that coin. But he still felt a nagging guilt, as if he had somehow betrayed the man by surviving him.

"Any trouble sleeping?" Gena asked.

He paused, wondering how truthful he should be. "Not great," he admitted.

"Because of the pain?"

"Sometimes."

"Any other reasons?" she persisted. "Headaches? Nightmares?"

"Yeah, sometimes. But that's pretty common, I hear, for someone like me." He looked up at her. "Are you a shrink, too? It was my understanding that you just covered the physical repairs. I didn't know you were qualified to get into my head."

His question held a challenging edge. If he wanted to see a psychiatrist, he would make an appointment with one. Why did she need to ask him all these questions?

She tucked the folder under her arm and met his gaze. "Everything's connected, David. Your emotional state, your attitude, your body. Your physical recovery is greatly impacted by your psychological state. And so is any work that we do together."

"Well, maybe, but it seems to me if I go to a gym and press weights for a month, I still get a muscle in my arm. Whether I'm smiling or crying."

She tilted her head. "Maybe. But this is different. This isn't just bodybuilding. It's healing, inside and out. Have you met with a counselor at any point to talk about your night traumas or your feelings about the friends you've lost?"

David sighed and sat back. She wouldn't give up, would she? "Yeah, once or twice. I didn't get much out of it. I'm okay," he insisted. "I mean, considering what I went through. Hey, anybody would feel down, a little messed up. I need to start walking again. That's what I need. Talking isn't going to help me. Walking is."

He knew he sounded angry but he couldn't stop himself. She had pushed his buttons with all her questions.

"If that's how you feel, counseling probably won't help you," she agreed. "But you ought to think about it, reconsider."

"Okay, I will," he said just to close the subject. "What do you think about my condition? About my physical therapy? Any ideas about that?"

She took a moment before answering. "If all you want to talk about is your body, I'd say you ought to consider yourself lucky. You didn't come out of it badly at all."

David knew that was true. All he had to do was look around at his fellow patients. Take the guy on the next table, who was missing an arm, for instance. What would it be like coming home in that condition?

He took another swallow of water, feeling like a self-absorbed slug. "Listen," he said, "I know everybody's got a story. I know I'm damn lucky to have come back in one piece. You don't have to tell me that. But it still stinks to be trapped inside this walker, dragging a half-dead foot."

She nodded, the same, serious expression that didn't reveal one hint of emotion or what was really going on in her head.

She thought he was a spoiled, whining baby, David decided. Well, so what if she did?

"You want to get rid of the walker. Is that your priority?"

"My priority? Actually, no. My priority would be to have

my legs working again. To be able to apply for a job as a cop or a firefighter, which was my plan once my enlistment was up. Until I got hit."

David quickly realized that somewhere during his explanation his voice had grown progressively louder. He was practically shouting at her. As if this physical therapist had anything to do with his condition, any say in what would be.

Well, she had asked him the question hadn't she?

He stared at her, feeling awkward. He should apologize, he knew. But Gena seemed unfazed, unmoved by the angry, crazy, disabled soldier yelling at her. She probably got that all the time.

"I read the medical report," she answered evenly. "There's still some chance you could regain feeling in your foot. But we have to assume that you won't and build up other muscles so that you can manage with a cane and the brace." She waited a moment for him to reply. When he didn't she continued. "It appears, at this time anyway, that any job with demanding physical requirements is off the table. I'm sorry."

David was not shocked by this assessment. He had heard this prognosis before from his doctors. But it was still discouraging to be reminded of his losses.

Maybe he had come here today expecting this new therapist to know something that the doctors didn't. To look him over, broken parts and all, and say, "Hey, no problem. I can fix that. You're going to be one hundred percent in no time, pal."

Maybe that's what he had secretly been hoping for. Not this flat-out, in your face, no icing on the cake honesty.

He took a long breath and shook his head. "Great. Just what I wanted to hear. I'm going to have a limp and need a cane the rest of my life? Is that what you're saying?"

She stared back at him, meeting his angry glare with a cool gaze. "That might be the final outcome. A lot depends on you, David, on your attitude and goals. What you're willing to put into your therapy." She paused, and closed his folder, neatly lining up the pages inside. "Think about it. Get back to me."

"What do you mean, get back to you? I thought I was assigned to you. I don't know much about VA hospitals, but I know they're part of the army. Which is not big on choices, last I heard."

"There are assignments and rules I have to follow," Gena conceded. "But if I meet a patient whom I think isn't going to be a good fit, there are ways to pass that case to another therapist."

So, he was reduced now to just a "case"? What was going on here? He had expected some gentle handling and sympathy—lots of sympathy, actually.

"So you don't want to work with me, is that it?" he asked.

"I didn't say that. I'm being honest with you, giving you the complete picture. I give my all, David. I don't like to work with patients who aren't making the same effort." When he didn't answer, she added, "Would you rather I didn't treat you like an adult?"

"Of course not," he snapped. Though secretly he wasn't sure. His father and Julie had been handling him as if he were made of glass. Signing on with this woman was like re-upping.

"Think about it. This is a partnership. I don't fix you like a mechanic repairs a car," she clarified. "Your next appointment is Wednesday. If you want to be assigned to a different therapist, you can ask at that time. No problem."

Before David could reply, Gena checked her watch. "I'm due at my next appointment. I'll see you on Wednesday."

"Right. When pigs fly, ma'am," he wanted to say. But he decided it was best not to say anything.

Flipping the curtain aside, she was gone. George soon

appeared as David sat struggling to get off the table. His arms felt weak and rubbery from all the exercise, and he rested for a moment, before trying to lift himself up and off.

Without saying a word, George gripped him around the waist and helped him down, then held the walker in place.

"Thanks," David mumbled.

"Don't mention it. That's what I'm here for."

"Really? You'd never know it from talking to your boss."

George laughed. "Gena? She's got her own style, that's for sure. But she gets results. Nobody will argue with that."

George delivered him to the waiting room door where David immediately spotted Jack, who sat reading a newspaper.

"So, how did it go?" Jack asked, stepping to David's side.

"My new physical therapist reminds me of my drill sergeant in basic training," David reported. "Except even wor—" He broke off as he noticed Gena on the other side of the waiting area, speaking to a patient in a wheelchair. "That's her."

Jack followed David's glance and looked back at his son with a surprised smile. "You must have had some good-looking officers in the army, son."

David didn't answer. His father didn't realize. Once you got past the looks, all you got was cold, mean . . . and meaner.

REVEREND BEN HAD DECIDED TO LEAVE HIS OFFICE early on Monday. He often took Mondays off, needing at least one day of rest after the weekend. But there were a few things he had to take care of today. Christmas was the busiest time of the year at church, with the Christmas fair, the pageant, and the special services. Ben could already feel the momentum building.

As he closed the door of his office and checked the lock,

he saw Laura Miller, one of his parishioners, in the long hallway, standing by the bulletin board.

She turned, looking startled when she saw him. "Oh, Reverend Ben . . . can I put this sign up somewhere? I can't seem to find a space."

Almost reluctantly, she handed him an index card. He quickly read the note written in bold block letters:

REFRIGERATOR NEEDED. ANY AGE OR CONDITION. IF IT RUNS, WE'LL TAKE IT.

Her name and phone number were written on the bottom.

Well, that was clear and to the point, Ben thought. "Having problems with your refrigerator?" he asked kindly.

"It's been on its way out for a while. Then it broke down a few days ago. It isn't worth fixing . . . but we really can't afford a new one right now," she explained. "We're hoping to find something secondhand. Sometimes people are redoing a kitchen and they want everything new. They'll throw out perfectly good appliances or stick them in the garage, you know?"

Ben knew that type of person existed. There just weren't many in his congregation.

"That's true. Maybe someone will come forward," he said encouragingly. "How are you managing in the meantime?"

"We've got a cold chest in the kitchen and some frozen food stashed at my neighbor's house, and we're buying just small amounts of perishables at a time. Luckily, it's been so cold out, we can leave some things on the porch."

Laura's tone was light, but the improvisation sounded inconvenient and complicated to Ben. He knew the Millers had three children and had to be using more groceries every day than could fit into a picnic ice chest.

But Paul Miller had been laid off from his factory job in September and hadn't found any work yet. Laura worked part-time in a clothing store in the mall, but that job surely didn't pay much.

She was still searching for a spot to stick the index card. Ben took down a notice for the youth group that was out of date and put the card up in the middle of the board. "People should see it there. I can announce this before the service if you like?"

Sometimes families preferred to keep their needs private. They felt uncomfortable advertising their financial downturns. He knew it was important to be aware of that.

Laura thought it over a moment. "We don't mind. I'd appreciate it if you would say a word. There's no sense being proud about it. We are in a jam."

"Okay, I'll do that," Ben agreed.

He walked to the door with Mrs. Miller and held it open for her. He saw Jack Sawyer coming up the path toward the church. A Christmas tree was balanced on one shoulder, and his arms were full of pine wreaths and roping.

Ben remembered Jack had promised to deliver decorations for the church today. He told Ben he would be around in the late afternoon, but Ben had forgotten. He was glad now they hadn't missed each other.

Jack was donating everything, including trees, for the sanctuary and Fellowship Hall. A very generous gift, Ben thought, and somewhat surprising.

But then Jack had changed a lot the last year or so. He had been coming to church regularly, too, which he had never done while his first wife, Claire, was alive, even though Claire had been an active member of the congregation and their son, David, had gone all through church school and been confirmed.

But Ben thought the changes in Jack's personality owed much more to his marriage to Julie than to sitting through sermons. Either way, it gave Ben hope to see how a person could experience a personal renaissance. If it happened to Jack Sawyer, there's hope for us all, he thought.

"Looks like you're getting a delivery, Reverend," Laura Miller said with a laugh.

"Yes, it does," Ben said. "I'd better help." He quickly said good-bye to Mrs. Miller, and trotted down the path toward Jack.

"Jack, let me give you a hand."

"That's okay. I've got it." Jack held the bundle up to his chest with little effort. Though he wasn't a very tall man, he was quite strong. "There's some more roping in the back of the truck. I couldn't grab it all on the first trip."

"I'll get it," Ben offered. "The sanctuary doors are open," he added. "You can leave all that in the back."

The deacons were meeting on Wednesday night to decorate so that the church would be decked out in its holiday finery for the weekend, the second Sunday of Advent.

While Jack continued toward the church, Ben headed for the truck, which was parked at the end of the path. He noticed there was someone in the passenger seat and soon realized it was Jack's son, David.

Ben hadn't seen David since his return from Iraq. He felt bad that he hadn't gone to visit the young man at home, but when he offered once or twice, Jack and Julie had put him off. Politely, of course, but Ben got the hint: David wasn't interested in a visit from his former minister—or maybe just any visitors.

Which was all the more reason he should have persisted, Ben reminded himself.

But here he was. Ben didn't want to miss this chance to say hello and wish him well.

He walked up to the truck window and waved. "Hello, David. Good to see you."

David nodded. Ben could tell the young man wasn't in the mood to socialize. For a moment, he didn't think David was even going to roll down the window. But he stood there patiently, and finally David hit a button and the glass rolled down.

He looked older, Ben thought. Ben had seen him briefly last winter when Jack had brought David to church, before he left for the Middle East. Ben remembered distinctly, because last year a Sunday had fallen between Christmas and New Year's. He had been surprised to see Jack without Julie; they had looked so comfortable together on Christmas, just days before. And he had been positively shocked to see that David had come home after so many years estranged from his father.

David's features had changed in the last year. A certain softness, left over from the teenage years, had hardened. His face looked leaner, his jaw and cheekbones sharper. But it was in his eyes that Ben saw the greatest difference. David's blue-gray eyes looked shadowed and dull, as if the intensity of what he had seen in the war had robbed them of their light.

Ben extended his hand through the window, and David shook it automatically. "How are you, David? How does it feel being back home?"

"Pretty good, Reverend. Pretty good." David forced a smile.

"How are you doing physically? Your father told me you're still recovering from surgery, and it's not been easy for you."

"It has not been easy, no sir," David agreed. A muscle in his cheek twitched, and Ben realized his innocent comment had hit a nerve. "I'm starting physical therapy. I had the first appointment today, at the VA hospital in Beverly."

"Good. I hope it goes well for you." Ben paused, moved by the expression on David's face. He could see how David was struggling to act and sound normal. To say what he believed was expected—nothing challenging, or even necessarily true.

But Ben could see clearly that the young man was hurting inside, his spirit wounded as deeply as his body. Ben wished there was something he could say to cut through the disingenuous script they were both reading from right now. Some meaningful words that would help the boy, if only to give a sign that he, Ben, recognized that everything was not okay, that things were not "coming along" all that smoothly.

Shouldn't a minister, of all people, know what to do, what to say? he asked himself. It was moments like this when Ben felt tested, wondering if he was any good at all at his calling.

"I know a little about going through physical therapy. Secondhand, actually," Ben said finally. "From what I can see, the first session is the hardest—and the second, not much better. The third one . . . that might be even worse than the first."

David stared at him with a confused, bewildered look, as if he thought his old pastor had gone a little soft in the head. "Thanks for the warning."

"That's how it went for my wife, anyway," Ben explained. "Carolyn had a stroke about six years ago. She lost the ability to speak clearly and lost some feeling in her right hand. She's a pianist, so that was devastating for her."

"I remember. I think I still lived at home then."

"You were probably in high school at the time," Ben calculated.

"How is she now?" David asked.

"She's fully recovered. Her speech returned first. But her hand was the problem. She didn't regain full use of it until two years ago. Pretty amazing how it happened. She had actually given up on ever playing the piano again with two hands. Then it came back . . . out of the blue."

Ben didn't elaborate. The truth was, the muscle control in Carolyn's hand had come back through an effort of faith and prayer. Ben still wasn't sure if he would call it a miracle, though his dear wife did.

Ben was afraid David would be turned off by the story. Too much spiritual talk quickly shut young people down. You had to go slowly, Ben had learned.

"—and her speech is perfectly clear now, too. She hasn't

lost her Southern accent though. Carolyn was determined to hang on to that," he added with a smile. Ben's expression turned serious again. "I guess what I'm trying to say is, it was a long road. Longer than we thought. But she made it."

"I'm glad she's better," David replied.

Ben wondered if the boy thought he was just a rambling windbag. He had said enough, probably more than enough. He reached through the window and briefly patted David's shoulder.

"Good luck, son. I hope to see you again soon."

"Thanks, Reverend." David's voice finally sounded sincere.

"It was nice talking to you."

"Nice talking to you, too."

Ben turned and walked to the back of the truck, to take out the rest of the pine roping. He saw Jack approaching on the path, and they reached the truck's tailgate at just about the same moment.

"Sorry to keep you waiting, Jack. I was just saying hello to David."

"That's all right." Jack glanced toward the front of the truck and lowered his voice. "I'm glad you had a minute to talk to him. Coming back and dealing with an injury has been hard. He's not doing that well."

Ben could tell Jack was worried. At least he was aware of David's state of mind, not in denial or so elated over his son's survival that he couldn't see what was going on with the boy.

"He has a lot to deal with, Jack. It's a lot for you and Julie, too, I imagine."

Jack nodded quickly, looking down at his boots.

"If you need to talk with me, about anything at all, just give a call, okay?" Ben offered.

"Yes, I will." Jack reached into the truck bed, lifted out the big coil of pine garland. "I've got it," he said. "Let me bring this in for you."

"Well, thank you, Jack," Ben said, following him back into the church. "And thank you for this wonderful donation. It's very generous of you."

"No problem. We're happy to do it." Jack set down the roping with the rest of the greenery. "Thanks for talking to David. I've been trying but . . . I'm not very good at it."

"I'm sure you're better at it than you think. Just stay with it. It can be very frustrating, watching him struggle. Keep believing in his recovery, even when he doesn't. Especially when he doesn't," Ben clarified. "That might be the hardest part."

"I'll do my best," Jack said quietly.

"That's all we can do. And pray. Then, leave the rest to God."

"I'll try to do that, too."

Leaving the rest to God was hard, especially when a parent had to stand by and watch his child flounder, even suffer. Ben knew something about that.

There was no doubt that Jack Sawyer loved his son and would do anything for him. Ben hoped that love would help pull this ex-soldier through.

CHAPTER FIVE

ᴰAD, LOOK WHAT I FOUND. IT'S PERFECT." GRACE Hegman practically ran right up the full flight of stairs. She entered the apartment over her shop a bit winded.

Her father sat in the parlor in his favorite wingback chair, reading the newspaper. It was nearly eleven, time to open the shop, but he could no longer handle that duty on his own.

Grace wasn't worried. Wednesday was the slowest day of the week, even during the Christmas season. Besides, they had important business to discuss right here. A treasure had dropped into her hands this morning, and they needed to do something about it.

"What is it, Grace? You seem so excitable lately." Digger put down the newspaper, greeting her with a curious stare.

She tugged loose the silk scarf tied at her neck with one hand, the other hand digging into the pocket of her jacket.

"Here, read this card, Dad. Just what we're looking for."

Grace handed down an index card, a message written in neat, block letters.

Digger wore his glasses but still held the card at arm's length to read aloud. "Refrigerator wanted. Any age or condition. If it runs, we'll take it. . . ."

Grace saw his eyes widen first, then his smile. "Good work, Gracie. Where the devil did you find this?"

Grace felt pleased by his praise. She slipped off her jacket and sat on the antique couch, a velvet-covered camelback with claw feet. "I was over at church this morning, dropping something off for the Christmas Fair. I was just walking out when I took a look at the bulletin board, and there it was, stuck right in the middle. As if someone had planted it there on purpose, for me to see. I wasn't sure if I should take it home. But I had no pen or pencil handy to copy the phone number. And I didn't want anyone else to see it and call and maybe offer that family some old hunk of junk—when we could buy a nice, new fridge for them."

"Good thinking." Digger dipped his white head in agreement. "You did the right thing. We've got this covered."

"Yes, we do. Or we will very soon." Grace smoothed down her cardigan sweater. "So, when shall we go shopping?"

"How about tonight, right after you close up?"

Normally, Grace planted herself in the Bramble from sunup to sundown. The antique store, taking care of her father, and church were the three compass points that defined her life. They were usually more than enough to keep her busy and content. But this morning it felt as if five o'clock were days away. She couldn't wait to buy this important gift and know it would soon be delivered.

She glanced at her watch then back at her father. "I think we should go right now. Get it over with. There's a big appliance store on the turnpike. The salespeople are pretty helpful, and I bet the place is empty in the middle of the day. If we wait until tonight, it will be more crowded and confusing."

Lately, her father didn't do too well in a big noisy place like an appliance store. That was also a consideration.

"What about the shop? Your customers?"

"Oh, nobody comes by this early on a Wednesday, and we won't be gone long. If we go right now, we'll be back in an hour or so. I'll put a note on the door."

"All right. If you say so." Digger rose from the chair and jingled the change in his pocket. It was a welcome sound. She knew he only did that when he was happy. "Now, don't forget, we need a wad of that money."

"Don't worry, I'll run down and grab some before we go. I can look up the Miller family's address in the church directory, for the delivery."

Grace put her jacket back on and picked up her purse. Her father found his big wool peacoat and stocking cap on the bentwood coat tree that stood on the landing.

When he was dressed, he stood with his shoulders back, waiting for Grace's attention. "So, do I look like Santa Claus?"

Grace looked him over. "Not quite. But you're getting there."

"You know I don't eat cauliflower, Jessica. It doesn't agree with me, never has." Lillian removed the offending vegetable from the plastic shopping bag and handed it to her daughter. "Here, take this home for your children. They need the vitamins."

Jessica set the cauliflower aside and tried to finish unloading the bags of groceries as quickly—and as surreptitiously—as she could. Her mother had sent her off with a very detailed list but somehow, by the time Jessica returned with the requested items, Lillian's needs and preferences had changed.

Amazing, Jessica thought. She turned to see her mother

slipping on her reading glasses in order to scrutinize the label on a box of muesli cereal. It was the same brand her mother had been eating all her life, or at least since Jessica had been a child. She was sure her mother could recite the information on that label by heart. Still, Lillian looked positively engrossed.

"This doesn't have as much fiber as I thought." Lillian peered up at her daughter. "Is this a different type from the one I usually get?"

"No, Mother. The exact same. I don't think they make any other type of that stuff." Jessica had tried eating it once. It tasted like bark scraped off a tree.

"Hmm." Lillian put the box down, looking unconvinced. "Take out the one Sara bought for me. I want to compare the labels."

Jessica found the cereal box and handed it to her mother, all the while suppressing a smile. If only Sara were here now to see this. Jessica knew the irony of it would not be lost on her dear niece. For three years, poor Sara had put up with her grandmother's grocery inspections and now, suddenly, everything Sara had bought was the high-water mark, the very standard, of Lillian's needs.

Jessica had arrived early. She had done some picking up around the house and two loads of laundry before going out to do the shopping, which was taking forever to unpack.

She wanted to get home before Tyler got home from school, but she needed to make her mother lunch and then make her something for dinner and leave it in the fridge.

These were but a few of the tasks for a housekeeper or home aide. There was a growing list of them—if someone would be allowed to write it all down without starting World War III, Jessica thought.

A knock sounded on the side door. Right on time, Jessica thought.

"Who's that? I'm not expecting anyone." Lillian looked

over to the door where they saw Emily standing outside, waiting to be let in.

"Hmmph." Lillian made an irritated sound. "Doesn't she have a key? And what is she doing here at this time of day?"

Her mother was right. It was only a few minutes past eleven, an unlikely time for Emily to visit.

"She must have been in the neighborhood and just wanted to say hello." Jessica walked over to open the door for her sister.

Jessica knew why her sister hadn't used her key. They both knew their mother disliked it. The keys were supposed to be saved for emergencies. Lillian felt it was a sign of bad manners, even disrespect, when they came "barging" in, unannounced.

"Hello, Mother," Emily said cheerfully. "Hi, Jess. Did you just get back from shopping? I'm glad I didn't miss you."

"It only looks that way. She's been back awhile now," Lillian noted, casting a look at Jessica—one that said, *It's taking you an awfully long time to put away these groceries today, isn't it?*

If her mother didn't question every can or box that came out of the bags, the stuff would have been stored hours ago, Jessica wanted to explain.

Fortunately, there was no need to explain anything to Emily. Her sister knew exactly what had been going on here.

Emily picked up the head of cauliflower from the counter.

"Fresh vegetables. Very healthy," she said.

"Not that one, it disagrees horribly. I don't know how it found its way into the cart. Would you like to take it home?" Lillian offered. "It's up for grabs, an orphan cauliflower."

Jessica ignored their mother. "Want some coffee, Em? I just made a pot."

"I would love a cup, thanks." Emily took off her coat and sat down at the table.

"So, what brings you around at this time of day, Emily?

Why aren't you running some important meeting? Or solving the village crisis du jour?"

"The crisis du jour has been solved, Mother," Emily said lightly. "So I gave everyone at village hall the rest of the day off."

"Hah." Her mother gave a mocking laugh. "I sincerely doubt that."

Jessica served Emily a cup of coffee and offered one to her mother.

"None for me, thank you." Lillian held out her hand, like a crossing guard. "I'm elated enough, finding both my devoted daughters here so . . . coincidentally. Isn't this an unexpected pleasure?"

Emily sipped her coffee, her eyes wide and innocent looking.

Jessica fixed her own cup at the counter, not ready yet to join them. Ninety-nine percent warm milk with just a spoonful of decaf. That was one thing she hated about being pregnant, cutting out coffee. Some women never went back but she would never get used to doing without.

Finally, she sat down at the table and took a sip, glancing at Emily over the rim. Their mother had definitely caught the scent of something. Lillian was like a finely bred hunting dog. She wouldn't give up until she tracked down her prey.

"Sara called last night. She sounded very happy," Emily reported. "Everything's going well at work, and they're almost unpacked. Luke is building some bookcases for her in the spare bedroom."

"Building bookcases?" Lillian scoffed. "Didn't he find a job yet?"

"He just interviewed on Monday, Mother. Even if he gets the job, it's going to take a little while to find out."

"Well, she can't say I didn't warn her. If he would rather build bookcases than look for a paying job, I say that's cause for concern. She never told me anything about book-cases," Lillian added with a touch of indignation.

"So you've spoken to Sara, too?" Jessica said.

"Of course I've spoken to her." Lillian tugged the edges of the cardigan that was draped over her shoulders. "I've spoken with her several times since she moved."

Jessica cast Emily a look. Their mother could go weeks without calling either one of them, unless she needed to report one of her emergencies. But she obviously had been calling Sara.

"I guess you miss them, don't you?" Emily asked bluntly.

"Miss them? Not one bit," Lillian insisted. "I was just concerned for her. You seem to think anything that knuck-leheaded husband of hers does is just hunky-dory. Some-one has to look out for her welfare. I told her not to rent in a bad neighborhood and to be very careful about signing any long-term lease."

"The neighborhood is lovely, Mother. It's Cambridge, for goodness' sake," Jessica assured her.

"Well then, case closed." Lillian shrugged. "I won't give those two another thought. Honestly, I much prefer the sol-itude, the blessed peace and quiet. I can hear myself think again." She looked at each of her daughters in turn. "You have no idea what a racket they would make, with their music and TV shows. Cooking in here at night, banging pots and pans."

Emily glanced at Jessica, a silent signal that their mother was leading them way off track. They had a plan and needed to stick with it, or this afternoon's sneak attack would be another victory for Lillian.

"Mother, I don't believe you," Emily challenged her. "I'm sure that you miss both of them, banging pots and pans and all."

When their mother just sat back with a frown, Jessica saw a chance to speak up and help the cause. "It's only logical that after three years you would miss them, Mother. And everything they used to do for you."

"Why is it logical? I never asked them to stay with me. It was a complete intrusion to have them living here." She turned to Emily. "Why, the only reason your daughter and her layabout husband came to live here was entirely for their benefit. They had no place else to go, so out of the goodness of my heart, I took them in."

Emily sighed loudly. "Mother, please, that was not the way it was at all, and you know it. You were in the hospital after your fall, and the doctor wanted you to go into a rehabilitation center, but you refused. He told us you could only go home with live-in help, meaning a nurse. But you refused that, too. And Sara offered to stay with you, because you were so stubborn and unhappy and had to come home on your own terms. You can't rewrite history. That's how it was, Mother."

Lillian's head snapped back as if she were sailing into a strong wind. "Balderdash. That's not how I remember it, not at all. For a relatively young person, you don't have a very good memory, Emily."

Jessica saw her sister's face go red. She reached over and squeezed Emily's hand. Jessica had always disliked confrontations, especially arguments with their mother. Emily was much better at it. All through her childhood, whenever the two of them butted heads, Jessica had lain low. But today, she had to stand with her sister. She couldn't let Emily take on this lioness in her den, all alone.

"Listen, we can sit here and argue all day about why Sara and Luke came to live here," Jessica said in a reasonable tone. "The point we're trying to make, Mother, is that they are gone now. Totally gone. And now you're alone and need some help around here."

"Exactly," Emily agreed. "That's the point we're trying to make. Maybe you didn't really need their help a few years ago, when they first came, but you certainly need some help now."

"Just a few hours a day," Jessica added. "Someone to help you keep the house in order, to go shopping and cook for you."

"I see. To relieve both of you of your jobs, you mean?" Lillian said shrewdly.

"We'll still come all the time. You know that. But we can't always be here when you need us," Emily answered her. "Once Jessica has her baby, it's going to be even harder for her to rush right over when you call or stay all day to help you. And she'll have to bring the baby with her."

Jessica saw her mother make a face. Lillian did not much like the grandchildren she had now, except for Sara, who was an adult and could carry on an intelligent conversation. She tolerated the younger ones, but had almost no patience for babies, whom she saw as disruptive and messy little creatures, always interrupting things.

Jessica had left her job at the bank over a month ago. Working full-time, running a house, and taking care of her boys while pregnant had just been too much for her. Since she'd been home, her number was first on Lillian's speed dial. Even with Sara and Luke around, there was always some emergency.

But Emily was right, once the baby came she couldn't just toss on a jacket and run over here every five minutes. It wasn't realistic or fair to her own family.

Lillian straightened her spine. "You girls don't want to help me, is that it? Well, who needs you? I can get along fine, don't worry your pretty heads. Grocery stores deliver, you know. I can get anything I need by just picking up the phone—complete dinners, hot and ready to eat. I don't need to burden you two, with your busy lives."

Lillian had tossed down the guilt card. Jessica had been wondering how long it would take for that one to be pulled from her bag of tricks.

"Mother, that is not what we're saying. We'll still come by, as much as ever. We would just feel better if someone was here with you," Jessica explained.

"You definitely need someone here, at least for some part of the day," Emily continued. "There's no use arguing about it anymore."

"Oh, really?" Lillian tilted her head with interest. "How could that be? You make it sound as if I have no choice in the matter."

Emily glanced at Jessica. Jessica knew what was coming and braced herself. Emily took the plunge. "We've tried to speak to you about this, Mother, several times. We had to move forward, for your own good. I spoke to an agency yesterday, and arrangements have been made. They're sending someone over tomorrow."

"Sending someone over?" Lillian's pale blue eyes widened with shock. "Who is this someone?"

"We don't know yet," Jessica admitted. "It's more of an interview."

"But they're good and reliable . . . and friendly," Emily insisted. "I've found a terrific agency. They screen their aides carefully and train everyone they send out."

"We thought you could meet a few candidates and decide," Jessica piped up.

"Two or three, tops. They're all highly recommended," Emily assured her. "It shouldn't take long to choose someone you like."

Someone her mother liked? The baby in her belly would be in college by then, Jessica wanted to say.

Emily, of course, knew the odds. They had already covered this ground privately, debating over whether to choose someone for their mother or let her do the interviews. They both doubted their mother would find anyone acceptable, no matter how many people she interviewed, but the process would give her some sense of control. Which was vital, they both knew.

Lillian squinted at them. "You've ganged up on me. This was all planned. That's why you left work today, Emily. To corner me here, with your sister. To ambush me."

Jessica didn't reply. It was true, they had planned this ambush and what they would say. And they both knew their mother would figure it out sooner or later.

Emily sat back and raised her chin. "We're only thinking of you, of your well-being and safety. For goodness' sake, you act as if we're trying to punish you."

"Mother, won't you at least consider the idea?" Jessica leaned across the table to appeal. "Meet a few of the people from the agency?"

Lillian paused and took a long breath. "I'll think about it, I suppose. If you both insist." Then she looked at Emily. "I'm just warning you, don't start sending people over here without my approval. I'm not agreeing yet to having a parade of strangers coming through this house."

"It doesn't need to be a parade, Mother," Emily pointed out, "if you could simply settle on one quickly."

"No need for sarcasm, Emily. This isn't a town council meeting where everyone jumps when you snap your fingers," Lillian retorted. "Why, just last week I read in the paper how some helpless old woman was robbed blind by one of these so-called certified, responsible companions. Robbed blind, I tell you. Is that what you want to happen to me?"

"Of course not, Mother," Emily said. "The point is just the opposite. We want you to be safe."

"We don't want to worry about you," Jessica repeated.

"Of course, that's the intention. But you girls have always been so naive. You have no idea what really goes on in these situations. Or perhaps you just don't want to face it."

It was hard for Jessica to remain patient when her mother got this way. She was ready to give up and go home. She could see her sister struggling to hold on to her temper and hoped Emily wouldn't blow up. That wouldn't help at all. Lillian had a way of provoking them both, but especially Emily. Situations would build and build and then explode in some big drama, which played right into Lillian's hands. Once they lost their temper, she could dismiss anything they said.

"Mother, the reality is this," Emily said in a strained tone. "You can't live completely on your own in this big house any longer. It's not safe or even practical. We would be very irresponsible to let you. If you can't abide having a housekeeper or part-time help here, then we'll have to think of some other solution, which I am sure you would like even less."

"Such as?" Lillian asked, looked genuinely alarmed.

"Such as selling the house and having you move in with one of us," Emily proposed.

Oh, dear. Now she'd done it. Jessica looked over at her sister. Hadn't they agreed to hold back on that ultimatum? But of course, their mother had pushed Emily to her limit. Who could blame her for putting all the cards on the table— even if they were cards that they both knew their mother would hate. Never mind that they both knew the "moving in with one of us" idea was also a disaster scenario.

Jessica saw her mother's face go pale as paper. She half rose in her chair then dropped down again. "Sell this house? Not while I have breath in my body!" She clutched her chest, gasping for air.

"Oh, dear . . . get her pills, Emily. The case should be in her purse." Jessica jumped up and put her arm around her mother's thin shoulders. "Calm down, Mother. Just try to calm down and take deep, slow breaths."

"I'm going to die in this house, I've always told you that," her mother railed. "I'm going out feet first. Maybe today if I'm lucky . . ."

Emily ran back with the pill case. Jessica could see her sister's hands shaking as she fumbled to open the zipper.

"Which one do you need, Mother? Should I call the doctor?"

Lillian just moaned and closed her eyes. "I'm not at all well. . . ."

The phone rang, and Lillian's eyes peeked open. "Should I get it?" Jessica asked her.

"Wait, see who it is. I don't want to speak with anyone. I can't talk . . . I can hardly breathe," Lillian insisted, though Jessica noticed she seemed to be breathing—and talking—quite easily. Except for her very pale complexion, she didn't seem nearly as bad as she had a few moments ago.

The women waited for the outgoing message and then heard the sound of a familiar voice. "Lily, are you there? Pick up the phone, for Pete's sake." A long, noisy sigh followed. "All right, take your time. Don't break a hip. It's only me."

"Ezra. Give me the phone, please!" Her mother stretched out her arm, as if grasping for a lifeline. Jessica leaned over, picked up the receiver, and handed it to her.

"Ezra? I'm here," Lillian greeted him. "Emily and Jessica are visiting. They're plotting against me now. They've come to torment me. . . . Yes, that's exactly what I said. . . ."

Lillian waited, listening.

Jessica tiptoed over to the sink carrying her coffee cup and waved for her sister to join her.

"She's fine, thank heavens," Emily whispered.

"What an actress," Jessica whispered back. "She had me going for a minute there."

"A miraculous recovery," Emily quipped.

Lillian turned her head, her hand covering the phone. "You two, what are you whispering about back there? Giggling like schoolgirls. It's very rude."

"We were just wondering what we should fix you for dinner. It's getting late," Jessica replied. It *was* getting late. Time to give up and fight another day.

Lillian ended the call and placed the receiver on the table. "That was Ezra," she announced. "His housekeeper,

Mrs. Fallon, is making a roast chicken and if I can provide a few side dishes, he'll bring it over tonight to share. So neither of you need to make me dinner. I'm sure that is some relief of your great burden."

Plain old unseasoned roast chicken, her mother's favorite. How did Ezra know? The question made Jessica smile.

"That's very nice of him," Emily said.

"We planned to watch a show on the History Channel tonight," Lillian informed them. "Ezra prefers my television set, so he's getting something out of the bargain."

She stood up, adjusted her sweater around her shoulders, then took hold of her cane, which was propped against the back of the chair.

"I can make a vegetable and some potatoes for you," Emily offered. She pulled open the refrigerator door, but Jessica saw her mother walk over and push Emily aside.

"I'm perfectly capable of boiling a few potatoes and a pot of string beans."

That was her mother's favorite cooking method. Boiling everything. Jessica was sure that if Emily made the food it would taste a whole lot better—and Emily was no cook, not by anybody's definition.

But it was good for her mother to take an active role. They could trust her alone until Ezra arrived, Jessica thought. Though she would call later, to make sure her mother remembered to turn off the stove.

They both kissed their mother good-bye, a gesture she barely acknowledged.

"Good-bye, Mother. Have a good time," Jessica said. "I'm glad you have some company tonight."

"Oh, Ezra isn't company," she scoffed.

"He isn't?" Emily challenged her. "What is he then?"

"Oh, I don't know. He's . . . Ezra," she replied, sounding annoyed by the question.

Outside at their cars they consoled each other.

"I nearly thought we had a nine-one-one call on our hands there for a minute," Emily confided.

"Thank goodness for Dr. Elliot. Mother was instantly revived by the mere mention of roast chicken."

Emily laughed. "Yes, she was, wasn't she? We'll have to remember that next time she fakes a collapse."

"At least we got her to talk about the problem," Jessica pointed out. "She did say she would consider the idea."

"Oh, Jess, those were the words of a desperate woman. She would have said anything at that point. I don't believe her for a minute." Emily fished through her big purse and pulled out her car keys. "But I meant what I said," she added. "If she won't accept live-in help, then we'll have to move her out of the house. Which won't be any picnic either."

Jessica could only picture her mother being carried out, kicking and screaming. "I hope she'll see reason. I hope it won't come to that."

"I hope so, too," Emily said.

DAVID SAT IN THE WAITING ROOM, HIS GAZE FIXED ON the closed door. Any moment now either George Henson or Gena Reyes would open that door and call him in. For the past few days, he had thought about asking for a new therapist.

When his father had dropped him off today at the front of the building, he still wasn't sure what he would do. By the time he reached the check-in desk, he knew. He would stick with Gena, see how it went. She was tough, no question; a hard-nosed bully when you got right down to it. But maybe he needed someone like her to get him moving again. The door to the treatment room opened, and George appeared. "Hey, David. Back for more fun and games?"

"That's right. I can hardly wait," David grunted as he lifted himself on the walker and made his way to the door.

George led him to a curtained cubicle where Gena was waiting, clipboard in hand. It was hard to tell if she was pleased to see him or surprised that he had not asked for a new assignment. He did want to show her something by coming back, he realized, maybe that he was tougher than she thought.

"Morning, David. Ready to dig in?" she asked evenly.

"Yes, ma'am, I am," he answered, sounding all army. "I know you're a slave driver, but maybe that's a good thing. In my situation, I mean."

She glanced at him, then set the clipboard on a side table. "Maybe. I guess we both have to wait and see."

"Right," he said, wondering if the word *optimistic* was even in her vocabulary.

"Okay, let's start with some stretches. Lie back on the table, please."

David did as he was told, suddenly remembering Reverend Ben's story about his wife's recovery. What was it he said? The first visit is hard. The second not much easier. And the third, even worse than the first?

It was better not to keep track, David decided, not to keep watching the mileage on the meter. All he knew for sure was that a long road stretched out ahead of him.

Gena and George worked him hard. They started off with stretches, then the weight machines for both his upper and lower body. Gena told him he needed to build strength—not necessarily bulk—for better balance and muscle control. With injuries to both legs, he would have to work doubly hard to get back in condition. Then they went to the exercise bike, where his bum foot had to be strapped in. It was a struggle just to pedal. David was ready to quit after the first three minutes, but Gena pushed him until he pedaled out of sheer anger.

He thought the workout was over at that point, but after a short rest, she had him back on the floor again for more stretches, then up on a treadmill. That was even harder than the bike. David slipped off twice, and George had to catch him and stick him back on. When it was finally over, George gave him a massage.

David hardly spoke two words to his father during the ride home. Every muscle still ached. He went straight to his room for a rest before dinner.

David tossed around for a while on his bed, trying to get comfortable. No use. Though he was exhausted, he couldn't sleep. The pain was too much.

He leaned over and shook a capsule from a bottle, then drank some water from the glass on his nightstand. He closed his eyes again and let his head sink into the pillow. The pills weren't that strong, and even though the doctor would have given him something stronger, he didn't want to get dependent on medication.

But it wasn't just the pain that chased sleep away. David didn't want to watch the images that floated into his head whenever he closed his eyes. Images of combat, the sound of gunfire, the flare of rockets and fiery explosions as they struck in all directions. The way the landscape looked afterward, torn and smoldering, the buildings knocked to pieces, as if they were built of toy blocks and kicked down by an angry child. And all through the rubble, the bodies scattered like broken dolls, torn and bleeding, carelessly tossed aside.

If only the doctor had a pill that could erase the tapes in his brain, he would ask for that one. David turned his head to the side and finally fell asleep.

KATE CAME TO WAKE HIM, GENTLY TAPPING HIS HEAD with her favorite stuffed toy. It was a funny sensation and David swatted the air, feeling caught in a swarm of insects.

Kate's small whispering voice finally roused him. "David, wake up now."

"Oh, hello, Lester." David took the stuffed rabbit and sat him up on his chest. "Were those your ears tickling my nose? Or . . ." He turned the rabbit around, and made the animal do a little dance. ". . . that big old tail?"

Kate giggled. "It was his ears, silly. I wouldn't stick his tail in your face."

"Well, thanks." David smiled, handed the rabbit back to her, and sat up.

"Your hair is sticking up all crazy, David. You need a haircut," Kate told him.

He glanced in the mirror. "Yeah, I do."

"I can do it," she offered. "I cut my doll's hair all the time."

He laughed. "Nice. What does your mom say about that?"

"She says not to do it, because it won't grow back," Kate answered, looking very serious.

"I bet you give great haircuts. But I need to see a barber. You know, just for guys."

"Oh . . . okay." She tucked Lester under her arm and headed for the door. "Mommy said the food is on the table."

David's nose confirmed that message. Dinner smelled good, and he had worked up a real appetite today.

Kate disappeared, and he went into the bathroom, splashed his face with cold water, and combed his hair. The pain in his leg was building, probably from the extra activity. He took two ibuprofen pills, not wanting to take anything stronger. He was trying to get away from the meds. They helped in one way, putting the pain at a distance, muffling it in cottony wads, but the rest of the world went with it and that wasn't helping him any, he decided.

When he got out to the kitchen, his father and Kate were at the table, and Julie was ladling out dishes of beef stew. He set the walker aside and practically dropped in his seat, accidentally rocking the table. Jack reached out and grabbed Kate's glass of milk before it tipped over.

"Whoa there," Jack said, making Katie laugh.

David felt embarrassed. "Sorry."

"You must be tired from the therapy session. You were

there a long time." Julie set a dish of stew in front of him. It looked really good, but he suddenly didn't feel that hungry. The ache in his hip was stealing his appetite.

"Yeah, how did the therapy go today?" Jack asked. "You didn't say."

"Oh, you know. You warm up for a while and then she makes you do exercises—for core strength and others to build the leg muscles."

Julie leaned over to help Kate cut her food. "Is it hard, getting started again?"

"Yeah, it's hard. It's very hard." David didn't mean to snap at her, but it was sort of a dumb question, wasn't it?

"Of course it is," she said quickly. "What a question. . . . Do you like the new therapist?"

David didn't answer right away. He pushed at a bite of food with his fork. "She has her pluses and minuses. I'll have to see how it works out."

Julie seemed concerned by his reply. "Can you change therapists if you don't like her?"

Before David could answer, his father jumped into the conversation. "It's important that you like the person, don't you think?"

David stared down at his food and let out a frustrated sigh. He didn't need all these questions right now. He was tired and in pain, and he had been thinking about little else but this issue for days.

He didn't know why, but they both just got under his skin.

"Actually," he said, "I don't think it matters squat if I like the person or don't like them. I'm not looking for a best friend, you know? Just somebody who's good at what they do and can get me out of this walker."

He could see both his father and Julie shrink back, their expressions growing tense. Jack picked up a forkful of noodles and continued eating. Julie looked grim, and even Kate looked confused, staring around at the adults as if she was wondering why everyone was so quiet.

Jack took a sip of water and cleared his throat. "Good point," he said finally. "As long as you see improvement, that's all that counts."

"Mommy, I'm done. Can I watch TV?" Kate asked.

Julie leaned over and looked at Kate's plate. "You didn't eat your vegetables. There, hidden under the noodles."

David saw them, too, carrots and peas, cleverly tucked under the leftover noodles.

"Hey, pal. You need to eat those," David encouraged her. "Lester likes carrots. He eats them for dessert instead of cookies."

"He can have mine," Kate offered.

This generous impulse made the adults laugh. "I'll tell you what—if you finish everything on your plate, I'll play a game with you," David said.

The deal definitely caught Kate's interest. Julie smiled a silent thank-you at him.

"Candy Land?" Kate asked eagerly.

David sighed. He hated Candy Land. He always pulled a card that got him stuck on Gum Drop Mountain. But he was too tired tonight for hide-and-seek, Kate's other favorite.

"No problem. Whatever you like."

"But you have to eat a few more carrots," Jack reminded her.

"And drink your milk," Julie chimed in. Then she glanced at David's plate. "You hardly touched your food. Would you like me to fix you something else?"

David shook his head. Julie had enough work around here without fixing him special orders, as if it were a restaurant.

"No thanks. The stew is great," he replied quickly. He turned his attention back to his plate, then caught Kate's eye and winked.

He knew his foul moods upset the household at times, a household that before his return had been a picture of harmony. But when a dark wave hit, he couldn't see it coming and he couldn't control it.

Though Julie treated him with unfaltering kindness and sympathy, he could tell that his presence here was causing tension between her and Jack. The last thing he wanted to do was create problems in his father's new marriage.

David glanced over at his dad. It was bad enough his own life was messed up. He didn't have to spread his unhappiness around, like some contagious disease.

The sooner he recovered and got out on his own the better.

Better for everyone.

WHEN THE SHOW ON THE HISTORY CHANNEL ENDED and the credits appeared on the screen, Lillian shut off the TV. She didn't believe in random viewing. She chose her shows carefully from the weekly guide, then turned off the television.

"Well, that was very interesting. I'd love to go back to Egypt someday," Ezra said. "It's one of the most exciting places in the world to visit."

Ezra was an amateur Egyptologist. He knew more about the subject than anyone Lillian had ever met, and in the days before her marriage, she had been an assistant curator of the Egyptian department in the Boston Museum of Fine Arts.

Ezra had been to Egypt twice and knew every treasure in the collections of the Metropolitan Museum in New York and the British Museum in London. There were probably more ancient artifacts in those two institutions than remained in the entire Mediterranean. Still, to actually walk in the footsteps of the ancient kings would be exciting, Lillian had to agree.

She set down her teacup on the end table. "I wouldn't wait much longer to make your travel plans. Not at our age."

Ezra laughed. "Good point. You can't put these things off. Why don't you come with me, Lily? Can't you see yourself floating down the Nile on a barge? Just like Cleopatra," he teased.

"What a picture." She let out a long breath and shook her head. "Maybe I will visit the Sahara. And stay there," she added curtly. "My daughters would be pleased to learn I'd settled in some cozy tomb or pyramid."

"Your daughters? What do they have to do with it?"

Lillian briefly related the debate she'd had with Jessica and Emily that morning. "They had it all planned out. They cornered me," she complained. "When I wouldn't give in, Emily threatened me. She said they would sell the house right out from under me, and I would have to go live with one of them."

"My, my . . . the vipers. What horrid children, Lillian." Ezra's tone was laced with sarcastic sympathy. "They want to take care of you? They want you to live with them? What an outrageous threat. It's blackmail. It's . . . parental abuse. Maybe there's some hotline you can call."

Lillian glared at him. "Easy for you to say. No one is handing you ultimatums. Do this, do that, or we'll take your house away."

Ezra leaned toward Lillian's chair. "I agree their tactics are extreme. But perhaps these threats are necessary to get your attention?" When she didn't answer, he continued. "I think your daughters are rightfully concerned about you. Would it be the end of the world to hire someone to help with the housework and watch over your well-being? It's not just a good idea, Lily, but a necessary one if you plan to stay here."

"Yes, yes, that's what they both say, over and over and over again." Lillian stared down at the carpet, a sulky expression on her face.

"Your daughters have busy lives, just as it should be. Children and husbands. Jobs and responsibilities. You can't expect them to be here every day, doing for you—or drop everything when you have the least little problem."

"When do I ever ask them to drop everything for me?"

Ezra tilted his head back and laughed. "You're not seriously asking me that question, are you?"

"If I call upon them once in a great while, is that a crime? Does that mean I must employ some meddling somebody, hovering over me? Some dreadfully annoying babysitter and bodyguard? Is that how I'm supposed to endure my final days in this world?"

"Why must you paint such a grim picture? I'll give you an even grimmer one, if you like. You get your way and remain all alone in this house, no bothersome intrusions. You fall again, the way you did three years ago. You were lucky that time, Lily. Sara came by and found you," he reminded her. "But what if no one had come? You would have been lying there for hours, possibly days . . ."

Before she could come back with a clever reply, he added, "Anyone with common sense would realize that they dodged a bullet that time. You might not be so lucky if you cling to this foolish notion of total independence and it happens again."

Lillian shifted in her seat. It had been awful to fall like that and lie there in pain, so helpless, wondering if anyone would come. She hated to think about it.

She drew in a long, shaky breath. "Thank you, Ezra. I think you've made your point."

"Have I really?" he persisted. "I don't think I've changed your mind any. Look at me, Lily. I have a live-in housekeeper who's been with me now for years. Mrs. Fallon is a lovely woman, does everything for me. I couldn't survive without her. What's so wrong with that, can you tell me, please?"

"Absolutely nothing," Lillian snapped back sharply. "If it makes you happy, I say, bravo."

"Oh, for pity's sake," Ezra replied with disgust.

"Really, Ezra. I hope you and your housekeeper are very happy together. Why don't you take *her* to Egypt? Now, if you'll excuse me, I'm tired. I think you had better go."

Ezra stood up, gave her one last exasperated look, and

headed for the front door. "Now that you mention it, I'm tired, too. Tired of arguing with you, Lillian. You've worn me out."

She felt her cheeks get warm at this, though she didn't know why. What did she care about Ezra's opinion? She never did and never would.

He paused at the entrance to the foyer and glanced back at her. "I've known you all of my adult life, Lily. You're one of the most intelligent women I've ever met—and easily, the most pigheaded. Don't you get it? We're all concerned about you."

Lillian stared straight ahead. "Can I show you out?" she asked in her frostiest tone.

"Don't trouble yourself. I know the way out by now. I'll be sure to lock the front door. Please check the side door before you go to bed and put the alarm on."

"Yes, Ezra, I will. Good night now."

"Good night, Lillian."

She sat in the parlor, listening as he put on his coat and hat then firmly closed the front door behind him.

She could tell by the way he had said good night that he wasn't really mad at her. He would be over it by tomorrow. That's the way he was, fortunately.

For goodness' sake, she had expected more sympathy from him when she told him how Jessica and Emily had cornered her. But she didn't want Ezra angry at her, too, when she was really all alone here.

And why did people keep reminding her of that fact? Over and over again, like a recorded announcement. She was going to scream if she heard it one more time.

Lillian rose to check the side door and set the alarm.

Didn't the fools realize she knew how alone she was now? Better than all of them.

CHAPTER SIX

⟋⟍

The four weeks of Advent were Reverend Ben's favorite time of the liturgical calendar. While every season had its own spiritual meaning and inspiration, Ben loved Advent best because it seemed to resonate with such great anticipation and hope, encouraging all to put forward their better selves.

He loved the way the sanctuary looked this time of year, decked out with pine garlands and a Christmas tree to one side of the pulpit. He loved the blue banners that hung on either side of the altar, delivering messages of faith and peace, the rich color reflecting the midnight sky over Bethlehem.

A crèche had been set up on one side of the altar, with all the figures of the great story present, except for the infant, who would be added to the tiny wooden cradle on the big night. On the other side of the altar stood the Advent wreath, four candles surrounded by an array of fresh greens. Two of the candles were lit so far. One for last Sunday, and one today.

Each Advent Sunday, at the start of the service, one family in the congregation was invited to the altar, where they would light the candles and recite the traditional prayers.

The Sawyers had come up this morning, Jack, Julie, and Kate. Ben wished that David was at church today for this special ceremony, but he wasn't surprised by the young man's absence. It would be some time, he thought, before he would see David in church again. If at all.

When it was time for "Joys and Concerns," the segment of the service when the congregation shared their celebrations and worries, Ben saw Jack slowly raise his hand. Ben nodded to him at once. Jack was a shy man, not usually prone to speaking in church.

Jack stood up and cleared his throat. "I'd just like to ask for a few prayers for my son, David. We're still so thankful that he's home safely. But his injuries are serious. He's started physical therapy and he's got a long way to go. I have to say, he's feeling very discouraged right now."

Jack quickly sat down again. Ben saw Julie take his hand.

"Thank you, Jack," Ben said. "I'm sure we all wish David progress with his recovery."

Laura Miller, who was sitting in the back of the church waved her hand, and Ben quickly acknowledged her. "Oh, gee," she began, "I don't know where to start—"

Ben gave her an encouraging smile. "It's all right, Laura. Please start anywhere."

"Well, last week our fridge broke down. It made the most awful sound, then it just died. We couldn't afford to have it fixed. It wouldn't have paid, it was so old," she added. "And with Paul still out of work, we can't afford a new one. I posted a sign on the bulletin board last week, to see if anyone had a used fridge to sell or donate. I didn't get any calls, and I didn't think anything of it. But when I came to church on Wednesday afternoon, the card was missing."

Ben sighed inwardly. This was getting long, and he did need to finish the rest of the service. "Go on, Laura. Please?"

"Oh, yes . . . sorry. Well, this is the amazing part. On Thursday morning last week, a truck pulls up at our house and two deliverymen come right up to my door with a brand-new refrigerator. I thought it was a big mistake, some kind of strange coincidence. In fact, I was laughing at them at first. Then they showed me the paperwork—all paid for and it really had my name on it. But they wouldn't say who bought it or sent it . . . or anything," she added. "I even called the store, but no one would tell me. They said it was paid for in cash and they weren't permitted to tell."

Ben hadn't expected the story to wind up that way. "What an amazing story," he said. "What a wonderful gift for your family."

"Isn't it?" Laura's cheerful composure suddenly slipped and for a moment, Ben thought she was going to cry. "It's been very difficult for us these past few weeks. I know it has to be someone in the congregation who sent that wonderful gift. I just want you to know how much it means to us. I just want you to know how very grateful we are. God bless you, whoever you are."

"Yes, bless you for your generosity," Ben echoed quietly.

Ben continued the service, but he could see that Laura Miller's story had sent a ripple through the sanctuary. He was still thinking about it as he said the final prayers.

When the service ended, Ben stood outside the big wooden doors and greeted everyone as they left. He saw Laura Miller near the front of the line, looking eager to speak to him.

Grace Hegman and her father were the first in line, however.

"Very nice sermon, Reverend," Grace said as Ben shook Digger's hand.

"Why, thank you, Grace."

Grace seemed unusually cheerful this morning, Ben thought. She was typically such a reserved woman, he wondered what had gotten her in such a good mood. His sermon hadn't been that uplifting.

"Yes, nice service," Digger echoed. "I like seeing these young families light the candles. And how do you like that story about the refrigerator?" he added with a laugh. "Don't that beat all? Now who could've done a thing like that?"

"I have no idea. It is very surprising," Ben agreed.

Before Digger could say more, Grace took her father's arm. "Thank you, Reverend," she said curtly, sounding more like her usual self. "We have to hurry home to open the store. Have a nice day."

She whisked her father away and steered him out of the church before Ben could say good-bye.

When he turned, Laura Miller stood next in line.

"Laura, it seems Christmas came early to your house."

"I've never had a surprise like that in my life. I nearly fainted. It was just like winning a game show or a sweepstakes," she said. "It's been such a big boost to our family. We feel so much more hopeful about things now. If something like that can happen out of the blue, who knows? Other good things can happen, too, right?"

"Absolutely," Ben had to agree.

Laura smiled at him. "If anyone knows who did that for us, it's you, Reverend. Come on. Couldn't you just give me their initials?"

"I have no idea who did it, Laura. This is the first I've heard of it, honestly."

Laura shrugged. "Well, maybe someday we'll find out and we'll be able to thank them properly."

"I hope that person was here today and saw how pleased you are. I'm sure that would be very gratifying for them."

"I hope so. It's funny, but that gift landing on our doorstep out of the blue, it's made me want to do something nice for someone else. For someone I don't even know," she confided. She seemed surprised by this reaction but Ben wasn't. Before he could reply she said, "You mentioned in the announcements that the church is starting up a program to send food out to people in need?"

"Yes, we are," Ben replied. "It's just starting up. I think the group had their first meeting last week."

"I'd like to help out and do some cooking," Laura said.

"That would be great. Sophie Potter is coordinating everything. I'm sure she would welcome your help."

"Thanks. I'll go look for her." Laura Miller said goodbye and moved on.

Reverend Ben turned to greet the next congregation member in line. Lillian Warwick was approaching slowly with the aid of her cane and her daughter Emily.

He braced himself for some backhanded compliment about his sermon or critique of the way the sanctuary had been decorated. Lillian Warwick had never been shy about making her feelings known. He wondered briefly if Lillian might have been Laura Miller's benefactor—and immediately dismissed the idea. Though Lillian certainly had the means to send each family in the church a refrigerator, he was almost sure she had not been the anonymous donor.

Then he caught himself for such an uncharitable thought. He didn't know that for sure. It could have been Lillian. It could have been many church members.

A real mystery, he thought. Life was full of mystery, wasn't it? God likes to keep us on our toes.

I'll have to keep my ears open, Ben decided. Such a grand gesture couldn't remain a secret for too long. Many people start off thinking they don't want recognition for a good deed but later find it's disappointing to remain without notice or thanks.

The mystery Santa would soon make his or her identity known. Ben felt certain of it.

AS IF THE GRUELING THERAPY SESSIONS WERE NOT ENOUGH, Gena had sent David home with a set of huge rubber bands for stretching his arm and leg muscles, and a set of hand and ankle weights for keeping up his exercise over the weekend.

He worked out in his bedroom, where no one could see his pained expression or the sweat dripping down his forehead during the simple routine.

He had just gone into the kitchen for a glass of water when he heard a tapping sound on the windowpanes of the back door. The tree stand had been insanely busy this weekend. But his father had purposely left a sign there this morning, before the family left for church, so that David wouldn't be disturbed.

David was sure that some pushy customer had decided his father's polite words didn't apply to them.

David made his way to the door with the walker and soon spied Christine through the window. Sunday morning was her surprise visit time, it seemed. Twice in a row and she still caught him off guard.

She had on a purplish-blue hat today, pulled down over her blond hair. The shade of the wool matched her eyes.

What could he do? Just like the last time, he leaned over and opened the door to let her in.

"Hey," she said quietly.

"Hey, yourself," he answered.

She looked him over. "Are you working out or something? I don't want to interrupt."

"More in the something category. I just finished up."

He knew he looked sweaty, his T-shirt sticking to his chest. He had a towel around his neck and quickly wiped his face. "I was just getting a glass of water. Can I get you anything?"

"No thanks." Christine sat at the table and watched him at the sink. He felt clumsy and tried not to fumble too much as he balanced the water while moving along with the walker.

She turned away, maybe realizing she had been staring.

He was glad she didn't jump up and offer to help. That would have been worse. He finally made it to the table and sat down across from her. He was surprised to see her, even though he had been thinking about her all week. He had thought about calling her or sending an e-mail, just thanking her for dropping by last Sunday. But he never got around to it; he wasn't sure what he would accomplish by staying in contact—and drawing out the agony.

"So, how's it going?" he said. "Still like school? Think you'll stick with it?"

She smiled at his teasing. "I don't like it very much this time of year. Too many finals and papers to write."

That did sound tough, David thought. But if she was so busy studying, it didn't leave much time for her boyfriend, did it? There was a happy thought.

"I think you'll do okay. You never minded studying. Not like me," he reminded her.

"You seemed to get good marks anyway," she replied. "I was such a grind, and it killed me when we got the same grades."

Her recollection made him laugh. "That is so not true."

"Yeah, it is. You're pretty smart, David. You just don't want too many people to know. You don't want people to see you that way, or you need to keep it a secret or something."

David stopped to think about that observation. Was he really like that? Something about it felt uncannily true.

Christine opened the buttons of her big shearling jacket.

She looked so cute and cuddly with the lamb's wool around her face, David felt like reaching over and putting his arms around her.

"I was cleaning out my bookcase and I found this book I thought you might like." She took a paperback from her coat pocket and held it out to him. "Remember that writer we used to like in high school, Tony Hillerman? Those mysteries in the Southwest," she reminded him.

"Sure, I remember him. Those books were great."

"This is the last one he wrote, *The Shape Shifter*. Have you read it?"

David took the book and stared down at the cover. "No, but it looks good." He felt touched that she had remembered such a thing. "Thanks. Thanks a lot. That was really nice of you."

She seemed embarrassed. He saw her cheeks redden, and she looked away.

"It's okay. I was going to toss it otherwise. I thought it was pretty good, though. Let me know what you think."

"I will," he said.

"So, what have you been up to?" she asked, suddenly changing the subject. "Did you start physical therapy?"

"Yes, I did. I'm going five days a week."

Christine looked impressed. "That sounds intense."

"Yeah, it is," he admitted. "The sessions take a few hours. I'm working like a dog just to get rid of this walker. I may never get the feeling back in my foot again, though. I may never walk normally."

He wasn't sure why he added that. He hadn't planned to. It just came out. He watched to see her reaction.

Christine looked surprised. "That's not what your father told me."

"My father doesn't know the whole picture—or maybe he just doesn't want to face it."

Christine pulled her hat off, then fiddled with it on the top of the table. "At least you're alive, David," she said after a moment. "When I hear stories about the way some men and women come back—"

"Yeah, I know," he interrupted her.

He not only had heard the stories, he had been on the ground, while it was happening. Didn't she realize that?

Still, he felt touched by her concern. She worried about him while he was away, David realized. She really cared about him. But that made it even harder to sit here, facing her. It wasn't enough to be alive. It wasn't enough to offer her, David thought angrily.

"You know, when people say that, I know it's true," he began slowly. "That was my first reaction, too. I know I should be grateful. Of course I am. But I have to tell you, it's darned cold comfort if you're sitting here, unable to get up and walk across the room and just get yourself a glass of water." He heard his voice getting louder, harsher. He saw the tense look on her face, but he couldn't control it or stop himself. "Like, 'Gee . . . it could be worse. I could have come back without any legs.' Now that would have really been bad. . . .'"

She stared back at him. She looked stung. As if she might just turn and run out on him.

He wondered if she would. Well, that would tell him something, too. He wanted to be honest with her, of all people. If she couldn't take the plain truth about what he was going through, well, that would just make it easier for him to get over her, wouldn't it?

But Christine didn't run. She looked down at her hands a minute and then back up at him.

"Sure," she said quietly. "I understand."

He wondered if she really did. He could see she was trying. He had an urge to reach across the table and take her hand. He wondered what she would do. Probably pull away from him.

"I just feel so . . . frustrated sometimes," he said in a more reasonable tone. "Everyone keeps telling me I have to be more patient."

"Everyone is right." She still wasn't smiling, but she didn't look as if she wanted to run out of the house anymore. David felt relieved. He wanted her to stay a little.

"How's the therapist? Is he good?" she asked.

"The therapist is a she. And she's very tough."

"Well, tough is probably a good thing, right?"

"That's what she tells me," David replied.

He caught her gaze and held it. There were so many things he wanted to say to her, important things. All of it, whirling around in his head at once, so that finally, he couldn't say anything at all. Nothing that was very important, anyway.

They both turned at the sound of the front door opening.

"Hey, Dave, we're home," his father called out.

"I'm back here, in the kitchen," David called back. He realized Christine had parked behind the house, so his family hadn't seen her car and didn't realize he had a visitor.

Kate ran ahead of the grown-ups and soon appeared in the kitchen doorway. She flung herself at David, and he caught her in his arms and lifted her into his lap.

"Hey, Muffin-Head. What's up?"

"We stopped at the bakery. I got cookies." She held up a small white bag. "For after lunch."

"Hmm. Any for me?"

She thought about it a moment. "Maybe," she said seriously. She patted his head. "You're all sweaty. You need a shower, David."

"Yeah, I do," he agreed.

Christine laughed, and Katie suddenly noticed her.

"That's my friend, Christine Tate," David explained. "Christine, this is my little sister, Kate."

"Hi, Kate," Christine said. David could tell by the look on Christine's face that she was totally charmed.

"Hello," Kate said, suddenly shy. "I'm David's *new* sister," she explained.

Jack and Julie walked into the kitchen. David saw his father's expression change when he saw their visitor. Julie smiled curiously.

"Christine . . . for goodness' sake." His father's happy reaction was deeply embarrassing. "I didn't know you were here. How are you?"

"I'm good, Mr. Sawyer."

"Do you remember Julie? I think you met last winter, when we ran into you at the drugstore?"

"Yes, I do," Christine replied.

Julie and Christine said hello to each other. Kate slipped off David's lap and walked over to her mother.

David took a breath, wondering how long this tea party was going to last. With the noisy arrival of his family, the magic spell in the quiet, dim kitchen was suddenly gone.

Christine stood up and started buttoning her coat. "I guess I better be going. Nice to see everyone . . ."

"What's the rush?" Jack asked. "Why don't you stay and have lunch with us?"

"Yes, please stay," Julie urged her. "We're just having sandwiches, nothing special."

Christine looked at David. He could tell she didn't know what to say.

"I think Christine has to get going. She has a lot of studying to do," he said. Then he saw her expression change and realized she had wanted to stay.

She reached for her hat. "Um . . . yeah, that's right. I have all these finals and term papers to write."

"Oh, sure. Busy time for everybody. We've got our hands full at the tree stand this year," Jack said, commiserating.

"That bell just does not stop ringing," Julie agreed as she set platters of cold cuts and cheese on the table.

Jack stood at the counter, cutting bakery rolls on a board. As if to prove Julie's point, the bell at the stand began to sound. Jack glanced outside, then put the knife down. "I better get out there."

"I'll bring your lunch out later," Julie promised as he left. She turned back to David and Christine. "We really need some help this year, even for a few hours a day or just on the weekends."

David knew what Julie said was true; they needed to hire someone this year. But the innocent comment hit a nerve, reminding him that he should have been out there with his dad. He felt embarrassed for Christine to see how useless he was around here.

"I'm looking for a Christmas job," Christine said to Julie. "I need to earn a little money for shopping."

"Really? That sounds lucky for us." Julie set down a pile of dishes on the table. "Why don't we go outside after lunch and talk to Jack about it?"

David felt his stomach clench in a knot. He stared at Julie, trying to catch her eye. She didn't seem to notice. Did she know how he felt about Christine?

Of course, if his father had kept private conversations private, then she couldn't know the whole story, that he had given up on winning his old girlfriend back—and that having her around all the time would be sheer torture for him.

In fact, David suddenly realized, Julie might even think she was doing him a favor by hiring Christine. How ironic was that?

"We also need someone to help make items for the Christmas shop," Julie continued. "And to keep an eye on Kate at times."

"I love kids," Christine said. "I'm majoring in elementary ed at school. I'll be student teaching next semester."

"Really? I teach art at the elementary school in Hamilton. I just started there in September. It's a great district. . . ."

The two women began talking about the ups and downs of teaching. Meanwhile, Julie persuaded Christine to stay for lunch, after all. David could see that Julie also wanted Kate to get to know Christine a bit, since it seemed very likely Christine would be her new babysitter.

David made himself a sandwich and began eating. He wondered if anyone would notice he was still in the room.

Katie seemed smitten with Christine, peering at her across the table. Finally, Kate interrupted, drawing Christine's attention. "This is Lester," she said, introducing her favorite toy.

Christine gave Kate and the stuffed rabbit a wide, warm smile. "Wow, he's a big guy. What's in his backpack?"

Kate quickly opened the pack to show her.

That did it. David felt instantly displaced. Kate had a new favorite.

He never minded babysitting for Kate. But he didn't always feel up to it, and Julie knew it was not realistic to count on him. He knew that his stepmother was just trying to be considerate, but he suddenly felt as if his one responsibility in the household had been taken away now.

As Julie prepared to serve some tea and a carrot cake from the bakery, Christine quickly rose and helped her clear the table. She came over to David, ready to take his dish. "Finished?"

"I can do it," he said quickly. He used the table to lever himself up, then grabbed his walker and carefully carried the plate to the sink. With about two steps left though, his fork and knife slid off, along with the remaining bits of his sandwich. The entire mess hit the floor with a noisy clatter.

The sound of the silverware startled him, hitting a nerve. With a shout, he jumped back and crouched down, covering his head with his hands, as if protecting himself from gunfire. The plate fell to the floor as well.

The room went silent. Everyone in the kitchen was staring at him. David felt his face turn beet red. He stood up again, taking in a long, deep breath.

"Are you all right, David?" Julie asked. She had seen this reaction before and wasn't totally surprised. Christine, though, looked a little shaken.

"I'm fine. No problem," he snapped. *I just thought the*

kitchen was being fired on by the enemy. What's so strange about that?

Hanging on his walker with one hand, he made a half-hearted attempt to lean over and grab up some of the mess. But it had all fallen on his bad side, and he wasn't flexible enough or mobile enough to even touch it.

"Don't worry. I'll get it." Julie turned and grabbed some paper towels. Before he could answer, she had crouched down, grabbed the plate and silverware, and wiped up the food.

"I'm sorry," David mumbled.

"Don't be silly. It's nothing." She put the silverware in the sink and grabbed some more towels and the spray cleaner. David awkwardly turned the walker in the small space, hurrying to get out of her way. Or trying to hurry. He couldn't look at Christine as he ambled out of the room.

"Do you want some tea or coffee, David?" Julie called after him.

"No thanks." He kept moving and didn't turn around.

He knew he was being rude. He hadn't even said good-bye to Christine. Did it matter? Obviously, he was going to be seeing more of her around here. And she would be seeing more of him—seeing what his life was really like, the ugly truth of it. How getting a dirty dish from the table to the sink was a major challenge. Even inspiring a battle flashback.

That should make up her mind about him, once and for all.

That should really do it.

By THE TIME BEN RETURNED HOME FROM CHURCH, IT was late in the afternoon. Unlike most people, for him Sunday was a workday, the most important of the week. After the service there were often meetings or other events he needed to attend.

Today, he had met with the trustees right after the coffee hour in order to review bids for an emergency repair of the church boiler. Then there was a class with the middle-school students who would be confirmed in the spring. That was always an enlightening experience. No matter how often he taught that course, each group of adolescents had a lot to teach him.

He let himself into the parsonage and hung up his hat and coat on a coat tree in the foyer. The delicate notes of a piece by Handel floated out to greet him. Carolyn, playing one of her favorite pieces. He moved extra quietly as he walked through the house, careful not to interrupt her.

The music was lovely and instantly put him at ease. He was a lucky man to have such wonderful music in his life. After so many years of marriage, he had taken that gift for granted. But during the time Carolyn was unable to play, he felt a great loss. Ever since, he had remained mindful, certain that he would never take it for granted again.

By the time Carolyn finished, he was sitting in the family room, reading the newspaper.

"Ben, I didn't expect you home so early. Why didn't you let me know you were back?"

"I didn't want to interrupt you, dear. I was enjoying the private concert."

She sat on the sofa next to his chair. "So, did you ever find out who it was?"

Ben put down the paper. "Find out what?"

"Who gave the Millers the refrigerator."

"Oh . . . right." Ben had been so busy all day, he had forgotten all about the mystery. He shook his head. "No, I didn't hear a word about it. No clues so far."

Carolyn looked disappointed. "I was sure someone would have told you or at least given a hint. It's hard to keep that sort of thing a secret. And people do want to get some credit for good deeds from their pastor."

Ben laughed. "Yes, they do, don't they? Though I really don't have any more influence than the next person."

He meant, with God. It had always been a peculiar feeling, even uncomfortable at times, when people expected him to judge their actions. They didn't understand that his role wasn't to judge whether they did right or wrong. He was there to encourage and support them and to be understanding when they made mistakes.

"Well, who could it be then? It would have to be someone of means," Carolyn speculated.

"That would make sense. Though it often seems that the people who have the least give the most."

"That leaves the field wide open. It could be anybody."

"Could be," he agreed. "But it would require a combination of generosity and modesty. A fairly rare combination."

"As rare as hen's teeth," Carolyn said, more willing to speak frankly. "How about Sophie Potter? She's generous to a fault and wouldn't care about taking credit. But I don't think she has the extra money to spare right now."

Ben saw it the same way. Sophie would have motivation but not the means.

"Lillian Warwick? She certainly has the money," Carolyn said. "But how would she have managed taking care of all the details? I just can't see her making the effort for a total stranger. She hardly bothers with her own family."

Carolyn sounded a bit judgmental, he thought. But Lillian's distant, aloof air was well-known. She was not the type to go out of her way for a stranger, he thought, then felt bad for not giving her the benefit of the doubt.

Anything was possible, wasn't it?

"I honestly can't guess," he told his wife. "But I will say it's made me reflect about my own attitudes. It's a lesson in generosity for all of us. And maybe, for you and me right now, in not being so judgmental of everyone."

"I suppose." Carolyn nodded and picked up her knitting basket. "Still, it's fun to speculate."

"True. But maybe it's better not knowing. Then we can credit lots of people for being so generous."

"Of course you'd say that. You're a minister," Carolyn replied with a laugh. "I have to be honest, Ben. I still want to know."

Ben glanced at her. The truth was, he wanted to know, too.

CHAPTER SEVEN

✑

*M*OTHER? IT'S ME, JESSICA. I JUST WANTED YOU to know that I won't be by until three. I forgot that it's Thursday, and I have to see Tyler's teacher after school. But I'll pick you up in plenty of time for your appointment at the podiatrist. So don't worry. Call me on my cell if you want. I'm out doing some errands."

Lillian hit the flashing button on her phone machine, meaning to shut the annoying thing off, but only succeeded in replaying her daughter's message.

"Mother? It's me, Jessica. I just wanted—"

"Oh, fiddlesticks," Lillian said aloud, quickly pressing every button on the phone console.

Finally, Jessica stopped talking. Lillian heaved a sigh of relief.

Well, thanks for nothing, Lillian decided. She had been waiting since noon for Jessica to join her for lunch.

Time to take matters into her own hands. She peered

into the refrigerator, wondering what to eat. Nothing looked very appetizing. Another problem with getting old. So many foods disagreed now, and she had never enjoyed a terribly adventurous palate.

A lovely wedge of cheddar caught her eye. A grilled cheese sandwich would be nice. Not nice for her cholesterol count, of course. But she had not indulged in some time, and her next blood test was at least a month away.

Lillian figured she didn't have all that long left in this world, and it was important to have some small pleasures. Like a cheese sandwich, for pity's sake. Did they have to take that away from her now, too?

She carefully grated the cheese on a board, then set a pile of it between two slices of bread. She dropped a pat of the healthy spread Jessica chose for her in the fry pan and watched as it melted into a bubbly pool.

Lillian had never been interested in cooking. While she was growing up on Beacon Hill in Boston, her family had employed servants, a cook and maids, to do all the housework. She could never recall her mother making herself even a cup of tea.

Besides, Lillian always wanted to be recognized for her mind, not for her flaky piecrust or the height of her soufflé. Her husband, Oliver, had respected her intelligence, though he had also made her feel like the most beautiful creature in the world, which was hardly the response she got from most men.

Oh, she drew enough attention when she was young to know that she had a certain look. But very few admirers had any staying power, not once the conversation got going and they saw what she was made of.

These days, it was different for young women. But not necessarily better, Lillian thought. Look at her daughters: One was a banker and the other the mayor of this town. Her granddaughter was now a reporter on a big newspaper.

Meanwhile, they were all still expected to look like fashion models, be devoted mothers and wives, *and* bake a perfect soufflé. Jessica probably could, she reckoned.

Sometimes she felt relieved that she wasn't young anymore. Sometimes.

She poked the bread with a spatula and slipped on her reading glasses to check the progress. The bread was toasty, but the cheese had not melted much. Why was that? She wasn't sure. The flame was probably not high enough.

She turned the sandwich carefully, put a cover on top, and turned up the heat.

Out in the parlor, where the radio was tuned to the classical station, she heard the opening bars of one of her very favorite operas, Bizet's *Carmen*, with Maria Callas singing the role of the doomed temptress. There never was a better Carmen, in Lillian's opinion, and never would be. Callas's passion and voice were both at their height in this recording, the combination peerless.

She walked out, turned up the music, and sat in her favorite armchair. A copy of the *Boston Globe* lay on the end table, and she picked it up, scanning the pages for her granddaughter's byline.

Nothing yet, she noticed. Was that a bad sign? Weren't Sara's new editors letting her write news stories? She hoped Sara had not taken a job as some coffee-fetching lackey, just so she could say she was working at the *Boston Globe*. She was a sharp, talented girl, and Lillian didn't want to see her demeaned.

An article on global warming caught her eyes. Lillian began to read it. The music was very soothing. She loved the flute, such an elegant instrument. She leaned her head back and listened to the notes with her eyes closed. Music was such a great pleasure, one of the few pleasures she could still enjoy.

When Lillian woke, the beloved arias of *Carmen* had faded, replaced by the blaring shriek of the smoke alarm.

She sat up sharply and coughed. The room was full of acrid smoke, and her eardrums were nearly bursting from the screaming alarm.

She covered her mouth with one hand and fumbled for her cane, so excited that she nearly fell over. She caught herself just in time on the back of the chair.

"Merciful heavens. . . . What in the world . . . ?"

Lillian stumbled through the foyer and hobbled out of the house, silently coaching herself to go slowly on the wooden steps that led down from her front porch.

She walked out onto her lawn just as two fire engines and an ambulance came screaming up Providence Street. Her smoke alarm was wired to the fire department. Emily's idea, of course. Well, perhaps that was a good thing, Lillian conceded.

As if the thought of her daughter had the power to conjure her, Lillian spotted Emily's Jeep coming down the road as well. The Jeep pulled into a space across the street, and Emily jumped out and ran toward the house.

At the same time, a firefighter stepped up beside her. "Are you okay, ma'am?"

He was a big, burly fellow. Like a cartoon of a fireman from a children's TV show, Lillian thought, decked out in full gear, a black rubber slicker and big brimmed hat.

"Ma'am?" he said again. "Can you hear me?"

She blinked up at him, her eyes tearing from the smoke. "Certainly, young man. I hear you loud and clear. I'm not deaf, though all this noise is likely to cause some damage."

"Are you all right?" he repeated again.

"I'm perfectly fine," she insisted, pulling away from his hold on her arm. "I'm the mayor's mother, did you know that?"

Before the man could answer, the mayor herself appeared. "Thank you, I'll take care of her now," Emily said.

"Of course, Mayor Warwick. If you need anything, let us know."

Lillian turned to her daughter. "Emily, what in the world is going on here?"

Emily reacted with a look of astonishment. "Good question, Mother. You tell me. Looks like there's a fire in your house—probably the kitchen, judging from that plume of smoke out back."

Lillian saw several firemen run past with a large fire extinguisher. "Oh, dear. Where are they going with those things? Will they spray chemicals all over my house? Not on the Oriental carpets, I pray . . ."

"They'll spray it on the fire." Emily was tugging on her arm, trying to lead her across the lawn.

Lillian resisted. "What happened to water? Chemicals will damage everything. Can't you speak to them about it?"

"Just come with me, Mother. We need to get out of the way, so the firefighters can do their job."

"No need to speak to me like a child. I haven't gone all addlepated yet."

The next thing Lillian knew, she was sitting in Emily's car, with Emily's coat wrapped around her shoulders. Two paramedics from the ambulance questioned her but soon determined her fit and unharmed.

Lillian watched as they jumped in the ambulance again and drove away. So, she was not very much of an emergency, was she? Lillian felt somehow slighted.

One of the firemen had come out in the meantime and reported that it was just a kitchen fire and would soon be extinguished.

"A kitchen fire. I see. Thank you," Emily said, turning to look at her mother.

Lillian lifted her chin and stared straight ahead, pretending not to notice. If only the TV had gone up in a state of spontaneous combustion, Lillian thought bitterly. That pitiful sandwich has given Emily plenty of ammunition.

But before Emily could start in on her, Jessica came running up to them. "Oh my God. Is the house on fire?"

Jessica and her family had survived a house fire just last winter. Their beautiful turn-of-the-century house had burned to the ground and everything they owned, in it. It was hardly surprising that Jessica seemed more upset right now than anyone.

Emily touched her sister's arm to calm her. "Just a kitchen fire, Jess. They say it's already out."

"Oh my goodness . . ." Jessica let out a long sigh. "That's a blessing. Are you all right, Mother? You didn't breathe in too much smoke, did you?"

"I'm fit as a fiddle," Lillian replied tartly. "I've just been examined by the ambulance crew. They gave me a clean bill of health and drove off, on to the next emergency."

"She's fine. Thankfully, she got out quickly and didn't have any mishaps leaving the house."

Any mishaps. Emily's polite way of saying, "She didn't fall and fracture any bones. Or give herself a heart attack."

Oh, this was not a good day. Not at all.

A short time later, the fire trucks drove off, and Lillian and her daughters were allowed to go back in the house. Emily and Jessica ran around, opening all the windows and doors. Lillian sat down on the sofa with a heavy sigh.

"We need to let the smoke out. Maybe you shouldn't come back in here today at all, Mother," Jessica said.

"So it smells a little smoky. No worse than the chimney backing up or sitting around a campfire."

Emily glanced at her. "When did you ever sit around a campfire, Mother?"

Lillian shrugged. "I'm sure I did. At one time or another."

She edged into the corner of the sofa and tugged an afghan around her shoulders. It was getting cold in the house with all the windows open. But, for once, she decided not to complain and draw more attention to her . . . mishap.

She sat quietly while her daughters surveyed the damage, feeling like a schoolchild who's been sent to the principal's office and is awaiting her interview. She had made an egregious error today, it was true. Her daughters were bound to make the most of it. Especially Emily.

"The firemen didn't get spray on the carpeting, I see," Lillian had noted as they walked back into the parlor. "That was fortunate."

"The kitchen isn't too bad," Jessica reported. "But you need someone to come in and clean before you can use the stove again."

"Use the stove? I don't think so." Emily stood in the middle of the parlor, arms crossed over her chest.

"Really? What am I to do, go on a cold-food regimen? Is that some new weight-loss theory? I hardly think it's wise to try fad diets at my age," Lillian grumbled.

"Mother . . . just stop." Emily held up her hands like a traffic cop. "Not another word. This event just proves what Jessica and I have been trying to tell you since Sara left. You can't live alone here anymore. Not another day. It's simply too dangerous."

Jessica looked at her with a sympathetic but serious expression. "We know it's hard to face it, Mother. But honestly, didn't the fire frighten you? Doesn't it say something to you?"

Lillian shook her head stubbornly. "It proves nothing except that I much prefer Bizet to cooking. Always have and always will."

"Bizet? What does he have to do with it?" Emily and Jessica exchanged puzzled stares.

"Oh, you two prosaic souls would not understand, not in a million years. The cheese wouldn't melt, and I came in to hear some music. On the radio. Selections from *Carmen*. I must have dozed off for a few minutes. . . . It could have happened to anyone."

Emily walked over to an armchair and sat down. Lillian watched her cross her long legs. *One of her better physical attributes,* Lillian noted, *for which she has only her mother to thank. But has she ever thanked me? Of course not.*

"Yes, Mother, it could have happened to anyone." Emily's mild agreement took Lillian off guard. "But since you were alone here, with no one else to smell the smoke, a minor situation nearly turned into a full-blown disaster. Therefore, we must make a change immediately. No more debates. No more delays."

"My, my. That directive has the ring of a political slogan if ever I heard one. *No more debates. No more delays.* That's a phrase you could run on, my dear. Though you won't get my vote."

"Mother, it could have been a real catastrophe here today," Jessica implored her. "Emily's right, we can't sit by and wait any longer to . . . to help you."

"To force me into some arrangement I'd detest, you mean?"

"Why don't you come live with one of us?" Emily suggested. "My house is small, but Dan and I have been talking about moving for a while. We would buy something larger, with a comfortable space for you."

"Comfortable space?" Lillian snapped. "Do you honestly think I want to spend the rest of my life in some 'mother-in-law' quarters, built over a garage? Really, Emily. Don't make me laugh."

Or cry, which is exactly what Lillian felt like doing. Oh, she could just picture it. Some cramped, patched-together space in a makeshift extension. She would be permitted to take her bed, of course, and maybe an armchair and a single rug. They would allow her a painting or two and a little cabinet for a few collectibles. The rest would be taken away, scattered to the four winds. They might as well put her in a jail cell—or put a pillow over her face and be done with it.

"You can come live with us, Mother," Jessica said quickly. "You practically paid for building the new house. It's only fair. And there's plenty of room."

"Once that baby comes, it won't feel that roomy to me," Lillian said. "What about your husband? I'm sure he isn't all that eager to take me in."

Lillian knew that Sam tried hard for Jessica's sake, but she and her son-in-law did not get along well. The man had no polish, no conversation skills, Lillian felt, at least not the kind she valued. Lillian had opposed Jessica's marriage to him, and the bitter words and arguments had never been entirely forgotten, she was sure.

Jessica shook her head, her long curly hair bouncing on either side of her face. "Sam's already told me he would love to have you come live with us."

"Ha! I doubt that's a direct quote, dear. But I can't fault you for trying."

"Honestly, Mother. He said if you don't want to live in the house, he would build you a cottage on the property, so you can have your own space."

"And he can have his," Lillian said. "A little cottage, how sweet. I'll be just like a witch in a fairy tale, pulling children into my lair to fatten them up—"

"Mother, be serious, will you? If you won't come live with one of us, we'll try the home companion route. Again," Emily said grimly.

Lillian met her gaze a moment and quickly looked away. She'd had her share of home companions over the years and had yet to find one that could last a week. Her record was eight minutes flat. It appeared she would soon have an opportunity to break it.

But before she could formulate a proper salvo, Ezra walked in. He fanned the air, doubtless reacting to the smoky smell.

"Good grief, what's been going on here?"

"Ezra, I realize our relationship stretches back decades, but don't you think a proper knock on the door is still appropriate?"

"The door was wide open, Lily, so I dispensed with the

formalities. This is, after all, an emergency. Fire engines flying down Main Street, headed for your house. And I still smell smoke in the air. Are you all right?"

"I'm fine," Lillian said dismissively. "It's been a big misunderstanding. High drama over a mere grilled cheese sandwich, for heaven's sake. Both of my daughters could have had brilliant careers in the theater."

"There was a kitchen fire, Ezra," Jessica explained. "Mother was cooking and left the room for a while—"

"And fell asleep out here," Emily clarified. "Listening to Bizet, selections from *Carmen*. Luckily, the smoke alarm sounded and she got outside safely."

Ezra turned to Lillian, looking shocked. "You fell asleep listening to *Carmen*? Who was the soprano?"

"Callas," she answered guiltily.

"Why, Lily . . . Maria Callas singing *Carmen*? That's one of your favorites."

Lillian shrugged. "I can't understand it myself. Perhaps I need my medication adjusted. No harm done, I suppose, though my daughters would have been delighted to see this place burn to the ground. Then I'd really have to live with one of them—or end up in some drafty old-age home."

"No one in this room ever said the words *old-age home*," Emily insisted. "Who even uses that term anymore?"

"It's called assisted living now, Mother," Jessica said.

"Pish-posh." Lillian waved her hand. "The euphemisms improve, the reality remains the same. How's that for a slogan, Emily?"

"Old-age home? Assisted living? What is going on here?" Ezra wanted to know. "Have you finally agreed to sell this place?"

"Ask them." Lillian pointed at her daughters. "They seem to think they're calling the shots now."

"We are not calling the shots, Mother," Emily argued. "But after this latest near miss, we think the situation here must change. The choices are very clear. You can either live with one of us or have some help in here. This kitchen fire could have been a serious matter."

"Your daughter is right," Ezra said. "This was a very close call. Stop being so stubborn and let someone in here to help you. It's not the end of the world. Your position in this matter is positively irrational."

"Traitor! Why, I ought to call you Benedict Arnold from now on. Are you ganging up on me, too?" Lillian demanded. "Of all things, Ezra. I expected *you* to be an ally, not help them herd me through the fence to be sent out to pasture."

Ezra sighed. "If your daughters are dramatic, I can see where they get it from, Lily. But if we can all put the theatrics aside for a moment, you'll see that they have a good point and only the best intentions for your welfare."

"So *you* say. I hardly see it that way at all . . . Benny."

"What are your alternatives?" Ezra asked. "You will either risk losing your house and the autonomy you have now. Or, the next time you fall asleep with something on the stove, you'll harm yourself for sure. Take your pick, Lillian, though neither choice seems worth maintaining this pose of utter obstinacy."

Lillian huddled in her afghan. She felt cornered, like a wild animal caught in a trap. Emily and Jessica were easy to spar with, to keep off balance. She knew how to elude their grasp.

But three to one? That match was weighted too unevenly, even for her.

"I choose . . . door number three. If I must choose something."

Emily leaned forward. "Meaning exactly what, Mother?"

"Home companion. The mysterious 'somebodies' from the very reputable agency you were rhapsodizing about just yesterday. Bring it on," she added, "as they say on TV."

"Well, that wasn't too tough." Jessica's tone was uncharacteristically sardonic.

"I suppose you have this helper all lined up, ready to roll out like a bowling ball?" Lillian inquired.

"Since you asked, I do, Mother. I can have her here tomorrow at nine thirty. I'll come over to meet her with you and get you settled. How does that sound?"

"Simply dreadful," Lillian said, her face taut with a false smile. "But what choice do I have? My fate is sealed."

"Exactly," Emily agreed. She glanced at her watch. "Sorry but I have to run. I have to pick up Janie at pre-school today."

"I can stay, Mother," Jessica said. "I'll clean up the kitchen and leave you some dinner. The microwave should be working."

"No, no . . . leave that work for the home helper. What else will she have to do? I might as well get my money's worth," Lillian noted. "I'll just have a cold supper, some cereal or something. You run along now. I'd like to enjoy my last few hours of freedom."

"Yes, enjoy, Mother. I'll see you tomorrow, bright and early." Emily leaned over and kissed her mother good-bye. Jessica did the same.

Once her daughters were gone, Lillian turned to Ezra.

"What do you have to say for yourself, Ezra Elliot? I'm not sure if I can ever forgive you for turning against me like that. I'm surprised I'm even speaking to you."

"If that's the price I have to pay, so be it. I did it for your own good," Ezra told her plainly. "I saw those trucks flying down Main Street, and Tucker Tulley told me they were headed for your house. Everyone in town was convinced that this place had burned to the ground and you in it."

"Officer Tulley." Lillian scoffed at the name of the town's most popular policeman. "You were sitting at the lunch counter in the Clam Box, I assume. That stretch of Formica is his beat."

"Yes, I was, as a matter of fact," Ezra replied with a laugh. "Tucker was sitting right next to me."

"Well, reports of my death have been greatly exaggerated," Lillian said crisply. "But I'll bet the news brought Charlie Bates a smile," she added, naming the owner of the diner and a lifelong foe. "Along with a few others. I'm surprised they didn't come running down here with a bag of marshmallows."

"Lillian, be serious."

"I'm perfectly serious. I've never won any popularity contests in this town, Ezra, and I never will. You should know that by now."

"I know all about you. I've been studying you now for years." Ezra reached down and took her hand.

"Maybe, but you *hardly* know everything," she continued arguing, though she didn't take her hand away.

"That's what keeps it interesting." He sighed. "Let's not be at odds, Lily. I'm glad you agreed to have someone in here. I worry about you now that Sara and Luke are gone. Anything can happen at our age."

"Oh, go on. You just like haggling with me. It helps your low blood pressure."

"That it does," he admitted with a grin. "If anything happened to you, I'd miss having someone to argue with. We go back a long way, my dear."

Lillian didn't know what to say. She looked into his faded blue eyes, twinkling at her from behind his spectacles, then quickly looked away.

They did go back a long way, no debating that. She was still annoyed that he had sided against her, but he was her closest friend. Her only friend, when you came right down to it. She couldn't stay angry with him for long.

Ezra sat down next to her on the couch. "Do you remember when I took you to the opera on our first date?"

"Our first and last," she reminded him. "It was *Turandot*. Not a very distinguished production but the tenor was first-rate."

"Yes, he was," Ezra agreed. "You were first-rate, too.

Very fine indeed. I recall you had on a black dress and pearl earrings. I still remember the way you looked, walking down the stairs in your father's house to greet me. So elegant. Like a queen."

She glanced at him, surprised and touched that he could recall the moment so clearly, after all this time.

"You looked very handsome, too," she replied graciously. "You brought me a wrist corsage, I think."

"A gardenia. I wanted to choose something unusual. Something that would make an impression on you."

"You've always made an impression on me, Ezra. That goes without saying."

It was true, too, though not the impression Ezra had once hoped to make.

When Lillian was in her early twenties, she had come to stay with her cousin who lived in nearby Newburyport for a short vacation toward the end of the summer. She had met Ezra Elliot at the recently opened Clam Box diner, the Grand Opening sign still hung across the doorway. They were introduced by her future husband, Oliver Warwick, who had taken her out to lunch that day.

Lillian had met Oliver at a country club dance the night before. She didn't want to go out with him, but he had tracked her down at the beach and then insinuated himself into her party, a group of young women who fairly swooned over him.

Oliver was the most sought after, and notorious, bachelor in town. Handsome, charming, smooth-talking—the son of the richest man for miles around and sole heir to the family fortune. He had some scandals in his past, a divorce and some gossip about a young woman who had to leave town under mysterious circumstances. Which made him all the more interesting to some girls.

At first, Lillian found him intolerable and didn't want anything to do with him. Maybe that's why he found her so intriguing and challenging.

Ezra was one of Oliver's large circle of friends. They grew up together. Both served in the military during World War II, and upon his return, Ezra finished medical school. When he met Lillian, he was working at Children's Hospital in Boston. He had some advantage in the race to court her, as they both lived and worked in the city. She was an assistant curator at the Boston Museum at the time.

But, despite the many interests she and Ezra shared—art, opera, literature—and despite the fact that Ezra was an acceptable choice to her family while Oliver was not, poor Ezra never had a chance. Oliver already owned her heart.

From the first audacious hello, she realized later. In fact, her few dates with Ezra only served to clarify how much she felt for Oliver, the strong, passionate connection between them that simply defied logical analysis and explanation.

Ezra was a fine man with a kind heart and a keen intellect. He was a gentleman, certainly her intellectual equal, which was rare. But at the time, she felt nothing for him but friendship. And she knew that would never be good enough, for either of them.

Ezra may have enjoyed romances with other women throughout the years. If he had, Lillian had not been aware. He never married and she never asked him why, though from time to time she had been curious.

"I thought about that date, Lily, for a long time after," Ezra now told her. "I wondered if there was something I should have done differently, something to bowl you over. To shake you loose from Oliver."

Lillian wondered, too. Perhaps her life would have been much happier, ultimately, if Ezra had shaken her loose. Later in their marriage, Oliver inflicted great pain and disgrace on the entire family when he was caught stealing funds from the company retirement accounts to cover his gambling debts. The family lost nearly everything—their huge estate, Lilac Hall; the factory in town; and most of their investments and savings.

Oliver was left a broken man, and Lillian had been hard-pressed to hold things together, to sort out their situation and keep her husband out of jail.

At the time many in town seemed to secretly—and not so secretly—rejoice in the Warwicks' misfortune, happy to see the proud family fall from power and grace. Ezra was among the few who had stuck by her and Oliver, helping her navigate the rocky course as best as he could.

Everyone was gone now, like characters in a play who have left the stage. Everyone who had been so close to her, who had held such great roles in her life. Her husband, Oliver, a starring player, center stage. Her parents and siblings. Her relatives in Newburyport. So many who had lived in town, their peers and even their servants and employees at Oliver's factory. All dead now. Dead and gone.

Except for her daughters, of course.

And Ezra. He was the only contemporary left now. The only one who knew what she had been through and could really understand her.

But she didn't like to think of the past, to dwell on those dark days. Best to not look back, she had learned the hard way, not at the bleak times, or even the happy ones.

"Oh dear, let's not get all sloppy and sentimental now. Please?" Lillian asked, withdrawing her hand from Ezra's. "As they say in meditation class, be here now."

Ezra laughed. "When did you ever study meditation?"

"I've seen it on TV. It looks very beneficial. Though I won't be able to try anything like that now, with all these strangers underfoot, trampling on my solitude and privacy. With their endless false cheer and small talk—very small—and questions, questions, questions. I'm not sure I can do it, Ezra," she said. "It might be the old-age home for me, after all."

"Nonsense. You'll just have to get used to it. Change is healthy at our age, Lily. You don't want to get stuck in a rut. Change is inevitable. You can't fight it. You must have more patience, more tolerance. How else would we get by at our stage of life?"

"I don't know, obviously," Lillian admitted. "Old age is no place for sissies, that's for sure."

"Bette Davis," he replied, identifying the quote.

"Did she say that, too? She was right." Lillian thought he might be correct, but the observation had been totally original on her part.

Ezra did have a point. Change was inevitable, for better or worse, whether she liked it or not. She had already learned that hard lesson.

She was in the midst of frightening, unwanted changes right now and would have to manage as best as she could. Her daughters just didn't understand. But Lillian felt, even though he had taken sides against her in this argument, Ezra did. He would stick with her and tolerate her great wailing and gnashing of teeth . . . and everything that came after.

That was a comfort, she reflected, gazing over at him. Some comfort, indeed.

THE NEXT MORNING, WHEN THE DOOR CHIMES SOUNDED at a quarter past nine, Lillian realized that her daughter Emily was on time for once in her life. Ahead of schedule, in fact. For this visit of all things. It figured.

Lillian had showered and dressed and even made herself some tea, heating water in the microwave. But she hadn't fixed her hair properly or applied her requisite swipe of lipstick. She positively felt faded without it and hated to meet the new home companion feeling less than her imposing, well-groomed best.

But there they stood, her daughter and the stranger, side by side on the front porch. Lillian took a peek from the parlor window. The woman who stood beside Emily in a dark coat and muffler didn't look so bad. A bit young, wasn't she? So much the better. Easier to intimidate.

The door chimes sounded again. Lillian sighed and made her way to the foyer. "Let the games begin," she whispered under her breath.

The helper's name was Alyssa . . . or Alicia? Or maybe it was Melissa. Lillian hadn't paid much attention to the introductions. She appeared to be in her late twenties. Something in her dress and manner suggested there would be requests for soap opera viewing. And secret calls on the cell phone, when she thought Lillian wasn't aware. Lillian just got that feeling.

Emily made the introductions, then showed the girl around the house, finally ending up in the kitchen. She briefly explained about the fire, without too many incriminating remarks, Lillian was relieved to hear.

The girl was assigned the task of cleaning up the kitchen. An appliance man was coming tomorrow, to see if the stove could be repaired or needed to be replaced.

Next, Emily showed the woman a list of household chores and another of important phone numbers. How organized she was. Lillian was impressed. Had her daughter just whipped out these lovely lists on her laptop this morning? Or had she been saving them for months, preparing for this big day? The thought was thoroughly depressing.

"That's it, I guess," Emily said to the helper. "If you have any questions, just call my office or the cell." She turned to her mother. "I've got to run now, Mother. I'll call you a little later to see how things are going."

Lillian was surprised. She had expected Emily to stay longer, long enough to see if it was even safe to be left alone with this . . . person.

What did they know about this Alexis anyway? She looked harmless enough. But that didn't mean anything.

"Must you go so soon, Emily?" Lillian blurted out.

The girl smiled. "Don't worry, Mrs. Warwick. We'll be just fine. Your daughter has to get back to work now. After all, she is the mayor."

Lillian tried not to snap at the girl, but she couldn't help it. "Of course, I know she's the mayor. You don't need to speak to me as if I'm a child, being dropped off at pre-school."

"Mother, please!"

"Her tone was very condescending, very demeaning, Emily. I won't stand for it. You know I won't. If that's how it's going to be, she may as well leave right now with you."

The girl turned to Emily with a look of surprise.

"Oh, heavens." Emily was tugging on her coat and looking for something in her big bag. "Please, don't pay any attention to her, Felicia. She didn't mean that."

"I most certainly did," Lillian insisted.

To Lillian's great disappointment and chagrin, the girl didn't even glance at her but remained with her gaze fixed on Emily. "Don't worry, Ms. Warwick. I understand."

Finally, Emily fished out a large set of keys and snapped the bag closed. She hugged her brown wool coat around her middle and tied the belt, then gently took hold of Lillian's hand.

"Why don't you walk me to the door, Mother? So we can say good-bye."

Lillian allowed her daughter to lead her across the kitchen to the side door. "Good-bye, cruel world, is more like it," she muttered under her breath. "This Patricia person will surely be the death of me."

"Come on now, you promised," Emily reminded her.

"I did nothing of the sort. I was blackmailed into this, pure and simple."

"Let's not get into that again. She's a sweet girl, and there's no reason that you can't get along. I want you to promise that you'll at least try," Emily said. "I'm sure you remember the alternatives?"

"Indeed I do. The garage garret, with you and Dan. Or the witch cottage, with your sister and her handyman husband."

Emily sighed and pulled on a pair of leather gloves. "Correct. As long as we're all on the same page."

Lillian made a snorting sound and lifted her chin. "Well, don't let me keep you. I'm sure you have a full roster of browbeating ahead of you today."

Emily smiled and kissed her cheek. "As a matter of fact, I do. This was just a warm-up. I'll see you soon."

Lillian closed the door. Emily thought she had things well under control now, didn't she? She looked so smug, like the cat who swallowed the canary. Well, this game wasn't over yet, Lillian decided.

What did they say at the ballpark? "It isn't over until the fat lady sings."

How true. With any luck, Lillian thought, the fat lady will choose a score by Bizet.

CHAPTER EIGHT

~❦~

*D*AVID KNEW THAT CHRISTINE WAS STARTING HER job at the tree farm on Friday, but he didn't know what time she would come. He figured she would be there at night, when the place was the busiest. Especially with only this weekend and the next left before Christmas. He kept telling himself he would hardly see her, she'd be outside, and he would be inside most of the time she was working. But her presence still disturbed him, the mere sight of her, like salt rubbed in his wounded heart.

David wanted to ask his father about her but decided the less said, the better.

"How did your therapy go?" Jack asked as they left the hospital grounds. This was his father's standard question as they started the ride home.

"It was fine. Gena says I'm coming along," he reported. "Coming from Gena, that crumb is like a triple gold star."

His father nodded. "Sounds like there's some progress."

"Some," David conceded. He still couldn't do much without the walker, which was frustrating. But he was getting there, day by day. Today he was able to make it down the handrail lane pretty well, and he stood without the walker, totally balanced, for an entire minute.

Part of him wanted to report these small successes, while another part insisted it would all sound pretty pathetic. Best to just keep a lid on it.

"How was business today?" he asked, changing the subject. "You look a little tired, Dad. Customers got you hopping?"

"I'll say. Looks like we'll be running all weekend," Jack predicted. "I've got to get back and help Julie."

"Right." David stared out his window. What about Christine? Wasn't she there yet? He wanted to ask but didn't.

As if reading his thoughts, Jack said, "I've been meaning to talk to you about Christine. I wouldn't have offered her a job, but Julie didn't realize. I hope you aren't mad at her."

"I'm not. I know she didn't realize."

"If I'd been in the room at the time, I would have figured a way out of it. I still could, if you want."

David was surprised by his father's offer. "What would you say to her? I thought it was all set."

Jack shrugged. He turned the truck off the highway and followed the county road toward the village. "Oh, I don't know. I'd put it to her nicely. Something like we didn't need as much help as we thought, or we really couldn't afford it."

David didn't know what to say. "Why did you wait until now to ask me, Dad? Isn't today her first day?"

"I don't know why. I wanted to ask you. It never seemed the right time. Either you were worn out or in a foul mood . . . or I was worn out or in a foul mood," he said honestly, making David smile. "I know you hate to hear it, buddy, but the pinecone doesn't fall too far from the tree."

David stared out the window, the familiar landmarks

coming into view. They were getting close to home. He had to decide.

"I don't know what to tell you," David said finally. "I can't say I'm looking forward to having her around. But it doesn't seem fair to just pull the plug for no real reason."

"No, it doesn't. I was just thinking more about your feelings than hers, I guess. She's a nice girl. She'll get a holiday job somewhere in town."

"It's a little late to look now, don't you think?"

Jack glanced at him. "Well, maybe."

David knew more about Christine's family than his father did. He knew there were three other children in the Tate household, all younger. It had been a struggle for her parents to send her to college. Although she had been very offhand about her reasons for wanting a job, he guessed she really needed the money. It didn't seem right to tell her it wasn't going to work out after all.

"It's only a couple of weeks until Christmas," David said. "I mean, it's already the eleventh."

"One week and six days until Christmas Eve," Jack corrected him. "That's how I calculate. Christmas Eve, we close at five o'clock sharp. If you haven't bought a tree by then, that's not my problem."

"One week and six days isn't long. I can stand it. She'll be outside most of the time. I'll hardly see her."

"You'll hardly see her at all," Jack agreed.

"I don't want you to take her job away for no reason, Dad. Not because of me," David said quietly. "I can handle it. Don't worry."

Jack glanced at him. "That's what I was hoping you'd say."

His father's words made David feel good, as if he had lived up to Jack's expectations that he would make the right call here, one that favored fairness and a generous spirit.

The sign for the tree farm came into view. Jack turned the truck onto the long drive that wound up to the house.

Down below at the tree stand lot, David saw rows of cars already parked under the bright lights.

Jack parked the truck and turned off the engine. "I'd better get out there. Need some help getting into the house?"

David pushed open his door. "No, sir. I'm good."

He was tired and achy from the therapy session and probably could have used a little help, pulling his walker out from the half seat in the back of the cab and setting it up so he could balance once he got down. But tonight he felt better doing it himself.

As David let himself into the house he could tell it was empty. Even Katie was outside, helping Julie in the Christmas shop. He pictured her sitting at the counter, gluing random bits of ribbons to foam ornaments. Julie just let her play with the stuff to amuse herself, but sometimes Katie's concoctions came out really good and people wanted to buy them.

He took off his coat and stared out the front window, looking at the activity at the tree stand. He searched for Christine and finally found her, helping a couple pick out a tree. She was wearing her shearling jacket and a Red Sox cap tonight, her long blond hair pulled back in a ponytail.

His father was lucky to have such a cute salesclerk, David thought. She was going to sell a million trees for him.

He watched for a few minutes longer, then decided he'd had enough. Who was he kidding? He wanted to be out there. With her. With his folks. Working and feeling useful. The only time he felt productive lately was working out at the PT sessions.

The last week or so, while everyone was outside working, he had tried to help out around the house. Whatever he could manage to do—clean up the kitchen, empty the dishwasher, throw in some laundry. He even fixed a dinner or two with food Julie bought and instructions she left for him. A meat loaf one night—that had been easy—and breaded chicken, oven baked on another night.

When he had gotten stuck with the zucchini, he looked up a recipe on the Internet, instead of bothering Julie. It had turned out pretty tasty; even Kate ate her vegetables that night.

This past week, he spotted a good recipe in the newspaper for short ribs and told Julie what ingredients to buy so he could try it. The cooking was a help to her and Jack, and there was something about cooking that was getting him hooked. You put in the time and effort, and you ended up with something you could sit down and eat and enjoy.

Of course, there was a downside to it for him. It hurt to stay on his feet for any length of time, especially after a long therapy session. Once in a while, he sat down to chop, resting his hip, giving himself a break. And when even that didn't help, he just stuck with it, forcing himself to focus on the job and ignore the pain.

Feeling useful and contributing around here in some small way was worth a few aches and pains, he decided. Better than lying on his bed, staring at the ceiling.

He was going to make pasta with vegetables tonight, but it was too early to start cooking. David wasn't sure what to do with himself. He needed some distraction, or he would end up with his face pressed against that window all night.

He went into his room and turned on his computer to check his e-mail. An army acquaintance who had also been recently released from the service with injuries had written to him. They hadn't been close, but David empathized with the guy's story. He sent back a quick note, one that he hoped would be encouraging.

Then he got the idea to write a real letter to a pal in his old squad. They were still stationed in Baghdad but were due to return in a month or two.

David had grown close to a lot of the guys in his squad. They were like brothers, working together to take care of each other. But Buzz Murray was a special pal. Buzz had been the driver of the Humvee when the missile hit. He had also managed to get out in time before the armored vehicle's engine exploded. But Buzz was still over there risking his life every minute, and David was back here, living in complete safety.

That didn't seem right. It made David feel guilty, undeserving. Sometimes David wished he could go back to help them. He hated to hear of losses in his battalion, which was probably why he was so lousy at corresponding. The setbacks in his recovery hadn't helped any either. Every time he thought about writing, he couldn't think of anything good to say; he didn't want to send a letter filled with griping and complaints.

In his heart, David knew he owed his pal Buzz a long letter, the kind Christine used to write to him. If only to let Buzz know that he had not forgotten him, or any of the guys. Or what they were doing over there, every day and night. It was so easy to forget once you were home.

If he needed some worthwhile project to get his mind off Christine and his own pitiful little problems, maybe it was time to sit down and write that letter.

David wasn't sure how long he had been sitting at his laptop when Kate appeared in the doorway. He turned and smiled at her. "Hey, Muffin-Head. What are you doing?"

She put her finger to her lips. "Shhh! We're playing hide-and-seek. Don't tell Christine I'm in here."

Then she scampered across the room and crawled under his bed, yanking the bedspread down on one side of the mattress.

David turned back to his computer and tried to continue his letter, but deep inside he felt his heartbeat speed up, anticipating Christine's appearance.

Soon enough, she stood in the doorway and peered inside. "Any little girls hiding in here?" she asked.

David shrugged. "Not that I've noticed."

He tried not to smile. He tried hard not to even turn his head to look at her. He knew little Muffin-Head under the bed was listening to the conversation.

Christine did not seem convinced. Either his tone of voice had given Katie away—or it was the small pink sneaker, sticking out from under the quilt.

"Hmm . . . let's just make sure, shall we?" Christine walked slowly around the bed, then crouched down and grabbed Katie's foot by the ankle. "Got'cha!"

Katie shrieked, then laughed and slid back out, covered with dust bunnies. "How did you find me so quickly? David, did you tell?"

David frowned and shook his head. "No way."

"He didn't tell, honest," Christine said quickly. "But that was fast. You can go again, it's okay."

"Can David play? He's really good."

David often played hide-and-seek with Kate. It usually took her a long time to find him. He had the advantage of his army training, having been taught to hide from the enemy.

But play with Christine? He wasn't so sure about that.

"Sure, he can. It will be more fun with three." Christine smiled at him and he felt his heart melt—and all his excuses for skipping the game along with it.

"All right, I'm in," he said. He knew she was watching him. He didn't want her to see how awkward he was, getting up from his chair and grabbing his walker. He stayed put. "How about both of you hide?"

"Okay, close your eyes and count to twenty. Slowly," Christine told him.

David did as he was told, listening intently to the two sets of footsteps as they ran off into the far reaches of the house.

"Ready or not, here I come," he called. He rose from the desk chair, grabbed his walker, and swung his body into place.

Katie was a cinch. He found her in about ten seconds, hiding behind the shower curtain in his bathroom.

"I guess she's not in here," he teased her. Then he suddenly pulled the curtain aside. "Oh yes, she is!"

She shrieked at the sight of him, which was most of the fun for her.

"Let's find Christine. I bet I know where she hid," Katie whispered to him.

"Lead the way," he whispered back.

He followed her into the kitchen, moving as quietly as he could. They checked the broom closet and pantry and then the laundry room. They checked the living room, behind all the furniture and curtains, narrowing the choices down to the coat closet.

David signaled to Katie to be silent and pointed to the closet. Focusing his entire will on controlling his movements, he ever so quietly snuck up to the closet on the walker then quickly pulled the door open.

"Got'cha!" Katie called out.

Christine had not heard them coming. She shrieked then tilted off balance. David realized she must have been leaning on the door.

He quickly held out his arms and caught her as she pitched forward. The walker got stuck between them but his hands ended up clamped on her shoulders and her hands pressed to his chest. He was suddenly glad he'd been working out again. He felt the hard muscles in his arms and chest supporting her. At least he had gotten some reward for the grueling hours of PT he put in.

Her cheek and soft hair brushing his face, his senses filled with the scent of her flowery perfume.

"Oh my gosh . . . David," she said, righting herself.

She looked as embarrassed as he felt, her cheeks flushed and wide eyes glistening. They stared at each other a moment, both stunned by the close contact. David realized she had been close enough to kiss, if he'd dared.

Maybe he would have, too. If Katie hadn't been standing there watching them, the perfect chaperone.

"I'm so sorry. Did I hurt you?" Christine asked quickly.

Her question was like a dash of cold water. Totally deflating. Reminding him just how she saw him—a handicapped invalid.

"Of course you didn't," he said quickly.

She nodded, looking self-conscious, and quickly stepped out of his way. "I think I'd better go start Kate's dinner. Do you want something?" she offered.

He hesitated. He was hungry, but she hadn't been hired to babysit for him, too . . . had she?

"I'm cooking dinner tonight," he said. "Why don't you give Kate her bath? I'll have the food ready by the time you're done."

I hope, he silently added.

For a moment, Christine looked at him curiously, as if she didn't quite believe he was capable of keeping that promise. "Okay, sounds like a good plan. Come one, Kate. Time for a tub," she said cheerfully.

Katie followed her like a puppy. "Mommy bought me Little Mermaid bubbles. Want to see?"

"The Little Mermaid? She's my favorite," he heard Christine say, their excited voices disappearing up the stairway.

David pushed himself back to the kitchen as fast he could move the walker. Time for some speed cooking. He had a recipe and quickly pulled the ingredients out of the fridge. Large onion, garlic, parsley, bell pepper, box of mushrooms. He searched around a bit. Chicken cutlets. He added the package to the pile tucked to his chest, made his way to the counter, and dumped it.

Since he had started cooking, Julie left a lot of the pots out on the stove to make it easier for him. He set a big pot for boiling water on the burner then made a few trips back and forth from the sink with a smaller pot of water, until there was enough to boil for the pasta.

He grabbed the recipe again and followed the steps. First browning the chicken and setting it aside, then cooking the vegetables, starting with garlic and onions. When the mixture was cooked and seasoned, he cut the chicken into bite-size pieces and mixed it all up. Then he added the cooked pasta with a slotted spoon directly from the boiling water. He had seen a cook on TV do it this way, and it was sure easier for him. He still wasn't up to the task of carrying a pot of boiling water across the room to drain it in the sink.

David had never minded cooking when he lived on his own. Now he enjoyed it even more. He wasn't quite sure why. Maybe because he felt in control when he cooked. He was calling the shots—more salt, a little garlic, a dash of ground pepper? Sliced or diced? Pasta or rice? He was the one to decide. He liked that feeling and liked ending up with something to show for his efforts. Most of the time nowadays, he felt out of control and acted upon, just taking up space and not being very productive.

When he cooked, he forgot about his bad leg, his worries about the future, and even the haunting images of his recent past. It was just him—and a chicken cutlet sautéing in a pan. And that was a good thing, like a minivacation. He was even starting to wonder if this was something he could make a career out of. Maybe it was nothing like being a police officer or a firefighter, but it might not be so bad. . . .

Christine came into the kitchen followed by Kate, who looked fresh as a flower after her Little Mermaid bubble bath, dressed in her flannel pajamas.

"What's for supper?" Christine walked up to the stove and watched him add the finishing touches, some chopped parsley and grated cheese.

"Pasta with chicken and sautéed vegetables," David

announced. He managed to keep his voice smooth and even, though her nearness had him all jittery inside again.

"It smells good, David," Katie said.

"You smell good, too." He dipped close to her head. "You smell like . . . a mermaid."

Kate laughed, looking surprised. Christine laughed, too. "We used half a bottle of bubbles. I'd be surprised if she didn't smell like a mermaid by now."

Christine quickly set the table, giving Kate the task of folding some paper napkins. "Should I set a place for Julie and Jack?" she asked. "Maybe I should go out and help while one of them comes up here?"

"Right. I'll call down there and see," David said, though he sure hoped they wouldn't take Christine up on the offer.

David grabbed the kitchen phone and dialed his father's cell phone. He knew Jack and Julie had been outside a long time and were probably hungry by now. But all the time he had been cooking he had been anticipating eating dinner alone with Christine. He knew it was part of her job, but he would hate it if Christine had to run out now to the tree stand.

The cell phone rang a few times. Finally, Jack picked up.

"I made some dinner. Do you guys want to come up and eat?"

"I can wait. Let me ask Julie." David waited. Finally, his father came back on the line. "She says she's okay for now, too. She'll come up in a little while and tuck Kate in, then bring me down something. Can you just save it for us?"

"Sure, no problem." David hung up, feeling suddenly lighthearted again. "He said they're all right for now. Julie is going to come up in a while and put Kate in bed."

"Okay, thanks." Christine nodded. She seemed unsure of what to do next. "Can I help you with anything?"

He did hate that question. But it wasn't so bad, coming from her, David decided. It was more the way she said it, like anybody could need a little help. It didn't have to do with his leg or being in a walker.

"Why don't you hand me the plates, and I'll serve the food from here?" he told her.

Christine handed him the empty plates and then set them back on the table.

"Wow, this looks great. I didn't know you could cook," she said as she took a seat next to Kate.

"I didn't either," he admitted. "It's just something I've gotten into lately, hanging around the house. Gives me something to do with myself while everyone's out working."

"It's a big help for Julie," Christine said. She tasted a bite, and he waited to see if she liked it. "Mmm. This is really good. I love the sauce."

"It's just some butter and cheese and stuff," he tried to explain. "I googled 'chicken cutlets' and found the recipe on a cooking show website. How do you like it?" he asked his little sister.

Kate mimicked Christine's response perfectly. "I like this googled chicken, David. It's really good."

David and Christine laughed at her. David felt more at ease. They talked easily with each other, as if they hadn't spent years apart since high school.

But that's the way Christine was, easy to get along with. To a fault. She probably should have been mad at him for the way he had left town and faded out of her life. But she wasn't one to hold a grudge. That's why he had thought he might still have a chance with her—if he'd come home in one piece.

Kate ate quickly and asked to be excused so she could watch one of her favorite TV shows. "I guess that would be all right," Christine said, looking at the clock.

Kate grabbed Lester and happily ran off toward the family room. "She's too cute," Christine whispered, watching her go. "You always said you missed having siblings. I bet you didn't expect to get one now."

"No, I didn't," David admitted. Of course he'd known his father might marry again someday, but he had never given much thought to the consequences, one way or the other. He hadn't been back in touch with his father until last Christmas.

"Kate is amazing. I really get a kick out of her," David said.

"I can see that. She's crazy about you, too."

David felt pleased by her words. "Just goes to show, you never know what's going to happen."

"That true. You never know, do you?" As she gazed at him from across the table, David wondered what had put that thoughtful light in her blue eyes.

"So what does your boyfriend think of your new job?" he asked, then wondered what in the world had made him say that.

"My boyfriend? What does he have to do with it?" Christine looked confused and surprised by the question.

"Your fiancé, I mean," David corrected himself. "Maybe he doesn't like the idea of you working here, since I'm your old boyfriend?"

"Oh, that." Christine looked down at the table. "He doesn't care. I mean, he doesn't mind." She looked up at David and shrugged. "It's only a week or two. I need the job. He understands."

Christine rose and started clearing off the table.

David got the distinct feeling she hadn't told her fiancé about the job. Or about him. Which sparked a tiny flicker of hope.

He swatted the feeling down. What was the difference if she told her boyfriend or not? She was still marrying the guy a few months from now. Nothing was going to change that.

The back door opened and Julie came in. Her cheeks

were red from the cold, and she pulled off her gloves and rubbed her bare hands together. "It's freezing out there. Loads of customers though," she added cheerfully. "We must have sold a hundred trees tonight."

The conversation quickly turned to Kate. Christine gave Julie the update, and Julie headed for the family room.

"Guess I'd better head outside and help Jack awhile," Christine said. "Thanks again for dinner. I'm sort of stove-challenged in the kitchen," she admitted.

"If I can figure it out, anybody can," he assured her.

"See you," she called out from the back door.

"Right, see you." He watched her go then stood staring at the closed door a moment.

He would see her, too. Every day until Christmas.

Think you can stand it? he asked himself, realizing that this situation was not quite the hardship he had thought it would be.

Um . . . yeah, he answered his own question. *I think so.*

CHAPTER NINE

❧

*Y*OU DON'T HAVE TO STAY. THAT'S ALL RIGHT. I CAN manage on my own, Emily," Lillian said.

Meanwhile, she gripped Emily's arm for dear life as they walked up the driveway heading for the side door.

Right, Mother, Emily wanted to reply. *You can't even get into the house on your own. Do you really expect me to believe you can manage just fine once you're in there?*

But she didn't say that, of course. And it was slippery. Flurries during the night had left a few inches of fresh snow on the ground, and Emily had to make the choice this morning to either shovel a path from her mother's side door to the car, or risk walking in late to the church service. Which her mother hated more than risking a fall. So now there was no path and they struggled to get inside, without Lillian ending up in the snow.

Finally, they made it.

"I'm going to shovel a bit and then I'll make lunch," Emily said as they entered the house.

"I can make the lunch," Lillian insisted. "Cold foods, nothing that requires turning on the stove," she added with special emphasis.

Of course her mother had started using the stove again. Just not when either of her daughters was around, Emily knew.

"A sandwich would be fine. Anything you have on hand," Emily said, holding on to her patience. She found an old wool scarf on a hook near the door and wrapped it around her neck before heading out again.

Emily quickly shoveled a wide path from the side door to the driveway, then another path from the sidewalk up to the porch. The cold dry air had a bite today, though the sky was perfectly clear, a brilliant blue. She really didn't mind shoveling; she needed the exercise. But she did have a lot at home to do.

If only her mother would tolerate some help. Felicia had not lasted long. Her mother had fired her for some odd reason—mixing white clothes with colored items in the laundry?

It seemed an unlikely error for a trained home-care worker to make, Emily thought. More likely, it was one of her mother's tricks to create a valid cause for banishment.

Like an unscrupulous detective, planting evidence.

Emily had not bothered to confront her mother about it. Yet. But her mother had to realize she was playing a dangerous game. Three strikes and she was going to be out of this house, if Emily had any say about it.

By the time Emily finished shoveling and came inside, the kitchen table was set for lunch. Her mother had made two sandwiches, each containing a single slice of yellow cheese and a wispy leaf of iceberg lettuce balanced within slices of toasted white bread.

Emily wasn't sure why she found the sandwiches so amusing. Maybe it was the combination of obvious, painstaking care in assembly with extremely meager ingredients.

"You made lunch, how nice." Emily said, sitting down.

"And some tea. It's cold out there," Lillian noted. "That man who spoke up in church today . . . that Mr. Healy. Isn't he fortunate that his family won't be doing without heat tonight?"

"Yes, he is, very fortunate. That was an amazingly generous gift someone gave him."

Once again during "Joys and Concerns," a member of the congregation reported that his family had received an anonymous gift. This time, a new furnace.

"He was so grateful," Emily recalled, "he was practically in tears."

Along with his heartfelt thanks, Howard Healy reported that he had been injured at his job in a warehouse several months ago and was still unable to return to work. His family was struggling to live on his disability benefits and the small paycheck his wife brought home from her job at a food store. When the furnace went, they really had nowhere to turn.

"I wonder who's giving these amazing gifts to everyone." Emily took a sip of her tea. It was weak as dishwater, just the way her mother liked it, but hot at least.

"Yes, I wonder. It must be someone with money to spare," Lillian speculated. "That leaves out most people in that church."

Emily glanced at her. "In that case, your name would be at the top of the list of possibilities."

The observation was simple fact. Her mother was among the wealthiest church members. And Emily was curious to see what her mother would say to that.

Lillian sputtered a bit as she put her teacup down. She patted her mouth with a paper napkin. "Yes, I suppose some people might think I was the Yuletide Robin Hood. With some assistance, of course."

"You would need some help to carry it off. But it's not

really like Robin Hood, Mother. Robin Hood *stole* from the rich to give to the poor."

Lillian shrugged. "For all we know, the person giving these extravagant gifts might well be stealing the funds to do so. This situation seems so heartwarming from a distance, but we don't really know what's going on, do we? Who is doing this and why? And where are they getting the money? I will find it heartwarming when those questions are answered satisfactorily. It is most . . . peculiar. Most likely, the act of someone who is mentally unbalanced, I'd say."

Emily was shocked into laughter. "Mother, do you really think that? Do you really think it's a sign of mental illness to be generous to strangers? What about donating to charities for different causes? You sometimes make those kinds of donations, and very large ones, too, I've noticed."

Her mother gave substantially to causes that moved her. A famine in Ethiopia. Or Hurricane Katrina relief. She was an avid news watcher, and these were often situations that came right into her living room.

"That's different," Lillian argued. "This is so . . . personal. It must be someone in our church who knows all these families. It strikes me as very inappropriate somehow."

"I think it's wonderful. It's the real spirit of Christmas and a lesson for all of us," Emily said quietly.

"Oh, balderdash. Now you sound as if you're reading out of a greeting card," Lillian scoffed. "Speaking of the spirit of Christmas, don't you think it's time to bring down my boxes from the attic? I want to do a little decorating around here."

"I can bring them down for you," Emily said. "But I need to go soon, and you can't decorate by yourself. So what's the sense? You'll only be tempted."

Lillian made a face and crossed her arms over her chest. "I knew you were going to say that."

"You could have had your decorating finished by now if you hadn't fired Felicia," Emily pointed out.

"Felicia was not as capable as you think. I was the one who was here with her and subjected to her incompetence. If I had sent her up to the attic on Friday, she would still be up there, looking for the boxes."

"Well, we'll have to see if the person coming tomorrow can manage to find your decorations and find their way downstairs again," Emily said dryly.

"The person coming tomorrow? Good grief—"

"You didn't think that was going to be the end of it, did you?" Emily asked. "Her name is Nancy. She's very experienced, older than Felicia. She used to be a nurse, so you can't claim she lacks training."

"Maybe so, but she must lack plain common sense if she gave up a good career like nursing for this sort of work."

"I wouldn't be so quick to find fault before you've even met her. We're giving you another chance. Don't blow it," Emily advised.

"Thanks for the warning. Are you done with your lunch?" Lillian asked tartly.

"Yes, I am. Thank you." Emily picked up her empty plate, and her mother's. The sandwich had been so flimsy, she would be hungry again by the time she got home.

"Just put those dishes in the sink," Lillian said. "I'll take care of them later."

"Don't bother, Mother. Nancy will do it for you tomorrow."

Her mother gave out a short, harsh laugh. "Yes, Nancy is coming. Be still, my beating heart. I can hardly wait."

Emily slipped on her coat and grabbed her purse. "Jessica said she'll drop by later, on her way home from the mall. She wants to bring you some dinner."

"She needn't bother. Cold cereal would be fine with me. I can wait for Nancy to fix me a real meal."

Emily had to laugh out loud. "Mother, you are sui generis." She leaned over and quickly kissed her mother's cheek.

"My, my . . . I am impressed. If you think you can butter me up with a little high school Latin, think again, my dear. Sui generis, my foot," Lillian grumbled as Emily headed for the back door. "Wait a minute. Does this Nancy know any Latin? That is one of my requirements, you know."

Emily glanced over her shoulder and waved good-bye. Then she slipped outside, into the bracing, head-clearing cold air.

She didn't dare reply.

ON MONDAY MORNINGS REVEREND BEN USUALLY SET out early to visit members of the congregation who were sick in the hospital or confined to a nursing home. By lunch time, he had visited all four on his list and headed back to the village. But instead of going straight to the church, he parked near the Clam Box diner on Main Street.

As Ben entered, the bell over the door rang, and Officer Tulley turned on his stool at the counter to see who had come in.

Just the man I want to see, Ben thought, waving at his friend. He walked over and sat on the empty seat next to Tucker.

"Hello, Reverend. How's your Monday going?" Tucker asked.

"Fine so far. It's my Sunday that still has some wrinkles to iron out."

Tucker smiled. "You mean the Phantom Santa?"

"Exactly. He—or she?—has struck again and made Howard Healy and his family very happy and grateful."

"And warm," Tucker added.

"And warm," Ben agreed solemnly.

It was hard to think of anyone doing without a properly

heated house in this weather. But Ben knew that even
families with perfectly good heating systems were turning
their thermostats down low this year because they couldn't
afford the heating bills.

Charlie Bates bustled out of the kitchen. He dropped a
plate with a turkey sandwich in front of Tucker then turned
to Ben. "What'll you have today, Reverend?"

Ben noticed that Charlie hadn't bothered to give him a
menu. Not that he needed one, but he did like the pretense
of looking it over, as if he didn't know it by heart.

He glanced up at the blackboard over the counter where
the specials were listed. "How about the corn chowder?"

"How about it?" Charlie quipped, with a nasal laugh.

"I'll have a bowl, Charlie. Thank you," Ben answered
evenly.

"Coming right up. Sorry if things are slow. We only have
one waitress on today. That other one, the new one, she didn't
show up, didn't even bother to call. You just can't find good
help these days. . . ." His grumbling voice disappeared into
the kitchen.

Tucker leaned close to Ben, his voice low. "The only
waitress that ever stuck with this job was Lucy. Because
she's married to him. And even she found a way to escape,"
he observed in an amused tone.

Tucker had known Charlie since kindergarten and was his
closest—and sometimes, his only—friend. So Ben figured he
had the right to comment in this way. Besides, it was true.

Lucy was Charlie's wife. She had worked here day and
night, waiting on tables while Charlie cooked and managed the kitchen. But a few years ago, Lucy decided to get
out from under Charlie's tyrannical thumb and return to
school. It was no small struggle, but she finally managed
the dual accomplishments of earning her nursing degree
and staying married to Charlie.

"That waitress covering the tables today?" Tucker said,
glancing over at her. "Her name's Trudy. She's been here

since the summer. That's probably a new record for anyone other than Lucy."

"Probably," Ben agreed. He hadn't realized the woman had been working here that long.

Charlie arrived with a bowl of soup and dropped it down in front of Ben along with a bag of oyster crackers. "Corn chowder, piping hot."

"Thanks," Ben said.

"More coffee?" Charlie held the pot over Tucker's mug.

"No thanks, Charlie. I'm fine."

"Suit yourself." Charlie sounded insulted, and left them again.

"Tucker," Ben said, his mind returning to their earlier topic. "You hear a lot around town and at church. Who do you think is giving out these extravagant gifts?"

Besides being a police officer, Tucker also served as a deacon at church. Ben knew those two roles covered a lot of ground on the town grapevine.

"I don't have a clue," Tucker replied. "But I think it must be someone in our congregation. How else would they find out that these families are in need?"

"Good point. What I can't figure out is how they knew about the Healys' furnace. Did Howard Healy put a sign up on the bulletin board, too?"

"I don't think so." Tucker rubbed his chin. "Howard is on a lot of committees and so is his wife. There's a lot of personal chitchat at the meetings, you know how it is. One of them must have mentioned that the furnace was on the blink, and the right person must have heard them."

"Yes, it could have happened that way."

Tucker shrugged. "It's not that hard to figure out. You know I could have made detective, Reverend. I just like being a uniform, on a beat."

"Yes, I know that," Ben replied with a smile.

Tucker would have been a good detective, too, he thought, the unobtrusive type that criminals underestimate.

"I know our Secret Santa wants to be anonymous, but I'm really curious now about who it is," Tucker admitted.

"I'm curious, too. I think everybody at church must be. It's amazing to me that this person—or persons—have managed to remain anonymous all this time. I mean, one gift. But now two? And such big gifts, too. How do you think they've managed it?"

"I'm not sure. But it must be someone nobody would expect. And someone who's able to keep a secret," Tucker said. "The thing is, most people carrying on some covert activity—for better or worse—eventually slip up and give themselves away. It's just human nature." Tucker took a sip of coffee and looked over the check that had been slipped under his plate. He left a few bills on the counter and then put on his brimmed hat.

"Human nature, yes." Ben nodded. "And probability, too. I mean, the longer this goes on, the more likely it is that the Secret Santa will be discovered, don't you think?"

"I expect before Christmas is over, the Secret Santa will slip up or leave some telling clue. Don't worry, Reverend, we'll figure it out." Tucker laughed and patted Ben's shoulder as he walked past him and headed for the door.

Ben sat alone, finishing his soup. He didn't know why it suddenly felt important to him, but he did want to know the identity of this Secret Giver. It would probably turn out to be someone well-known to him, he realized. Would he see that person differently once he discovered that they were responsible for these grand gestures of generosity?

The bell over the door sounded, and Ben turned to see Grace Hegman and her father, Digger, enter. Ben waved hello, and a wide grin spread over Digger's wrinkled face. The old man looked as if he intended to walk over, but Grace quickly tugged at his sleeve and steered him in the opposite direction. She glanced back at Ben with a small, tight smile.

Grace had her hands full now with her father, Ben thought as he turned back to his lunch. It was just as well they hadn't joined him. Digger's conversation would have been a rambling one, and Ben had to be on his way. He couldn't linger here all day, gossiping about the Secret Santa.

ON MONDAY IT WAS HARD TO GET BACK INTO THE PT routine. Or maybe Gena the slave driver was just working him harder, David thought. He was doing a little better on the handrail lane and able to stand longer without the walker.

Gena had let him try a cane, but he hadn't been able to manage more than a few steps before his bad leg slipped out from under him. A discouraging debut. But she was trying to work with him to meet his goal to be walker-free by Christmas. "We'll get there," she told him, one of the few times she recognized his effort. He had not answered but hoped that was true.

When they finally finished he practically crawled back to his table and lay back exhausted while she massaged his aching legs.

"Been out last night, David? You were really dragging your butt out there."

David laughed harshly. "Yeah, it was a wild night. A real party night. I got trashed."

"Still having trouble sleeping? Bad dreams?"

"Yeah, I am."

Nightmares about the war zone plagued him, keeping him up several nights a week.

"It wouldn't be so bad if I was living alone. But I scream so loud, I wake the whole house," he confessed. "My little stepsister wakes up and my stepmother has to go and take care of her. And my dad comes down to wake me. . . . One night, I wouldn't wake up that easily and I socked him in the face."

"Really? What did your father think about that?"

"He didn't like walking around with a black eye. But he got over it. He says he's going to put on boxing gloves now when he comes into my room."

Gena nodded. He noticed she didn't laugh at his joke.

Okay, maybe it wasn't that funny. He was just trying not to make such a big thing out of it.

"Your night terrors are a symptom of traumatic stress, David. We've spoken about this before. Have you thought any more about seeing a counselor?"

"No, not really," he admitted. "I did a few sessions when I first got out. I don't think it helped any. It made me keep remembering. I just want to forget."

"Forgetting isn't always an option," Gena said. "Some memories stay with you all your life. That's why I think counseling could help. If you feel uncomfortable in one-on-one treatment, maybe a support group would work for you. Talking with other soldiers who know what you've been through, what you're feeling now. Some of them will be further along and have some worthwhile insights to share. It might help you sort things out and get your life back on track."

"I am getting back on track," David insisted. "You told me I was making progress."

"You are. Some. But you could do better. It's all connected, David. I've told you that before." She completed the massage then put an ice pack on his leg.

David sat up and took a sip of water. "Right. But you never said *how* it's all connected."

"It's simple. If you can get some picture of your future, you have something to work toward." She paused and took a step back from the table and gave him a serious, appraising look. "Right now, David, I think you're stuck. It's not uncommon," she added quickly. "It's pretty normal, in fact. There are a lot of emotional stages you need to go through as you deal with this injury. Denial, anger, mourning. Acceptance, finally."

"Great. Sounds like a long list. When do I get to the last one?"

"If you keep flip-flopping between the others, never. If you get stuck. See what I mean?" she asked quietly.

David did see. But her words made him angry. She was such a know-it-all sometimes. He should have switched to another therapist when he had the chance. He didn't need to take this garbage from her.

"Hey, I'm doing the therapy, putting in my hours. Working out at home, too. What else am I supposed to do?" He knew he ought to control his voice and his temper, but he could feel them both rising. "Aren't you blaming the victim a little here, Gena?"

"I'm sorry if it sounds that way. I'm not blaming you. But you asked me what else you can do? Well, what about having hope?" she said in her quiet, serious way. "That's something that would help you move forward, David. Something to work toward, a goal. Besides getting rid of the walker," she added. "If you had complete physical health right now, what would you want to do? What would your plan be?"

"That's a pretty useless question, don't you think? I may never be able to walk normally again. What good does it do to fantasize about it? My plan was to go into the police force, or be a firefighter. I've told you that."

"Yes, you did. We discussed it."

"And you said it was off the table. So I have no idea what I'd do. If I could walk out of here on my own two feet? . . . Probably buy a car and get the heck out of town."

She leaned back and met his gaze. "Okay, that's a start. Where do you want to go, David? What's your destination?"

He didn't answer her. He didn't have an answer.

"There's got to be something you really want," she persisted.

I want Christine, his heart shouted back at her. *That's all I want. But that's not going to happen. And I can't admit it to this woman anyway.*

He looked straight at Gena then down at his lap again.

"I think there is an answer," she said quietly. "You don't have to tell me. But use it, David. Build on it."

She checked the pack on his leg. "I'm going to get you some more ice." He nodded, not even looking at her. She stepped away and closed the curtain, shutting out the view of the therapy center.

Gena was right. He had to admit it. He had been living in limbo. It was hard to look ahead. He couldn't do it.

He suddenly missed the army, where everything was spelled out for him. All he had to do was follow orders. He had thought it was tough at the time, but it was tougher in the real world where he had to sort out this mess—what to do with his life now that he was handicapped. What was the answer? He didn't know. He just didn't know.

What he told Gena was true. If he were fit and strong again, he would get a car and drive away. That's what he did the last time, right after he graduated high school. He just ran away.

There seemed little chance of pulling that stunt again, not in his present condition. Which left him exactly nowhere.

EMILY ARRIVED AT HER MOTHER'S HOUSE AT THE SAME time as the blue and white police car. She was relieved to see Tucker Tulley jump out and run to the front door.

Emily got out of her Jeep quickly but hardly with the same sense of urgency. She had a strong sense that this latest emergency on Providence Street was just another in the growing list of false alarms. She almost didn't want to know what was going on.

The door flew open before Tucker was halfway up the path. Her mother stood in the doorway, wild-eyed, still wearing her nightgown and robe, though it was well past ten on a Tuesday morning.

"Mrs. Warwick, is everything all right here?" Tucker asked. "Your burglar alarm went off. We got the signal down at the station."

"Everything is not all right," Lillian huffed at him. She suddenly stepped back as another woman literally marched through the doorway, her shoulders hunched like a football player determined to make his way through the defensive line.

Tucker jumped back. "Whoa there, not so fast. Can I have your name please, ma'am?"

Though Emily had never met her, she could guess the woman's name. She cringed at what would come next.

"For goodness' sake, let her go," Lillian ranted from the doorway. "Let her go and let's be done with it. She's learned her lesson."

The woman turned to face Tucker. "I'm Catherine Hatcher. I work for Mrs. Warwick. That is, I was *supposed* to start work this morning, but instead I'm quitting." Catherine Hatcher fixed Emily with a furious look. "Your mother needs medication. You ought to look into it."

Emily knew the former nurse did not mean more blood-pressure pills. "I'm sorry it didn't work out," she said.

"No problem. I'll have a new job tomorrow. She'll still be mad as a loon."

Lillian's eyes nearly popped out of her head. "Do you see how she speaks to me? Is that the kind of person that's sent here to care for me?"

"But you have no complaint against Ms. Hatcher?" Tucker was still trying to sort it out. "No reason for me to hold her here?"

"No reason," Lillian said, crossing her arms over her chest.

"All right then, you can go," Tucker told her. "Sorry for any confusion."

"So am I," Catherine Hatcher snapped as she trotted past Tucker and Emily.

Emily stepped up to the porch to join Tucker at the front door. "Mother, how did this happen? Why did the alarm go off?"

"I fired that woman yesterday. I'm absolutely positive she returned her key. See, I have it right in my hand." Lillian produced a key from her bathrobe pocket. "But she must have made a copy. She opened the door, walked right in here. She must have thought the house was empty—or was trying to sneak up on me in my sleep, knock me over the head, and make off with my valuables."

Tucker looked concerned. He glanced at Emily who sighed heavily. "Mother, I know you fired the helper who came yesterday, on Monday. That was Nancy Cunningham. This was a new person. I told you last night, someone was coming and they have the key. I was going to drop by later to meet her. Don't you remember?"

"I never heard any such message. Are you sure you dialed the right number?" Lillian asked. "I know how busy you are. Perhaps you thought you called but forgot."

Emily suddenly got it. At first, she had been alarmed by what seemed to be her mother's confusion. But now she could plainly see that it was all pretense. Lillian hadn't been caught unawares by a new companion coming into the house; she simply manufactured an excuse to get rid of her newest aide. Score another point for Lillian.

"Mother, you know very well that was an entirely different person," Emily said, determined not to let her get away with it.

"Are you sure?" Lillian managed an innocent expression. "She looks just like the other one to me."

"And this looks like a setup to me," Emily replied. "You purposely did this to get rid of her. Admit it. I had to beg the agency to give us one more try. I'm running out of options here, Mother."

"So, the alarm went off by accident?" Tucker asked. "You don't need me to check the premises?"

Lillian favored him with an aristocratic wave of her hand. "Go ahead, by all means. Do your duty, Officer Tulley. There may be several of these home companions lurking around—in the bushes, in the basement, in the attic. They seem to be multiplying, coming out of the woodwork. . . ."

Before Emily could argue, she noticed a cab pulling up to the curb. The door opened and Dr. Elliot came out. He stared up at the group on the porch then marched toward them with an impressively quick gait.

"What is going on here? Why am I finding emergency vehicles parked at your door every time I come to visit?" he asked Lillian. "Is this a cry for help, as they say on the talk shows?"

"A cry for help, my foot. Your brain is turning to mush from too much daytime TV, Ezra," Lillian shot back.

He hopped up the steps to the porch and faced her. "*My* brain? Do you plan on attending the luncheon at the museum in your dressing gown? As a doctor, I would have to consider that lapse a clear symptom of brain mush."

Emily saw her mother shocked into silence. Lillian gazed down at herself and gripped the lapels of her robe around her neck.

Emily remembered that her mother did have a plan to go out with Ezra today. But she must have gotten sidetracked by her scheme to derail the new home aide.

"You'd better get dressed, Mother. It's getting late," Emily said mildly.

Lillian retreated into the house, muttering, "I hope that woman did not walk off with my diamond earrings."

"I sincerely doubt it," Emily said. She turned to Tucker. "Sorry you were called out here for nothing."

"Not a problem, Mayor. I'm happy to help when I can." Tucker smiled at her as he turned to go, his face shaded by his cap.

"I'll stay and wait for her with you," Emily said to Ezra.

"I'm sure you have more important things to do today than mollycoddle your mother. Don't worry," he said. "I'll take care of her. I'll make her toe the line."

Emily had to smile at that last promise. "Thank you, Ezra. If anyone can do it, you can. Tell her I'll call her tonight."

Emily headed for her car. Once again, Dr. Elliot was a lifesaver. She was greatly relieved he was keeping her mother company today. She was also relieved there had been no time for another long debate about the situation. She knew she had been close to losing her temper.

It was becoming very clear, very quickly. This routine couldn't go on much longer. Her mother was making a choice, whether she intended to, or not.

SNOW THAT HAD BEGUN AT NOON ON WEDNESDAY WAS falling heavily by the time Jack picked up David after his physical therapy.

"There won't be any tree shopping tonight," Jack predicted as the truck's wipers worked hard to whisk off the falling flakes. The traffic on the highway was backed up, and the truck crawled along at a pace David found painfully slow. "Julie thought we should just close the stand and put up our own tree tonight."

"What's the rush?" David teased him. "Christmas isn't until next Friday."

Jack glanced at him and laughed. "I always leave it for the last minute, don't I? Sort of ironic, right?"

"Very ironic. But it's a family tradition by now. It wouldn't seem right if we did it any earlier."

"No, it wouldn't," Jack agreed.

They soon entered the house to find the living room full of cardboard cartons. Kate was running from box to box, lifting the lids and pulling out Christmas decorations. She looked like a little Christmas elf, David thought.

"Look, I found my stocking!" she greeted them. She held it up and waved it around like a flag, a long red flannel stocking trimmed with white fur on top and her name spelled out in silky green letters. David guessed that Julie had made it for her.

"I'm going to hang it on the fireplace," she told David.

"Good idea. Hang it right in the middle where Santa can see it," David told her.

He doubted she could reach the mantel, and his automatic response was to follow and help her. But it was tough to maneuver around the boxes with his walker. He didn't want to fall and break the ornaments and decorations. He stared down as he angled the metal legs, making slow progress from the door.

"David, let me move some of this stuff. I'm sorry we left it all over the place." Christine appeared in the passageway that led to the kitchen then rushed over to clear a path for him, pulling boxes aside.

What was she still doing here? Didn't she have a family and a Christmas tree at home to decorate? For crying out loud, he hoped she wasn't going to stay.

And he hoped she would. Being around her was both wonderful and pure torture. Ever since last Friday, when he cooked dinner for her and Kate, he had pretty much stayed out of Christine's way. She was outdoors a lot at the stand when she worked, so that helped.

"Thanks," David mumbled, silently cursing the walker and his need for it. He was almost able to support himself on a cane but right after his therapy session, his leg muscles were too tired, his hip too achy.

While Christine pushed the boxes aside, David made his way to the couch and flopped down in a spot near the tree. Jack and Julie had selected a tall, full pine. They had set it in the stand and already put most of the lights on.

"Pretty tree," David remarked. "It has a good shape."

"It's a nice one. But your folks do have their choice," Christine added with a grin.

"No excuses for a scrawny tree here, that's for sure."

She walked over to the tree and continued working with the strand of lights. David immediately felt antsy just sitting there, watching her. He forced himself to get up and maneuvered the walker close to the tree.

"Here, let me help. I can get the top," he said.

She stepped back, looking at him, about to object, he was sure, and make him feel like a useless idiot. Then she quickly nodded and handed him the strand of lights. "Good idea. I can't reach up there. Go for it."

David took the lights without looking at her. It wasn't easy to string them up on the highest branches, but he wasn't going to let her know that. Not if he could help it. He tried reaching with one hand but found he needed both and finally had to keep his balance without holding the walker. He was doing all right at first. Then reached too far, and for one horrible moment, felt himself pitching forward, about to fall right into the tree.

Christine leaned over and quickly grabbed him at the waist, holding him steady. Not really a hug but close enough to make his heart start racing.

He leaned back against her for one heavenly moment. "Whoa, close call. I almost took the whole thing down."

"Almost doesn't count," she said quietly.

She stood there for a moment, close to him. He felt her warm breath against his neck. Then he felt her hands drop away, and she turned to untangle the rest of the lights.

David braced himself on the walker with two hands, not sure of what to say, whether he should say anything at all. Julie, Jack, and Kate came into the room then.

"Okay, let's get this show on the road." Jack clapped his hands and happily rubbed them together. "I picked out the absolutely, very best tree on the lot for you guys. I want to see it decked out to perfection."

"Can I put the angel on top?" Kate asked.

"Of course you can. That's your job, Peanut." Jack lifted her up in his arms easily. "But we have to put everything else on first. The angel's the very last thing, the finishing touch."

"I can do the other ones, too." She squirmed in his arms, and he let her down.

Julie took the ornaments out, unwrapped the tissue that surrounded them, and put the hooks on top. Then she placed them on the coffee table, and everyone crowded around, picking out their favorites.

"I'm doing the dog and Elmo," Kate announced, snatching her choices off the table.

"I've got the Nutcracker and Larry Bird," Jack said. "Hey, David, here's one of yours, the Red Sox World Series ball."

David gazed at the Christmas ball, shaped like a baseball with the Red Sox logo and the date of their amazing World Series win, October 2004. Only the second time in an entire century his beloved team had clinched the series, the year they finally broke the Curse of the Bambino. His mom was dying, and he and Jack were arguing, but he had been going out with Christine then, the one thing that had been right in his life.

"Well, I'd better get going," Christine said suddenly. She stepped back from the family grouped around the tree, heading toward the kitchen.

Julie looked up and turned to her. She was still at the coffee table, fixing ornaments for Kate to hang up.

"You're welcome to stay, Christine. It's awful out there. Why don't you help us do the tree and stay for dinner?"

"Yeah, Christine, come on. We have about a million Christmas balls to hang, and I don't like the idea of you driving around in this snow. It should stop in an hour or so. What the rush?" Jack asked.

David didn't like the idea of her driving off in the snow either. Even though she didn't live very far away, she had a small car, and he knew the driving was difficult right now. If he were his old self, he would have jumped up and offered to drive her. But he couldn't do that now, of course, which made him feel weak. He wondered if that was how she thought of him.

He watched to see her reaction. She seemed undecided—until Kate ran over and wrapped her arms around Christine's long legs. "Please don't go. We *need* you," she said, in her dramatic little girl way.

That did it, of course. Christine was persuaded, and David didn't know if that made him feel happy or distressed.

His father had not been exaggerating about the million Christmas balls. At least it seemed like that many to David. But he did get up to hang his fair share, without any more tipping into the tree—or surprise hugs from Christine.

Finally, when it seemed every bough and space between was filled with ornaments and lights, the Sawyers decided it was time for Kate to do her special job. Jack lifted the little girl up, and she carefully placed the papier-mâché angel on top.

"Well done," Jack said, kissing Katie's cheek. But before her feet had even touched the ground, he turned to Julie. "I'm starved. What's for dinner?"

Julie laughed. "Chili and corn bread. It's all ready. Come help me set the table."

"I'll put some of this stuff away," Christine offered. She

stood up and began putting the smaller boxes inside the larger ones. "Want to help me, Kate?"

"In a sec. I just want to get some corn bread," Katie said. Then she ran out of the room, following her mother.

David was suddenly alone with Christine and the big mess. "I'll help you." He got up and started gathering the empties, holding the walker with one hand for balance. The PT had really helped him a lot, he noticed. He had not been able to support himself like that a few weeks ago.

"The tree came out really nice. Your family has some terrific ornaments," Christine said.

"Yeah, we do have a few unique ones. That's my dad's thing, you know." David rolled his eyes but was still smiling.

"Now all it needs is a big pile of presents underneath."

"Yeah, it does. I haven't bought much yet, only a few gifts over the Internet," David admitted.

"Neither have I. I always put my shopping off for the last minute then run around like a nut."

"Me, too," David said. "I just hate the mall. It's such a scene." Though this year, it was a bit more than procrastination and mall-itis that had kept him from shopping.

"Yeah, it is. I can take about half an hour there before I get a huge headache." Christine placed a stack of small boxes in a big carton and closed the lid. She moved so gracefully, David thought, it was a pleasure just to watch her.

"I try to get most of my gifts up in Newburyport. The shops are interesting, and the prices aren't any more than the big stores. Sometimes I even find real bargains." She suddenly looked over at him. "I was going to go shopping there on Friday. Want me to pick up a few things for you?"

David didn't know what to say. It was sweet of her to offer, thoughtful and considerate. Still, he didn't want her to think he was incapable of getting out and picking up a few Christmas gifts. He wasn't that disabled, was he?

"Thanks. But I can go out sometime and shop. New-buryport is a good idea though. I didn't even think of it."

"It's pretty up there this time of year. They go all-out decorating the town and the shop windows." Christine was crouched near another carton, closing its lid. "Want to come with me Friday? I could pick you up after your therapy," she offered.

David felt shocked by the question. He had turned away to close another box and was glad he wasn't facing her. His mouth suddenly got dry and he swallowed hard.

"That would be great. If it isn't any trouble for you," he quickly added.

"No trouble. It will be fun. And I need someone to share the misery."

Christine continued to talk about her shopping list, what she planned to buy for her folks and sisters and brothers.

David nodded, but he wasn't listening all that closely, his thoughts suddenly whirling.

They had a date now, he realized. Not a real date, he corrected himself. She was just helping him out, like any friend would do. A friendly outing, you could call it.

He would have to bring some good clothes to change into after therapy. He usually left in his very sweaty sweats, not even bothering to take a shower there. He would have to tell Gena they needed to quit early. He didn't want Christine waiting for him, and he didn't want to be too tired to walk around with her afterward. And he definitely needed a haircut.

Julie called them in to dinner, and David was thankful for the interruption. He had a lot to think about.

CHAPTER TEN

❧

$\mathcal{D}$AVID FELT JUMPY AND DISTRACTED DURING HIS
therapy session on Friday, anticipating his date with Christine. His nerves gave him a boost of energy but also made
him lose his focus.

"What's up today, pal?" George asked him. "You're,
like, out there."

"Nothing's up," David replied with a shrug.

"You got a haircut," George said.

"Yeah, so?"

George patted David's head in a chummy way. "I just
noticed, is all. You're still ugly. But it's some improvement."

"Thanks." David tried to sound peeved, but couldn't help
smiling. He pushed himself to finish the last of the hand-weight reps, then dropped the weights at the side of the mat.
"I need to quit early today. I already told Gena," he said,
struggling to get up off the floor.

George stuck out his hand and David quickly levered himself up, putting most of his weight on his good leg.

Then he grabbed his new cane and headed for the locker room to shower and dress. George trotted after him, carrying the walker. "Hey, David, forget something?"

David paused to glance over his shoulder. "Oh, right. Guess I'll need that sooner or later. Can you put it out in the waiting area for me?"

"Will do, pal. Don't trash it yet. But you're looking good with the cane, David. Keep the faith."

David smiled at him. "I will. Thanks."

He had come very close to managing with the cane last week, but was "Not quite ready for prime time," as Gena told him. Today, he'd insisted on making the switch, and she gave him no argument.

From the moment Christine had invited him to go shopping, David decided he had to make it with the cane. No matter what. He didn't care how much his hip hurt or how difficult it was to keep his balance. This was a "must win" game, and he was going for it.

When he walked out into the waiting area, he saw Christine sitting nearby, reading a thick textbook. She wore a red turtleneck sweater under her shearling coat, and her hair was loose, a silky curtain falling across her shoulder. She looked so pretty, he felt his breath catch in his throat.

If I knew she was sitting out here waiting for me every day, I could run in a marathon by now, he thought.

She looked up at him and smiled. He saw her surprise at the cane and felt proud and pleased inside. But he tried to act cool, as if this advance was no big deal.

"No walker today?" she asked.

"I'm done with that contraption. I need to take it home though. For a souvenir," he said. He saw it propped next to the reception desk. "Do you mind taking it with us? It's not heavy."

"No, not at all."

Christine slung her book bag over her shoulder and picked up the walker and they made their way out of the building.

It was a clear, cold day, and it felt good to get out of the hospital's antiseptic-smelling rooms and hallways.

While David waited for Christine to unlock her car and toss the walker in the backseat, he noticed Gena leaving the building. She had a ski jacket on over her uniform and carried a leather briefcase. He realized she was also leaving for the day.

He was surprised when she walked toward him and even more surprised to see that, for once, she was smiling. "Well, you look nice," she said. "Going somewhere tonight?"

"Just some Christmas shopping."

Christine had come around to his side of the car and looked at Gena with interest. David felt obliged to introduce them.

"This is my physical therapist, Gena Reyes. I've told you about her, remember? Gena, this is my friend, Christine Tate."

Christine extended her hand. "Nice to meet you, Gena."

"Nice to meet you," Gena replied, eyeing Christine curiously. "This is the first day we're letting him loose with that cane. Don't let him tip over, okay?"

"I won't," Christine promised. She turned to David with a small smile. "Was that a joke?"

"I guess. Coming from her, it might be. She doesn't have a great sense of humor." He pulled the door open and got in, then lifted his bad leg and slipped the cane in beside him.

Christine sat behind the wheel and started the car. "I didn't picture her like that," she said.

"Like what?" he asked, surprised that she would try to picture his therapist at all.

"So young. And pretty."

"I never really noticed." He glanced at Christine and

knew she could tell he was lying, a little. Was she jealous of Gena? That would be . . . encouraging.

Their conversation flowed easily during the ride to Newburyport, and it seemed they were there in no time at all.

Christine looked for a parking space on the shop-lined streets but finally had to drive down to a large lot near the harbor. It was at the bottom of a long hill, which they would have to walk up in order to get back to the stores. David dreaded the idea. As she pulled into a space, she must have read his thoughts.

"Is this a bad spot for you, David? I can go back up and look again," she offered.

"No, it's fine," he lied. "We don't want to waste the whole afternoon looking for parking." He also didn't want to complain or admit he wasn't able to walk up a little hill.

They got out of the car. He stared up the hill and took a breath. It looked like Mount Everest to him, and he wondered why he had ever agreed to go out with her like this. He would end up asking to go back to the car in five minutes and be totally mortified.

He glanced over at Christine to see if she had sensed his hesitation and anxiety, but she was oblivious. For someone who had moaned and groaned about shopping, Christine seemed pretty into it once she caught a whiff of the stores. As he slowly crawled along, she practically ran ahead to check out the first windows. He hurried to keep up, afraid he would fall with the cane.

Was he holding her back? Was she going to be annoyed with him? When he finally caught up with her, peering into the window of a trendy boutique, she didn't seem to notice his delay.

"The clothes in here are great. I think I can find something for my sister, Leah, like that embroidered blouse. Let's go in, okay?"

"Okay," David agreed. How could he argue? She seemed

lit up with excitement, even if she claimed to despise shopping. Maybe she just enjoyed giving presents to people, which was very much her personality. Either way, he liked to see her so happy. He knew he could follow her around all afternoon.

As they steadily made their way up the street, Christine seemed more aware of his slow pace but never commented on it. Instead, she held his arm, in a comfortable, affectionate way, though he knew she was secretly helping to move him along and steady his steps. He loved being close to her; he didn't mind this kind of physical therapy at all.

They both managed to find lots of good gifts, and David crossed most of the names off his list.

From time to time they stopped just to gaze at the elaborate window displays. Christine had been right when she said the village went all-out for the holidays. Every antique street lamp held a pine wreath and red bow. Every shop window and doorway was carefully decorated with lights, fake snow, pine boughs, elaborate ribbons, and carefully wrapped packages.

Sometimes she pointed out items that had caught her eye, a special brand of perfume, a big wide scarf that had fringe on the edges, a set of thin, shiny bracelets. David secretly tucked away the information. He wanted to buy her a gift, he realized, something special. He didn't care if it wasn't the right thing to do. He just wanted her to know that he cared.

They were both carrying several shopping bags, filled with presents, when David spotted a café. He was getting tired, and walking with the cane hurt more than he had expected. He hoped he was hiding his discomfort from Christine, but he did need to sit down for a few minutes.

Christine was ready for a time-out, too, and they were soon seated at a small table in the café, looking out on the avenue. They ordered cappuccinos and shared a brownie.

"Thanks for helping me pick out those earrings for Julie," David said. "I hope she likes them."

"I can't see how she wouldn't. They're really beautiful . . . and expensive."

He shrugged. "I wanted to get everyone something nice, that they would really like. I have the money, and they've been putting up with a lot from me, lately."

"That's sweet, David. But your family loves you. I think they all understand that it's hard for you right now."

"I know they understand. But it doesn't excuse my behavior altogether." He looked across at her. "I've been difficult with you, too. Pretty nasty at times." She seemed about to argue, and he lifted his hand to stop her. "I know I have. I'm sorry. A lot of other people wouldn't have put up with it."

It sounded weak, a lot weaker than the feelings he had inside. But it was the only way he could put it.

"I'm not a lot of other people," she said quietly.

He reached over and took her hand. He couldn't help himself, he just had to touch her. "You're different from everyone. You're . . . the best. I always knew that."

"You did hurt my feelings sometimes, David," she admitted. "I won't lie and say you didn't. But I guess you're worth it," she added with a small laugh.

He smiled across at her. They'd known each other for so long. But he wanted her to know who he was now. He wanted her to know what he'd been through and how it had changed him. That was important, too.

"Sometimes I feel so much coming at me, at once," he tried to explain. "It's like, I'm a computer or something and there's information overload. But instead of shutting down, I feel angry," he admitted. "And confused. And sort of . . . out of control. It's not good."

"That must be a really bad feeling," she said.

"It is. It's like I don't know who I am anymore. I've changed a lot since I went into the army. I know I have, but sometimes I just can't get a handle on who's in here right now." He tapped his chest. "I'm glad you stuck it out and kept trying to see me. That was . . . really great. But I'm not the same guy you dated back in high school, Chrissy," he said, using the nickname he had used way back when. "I'm sorry if I disappoint you sometimes. I know I must."

"I like that you called me Chrissy again," she said. "No one else ever called me that. But I'm not the same girl you knew either. I've changed a lot, too."

"I know that, believe me. You're so mature and together now. You're ready to take on the world, more ready than I am."

She didn't reply, casting a wistful smile his way. She had changed, it was true. But some things about her had not altered one bit. She was still the sweetest, most loving person he had ever known.

"Thanks for taking me out today. I need to get into the real world more. I need more shopping," he joked. "Maybe that could be some kind of new therapy."

"Maybe," she agreed.

David held her hand in both of his. Her skin was so soft, hard to believe, considering the way she had been tossing around those Christmas trees lately.

Then his fingertips felt the hard edges of her engagement ring. He looked down to see it sparkling at him, mocking him. He had almost forgotten for a moment that Christine was spoken for.

He took a calming breath and tried to keep his cool. He let her hand slip from his and sat back in his chair. "So, what did you get for your boyfriend? You didn't tell me."

"I got him a sweater and CD he wanted. I still want to get him a really nice leather briefcase. He can use it when he goes out on job interviews."

"That sounds great." David forced himself to act positive. "Guess he'll be home from school any day now."

"He won't be back until Christmas Eve," she replied. "He has a job on campus and can't leave until then."

"Oh, too bad," David said, though he didn't mean it.

Once her boyfriend came home, he wouldn't see her any-more. Her job at the tree farm would end on Christmas Eve, so the timing worked out . . . sort of.

"What's he studying? You never told me."

"I didn't? I thought I had."

She had said very little about her boyfriend, and David wasn't really sure why or what that meant.

"No, you didn't. I would have remembered. You've never even told me his name, come to think of it."

"Oh . . . his name is Alex," she said, looking embarrassed. "Alex Regan. He's studying computer science—designing websites, creating software, that kind of thing."

"Pretty good." David tried to sound enthusiastic. "There are a lot of jobs in that field."

"He's already interned at some good companies. He might find a job in one of those places."

This guy sounded like a tough act to follow—responsible and smart. Ambitious, too. Mr. High-Tech. That was not good news.

"So . . . when's the big day?" he forced himself to ask. He had been wondering ever since he saw that ring. But he'd never had the guts to ask her.

"In June, June fifteenth. We're planning a small wedding," she explained. "Just close family. I didn't want one of those huge productions. My folks can't really afford a big party, and I don't want to burden them."

"I'm sure it will be a great day, whatever you've planned," he said graciously.

It hardly mattered if there were five guests at her wedding or five hundred. Christine would be the most beautiful bride anyone had ever seen. He was sure of that.

He wished he could tell her that, too, but it didn't seem right. She looked suddenly ill at ease and self-conscious as she stirred her cappuccino.

"Thank you, David. Thanks for your good wishes. I hope it will be a great day, too," she said quietly.

Though it was just past five, it was dark outside by the time they left the café. It felt late to David. He was very tired but didn't want to admit it. The talk about Christine's wedding and boyfriend had deflated his spirits and energy.

Rain had begun to fall while they were inside. As they walked to the car David felt as if his slow gait was holding her up and making her get more wet than need be. But she walked alongside him patiently. At least it was downhill this time.

They tossed their shopping bags in the trunk and got inside the car. Neither of them spoke much as they headed back to Cape Light. "I hope this rain doesn't turn to snow," Christine said finally.

David glanced out his window. "It's a mess any way you look at it."

The raindrops had turned to icy pellets that made the road slick and treacherous. Christine was driving slowly, and David could tell she was nervous.

"I'm going to pull over a minute and see if this gets any better, okay?"

"Sure," he said. "Up ahead, that's a good spot."

Christine pulled the car over and David sat, staring out his window. He felt frustrated and helpless. He wanted to take the wheel and keep driving. That would be the manly thing to do. Not pull over and wait. The rain wasn't so bad.

Her boyfriend, Alex, would have taken the wheel. David was sure of it. She had to be thinking he was weak and inept. Unable to take care of her when it counted. A real loser.

They sat in silence, other cars and trucks whizzing by on the icy road. It didn't seem as if the rain was getting any better. To David, it seemed to be getting worse.

"What do you think?" He turned to her. "Should we get going again? I don't think it's going to change any."

He could see she felt anxious about driving. "Let's give it another minute or two. No rush, right?"

"Right, no rush," he agreed.

But as he sat there, listening to the icy rain beating on the car roof, he felt his heartbeat accelerate, faster and faster. He suddenly felt as if he were choking and couldn't get a breath.

The icy rain had turned to small hailstones, and the sound of them striking the metal roof transformed in his mind to the sound of gunfire.

David lost all sense of where he was and what he was doing. He was back in Baghdad, riding in the Humvee. They were under fire, and he heard the missile whining in the air above, coming closer, ready to strike them and explode.

He hunkered down in the car seat, giving in to the wave of terror that had taken over his mind and body. He held his arms over his head and when he felt Christine's touch, he shouted at her, violently pushing her away. "Take cover! It's coming. . . . Get down, damn it. . . . Cover your head! . . . God, please, don't let it hit again, please don't. . . ."

"David, what is it? What's going on? Talk to me, say something!" She sounded afraid, almost hysterical.

Outside the car, a truck horn sounded twice, breaking through his waking nightmare. David lifted his head and finally saw Christine, staring at him, her eyes wide and her expression shocked.

He sat up slowly and took deep breaths, the way they had taught him in the hospital. He felt so embarrassed, he wished he could have died, right there.

"Gee . . . I'm sorry . . . I really lost it . . ." He swallowed a few times, catching his breath. "The hail, it sounded like we were back in Baghdad being fired on."

Her frightened expression melted into sympathy. "I'm so sorry. Are you okay now?"

He nodded quickly and wiped his hand over his face, feeling like a complete fool. Christine reached out and rubbed his arm with her hand, trying to soothe him. David stared straight ahead.

"Did it remind you of the night you were injured?" she asked quietly.

He nodded. "Like I was right back there. Time traveling or something. I have nightmares about it sometimes. This was different. It wasn't like a dream. I was right there, all over again."

"How awful," she said. "How did you get injured, David? You never told me."

He looked over at her, unsure of what to say. "Do you really want to hear this?"

"I want to know." When he didn't respond, she added. "I'm not saying it just to be nice, David. It's important to me."

When he met her glance he knew she was telling the truth. It was important to her, though he wasn't sure why it would be. Maybe so she could figure out why he wasn't the same anymore, why she couldn't fall in love with him again?

What did it matter? She wanted to know the whole story? He'd tell it to her. Maybe it would help him, too, to get some of this off his chest. He hadn't really talked to anyone outside of his buddies in the squad about it. Not even his father.

David took a deep breath and stared straight ahead, going back again to the base in south Baghdad. "When you're in the army, everyone has a job to do. I was in the motor pool, trained as a mechanic."

"Really?" Christine looked surprised by this admission. "Is that what you want to do now? I mean, once your leg is better."

"No, not really. I didn't like it much. I learned enough to figure out it wasn't for me." Even if he had liked pulling apart engines and machinery, David knew that sort of work would always bring back difficult memories.

"Our base was in south Baghdad. There was a lot of fighting, a lot of insurgents. You were always anxious when you went off base. Always on alert, hyped up, watching everything that moved on the road. The wind lifting a scrap of paper. I wasn't assigned to patrol or guard officers, or anything like that. But when we went off base, anything could happen. You had to be sharp, prepared. If you passed a car on the road, and it got too close to the Humvee, that could be the one that would drive up next to you and explode. You just didn't know. I still get the jitters sometimes, driving along, looking at the traffic on the highway. Watching some guy behind my dad's truck who's tailgating . . ."

David paused. His mouth felt dry. He knew he was rambling and tried to get back on track again. "When you were fired on, you fired back. You didn't think about God or country or even 9/11. You were just trying to protect the guys on either side of you. Your pals. Your brothers. You didn't have time to think. It's kill or be killed. Just that simple. We all worked every day just to keep each other alive."

Christine sat listening to him with an awestruck expression.

Had he shocked her, confessing that he had been in battle and taken lives? Did she think of him differently now?

"Your legs, how did that happen? What were you doing?" she asked.

"A truck carrying supplies to the base had broken down a few miles down the main road. We had orders to go out and take a look. It was daytime. We had no cover. But sometimes traveling at night is even worse. You can never tell. My team went out in a Humvee. It was me, a pal of mine named Buzz, and Sergeant Nolan. Nolan was career army, on his third tour of duty." David stopped. He wasn't sure how much more he could get out. He didn't want to lose it again in front of her.

She sat silently, barely breathing, willing him with her eyes to continue.

"We didn't see anything or hear anything. The road

looked perfectly silent. Then the Humvee was fired on.
A grenade launcher. We were hit, and the truck turned
over. That's when my legs were crushed. I sort of blacked
out, I guess. Next thing I knew, Sergeant Nolan was pulling me out, away from the vehicle. Somehow Buzz had
jumped clear. But Nolan didn't know that. There was so
much smoke. He ran back, calling for Buzz." David took
a ragged breath. "Then the truck was hit again and the
engine exploded."

"Dear God. That poor man."

David nodded, a sick feeling in his gut. "He was the
greatest guy, too. Everybody loved Nolan. He had a wife
and two kids. Their pictures were all over the place." David
paused and felt a shudder rip through him. "I think a lot
about that day, about him. How it should have been me
instead. I was the one who was stuck. He was up, he was
mobile. He didn't have to save me. He didn't have to go
back for Buzz."

"David, you would have done the same thing if the situation had been reversed."

"Would I? I'd like to think so. I guess I'll never know
now." David took a deep, shaky breath. "I sometimes wish
we could have traded places," he confessed. "Nolan and
me. I mean, the guy had a real family, people depending
on him. He left a big hole in the world. I wouldn't have left
much of one. No one would have missed me, really. My
father, I guess."

"I would have missed you," Christine said.

He stared at her, shocked by her admission. Then he
brushed the spark of hope aside. She was engaged to be
married, in love with some guy named Alex. She only
meant it as a friend. Not the way he wanted her to mean it.

"Thanks, but . . . well, I know it's just chance or fate or
something, but I feel as if I screwed up and let those guys
down."

Christine sighed. He could tell she didn't know what to say.

"This is what I mean about not being the same, Christine," he said finally. "I might always be like this. Dragging around all this heavy baggage. Jumping out of my skin at the sound of rain on the roof of a car. You don't need this," he said bluntly. "You're lucky we didn't stay together. You're better off with Alex. Way better."

Christine sat back and turned away from him, facing forward again. After a few moments she said, "Looks like the rain stopped. We can go back."

She steered the car off the shoulder of the road and turned back into the flow of traffic. They would be back to the tree farm soon; they weren't far. David couldn't wait.

This afternoon had started out so well. So promising. Dressed in his new clothes, finally walking with the cane. How had it ended up this way? So bleak and hopeless.

"LOOKS LIKE THE RAIN FINALLY STOPPED, GRACIE. WHAT do you think?" Digger stood by the parlor window. He held the lace curtain back and gazed down at Main Street, the street lamps and car lights reflecting in the wet pavement.

"I'd rather not take the chance of it starting again. That was hail coming down a little while ago, Dad. I would hate to be caught driving in it." Grace gently drew him away from the window and steered him back into the parlor. "We don't have to go to the store tonight, Dad. We can go tomorrow. Let's sit down and figure things out a little, shall we?"

"Okay, Grace. What do you want to figure?" He took a pipe from a handmade wooden box on the mantel and then sat in his favorite wingback chair.

Digger had given up smoking some years back but still liked to hold the pipe in his mouth. Especially on a cold, nasty night, like this one. He still liked the feel of the hard mouthpiece and the rich, comforting scent of the tobacco.

"Well, here's our list. I think we've done pretty well so far." Grace sat across from him on the sofa with a yellow legal pad in her lap.

"We've done very well," Digger agreed. "Just seeing the look on those folks' faces when they get up in church and tell their stories . . ." He shook his head, grinning from ear to ear. "Does my heart good, Grace. You know what Charles Dickens said about doing a good deed?"

Grace didn't know what Dickens had said about good deeds, but she had a feeling she was about to find out.

"What was that, Dad?"

" 'No one is useless in this world who lightens the burdens of another.' " Digger clamped his teeth on the pipe end and nodded. "That's the truth. You feel like you've done one good thing in the world, just helping out one single person, and that's something money can't buy, you know?"

"I know, Dad. It is a good feeling."

"So, where are we at on that list?" he asked with interest.

Grace was surprised at his question. She had not seen him this clear and focused in years. She felt quietly happy inside.

"This week we paid the three months' owing on Elsie Farber's mortgage and three months into the new year. That ought to give her a good cushion. She told everyone at the Christmas fair committee that she's renting out the second floor of her house, starting the first of next month, so she can cover the payments easier."

"That was good thinking on her part. 'God helps them that help themselves,' " he said, adding his favorite quote from Ben Franklin.

"People just need a little hand up sometimes. They don't expect much more." Grace looked over the long sheet of notes, the list of names and dire situations she had compiled over the last few weeks. The challenge had not been finding folks in need; it had been choosing the most pressing situations.

"I wish we could help everyone," she went on. "But we have to pick and choose. We don't have a million dollars down in that freezer, not unless the bills have multiplied."

"You never know," Digger said. "We could find ourselves with a real miracle going on. Like the loaves and fishes."

"Mostly fishes," Grace added tartly. She peered at him, but he had not understood her joke.

Grace scanned the list again. "Oh, here's a good one. I just overheard this today, in the Clam Box," she explained. "You know that waitress in there—Trudy? The one with the red hair?"

Digger nodded. "I remember her. She looks a lot like Lucy Bates," he remarked.

"Yes, she does," Grace agreed. "I never thought of that before. Maybe that's why Charlie hired her. Well . . . I was having a cup of tea at the counter, and I heard her talking to Tucker Tulley about her car. It's very old, past a hundred thousand miles. The car didn't pass inspection, it has so many things wrong with it. She can't afford to fix it either. She was telling Tucker that she didn't know what to do, asking if he knew a good mechanic who would let her pay on time. She's a single mother and needs a car to get to work and take care of her children. I know it's ambitious, but I think she's a perfect candidate."

Digger chewed on the tip of his pipe, considering the suggestion. "A car, huh? That is a big ticket, Gracie."

"Yes, it is. I was actually thinking we might find a gently used car, say one or two years old? You can find one with a good warranty and not so many miles on it. I don't want to stick the woman with the same problems."

"Of course not. It wouldn't be any help to her to give her a newer car that breaks down like the old one."

"I think we can find something used but good quality. A compact model would be fine. One with good gas mileage, of course," she added.

"Yes, gas mileage. That's important." Digger took the

pipe from his mouth and peered into the empty bowl. "Sounds like you've thought this all out, Gracie. You have any color in mind?"

The question almost made her laugh. She had thought a lot about it. She was hoping to find a blue car for Trudy and had even figured out how they would manage to give it to her. She explained that to her father, too.

"The easiest way I think is to leave it for her on Main Street, parked outside the diner. After we buy it, I can park it there late at night, when nobody is out, and walk right home. We'll get all the papers in her name and leave them in the glove compartment."

"That's the way to do it," Digger agreed. "Oh, I wish I could be a fly on the wall to see that woman's face when she finds that new car. Wouldn't that be something?"

Grace wished he could be a fly on the wall, too. She had not seen her father so happy and animated in a long time. This secret gift-giving project had rejuvenated his mind and his spirit. It did her heart good, not only to give these gifts, but to give her father this pleasure. He might not be around for very much longer, she knew, but she would always have these memories to look back on, the Christmas they fooled the entire town in such a wonderful way.

"Well, let's see. That might be pretty simple," she told him. "Maybe we can get a front-row seat this time. I mean, if we just happen to be having lunch at the diner when she gets our note and goes outside . . . then we'd see it first-hand, right?"

"Yes, we would. And nobody sitting there would know it was us that gave the car, either. We could act surprised just like the rest of them."

"We would absolutely *have to* act surprised," Grace said, reminding him of their promise to remain anonymous. "It might be tempting to tell in all the excitement. Is that going to be a problem for you?" she asked gently. "You're not going to forget yourself, are you?"

"No, Gracie, I swear." He lifted his hand with a solemn expression. "I won't give us away. That's the God's honest truth."

She held his gaze a moment, then sighed and sat back against the couch cushions. "All right. Then that's the way we'll do it."

She knew her father fully intended to keep his promise and fully believed that he could, but when the moment arrived it would be another matter altogether.

It would be risky to let him sit right there and watch Trudy find the new car. But it did mean so much to him. And he had given so much. Didn't he deserve the benefit of the doubt?

Grace decided it was a chance she would have to take.

CHAPTER ELEVEN

✦

"I'M GLAD YOU CAME OVER TO HELP ME, EZRA. IF I LEFT it to my daughters, or these inept companions they keep sending over, I wouldn't have a Christmas tree up until the Fourth of July."

It was Saturday night, less than a week until Christmas. Lillian had decided that if she didn't get her tree up this weekend, she might as well send the boxes back up to the attic unopened this year.

But luckily, when she called Ezra that morning, he was free and happy to come over and help her. He also brought another lovely roast chicken, compliments of his housekeeper, Mrs. Fallon. Altogether, it had been a very enjoyable night. After dinner, Lillian served tea and dessert in the living room, along with some classical music on the stereo, and they had gotten started on her Christmas tree.

Lillian held the small, tabletop-size pine tree while Ezra secured the screws in the stand. He had to crouch down to do the work and seemed a bit winded when he stood up, but the tree was perfectly straight, Lillian noted. "That looks fine," she said, surveying it from all sides. "There's a gap in the branches back here. I guess it had better go on the table facing the other way."

"As you wish, madam," Ezra said in a courtly manner.

He lifted the tree by the trunk, stand and all, and placed it on a marble-topped table that stood in front of a bay window, an antique in the Eastlake style.

"Very nice," Lillian murmured. "Now for lights. I don't care for too many, and make sure we don't put on any twinklers. Sara bought a package of those last year, and they gave me a migraine."

"No twinkling lights. Got it." Ezra plugged a string of lights into the outlet and tested it. "Good one right here. It looks plenty long enough, too. That should cover it."

While Lillian held one end of the strand, he worked the other around the tree, hooking it onto the little branches.

"A touch lower there," she told him. "Let it drape more, a little looser . . . Not that loose."

He stepped back and handed her his end. "You try. I'm going to sit the rest of this strand out."

She glanced at him then focused on the tree again. He sat on the sofa nearby, rubbing his arm.

"What's the matter, Ezra? Did you pull a muscle or something?"

"Perhaps," he replied. Lillian didn't like the way his voice sounded. She turned to look at him, then put the lights down.

"You shouldn't have moved the table by yourself. You must have strained something. I said that I would help you. Do you want some liniment? I'll go get it."

"It wasn't the table. I don't think so, anyway." His complexion looked ashen, and a thin sheen of sweat had broken out on his forehead.

"You don't look well, Ezra. Do you want some air?" Lillian rushed over to the bay window and pulled one side open. "Maybe you should loosen your collar, open your bow tie."

Oh, she didn't like the looks of this. He didn't look well at all. Now he was rubbing his chest in a most alarming way.

"I . . . I don't feel very well, Lily. I have a sharp pain in my chest," he told her, each word pronounced very carefully. "You need to call an ambulance. Dial nine-one-one."

"Yes, I will," she said, feeling a burst of fear.

She quickly walked to the telephone, dialed the emergency number, and spoke to the operator. "I'm at 33 Providence Street. We need an ambulance right away. My friend Dr. Elliot, he's having a heart attack or a stroke or something. Please come right away."

Ezra's eyes locked on hers a moment as she walked back toward him, then his eyes closed and his head dropped forward.

"Oh, good God!" Lillian cried. "Ezra, please! Wake up. Say something. . . ."

She sat beside him and put her arm around his shoulders and her hand on his clammy cheek. Thank goodness he hadn't fallen off the couch and onto the floor.

He opened his eyes a moment but couldn't speak.

"Hang on, dear. They'll be here in a minute. They come very quickly," she promised.

She knew very well how fast the emergency calls were answered in this town; she'd made enough of them lately. Lillian had a sudden chilling fear that this time the response to her call would be delayed. That someone would hear her name and think it was another false alarm.

Oh, dear heavens, she prayed that was not the case. She prayed that they would come right away and take care of Ezra. What had happened to him? She didn't even want to think of the possibilities as she supported him in her arms.

His breath was labored. At least he was still breathing. But he looked so horribly pale, and his eyes had drifted closed again, his hand pressed to the middle of his chest.

Was she losing him? Dear Lord, that couldn't be. How would she ever stand it?

"Ezra, please. I beg of you . . . hang on, dear. Don't leave me, please. I couldn't bear it. You must try to focus and hang on. Help is coming. They'll be here any second now."

His eyes fluttered opened for a moment and his gaze met hers. He didn't say a word, not even a murmur. But she could tell he had heard her.

A split second later, she heard the sirens coming down the street. Her body sagged with relief. She helped Ezra lean back against the couch and made her way to the front door as quickly as her old legs and cane would carry her.

The ambulance driver and paramedic came running up the walkway and through the open door. "He's in there." She pointed to the living room. "On the couch."

She followed them and continued talking even after they were out of view. "We were putting up the tree and he had to sit down and suddenly looked very pale. He said he had a pain in his arm, his left arm. Then he sort of fainted. Nearly collapsed."

The two men hovered over Ezra. They quickly had him positioned so that he was lying on the couch. Lillian heard one of them talking to him in low tones and heard Ezra answer.

At least he was still conscious. "Thank God," she sighed under her breath.

There was a big medical kit open on the parlor floor. She wasn't sure she wanted to see what they were going to do to him next.

While one man remained with Ezra, the other took her aside and coaxed her to sit down. "Mrs. Warwick, how are you feeling? Do you want me to call someone?"

She nodded quickly. "Yes, please call my daughter Emily. Tell her to come right away. Tell her what's happened. Tell her I said it's a real emergency this time."

* * *

BY THE TIME EMILY ARRIVED, THE HOUSE LOOKED AS IT always did. She did not see an ambulance or any sign of an emergency. She found her mother sitting in the foyer, with her coat on, her purse in her lap.

"Mother, what happened? How is Ezra?"

"They've taken him to the hospital in Southport. You have to take me there, Emily. Quickly. I don't want him to be alone there," her mother said as she stood up. "I'll tell you everything in the car. We have a long ride," she added.

They did have a long ride. The Southport hospital was nearly an hour away. Emily had not expected her mother to go along so willingly—Lillian hated long car rides—but she had rarely seen her mother this concerned over anyone.

They had hardly pulled away from the curb, when her mother began to speak. "It was all my fault. I wanted the Eastlake table in front of the bay window, the way I have it every year. I offered to help him move it, but he wouldn't hear of it. He said it wasn't any problem, he'd slide the table on the rug." Lillian shook her head. "I think it was too heavy for him. That's what did it."

"It's impossible to say, Mother. Dr. Elliot could have been sitting at home doing a crossword puzzle and had this heart attack—or whatever it is. You can't blame yourself. You just don't know."

Her mother sat staring straight ahead, her hands gripped in her lap. "Well, perhaps. We'll have to see what the doctor says. Poor Ezra. Life is fragile, Emily. Not just for old people like us. For everyone. Things can change, just like that." She snapped her thin fingers. "You never know."

When they reached the hospital, Ezra was being worked on in the critical care unit and was not permitted any visitors. Emily did most of the talking with the hospital staff in the emergency room. Her mother was too upset and agitated.

Finally, after what seemed like an agonizing wait, a doctor came out to speak to them. Dr. Bourghard was somewhere between Emily's age and her mother's, in his early sixties, Emily guessed. That was a good thing, she thought. Her mother never trusted a doctor who was under fifty and thought that anyone much older was in danger of senility. Which left a very narrow window for trust in the medical profession.

"Are you Mrs. Elliot?" he asked Lillian.

"I'm Mrs. Warwick, Dr. Elliot's friend. His very good friend," she quickly added. "How is he? Did he have a heart attack?"

"Yes, a mild one. He's very lucky. He got here quickly and we were able to prevent further damage."

"Thank heavens."

"He's going to need more tests. We want to see what's going on with the arteries in his neck and legs, and in his heart, of course. Then we'll be able to determine if he needs any intervention."

"An operation, you mean," Lillian clarified. She still had a good ear for sugarcoated euphemisms, Emily had to grant her that. "Like bypass surgery, or that Roto-Rooter job that cleans out your neck."

Dr. Bourghard fought a smile but finally gave in. "Yes, that's what I mean. You've got the picture."

"Yes, I do," Lillian said crisply. "May we see him? Is he awake?"

"You can see him for a few minutes, not too long."

"We just want to say hello," Emily promised.

A few minutes later, they were led back to Ezra's bed, in a private room with a big glass wall so that the nurses outside could watch him every minute.

He was hooked up to a lot of tubes and machines, and Emily could tell the sight frightened her mother. But Lillian just paused a moment to get a breath then sailed in, her head held high.

"Ezra, we're here—Emily and I." She walked over to his bed and took his hand. "How are you?"

"Hanging in there, Lily. Hanging in. You did me a good deed, calling for help so quickly. You always did have a cool head in a crisis."

"Nonsense. You frightened me to death. I did what I had to do."

"The doctor tells me I've had a heart attack, a minor cardiac episode," he said. "Imagine that. The irony of it."

"I did imagine it, watching you eat all that gravy and whipped cream on Thanksgiving," she scolded him. "There will be no more of that once you get out of here."

"Whenever that will be. I hope I don't need an operation," Ezra confided.

"He didn't say you did for sure. Let's hope for the best," Lillian added, patting his hand again.

"Hope for the best?" Emily echoed in a kind of delighted disbelief. She could not remember ever hearing her mother say anything so positive. She wished she had a tape recorder.

"Oh, Emily . . . I forgot you were here, too," Ezra said. "Hello, dear. Thank you for bringing your mother all this way to see me."

"We wanted to check on you, Ezra," she said honestly. "Mother had to see you with her own eyes."

Emily thought he looked small and frail in the big bed, the hospital nightgown gaping open around his neck.

"She did, did she? Well . . . that's something. I thought she came just to scold me," he added, making both women laugh.

A nurse walked in, carrying a plastic water pitcher and a small paper cup of pills. "I'm sorry, but you two need to go now. The patient needs to rest."

"Having too much fun were we?" Lillian asked tartly. She looked back at Ezra. "I'll be back tomorrow. I'm not sure when visiting hours start. I suppose I'll go to church first."

"You don't need to come back tomorrow, Lily. It's a long drive. Who will take you?"

"I'm sure I can find someone." She shrugged and glanced at Emily. "Everyone wants to help me lately. Helpers are falling out of the trees."

"Well, then I'll see you tomorrow." Dr. Elliot looked so cheered by the idea, Emily knew that she would have to drive her mother, or enlist one of Lillian's sons-in-law to be a chauffeur for the day. "Bring us a crossword puzzle from the Sunday paper, will you? And some nice sharp pencils."

"I already thought of that," Lillian promised.

She paused at his bedside a moment, gazing down at him. Then she leaned over and brushed his cheek with her own. It wasn't exactly a kiss, Emily noticed. But close enough for her mother.

Emily had to admit, of all the people of her mother's acquaintance, she could think of no one more deserving of the honor.

ON SUNDAY, THE SAWYERS STARTED THEIR COUNTDOWN. Only four more days to Christmas Eve. Then they would close the tree farm at five and be able to enjoy their own holiday.

The weekend rush had been frantic. Friday night's nasty weather had kept a lot of tree shoppers at home, Jack reasoned, and a herd of them rushed the place on Saturday morning.

On Sunday morning, Jack and Julie woke up at the usual time but felt so tired, they decided to skip church. Julie made a big breakfast, pancakes with bacon on the side.

Katie finished her pancakes quickly and ran off to the family room to watch TV. Jack took his time enjoying his breakfast, then read the paper at the kitchen table, not in any rush to run out and open up again.

"Look at all the ads and coupons in the newspaper today.

Guess I'm not the only one behind in my shopping." Jack started tearing a piece off the page he'd been reading then got up to look for the scissors. "All the coupons. Who can keep track of this stuff? I'd need a filing cabinet in my truck."

"I already bought Kate a few things on her list," Julie said. "Did you have anything special in mind? I can pick up something for you."

He glanced at her over his shoulder. "There was something special she asked me for—if I can find it in time. Not at the mall, though," he added with a slight smile.

"Jack, I know that look by now. What are you cooking up?"

He smiled even wider, returning to the table with a fresh cup of coffee. "She told me she asked Santa for a pony."

"A pony?" Julie kept her voice low, but her eyes were wide as pot covers, he noticed. Beautiful blue pot covers.

"You can't get her a pony, Jack," she quietly insisted.

"Why not? She really, really wants one," he replied, pleading Katie's case in almost the same voice his darling stepdaughter might have used.

"Every five-year-old wants a pony. That doesn't mean they get one. You'll spoil her impossibly." Julie's voice was firm, but in her eyes he could see a certain amused light that told him he had hope of winning this argument and granting Katie's wish.

"She's not spoiled. She's as sweet as pie," Jack insisted. "Every kid needs a pet, Jules, and we have plenty of property. I could put up a little corral. I'll find a little saddle and bridle somewhere. She sure would look cute riding a pony."

"If you want to get her a pet, get her a puppy," Julie suggested.

"A dog is nice. I love dogs. But you can't ride it. A pony is just like a big dog, Julie. There isn't that much difference."

"You aren't seriously thinking it's going to come in the house, are you?" Now she looked shocked for real.

He laughed and put his arms around her. He loved this woman so much. He didn't know what he would do without her. "What do you want for Christmas?" he whispered in her hair. "You didn't even give me a clue. I want to spoil you, too. How about jewelry? Would you like that?"

Julie sighed and hugged him back. "Oh, I don't know. I don't need jewelry. Anything you get me will be nice, Jack."

"Come on. There must be something," he coaxed her.

He pulled back so he could see her face. She smiled up at him shyly.

See, there was something on her mind. He liked that. He wanted to get her something she really wanted, too. Not just any old thing he could find at the mall.

"Jack . . . I've been thinking. I really want us to have a baby," she said finally. "Maybe for next Christmas?"

Jack felt his head snap back. He couldn't help it. If she had given him even a little warning, he would have tried harder to hide his reaction. He could see she wasn't pleased by his immediate, unguarded response.

"A baby . . . wow. I never would have guessed that one," he admitted.

"You wouldn't have? Gee, I thought I'd been giving you plenty of hints lately."

He glanced at her, still holding her in the loose circle of his arms. He'd thought about it, a little. There was always the possibility it could happen just by accident, right? But he had never really dwelled on it. Or thought it might really happen.

"Maybe . . . but we never really talked about it."

"No, we haven't," she agreed. "Not directly. We've been so busy lately with David and the tree farm. I'm sorry if this just seemed to hit you out of the blue."

She slipped away from him and walked toward the sink to do some dishes.

He felt bad. Her feelings were hurt. He hadn't meant

for that to happen at all. He just wanted to know what she wanted for Christmas. But a baby? He was just . . . blind-sided.

He didn't know what to do. He watched her work on the dishes for a moment or two. She had her head down and wouldn't even look at him. Jack knew he had to do something.

"Let's talk now. Come on, stop fussing with the dishes." He walked up behind her and made her come away from the sink and sit down at the table. Julie looked upset, though she was obviously trying hard to be calm.

"I don't know what to say," Jack began. "I never thought about having more children. For one thing, I'm too old. David's in his twenties. I could be a grandfather soon, for Pete's sake."

"Of course you're not too old. You're in your early for-ties, Jack. Don't you watch TV or read the newspaper? A lot of men are just getting started at your age."

"They're pretty slow off the block then, if you ask me," he replied quickly. He hadn't meant to make a joke out of it, but he couldn't help it. The entire subject made him ner-vous.

A baby? A tiny, helpless infant? At his age? He just couldn't see it.

"You're great with Katie. She adores you," Julie reminded him. "She's only five."

"Yeah, well, five is pretty grown-up. That's not a baby in diapers and all of that." He didn't mean to sound harsh, but he had to be honest. "I was never real good with David as a baby. I don't think I changed his diaper more than once or twice," he admitted. "I don't want to disappoint you and be a bad father."

"Jack, I know you, and you couldn't be a bad father if you tried. Maybe you didn't do the diapers and bottles and all that when David was born, but I think you'd get more involved now. Wouldn't you?"

He took a breath and nodded. It was true. He would get involved, not leave it all to his wife. That had not been right or fair, though Claire had never complained. Then again, Claire never had a full-time job like Julie did, and it was a more traditional kind of marriage. And he was young and different then, too, he realized. Very different.

He had to admit, now that she brought it up, part of him would love to raise a child with Julie. He loved Kate with all his heart, but it would be different to have their own baby, a child they had brought into the world together.

But there was another reason it didn't seem right. The child he had already brought into the world.

"What about David?" Jack asked. "He needs my help right now, more than ever. I'm not trying to find more excuses," he assured her. "I just don't know if I can have another child until David is better. I let him down once, you know? I have to be there for him now."

"I know." Julie nodded.

"Maybe I just need a little time with this idea," Jack told her quietly. He reached across the table and took her hand. "That doesn't mean it's not ever going to happen."

"Fair enough," she said with a small smile. But he could tell what she was thinking. Julie was in her late thirties, and she was wondering if they would miss their chance. He sighed. He couldn't fix everything, could he?

"I promise I'll think about it. We'll talk again," he said quickly. "Once David is back on track."

"I understand, Jack. We're a family now, and I care about David, too. I want him to get better and start living a full life again."

"I know you do."

"You may have made some mistakes when he was younger, but you're doing your best now. You are making up for it. That's what makes you a good father."

"Thanks. I'm trying," Jack said.

The bell sounded down at the tree farm. Jack looked at

his watch. He was surprised they hadn't heard it sooner. He hated to just rush off and leave Julie this way, but there didn't seem much more to say on the subject.

She rose first and went back to the sink. "You'd better get out there. I think you're being summoned." She looked over her shoulder at him with a smile. A small smile, but it made him feel much better.

"Yes, it's time. A few more days of this, then it will really be Christmas." Before heading out, he stopped and kissed her on the cheek. She leaned into him a second, her hand on his hip.

They would work this out. There was very little he wouldn't do to make her happy, Jack thought, pulling on his thick work jacket and gloves. Including another run at fatherhood.

DAVID HEARD THE BACK DOOR SLAM, HIS FATHER LEAVING the house to open the tree stand. He rolled on his side in bed, just in case Julie peeked in to see if he was awake.

They had obviously thought he was asleep in here all this time. Or had totally forgotten he could hear just about every word that was spoken in the kitchen, his room was so close.

He had heard it all, starting with the pony debate. Leave it to Jack to think of that present.

The rest of the conversation had been less amusing. If he'd had any doubts about it the last few weeks, it was pretty clear to him now. His presence here was definitely messing up his father's new marriage and causing problems. He was an intrusion in their lives, plain and simple.

Though she was always very kind to him, Julie must resent him. In a short and difficult time, they had forged a good relationship, David thought. But what could she think of him now? If he wasn't around, she and Jack would be starting a family, and that seemed to be what she really wanted.

His joking suggestion to Gena of getting a car and driving

off somewhere didn't seem so half-baked now. It would be better for everyone—Jack, Julie, even Christine—if he left again.

Just like the last time, he had to get up and go, David decided. As soon as he was able.

GRACE AND DIGGER HEGMAN ARRIVED AT THE CLAM Box at a quarter to twelve on Monday morning. They wanted to be sure to beat the lunch rush, so they could get their choice of tables.

Tables by the window were always the first to go, Digger had reminded his daughter. He didn't care if they had to start with breakfast and sit there all day.

That would serve their purpose but probably draw suspicious attention, she told him. They wanted to see everything, but they didn't want to give themselves away.

Oh, it was a tricky business, Grace thought as they walked into the Clam Box. The red-headed Trudy had just started her shift, Grace noticed. She had made sure to surreptitiously find out the woman's work hours and already knew Trudy would be here.

When Trudy met them at the door and showed them to a table, Grace felt her heart jump into her throat. She was almost positive her father would give their plan away.

"Well, hello, yourself," Digger greeted the waitress. "How is it going for you? Having a good day?"

Trudy handed them menus, glancing at Digger with a curious but tolerant expression. "Okay, I guess. For a Monday."

"Oh, Mondays ain't so bad sometimes. Good things can happen on a Monday, too," he told her. "Good luck doesn't follow the calendar, you know."

Grace nudged him with her foot under the table. "Don't mind him," she whispered to the waitress. "My dad is getting on, you know."

"Oh, I don't mind. I think he's sweet." Trudy smiled and pulled out her pad and pencil. "Can I bring you folks some coffee?"

Grace felt relieved by her cheerful tone. "I'll take a cup of coffee, thank you. Tea for my father. We need a minute or two before we order."

"No problem. Be right back."

As soon as the waitress was out of sight, Grace leaned forward and spoke in a hushed voice. "Just calm down now, Dad. Not another word to her, or we'll have to go."

"For pity's sake, Grace, I didn't say anything wrong. She has no idea about us." He glanced out the window and practically clapped his hands together with glee. "Look at that car. It's a beauty, so shiny and clean. Wished we could have put a ribbon on it."

"There is a ribbon," Grace whispered, holding up her menu so nobody could hear them. "On the rearview mirror, see?"

"Oh, yes indeed, I see it now. Just perfect." He looked back at her. "What time did you say the messenger was coming?"

"I asked that he come at a quarter past twelve. But you can't be sure. He might not be exactly on time."

Grace had thought of everything. They paid cash for the car and put the papers in Trudy's name. Then Grace went over to Hamilton and arranged for a messenger to deliver their card, the car keys, and all the documents to Trudy here—while they were in the midst of their lunch, just like all the other customers.

Grace just hoped that if her father did slip up, nobody would notice in all the chatter and excitement that would surely follow Trudy's discovery.

"Twelve fifteen. I got it." Digger pulled his gold pocket watch from his vest pocket and checked the time. "We don't have much longer to wait, do we?"

"No, we don't, thank goodness." This one was the most

difficult so far. Grace was glad their generosity would only extend over Christmas. Playing Santa Claus with her father was a bit exhausting.

The bell over the diner entrance sounded, and both the Hegmans jumped in their seats. Grace turned to see who had entered. But it was only Reverend Ben.

He greeted her with a wide wave then walked over to their table. Oh dear, he wasn't going to sit here with them, was he? Not today, of all days.

But she couldn't very well refuse their minister.

"Hello, Grace. Hello, Digger. Mind if I join you?" Reverend Ben asked politely.

"Not at all, Reverend. Sit yourself down. We'd love to have a bite with you." Digger slid over on the bench seat to make room for the preacher.

Grace forced a smile. "We didn't order yet. Here, take my menu," she said, passing it over to him.

"Thanks," Ben said. "I've just been up to Southport, to visit Dr. Elliot," he reported. "I brought Lillian Warwick. She's staying up there all day."

"She seemed quite upset yesterday when she told the congregation about his heart attack." Grace had known Lillian most of her life. She could rarely recall the woman standing up in church to announce anything—good or bad—and had never seen her so emotional. After the service, during coffee hour, more people had commented on Lillian's reaction than on the poor doctor's situation.

"How is he doing? Will he need an operation?" she asked Ben.

"So far, the tests suggest he won't need any procedures. It seems to have been a very mild heart attack, which was very lucky for him."

"Yes, very lucky," Digger repeated. He grinned, and Grace could tell he was pleased to be able to repeat the word. "Well, I hope he comes home soon. Home in time for Christmas."

"Sounds like he'll be released very soon," Ben reported. "Maybe by tomorrow."

"Oh, that is good news," Grace said sincerely. She hated the idea of anyone being in the hospital over Christmas. And Dr. Elliot was such a nice man. He had been their physician for years before he retired and handed his practice to Dr. Harding.

Trudy walked toward their table, pad in hand, coming to take their order. But just before she reached them, the bell over the entrance sounded, and she turned to greet the new customer. Grace glanced over her shoulder, her heart thudding so loudly in her chest, she was sure Reverend Ben could hear it across the table.

It was the messenger from Hamilton, no doubt. He spoke with the waitress a moment and handed her a big manila envelope—the one that Grace herself had personally packed and sealed. Trudy signed the receipt, and he was gone.

Digger stared at Grace, his eyes bugging out of his head.

She forced a smile, silently willing him not to give them away in front of Reverend Ben.

"Looks like our waitress got sidetracked," Ben said, glancing at his watch. "It's slow in here today."

Digger just blinked, staring straight ahead. Grace sighed and drummed her fingers on the plastic-coated menu. "We didn't even get our coffee yet," she replied. "You can't blame that poor waitress. She has to take care of everyone. Charlie Bates ought to get more help."

"That's true. She does have a lot of ground to cover," Reverend Ben agreed.

Grace barely heard him, her gaze fixed on Trudy. She had opened the envelope, and now the key dangled from her hand. Her face was frozen in shock, her mouth gaping in awe.

Ben waved his hand and called to her, "Miss? We're ready to order?"

Trudy held up her hand. "I'll be with you in one minute, sir. . . . Just . . . one minute, please."

Then she dropped her order pad on the floor and ran out the door. Ben looked at Grace and Digger with surprise. "What was that all about?"

"She got a bee in her bonnet," Digger said with a short, sharp laugh. "Look at her out there." He pointed out the window. "What's she doing at that car? Running around it like a chicken with its head cut off."

Grace swallowed a lump in her throat. She didn't dare speak. Her father was saying enough for both of them.

Ben leaned over to get a better look. "Yes, I see her. Nice car," he said mildly. "Pretty color."

Grace nearly said, "Thanks. I thought so." Then caught herself. She just smiled. She had wanted a blue car for Trudy. She wasn't sure why. It was just the way she had pictured it. She looked out the window now, too.

Trudy had gotten out of the car again and was running back toward the diner.

Oh, dear. This was it. She nudged her father again with her foot under the table and gave him a warning stare.

Trudy burst through the door at just the same moment.

All eyes in the diner turned her way. Charlie Bates, who had been back in the kitchen, stormed out of the swinging doors into the restaurant.

"What the devil are you doing outside?" he demanded. "Don't you see we have a dining room full of customers here, waiting for their food? That service bar is loaded—"

"Someone gave me a car. A brand-new car. Well, almost new," she clarified. "But it's a good car. It even smells new inside and only has eight thousand miles . . . and the papers are all in my name . . . and here's the key," Trudy said, breathlessly, dangling it in front of Charlie's nose.

She turned around and faced the dining room. "Do you see that car out there?" She pointed out the window. "The blue one? Someone gave it to me. Just for nothing. Just to be nice. Can you beat that? It's just . . . amazing. I can't believe it!"

She had turned so that she was looking at their table now. She looked overwhelmed, Grace thought. The poor woman pressed her hand to her heart and looked as if she might faint.

Reverend Ben jumped up from the table and ran over to her. "Sit down a minute, please."

Grace was greatly relieved when he led her to another table. If Reverend Ben had sat Trudy next to her father, that would have been the end of it.

Another diner brought her a glass of water. Trudy fanned her face with a menu. "Was this an anonymous gift?" Grace heard Reverend Ben ask.

"Sure was. Must be the same person who's been giving people things all over town. Did you hear about it?"

"Yes, as a matter of fact, I have heard."

Trudy pulled Grace's card from her pocket. "Here's the note. See? No signature. They just want me to enjoy the car and drive safely. And to have a very merry Christmas. I sure will now!"

Ben took the card and looked it over. Grace feared for a moment that he might ask to keep it. As evidence. She didn't think there was anything about the card that might give them away. It was just a note card she had taken from a box in her shop, nothing special. But that's how people got caught, right? They didn't realize they had left a clue for someone to find.

All the customers in the diner were soon up and out of their seats and crowding around Trudy. Some asked to see the note. Others asked to see the car. Trudy went out to open it up and proudly showed it off.

"Hey, what's going on here? Don't you want your food, anybody?" Charlie chased after the crowd, carrying cheeseburger specials in each hand.

He carried the dishes all the way to the open door but

couldn't lure his customers back inside. The place had emptied out, except for Reverend Ben, Grace, and Digger.

Ben stood by their table, looking out the window. "The Secret Santa strikes again. Never seen anything like it," he murmured.

"Yes, he did." Digger nodded heartily. "You never know when it's going to happen. You never know to who . . . But we don't want any thanks. That would ruin it."

"What are you talking about, Dad?" Grace countered, quickly trying to cover up for him. She hoped Reverend Ben hadn't been listening to her father's rambling confession. The Reverend looked deep in thought, staring at the blue car and the crowd outside. She couldn't tell for sure if he had heard or not. She cast Ben a helpless glance. "I don't think he should have waited so long for his lunch. He seems a bit light-headed."

Reverend Ben suddenly looked back at her. "What was that, Grace? Digger not feeling well today?"

"He'll be okay." Grace smiled and rose, urging her father to do the same. "We'll just get something to eat at home, Dad. I have to open the shop."

"The shop. Right. We have to open the shop," he said to Reverend Ben. He stuck out his hand and Ben shook it. "You have a good day, Reverend. You know what I told that waitress when I came in here? I told her, good things can happen on a Monday, too. Luck doesn't follow no calendar."

"That's very true," Ben agreed, looking a bit puzzled.

"You're darned right it is. The proof is in the pudding," he said, pointing outside to the car. "The proof is in the pudding."

Grace tugged on her father's arm and finally led him out the door. They could have crossed the street, but Grace could not resist walking past Trudy's new car. The proud new owner still sat behind the wheel surrounded by a circle of admirers, asking her questions. A young man stood on the sidewalk, taking a photograph with a professional-looking camera. He looked like he was from the village newspaper, the *Cape Light Messenger*, Grace thought. Someone must have called them.

Grace twined her arm in her father's as they strolled past and headed back to the Bramble.

"I'd call that a productive morning, Dad."

"I'll say it was. And we haven't even opened the store yet." He glanced at her and winked.

Quite out of character, Grace winked back.

ON SUNDAY, EZRA HAD BEEN MOVED FROM THE ICU TO a regular room. Lillian had argued for a private room and even offered to pay the extra cost if his insurance didn't cover it. Ezra had laughed at her. "Why must I have a private room, Lillian? Will it speed my recovery in any way?"

"Of course it will. It's more comfortable. More civilized."

He laughed again. "Oh, now I get it. I think the privacy angle is more for your benefit than mine."

"Nonsense," she snapped. "You've just had a heart attack. You need your rest—peace and quiet—not extra germs from some stranger."

But he knew her well. Too well, it seemed at times. She abhorred sitting at a hospital bedside, and hated it even more when the person she was visiting shared the cramped quarters with some awful roommate and a huge, noisy family who paraded in and out, bringing in all kinds of germs, and pulling all the sitting chairs to their side.

If *she* was going to endure during this crisis, Ezra had to have a private room. Lillian was glad she had won the debate, too. Ezra had only been in the hospital since Saturday night, but she had gone to visit him faithfully. By Monday afternoon, she was feeling a bit worn out and welcomed the quiet in his room. She sat by the window and worked on her embroidery in the last of the winter sunlight while Ezra took a nap.

He had been taking a lot of those the last few days. His energy was low. It worried her. But he looked and sounded far better than he had when he had come in, so that was encouraging. The doctor would be by soon, she expected. He did his rounds just before dinnertime. Ezra was hoping Dr. Bourghard would say he could go home. She was not nearly as sure that he was ready.

Oh, he had given her a scare. She would never forgive him. She told him that, too. Of course, he just laughed at her. "You can't be mad at a person for having a heart attack, Lily," he said.

"Why not?" she wanted to know.

"You just can't. That's all there is to it. It's just not done," he added, mimicking her. He had found the debate quite amusing, though someone else might have taken offense, she realized. But that was Ezra. He argued and haggled with her, talked to her as frankly as anyone she had ever known. But he rarely took offense at anything she said. More likely, he found her most outrageous pronouncements entertaining.

That was why they had gotten along so well all these years, she knew. He was the only one who could put up with her—cheerfully, as if he actually enjoyed it. Her daughters put up with her, of course, but not happily. Not the way Ezra did.

She heard his breath deepen for a moment, sounding more labored. She quickly put down her sewing to check on him. He sighed and rolled to one side. It was nothing, she realized. He was still sleeping peacefully.

She returned to her chair and watched out the window. The sun was low in the sky, beams shooting out from between the clouds, turning the horizon peach and gold, blue-gray, and lavender. She hoped Ezra would wake up soon and watch this sunset with her.

"That's God in the sky," Emily had once said when she was a little girl. She had pointed to rays of sunlight, breaking through the clouds. Lillian had not contradicted her. It did seem that way sometimes, didn't it?

She had said a lot of prayers the last few days. More than her usual, by far. Not that she didn't pray. But these prayers were not the rote, routine variety. They had been more like . . . conversations. Desperate conversations sometimes, she had to admit.

Contemplating life without Ezra was very bleak. She did not want to lose him. She hadn't thought much about it before, she realized. Ezra had always been there. She had taken him for granted. But she thanked God for His mercy now, for sparing her dear friend's life. For His mercy on her, as well. For sparing her the pain of that loss when she, in her long life, had already lost so many.

No need to dwell on it, she reminded herself. Ezra was on the mend. He had passed all the prodding and poking and every possible test in the hospital with flying colors. There would be no operations. The doctor was very positive about his prognosis.

Just a scare, she reminded herself. She felt her eyes growing watery and pulled a tissue from the pocket of her cardigan. She didn't want him to see her crying. She was just tired, that's all. It had been quite stressful, these last three days. Quite stressful for her. Distracting, too. She had hardly given a thought to her own crisis, her battle with Emily and Jessica to stay in her house. Perhaps that was why she had thrown herself into the crisis so wholeheartedly. It had been the perfect distraction.

But no, she knew that wasn't the reason she remained at Ezra's bedside. She was here because . . . because . . . because it all boiled down now to just the two of them.

They had to stick together now. Reduced by age, two halves that made a whole.

If such a thing had happened to her, he would have done no less. She was sure of it.

Ezra stirred and blinked his eyes open. He stared at her, looking a bit confused.

"Ezra, are you all right?"

He nodded, pushing himself up in the bed. "I didn't recognize you for a moment, Lily."

"You didn't?" She began to worry again. Was he really well enough to come home?

"I knew it was you, don't misunderstand. But with the light coming from behind you like that, you didn't look any different than you did the day I met you, all those years ago."

Lillian shook her head and gave him a doubtful look. "Ezra, please. It must be the medication."

"Not at all, not at all. I promise you, Lillian. That's what I saw."

"I'll show you something. Look at this sunset." She stepped aside so he could see it. The sun hovered over the horizon, a glowing orange orb sinking into purple and lavender-blue clouds.

"My, my. That is something. Quite beautiful tonight, isn't it?"

"Yes, quite." Lillian agreed.

They watched it silently for a few moments, the room growing dimmer. Lillian felt a deep peace. And a flutter of hopefulness. Uncommon feelings for her anxious heart.

She glanced at Ezra, wondering if he felt it, too. She couldn't find the words to ask him though. Some emotions were too subtle, too fragile to be expressed in words.

Finally, when the light was nearly entirely gone, she heard him let out a long sigh and she knew he had felt the same as she did.

"I'm glad I woke up in time to watch that with you, Lily," he said quietly.

"I'm glad you did, too, Ezra. I was hoping you wouldn't miss it."

She turned to him and graced him with a rare smile. She was so glad in her heart he hadn't missed it.

CHAPTER TWELVE

$\smallsmile$

$\mathcal{D}$AVID TOLD HIS FATHER HE NEEDED TO BE AT PHYSI-
cal therapy a little earlier than usual on Tuesday. He said
that Gena had moved up his appointment. His father had
not questioned this change in the routine. Why would he,
David reasoned.

But after being dropped off at the PT unit, David walked
to a different building on the hospital grounds, the department of neurology, where a special test on the nerves in his
injured foot was scheduled for ten o'clock that morning.

He had undergone the test once before, right after his
second hip operation, when the numbness in his foot had
first occurred.

Gena suggested that he take it again—maybe because
he had graduated to the cane? He certainly hadn't felt anything in that area of his leg. For some reason, though, she
thought it was time to see what was going on with those
muscles and nerves. It was scary to ask the question. One
part of him didn't want to know. The chance was fifty-fifty

he would get bad news. But after thinking it over for a few days, David realized he was ready to find out—whatever the answer might be.

The test did not take long. There were some electrodes attached to his skin, and a machine recorded the information. The doctor read it immediately, and David was soon sitting in his office while he reviewed a long printout.

"The results are not conclusive," the specialist told David. "Your nerves are healthy, undamaged. So that's good. We can see some activity, more than in the prior test, but not at the level yet where you might feel sensation or have more muscle control."

"I understand that part. What about it getting better? How can I make the feeling come back—more exercise or something?"

The doctor sat back. "Unfortunately, that's the part that we don't know. Exercise plays a role but it's not the whole story, or the sensation would have returned by now."

The doctor took an X-ray out of David's file and put it up on a light box behind his desk. "See that? It's scar tissue from your surgeries, built up around these nerves here." He pointed with a pencil. "That could be the cause of the problem, what's causing the nerves to shut down."

The news was not encouraging. "So, there's nothing that can be done?"

The doctor turned to him again. "There is an operation we've been trying that's successful in some cases. It's exploratory. We don't know what we're going to find until we get in there. The results are not immediate, either. Once you have the surgery, it takes time to find out if it's worked."

Successful in some cases. Exploratory. Time to find out if it worked. This doc was certainly hedging his bets.

He must have realized he was dealing with a desperate man. A guy who would have put his life savings down on a thousand-to-one shot.

"When can I try it?" David said quickly.

The doctor smiled sympathetically. "I'm not done yet. You have to understand that the reason your foot lost feeling may be due to trauma to the nerves from surgery. In other words, the nerves might be in shock and with time— and I do realize it seems like eternity to you already—but with more time, a year or even two, they will reawaken and resume normal function. But if you have another surgery in that area, it could actually aggravate the condition."

David sat back, finally understanding why this doctor was taking such pains to explain the situation. "That's a tricky one, then."

"Yes, it is," the specialist said with a grave expression.

"I suppose there's no way to know how my nerves would react? No clue on the tests or X-rays?"

"Not much, no. It's pretty much a personal decision, David. Only you can weigh the risks and the consequences for yourself."

David reached for his cane. "Thanks for your time, Doctor. I'm going to think about all this. I'll call you one way or the other in a day or so, okay?" He rose, shook the doctor's hand, and headed for the door.

"Take all the time you need. And please call if you have more questions. Or if anyone in your family wants to speak to me, I'm available," the doctor added.

David already planned to keep this test and its results a secret from his family. He didn't want to get everyone's hopes up and then feel ten times worse if it didn't work out. He also didn't want this latest drama to be the focus of the holidays.

Jack and Julie had been working so hard the last few weeks, David thought. They deserved a happy, peaceful Christmas without any more distractions or focus on his problems.

This was one he had to figure out for himself.

* * *

A STEADY FLOW OF CUSTOMERS STILL MADE THEIR WAY to the tree farm on the day of Christmas Eve. It was all hands on deck, too. Christine had come in early, as she had to leave early to help her mother with their family party. Jack and Julie had been outside since morning, and even Katie was playing in the Christmas shop, so excited about Santa Claus coming, she seemed about to burst.

Since he had started using the cane last week, David had been coming outside to help, too. Though therapy took up most of his time, he managed to put in a few hours. The evenings had been a busy time this last week before Christmas, and he liked to think he had helped his father some when an extra hand was needed.

He had also been on KP, taking over most of the cooking at night from Julie. It just seemed natural that he would cook Christmas dinner, too. Julie had been working very hard, and David thought it was the least he could do.

He knew his father was a real meat-and-potatoes type. But for Christmas dinner David had decided to take a risk and surprise them all with a traditional roast goose. He had seen a big feast prepared step-by-step on a cooking show and had looked up all the recipes online, printed them out, and studied them carefully.

They would start with a salad of mixed greens, pears, blue cheese, and candied walnuts. The main course would be the roast goose with cherry and wine sauce, chestnut stuffing, roasted vegetables, and whipped potatoes. And for dessert, a whipped cream trifle.

Even Julie didn't know his plan. He had managed to get Jack to drop him at a gourmet grocery store on Monday afternoon, and he had done all the shopping. He had prepped all the vegetables last night, and tonight he would work on the stuffing and trifle.

But as much as everyone loved his cooking lately, his family seemed happy to have him outside, working alongside them. Especially his father. David acted happy, too, but inside, he felt blue. He knew these were not only the last days before the holiday and the end of the Christmas tree farm's short but glorious season. These were the last days he would be close to Christine and most likely the end of his stay in Cape Light, in his childhood home.

His mind was made up. Now that he was more mobile and fit, he knew it was time to go. He didn't want to tell anyone about this plan, not until after Christmas. He knew his father would be upset by the news, and probably try to convince him to stay. David didn't want all that to muddy their family celebration.

He tried to forget his secret plans and worries and just focus on being outside on a beautiful winter day, doing some mindless physical work. It was really fun to sell people Christmas trees. He had forgotten that part. Everyone was so excited to pick out their tree, especially the kids. Everyone was so particular about the size and shape they wanted. When you helped them find a tree they liked, they were so happy.

He couldn't deny that he loved working with Christine. He didn't even have to be close to her. He liked to watch her from a distance, her friendly way with people and the way she ran around the place with so much energy. As if she were doing the most important job in the world.

She had on a red knit cap today with a design of white snowflakes. Her hair was fixed in shiny braids that hung down to her shoulders. Her picture could have been on a box of hot cocoa, he thought.

They had not talked much since the disastrous shopping trip last Friday and had not been alone in the house much at all. David had gone out of his way to avoid her. He had answered her attempts at conversation with curt, one-word replies, brushing her off. As precious as he counted his minutes with her now, he still felt exposed and even humiliated by his stress episode.

Even so, he bought a Christmas gift for her in town. He'd had his father drop him off in the village one afternoon and he searched every shop until he found something just right. In a way, it seemed even more important now that he was leaving again to let her know how he felt. And to know that she would have something to remember him by.

The trick was to find a time to give it to her. David remained watchful, looking for his chance, but they never seemed to be alone.

Finally, that afternoon, it was time for Christine to go. Julie was practically crying as the two women hugged good-bye. "Merry Christmas, Christine. Thank you so much for all your wonderful help. I don't know how we would have gotten through the season without you. I hope you'll come back and see us sometime?"

"I'll come and visit," Christine promised. She bent down and gave Katie a big hug next. David knew that Christine had bought Kate a present and left it under the tree.

Katie was crying, but Christine tried to soothe her. "I just live down the road, silly goose. I'll see you all the time. You have to call me on Christmas and tell me what Santa left under the tree this year, okay?"

Kate nodded, still sniffing a bit. "Will you come back and babysit me?"

"I sure will. Whenever your mom calls me."

David knew Christine meant to keep that promise, and she would for a while. Her college was nearby and she lived at home. But she would be busy student teaching next semester and getting ready for her wedding. She certainly wouldn't be babysitting after she was married in June. Her whole life would change by then.

Christine walked away to say good-bye to Jack, who was in the tree lot, helping customers. David watched them from a distance as his dad gave her a hearty hug.

Then he saw her start to walk toward him. He felt relieved. She wasn't going to leave without saying good-bye, even though he had been pretty aloof and impossible the last few days.

"I'm going now, David," she said. She tugged on the strap of a knapsack that was hooked to her shoulder, then picked up a roll of pine garland.

"Here, I'll take that for you." David reached out and took the garland. "Where's your car?"

"Out in the lot. Near the road," she replied, without looking at him.

They walked side by side out to an area near the road where cars were parked. David was glad she had parked in a far corner, out of sight from any curious eyes at the tree stand, especially his father's.

Finally, they came to her car. She opened the trunk, and he handed her the garland. "Have a good Christmas, David."

"Thanks. You, too." He stared down at her and held her gaze. "So, is Alex home yet?"

She nodded. "I'll see him tonight."

"That's good," he replied, not knowing what else to say.

"Do you get any break from PT this week? Or do they just keep going?"

"No session Christmas Day. Otherwise, no rest for the wicked."

Christine smiled and touched his arm. "You've made good progress. You don't want to lose ground."

"That's right. I don't want to get lazy and backslide."

She met his glance for a long moment, then reached into her knapsack for her car keys. David reached into his pocket and pulled out a small box. The careful wrapping and bow had gotten a little mashed traveling around with him all day, but it still looked pretty, he thought.

"Hey, before you go. I just wanted to give you this. Merry Christmas," he said, quickly. He held the box out to her.

She stared down at it with such surprise, he wasn't sure

she was going to accept his gift. Then she finally reached out and took it and started to peel off the paper.

Part of him had hoped she wouldn't open it in front of him. Now he waited to see her reaction, feeling as if he couldn't take a breath. There was a velvet case under the paper, and she slowly lifted the lid. He almost didn't want to look at her face but couldn't help himself.

He could tell instantly that he had made the right choice. Her eyes lit up and a big smile spread quickly over her lovely face.

"Oh my goodness . . . a cameo. This is so beautiful, David." She stared at him in wonder. "I love it. I really wanted one of these. . . . How did you know?"

Success, finally. The first thing he had done right in months.

He shrugged, trying to make light of his detective work. "I noticed the way you were looking at them in the jewelry store in Newburyport when I got those earrings for Julie. I found this one in the Bramble. It's an antique."

"Oh, wow . . . it's beautiful. Thank you. That was so unbelievably thoughtful of you." Unbelievable because he had been such a nasty lug to her all week. That's what she meant, he guessed. Well, at least he may have made up for it a little.

"I have something for you but it's at home. I was going to drop it off tomorrow, or sometime during the week."

The idea that she bought him something too made David happy. But he wondered if he would even be in town by next week.

"That's all right." He shrugged and smiled. "I'm just happy that you like your present. . . . I need to tell you something."

"What?"

This was hard. He didn't know how to explain it without hurting her feelings or having her think badly of him. "I've decided to leave town. After Christmas."

"Oh . . . so soon?" She looked so disappointed and surprised. He could tell it wasn't what she had expected him to say. "Don't you need to stay longer for your therapy?"

He shook his head. "Not really. I can continue pretty much anywhere."

"Where are you going?"

"I don't really know." He caught her clear blue gaze a moment and then looked away.

Rerun of their senior year in high school, he thought. She had to be thinking the same thing: Wouldn't he ever grow up?

Before she could say anything, he added, "My dad and Julie have been great, but I need to get out on my own now. They don't need me here anymore, either."

"I see." Christine nodded, hugging her bag to her chest. She slipped the little velvet box into her knapsack pocket and zipped it up. "Well . . . good luck. I hope you find whatever it is you're looking for, David."

I did find it. I'm looking right at it, he wanted to say.

"Good luck with all your plans, Christine. With school this year and . . . the wedding."

"Thank you." She held out her hand, and he took it in both of his. But somehow, he ended up drawing her closer, his arms wrapping around her in a hug. Which would have still been all right, he thought later, if she had not hugged him back so warmly, so that he couldn't resist putting his hand on her cheek and holding her face a moment to look at her and then, kissing her the way he wanted to all these weeks.

He wasn't sure how long they stood there. But finally, the sound of a car pulling up nearby broke his trance.

He slowly stepped back and let her go. She stared at him a moment, looking sad and confused. Then she turned, got into her car, and drove off.

David felt as if his heart had been torn from his chest, attached to the fender of her car, and was now being dragged down the road.

He would never get over Christine, he realized. She had always been the only one for him.

LILLIAN KNEW WHAT THE PARTY WOULD BE LIKE, AND when she arrived, escorted by Emily and Dan, she found it very much to her expectations. Too many people, too much noise, too many sugared-up children, running around like wild animals. Later, when the herd of guests attacked their presents, she would want to hide under a table.

But she couldn't insult her daughter and son-in-law. She had to make an appearance, at least for a little while. Jessica, understandably, wanted to show off her new house. It was a lovely house, well built, too, as Lillian knew. She had financed most of it.

She recognized the usual suspects—Sam's sister Molly and her husband, Matthew Harding, the doctor who had taken over Ezra's practice in town.

They were the first to greet her. "Hello, Lillian. Merry Christmas," Molly said. "You look well."

"So do you," Lillian returned.

Molly did look good. Success agreed with her. She had made a good catch with this second husband, and her catering business was thriving. Lillian didn't care much for Molly's food, but others in town obviously did. According to Jessica, Molly was now thinking of opening a restaurant.

"Merry Christmas, Lillian," said Matt. "How is Dr. Elliot doing? I hear he came home on Tuesday, but I haven't been able to visit him yet."

"He is home but needs to rest. He can't have many visitors. He tires easily," she reported.

"Please give him our best," Molly told her.

"I certainly will, thank you. If you'll excuse me, I think I see my granddaughter, Sara, has just come in."

Lillian slipped past Matt and Molly, and headed for Sara, whom she had spotted at the far side of the room.

"Grandma, I didn't see you in this crowd." Sara ran over to her and gave her a gentle hug.

Lillian hugged her back. "When did you get here? Was the drive all right?"

"We came this afternoon. I wanted to help Aunt Jessica get ready, and we're going to stay over here. There's no room at Mom's house."

"There's room at my house," Lillian reminded her. "Your old rooms. I haven't rented them out yet."

She felt hurt that Sara had not asked to stay over with her. Was she so easily forgotten?

"I know, Grandma. But Mom said you were over at Dr. Elliot's a lot, helping him, and it might be inconvenient for you to have company."

"Oh, well . . . that's true."

Since Ezra had gone into the hospital on Saturday night, she had been with him every day. First visiting at the hospital, and then helping at home, though he did have his very capable housekeeper, Martha Fallon. But Mrs. Fallon was not exactly company, not someone who would sit and read the newspaper to you, or a good book. Or work on a crossword puzzle and argue about the news.

"How is Dr. Elliot? I felt so bad when Mom told me he was sick," Sara said sincerely.

"He's coming along," Lillian conceded. "He had a scare, and he must change some of his bad habits. I'm trying to help him."

"I can't think of a better candidate for that job," Luke said, coming up next to Sara. Lillian gave him a dark look, but he just laughed and said, "Merry Christmas, Lillian."

"Merry Christmas to you. Have you found any employment up in Boston yet?"

"As a matter of fact, Luke was offered that job at the New Horizons Foundation, starting up new facilities. He'll be traveling all over the country," Sara explained. "He starts next week."

"Really? Well, good luck. Don't blow it. It's obvious you're not that easily employable," Lillian added under her breath.

"Grandma, what a thing to say," Sara scolded.

"I'm just observing what I see." Lillian checked her watch. It felt as though she had been at the party all night. It had barely been twenty minutes. Jessica was bringing out more trays of hors d'oeuvres. It seemed the entrée would not be served for hours. Lillian hated that. She picked up a glass of ginger ale and sat down in a chair near the Christmas tree. Everyone around her was talking and laughing. She could only think of Ezra, all alone tonight at home. Even Mrs. Fallon was going to leave him right about now to visit her family.

He always came with her on Christmas Eve. Ezra was better at socializing, getting into the spirit of the thing. It helped to have him here, made it so much easier for her, she reflected. She wondered if he missed it this year. She hadn't even asked him, she realized.

"Mother, are you all right?" Jessica stood leaning over her, her hand on Lillian's shoulder.

Lillian looked up at her. "I feel . . . bad," she said quietly.

"You do? Do you feel sick?" Jessica quickly crouched down to talk to her face-to-face.

"No, not that way." She shook her head. "It's a lovely party, Jessica, as always. Christmas with all the trimmings, just like a magazine cover. But . . ." She took a breath. "I feel bad for Ezra. He's all alone tonight after his horrible scare. Just out of the hospital and—"

"You want to be with him, is that it?"

Lillian nodded, her chin trembling. "Yes, I do. I'm sorry. I don't mean to insult you. It's not very good manners to just up and leave a party."

Jessica stood up again and patted her mother's shoulder. "Don't worry, Mother, I'll find someone to take you over to Ezra's house. I'll pack up some food for you. Would you like that?"

Lillian brightened. "Very much, thank you. Nothing spicy, of course," she quickly added. "Ezra is on a very restricted diet. I imagine Mrs. Fallon has made his meal, so not too much for us. Just a taste or two."

Some of Molly Willoughby's specialties were bound to be on the menu, she guessed, and that woman had a very heavy hand with the spices.

A short time later, Sara and Luke delivered Lillian to Ezra's door. She had called ahead, and he was waiting for her. He opened the door and ushered her inside.

"A visitor on Christmas Eve. How classic," he said. "It's practically . . . Dickensian."

"Indeed," she agreed, slipping off her scarf.

"Did you miss me at the party?"

Lillian took off her coat and laid it on an armchair. For a brief moment, she considered telling him the truth. Then she decided that was just silly. No need to get all maudlin.

"Nonsense. I thought there should be someone here, to make sure you didn't go off your diet while Mrs. Fallon was out."

"Oh, so you didn't trust me alone with the trifle Mrs. Fallon made for me? All those layers of custard and cream."

Lillian was horrified. "She made you a trifle? Is that woman mad?"

Ezra laughed. "Of course, she didn't. I'm teasing you, Lily. She used to make one for me every year, but all I got tonight was an angel food cake and some sugar-free Jell-O." He made a disgusted face.

"That's more like it," Lillian said approvingly. "There'll be some coal in your stocking yet, if you don't watch yourself."

Ezra chuckled and took a seat on one of the couches.

"Would you like me to get you anything? A cup of tea?"

"Tea would be nice, thank you," he said. "But sit awhile.

Don't run off yet. Let's just talk. You look very fine tonight," he noted, as she sat down on the couch next to him. "I like that dress. It's very becoming."

"Oh, this is an old dress, Ezra. I'm surprised you don't recognize it. It's very warm, that's why I chose it. Jessica keeps her house cold as ice, though there's always a big fire going. I hear that all the heat in the house goes up the fireplace. It's a grand waste of energy if you ask me."

"I've heard that, too. But a big, roaring fire is so nice on a winter's night. Especially at a Christmas party. Aren't you sorry to be missing your daughter's big get-together?"

"Not really. So much noise and confusion, everyone talking at once. I don't find all that hubbub very enjoyable. Never really did. I know my daughter and her husband believe that they're superb at entertaining, but to my tastes, their parties are a bit . . . overdone."

"But you can't even tell it's a holiday over here," he pointed out.

"Perhaps, but I do take a special pleasure ignoring it with you."

Lillian's confession made him smile.

It was true, she did feel more comfortable in this snug little house, in this peaceful, orderly setting. Maybe she was past the age of enjoying family gatherings.

Or maybe it didn't feel right taking part in that sort of thing anymore without Ezra.

THIS WAS THEIR LAST BLAST. NOT THAT THEY'D USED up all the money. They still had wads of bills to spare, packed away in the freezer. Grace had kept a scrupulous account, and there was enough left to do this all over again next year. With some careful investing, they might even build on their capital over the next twelve months, she figured.

But she didn't see this as a year-round project. It took up

too much time and energy. No, it was solely a Christmas activity. And Christmas Day was here. The clock had just struck midnight. They had decided to wait until most people had gone to bed before giving out the rest of the presents. Though some of the gifts were sent by delivery services, there were still quite a few that needed to be dropped off.

"Do you have the map, Grace, and the flashlight?" her father asked as they left the house.

"Yes, Dad." He had asked her the same question for an hour now. He was stuck in a loop, it seemed.

"The van is already loaded with the packages, and I have the list, too, right here," she said, patting her coat pocket. "The route is planned out so we won't backtrack. But it still might take about two hours."

"Let's get going then," her father urged. "We have a lot of work to do."

The roads were slick from a late snow flurry. Grace drove slowly down Main Street, her father in charge of the list and their carefully planned delivery route.

Quiet as two mice, they crept up to dark houses and left their special surprises in empty mailboxes and on doorsteps.

Grace was surprised that they worked through the pile of packages so quickly and efficiently, and not once had they been interrupted. A few people had spotted them—a man walking a dog, a woman coming home from a Christmas party, two teenagers, walking hand in hand down the snowy street.

No one seemed to notice them, or think the sight of Grace and her father, dropping off gift boxes and shopping bags with bows on top in the very dead of night, was particularly interesting.

Funny how little most people see, Grace thought.

They still had a few gifts left in the back of the van as they headed back toward the village on the old Beach Road. Digger was reading the tags and telling Grace what was left. She checked each name against the list in her head. She must have been distracted when the animal—something big and fur covered—waddled out in front of the van.

She shouted out and swerved, trying not to hit it. And ended up running the van off the road instead.

They bumped down a short embankment for a moment, then came to a dead stop, the vehicle tipped to one side.

"Oh my goodness . . . Dad, are you all right?" Grace reached over and grabbed her father's arm.

Digger was hunched over, with one hand shielding his head. He sat up slowly and looked around. "I'm okay, I guess. Nothing's wrong that I can notice. What in heaven's name happened? Did you skid on a patch of ice?"

"An animal," she said simply. "A raccoon or a possum. I didn't want to hit it."

"How good-hearted you are. We nearly ended up wrapped around a tree." He sighed. "Well, no damage done. Let's get out of here."

"I don't think it's going to be that easy, Dad." Grace peered out the driver's side window. "I think we're stuck in the snow. The wheels are all at a funny angle. I'll need a tow to get out of here."

Digger slapped his knee. "Of all the luck. And it's two o'clock in the morning, bless me. How are we going to get a tow truck out here at this time of night? How will we finish giving out all those presents?"

All good questions, Grace thought. Before she could answer any of them, a sharp beam of light flashed in her eyes. She put her arm in front of her face and peered outside. She couldn't see a thing.

"What in the world?" her father muttered.

Then a face appeared at the window on her side, and she heard tapping on the glass. It was Officer Tulley. Was he working on Christmas?

She rolled down the window, happy to see him. "Oh, Tucker. We had a little accident. I turned the van quickly to avoid hitting an animal and just skidded right off the road. Can you help us?"

He stared at her, looking very surprised and confused, she thought. But this sort of thing must happen often out here. She had heard this was a dangerous curve in the road.

"Is anyone hurt? Should I call an ambulance?"

"Oh, no. We're both fine," Grace assured him.

"Just shook up a bit is all," Digger told him with a short laugh. "It was silly of her, really."

"And what are you folks doing out here at two in the morning? Coming back from a party somewhere?"

Grace was surprised by the question. Everybody in town knew they didn't socialize much anymore. Her father's illness made it difficult to be in large groups or unfamiliar places. Not that they had ever received that many invitations.

But now that Tucker had asked, she didn't know what to say.

"We were just out . . . taking a little ride, looking at Christmas lights," she explained. "Dad loves to see everyone's decorations."

"Christmas lights? At this hour of the night?" Tucker squinted at her.

"That's right." She nodded. "He couldn't sleep. It soothes him."

Tucker didn't answer. He peered into the back of the van. "Nice load of gifts back there, Grace. Looks like Santa's sleigh."

"That's nothing. You should have seen it when we started off," Digger bragged. "It was piled so high, she couldn't even see out the back window."

Oh, dear. That did it.

Grace watched Tucker's expression as he quickly processed the information. Tucker was not like most people, who didn't really listen to what her father said anymore. He did listen. He did try to make sense of it. He was making perfect sense of it right now, Grace could see.

"Come on out of the car, you two," he coaxed them. "This Secret Santa operation is busted."

Tucker extended a hand and helped Grace from the driver's side. She felt so embarrassed to be caught. "Oh, Tucker, you won't tell, will you?"

"Your secret is safe with me, Grace. But you two are headed home, so climb in the cruiser. I'll get you back to town."

Digger came out of the passenger's side, shaking his head. "I don't know. Doesn't seem right. There's a load of presents still to give out. Folks really need that stuff, too. We had it all planned. Old Mrs. Bartow needs that electric blanket. Her house is so drafty—"

"All right, all right." Tucker raised his gloved hands in surrender. "I get off my shift at five a.m. I'll finish the deliveries for you then. Will that do?"

Grace smiled. She had been worried about the same thing but didn't have the courage to speak up. "Thank you, Tucker. That would be perfect."

"That's the spirit, son." Digger patted the police officer on the back. "Even Santa Claus needs a little help now and then. Give him the map, Gracie."

"DAVID, WAKE UP! SANTA CAME. HE CAME!"

David opened his eyes to see Kate jumping up and down beside his bed in her pink flannel pajamas. As if the shouting wasn't enough, she was also clapping her hands.

"Come and see what he brought for us!"

Then she dashed off, a pink streak. David sat up and rubbed his head. He knew what the big surprise would be, but he wanted to witness her reaction firsthand.

He stumbled out of bed, grabbed his cane, slipped on his sweatshirt, and then made his way into the living room just in time to see Kate opening a big box wrapped in gold paper. Jack and Julie, both dressed in their pajamas and bathrobes, watched her intently. She tore off the wrapping in an instant and pulled up the lid.

She looked in the box and then stared around at all the grown-ups, looking terribly disappointed.

"What is it, honey? What's inside?" Julie asked her.

"It's feathers. A box of big white feathers," she said sadly. "Why did Santa bring me that? I told him I wanted a pony, not a broken chicken."

David had to hold his breath in to keep from laughing out loud. Jack leaned closer to his stepdaughter. "Hmm, let me see." He searched through the box, too. "Oh, look. Here's a note."

He pulled out a note, written in big block letters on plain note paper.

"What does it say?" Kate asked. "David, will you read it for me?"

"Sure." David took the note from her. "It says, *'Dear Kate, you have been a very good girl this year. I did bring you something special. Go to the shed behind the tree stand and you will find a surprise . . . and the Feathers you've been looking for. Love, Santa.'*"

She looked up at Jack and Julie. "Can I go outside and see my surprise?"

Julie nodded solemnly. "Of course you can, honey. We'll all go out."

"I'll grab some coats and boots," Jack said. David saw his secret grin. Jack couldn't help himself. He soon returned, and everyone slipped jackets over their nightwear and put their boots on.

David did the same. Anywhere Jack had stashed this pony was bound to be a muddy mess, he figured.

They tramped outside with Kate boldly leading the way. The early morning air was bracing, and David saw his breath come out in little foggy puffs.

The pony was obviously not a late sleeper. Kate's surprise must have heard them coming, and it neighed loudly from the shed behind the tree stand.

Kate gasped and stood stone still. Then she turned to Jack and Julie, wearing a smile from ear to ear, her eyes wide as saucers. "Did you hear that?"

"I did," Jack said. "What in the world is back there?"

The pony whinnied. Kate didn't bother to answer. She ran off, headed for the shed. Jack and Julie dashed after her, Julie pulling a point-and-shoot camera out of her jacket pocket.

David did his best to pick up his pace, and managed to reach the shed just as Jack walked over to help Kate open the barnlike doors.

The doors swung open. A white pony stood right in the middle of the doorway, as if it had been posed there. Jack had done a great job wrapping it, with a big red bow tied to the pony's green wool coat.

"A pony. A real pony!" Kate ran toward it, and it tossed its head and snorted. She quickly jumped back.

Jack laughed. "Wow, she's a lively one, isn't she? Here, give her this. See if she likes it." He conveniently pulled an apple out of his pocket, making Julie laugh.

Kate didn't notice. She took the apple and held it out to her new pet at arm's length. The pony craned her neck and, more or less, sucked the apple out of Kate's hand, gently, David thought, for such a big beast. She bared her big yellow teeth as she quickly crunched it down.

"Whoa!" Kate was astounded.

Jack laughed. He walked over to her and scooped her up in his arms, then carried her over to the little horse. "Here, let's pet her mane. Isn't she pretty?"

"Oh yes, she's beautiful," Kate said with a sigh. She leaned over quickly and kissed the pony's ear. The ear flickered and the pony shook her head a little, as if reacting to a fly. Kate wasn't scared though. She just laughed.

"I think she liked that," Jack said. "She just needs to get used to you."

"We need to make friends," Kate said wisely.

Julie had walked over to the pony now, too. David knew Jack had finally persuaded her with a story about a pony that was going to be sent to an animal rescue shelter . . . or worse, because an old couple in town had to give up their property.

Julie picked up a ribbon that was looped around the animal's neck. David saw another note taped to the ribbon and Julie pulled it off.

"Look Kate, another note from Santa. It says, *'This is your new pony. Her name is Feathers. Please treat her kindly. Love, Santa.'* "

Kate took the note and stared at it. "Feathers. I get it now." She grinned at Jack. "I can't believe I have a real pony, Jack. Santa is so nice to me."

Jack started laughing. "That Santa is a good guy, that's all I have to say. He must love you a ton."

"He is a really good guy," Julie agreed. She put her arm around Jack's shoulder then kissed his cheek.

They looked so happy together, the three of them and the new pony. David wished he had a hold of Julie's camera. The scene would have made a perfect photograph— one for next year's Christmas card, maybe?

One he could take with him, when he left town.

He was here with them but outside their circle. Partly by his own choosing, he knew. But it seemed very clear to him. He had made the right decision. He would leave here very soon.

Once inside the house, their attention turned back to the gifts under the tree. For everyone but Kate, who remained glued to the front window, where she could keep Feathers in sight.

Of course, nothing in Kate's pile of gifts could rival her new pet. But she was very pleased with David's presents, a big trunk loaded with costumes for playing pretend, one of their favorite pastimes while he had been here. He also gave her a picture book, *The Little Engine That Could*, an old copy he had found in his room and one of his favorites. He had read it to Kate again and again, and now she loved it, too. He had written a little note in the cover and hoped she would save it as she got older. Something to remember him by.

Finally, there was a special doll she had been asking for, a fashion doll with long blond hair that could be twisted and pinned into elaborate styles. Kate was fascinated by her, almost as much as she was by Feathers.

"I'm going to call her Christine," she said. "She looks just like her."

David could not argue with that observation. He thought so, too.

Jack and Julie also loved their gifts. Julie was ecstatic over her new earrings. He could tell she really liked them and wasn't just trying to be nice.

Jack was pleased, too, by David's generous gesture to his stepmother. He shook his head. "Pretty good, David. You put your old man to shame. I didn't get her any fancy jewelry like that."

David sincerely doubted Jack had skimped one bit on his gift to Julie, but he played along with the joke.

His father had been hard to buy for. David had picked out a corduroy sports jacket, not knowing what his father's reaction would be. Jack hated dressing up, but he was going to church nearly every Sunday now and socializing more with Julie than he had in years. He really did need something more than the old blue suit he wore for funerals and weddings, and the few "good" sweaters in his closet.

"Wow, look at this." Jack took the jacket out of its box and twirled it around. "That's sharp," he said, his highest compliment to clothing.

"Try it on," Julie urged him.

Jack slipped the jacket on, over his pajama top. He

modeled it for everyone. "Fits well," he said, checking the sleeves. "How do I look?"

"You look terrific," Julie said. "Very handsome. Doesn't he?" she asked David.

David nodded. His dad did look good in the jacket.

"I don't have anything like this. Not nice and new, I mean," Jack admitted.

"I'll say." Julie shook her head. "I've been trying to get him to buy a sports jacket like that for months. Thank you, David."

"You're very welcome," David said. All in all, his gifts had been a great success. He would have to tell Christine, he thought, as they had picked out most of the gifts together. Then he realized he wouldn't speak to her again before he left.

David's father and Julie had already given him the laptop, but there were still a few more surprises for him under the tree. A sweater, leather gloves, assorted books and CDs.

All in all, it was a great Christmas morning, David thought, the best he'd had in years. While he and Jack cleaned up the wrapping paper, Julie made breakfast. "Oh, look at the time," she said as they sat down to eat. "We'd better hurry. Church will be packed today."

"Coming with us, David?" Jack asked.

The question took David by surprise. Yes, it was Christmas, but he hadn't even thought of going to church. When he hesitated, his father persisted. "Come on. It's Christmas. Everybody goes to church on Christmas. You haven't been since you got back. It's a good day to . . . check in."

David assumed his father meant it was a good day to acknowledge his good fortune, his survival and return from the war.

Well, maybe that was true. But it was also a good day perhaps to let God know he would never forget or forgive himself entirely for what he'd had to do as a soldier.

David glanced around the table. They all seemed to be

waiting for his answer. "Sure, I'll come with you," he said finally.

It could be the last time he had a chance to go with them.

GRACE AND HER FATHER USUALLY WALKED TO CHURCH on Sunday mornings, unless it was bad weather. But on Christmas Day they had no choice. Tucker had left a message that their van could not be pulled out of the snowbank until tomorrow.

Worn out from their late night, they had both overslept. As they hurried down Main Street, Grace knew they were late and would miss the start of the service.

She also knew she was taking a big chance bringing her father to church this morning. Except for Tucker catching them red-handed last night, they had managed to keep their secret. Besides, Tucker promised not to tell, and Grace believed him.

But the pressure might be too great today for her dad. Over the past few weeks, they had both enjoyed the reports of the mysterious, unexpected gifts and how those gifts had helped the lives of their neighbors. How the unexpected blessings had given many new hope and inspired some to pass on the goodwill.

All that time, her father had sat silently, acting as surprised as anybody. But could he keep up the act today? She wasn't sure. She would be relieved when it was over—and a little sad, too, she realized. She had enjoyed playing Secret Santa more than she ever imagined. She knew her father had, too.

As the church came into view, she took his arm and spoke quietly. "Now remember, Dad, we have to keep our secret. No matter what anyone says today. You mustn't give it all away."

"No, no. Of course not, Grace. We got this far, didn't we?"

"Yes, we did." She had to grant him that. Just an hour or so more and they would be home-free.

By the time they entered the sanctuary, the service had begun. Just about every seat was filled, and a few people were standing in the back. Sam Morgan, who was a deacon, greeted them and guided them to two empty seats in the front of the church.

Grace hated coming in late. She felt as if everyone was looking at her. Well, maybe they were. Looking at her father, more precisely. Digger was a big favorite in town, and everyone they passed had a little smile for him—Sophie Potter and Vera Plante, Sam Morgan's wife, Jessica, and their children. Mayor Warwick and her husband, Dan. Even Lillian Warwick, who was usually so haughty, acknowledged their arrival with a regal nod.

Finally, they reached their seats but unfortunately, the places were not together. Her father was seated directly in front of her. Well, at least she could tap him on the shoulder if necessary.

Before she sat, Grace helped her dad take off his peacoat, revealing his special Christmas outfit—a red flannel shirt, a green wool vest, and over that, green suspenders imprinted with Christmas trees. The perfect costume for a Secret Santa, wasn't it?

She sat in her place, her fingers crossed under her program as Reverend Ben delivered a thoughtful sermon about the importance of keeping the Christmas spirit alive all year long. Very true, Grace thought. Even if she and her father couldn't continue the gift-giving at such an ambitious level, there were many other ways they could share all year round.

Finally, it was time for "Joys and Concerns," and Reverend Ben began to recognize the church members, inviting them to speak.

Elsie Farber rose from her seat. "I have another story about that mysterious gift-giver. Since my operation last summer, I've been struggling. I haven't been able to work full-time, and I fell behind in the mortgage. It looked pretty grim, got so I was scared to even pick up the phone. Then someone called and said I was all caught up on the mortgage with a few extra months' payments besides, I didn't have anything to worry about . . ." Elsie's eyes got glassy. "Well, it was that person in this church giving the presents, of course. I just want to thank you, whoever you are, from the bottom of my heart. I wish you would let us know who you are—even in private—so I could thank you properly. God bless you and keep you well."

Grace bit down on her lip then quickly checked her father for his reaction. He was staring straight ahead, his hands on his knees.

So far, so good.

Trudy, the waitress at the Clam Box, got up next and told about her new car and after her, the Kreugers, who received a new furnace. Then some others who had received small gifts. Suzanne Tuttle, a single mother, thanked the Secret Santa for bringing her son a computer. He was a smart boy, Grace knew, the type to win scholarships.

"Boy like that needs a computer," she heard her father say to the woman sitting beside him. Then there were some parents thanking the Secret Santa for toys that their children had found that morning, outside their front doors— toys those children had their hearts set on, but pricey items their parents couldn't afford.

"A surprise like that, well . . . it was really special. That's what Christmas is all about," one young father said.

Grace had enjoyed the toy shopping, too. *Oh, that was nothing,* she wanted to answer. *That was the icing on the cake.*

But she sat back and held her tongue.

"I agree with Elsie," the young father added. "We wish you'd let us know who you are, Secret Giver, so we can all thank you."

The testimony continued. Reverend Ben looked

astounded and truly moved. "This is just . . . unbelievable," he said finally, his voice thick with emotion. "As pastor of this church, I feel blessed to be part of this amazing expression of charity and Christmas spirit. Truly blessed.

"I am sure, my friends, there's no sermon I've given, or could ever compose, that could impart this message so powerfully. A message we should live by every day, not just at Christmastime. An example of faith in action we should all strive to follow . . . 'faith, if it hath not works, is dead.'" he added, quoting a verse Grace knew well from the second book of James.

She and her father had simply seen the need and reached out to help. Though she didn't give herself too much credit. So many times, she'd seen the needy but turned away or felt unable to help.

If their actions had served to inspire anyone here to do more good in the world, then that was an unexpected bonus, wasn't it?

Reverend Ben turned, about to continue the service, and Grace felt herself relax. Suddenly, her father raised his hand and stood up to speak.

Oh no! He couldn't spill the beans now, could he?

Grace stood up, too, and touched her father's shoulder, willing him to turn around. "Just a minute, Gracie," he said, as if she were a little girl again, trying to claim his attention.

Reverend Ben smiled at him. "Do you want to share something with us, Digger?"

"I do, Reverend." Digger stood up straight and smoothed his long beard. "I know who the Secret Giver is . . . and you all do, too—"

"Oh, Dad . . . please?" Grace tugged at his sweater vest, imploring him to sit down.

"Now, Grace. Just give me a moment."

Grace stepped back, realizing there was nothing more

she could do, short of tackling him and stuffing her scarf in his mouth.

"I know I'm an old man and I get confused sometimes. But think about it a minute." He tapped his forehead with his finger and gazed around at his audience. "Everything we are given in this life, the clothes on our backs, the bread on our table, the good work for our hands to do. The flowers in our garden or the snow falling on the ocean waves, so that you can't tell the water from the sky sometimes. The love of our dear ones, our families and friends. That part especially. Everything good comes from God, don't it?"

Her father had everyone's complete attention now, and they all nodded in agreement. Even Reverend Ben.

"All these nice presents you folks got," he continued. "Someone in this town went out to the store and bought them. Wrapped them up and snuck them on your doorstep. I'm not saying those boxes fell down from the sky, or anything like that," Digger clarified, making everyone laugh. "But the Secret Giver is no mystery. It was God who sent those blessings to ease your burdens and bring you joy. God, who heard your secret prayers. I know, in my old heart, whoever done it would want you to give proper thanks where thanks is due. To the One Above. And that's probably why that Secret Giver person feels better staying secret. They know they were just doing the Lord's work. More like . . . Santa's helpers, you know? Like the Reverend said in his sermon, like we all should be, every day."

The sanctuary was so quiet, Grace could hear the sound of her heart thudding in her chest.

"Thank you for hearing me out. Merry Christmas and God bless." Digger gave everyone a brief wave and sat down. So did Grace, feeling stunned.

Her father was truly one in a million. One in ten million. Here she was, feeling frantic that he was going to give them away, and he managed to cut right to the heart of all their hard work and good intentions. Yes, they had shown a generous spirit. But they had just been an instrument, expressing the intentions of some far greater power. Wasn't that the real truth?

Reverend Ben stood stone still, without expression at first. Then he slowly smiled, his eyes growing very wide behind his glasses.

"Thank you, Digger. From the bottom of my heart, thank you for that inspired solution to our Christmas mystery. I don't think anyone in this church ever needs to wonder about it again."

CHAPTER THIRTEEN

$\sim$

"NEED SOME HELP CLEANING UP THE TREE STAND?"
David asked Jack. They were sitting at the breakfast table,
the day after Christmas. Katie was outside, feeding Feathers her oats, and Julie was helping her.

"Oh, I'm not going to start in on that today. I need a break
from those trees. I'm going to put up some fencing for the
pony later on. Want to help?"

"I guess. Sure," David said, though he didn't sound very
enthusiastic.

Jack could tell David was feeling blue again and looking
for something to keep himself occupied. He guessed it had
something to do with Christine, but he didn't dare pry.

"Want to come for a ride with me? I found a good bargain in the paper on a saddle and tack for Feathers. Thought
I would go out and get it today. I know Katie can't wait to
ride her."

"Sure, I'll come. Where are we going, into town?"

Jack gathered up some dirty dishes and brought them to the sink. "Out to Angel Island. Remember that place?"

David laughed quietly. "I sure do."

Jack could tell from the sound of his son's voice that they were good memories, too. It was a fine idea to ride out there this morning. It was just what they both needed to clear their heads after all the fuss and excitement of Christmas.

Twenty minutes later, Jack and David left the tree farm in Jack's truck. He drove down Beach Road, turning left toward the bay side. There was a land bridge down one of the roads that led to Angel Island. It was not always accessible and was often covered by water after a storm or at an unusually high tide. Of course, some people took a boat out to the island, but in this kind of weather that wasn't too much fun.

"Will the bridge be clear?" David asked.

"Should be. There hasn't been any really bad weather the last few days," Jack recalled. "Not the most convenient place in the world. I guess that's part of its charm. There are going to be some big changes out here," he added. "The island has been named part of the National Seashore, or something like that. They're going to start a ferry service from Newburyport and improve the beaches. It's going to be a pretty busy spot next summer, I guess."

"Really? I can't picture it," David said honestly. "I hope they don't ruin the place. Its wildness is the best part."

"I agree. But a ferry is a good idea," Jack said as he drove the truck over the land bridge. Minutes later, they were on the island, following one of its few main roads.

"Where's the tack?" David asked.

"The fellow owns a general store," Jack replied. "Shouldn't be too hard to find."

"I think I remember that place," David said. "Remember when we used to camp here? Mom hated it. She would last one night in the tent, then we would wind up at that inn."

Jack smiled. "Your mother was a good sport. With the landscaping business it was hard to take real vacations in the summer. So this place was our compromise. We'd camp and hike around here. Sometimes we'd fish. You loved it. You thought it was paradise."

"I did," David admitted.

Jack was driving along a narrow road edged by stretches of open, grassy land interspersed with clusters of old cottages. A few looked occupied, but most appeared to be summerhouses only.

"Is this the way to the general store?" David asked.

"Could be," Jack replied cryptically. "I don't really remember. Hey, look at that. I knew there was something down here." He slowed the truck and pointed.

David looked out his window to see an old Victorian house, Queen Anne style, with bay windows on the first and second floors, a huge wraparound porch, and a turret.

The Angel Inn, the bed-and-breakfast they used to stay at, his mother's favorite refuge from soggy tents and mosquitoes.

"Remember the night we found this inn?" David said. "Our tent got blown away in a storm, and Mom was fit to be tied. We thought we were all going to sleep in the car. We knew the land bridge would be flooded so we couldn't even go home. Then we just drove a bit and here it was."

"Yeah, here it was. Your mom liked it so much, she never wanted to stay anyplace else." Jack leaned over to get a better look. "It's a little frayed at the edges, but it was once a beauty. Could be again, with some time, attention, and money."

"I wonder if it's still open for business?"

"Looks like it. I see a vacancy sign."

David took another look. He saw it now, too.

They drove on a bit more, just looking around at familiar spots. Some had changed, others had not changed at all. The farmhouse and barn were still there, as was the sheep pasture, a snowy meadow dotted with brown sheep.

Finally, they came to the small town center, where there was a small general store and an even smaller building with a large sign that read, DAISY'S TEA ROOM & LENDING LIBRARY. A few more commercial spaces all looked closed for the winter.

Jack jumped out of the truck and went into the store. David decided to wait outside while his father asked about the saddle.

He walked around and peered into windows. There wasn't too much to see, though the tea shop looked interesting. The room was filled with small tables, the wall lined with shelves up to the ceiling, brimming with books.

His father soon came out of the store, carrying a worn but reasonable-looking saddle. He hoisted it into the back of the truck then went in again and returned with the tack, a harness, and other necessary items.

Back in the truck, his father said, "Let's go out to that beach we used to like and take a look. I'm curious to see it."

They drove back the way they had come and then down a very narrow, twisting lane, where the beach came into view.

Jack parked the truck on the side of the road, and they both got out of the cab. It was a clear, cold day, and the wind off the water was icy cold.

David dug his free hand into his pocket, flipped up his collar, and followed his father. A narrow wooden walkway led out onto the sand. At the bottom, Jack turned to him. "We don't have to walk if it's hard for you."

"I can do it," David answered. He wasn't quite sure how well the cane would work in the sand, but he was determined to try.

They walked on the packed sand, above the shoreline. Jack slowed his pace to David's but not in an obvious way.

"So David, you won our bet. You got rid of the walker by Christmas," Jack said. "How can we celebrate?"

David still had visions of running the darn thing over with Jack's truck but didn't share the fantasy. "I don't know, Dad. It just sort of happened. Now I need to get rid of the cane."

"All in good time," Jack promised him.

David glanced at him. Jack knew that look; he wondered what was coming.

"Speaking of time, I need to talk to you about something."

"Yes?" Jack was already bracing himself.

"It's time I moved on, Dad. You and Julie have been great, but I need to get my life together and figure out what I'm going to do with the rest of it. That's not going to happen in my old bedroom at home."

Jack felt as though he had just taken a blow to his gut.

He knew this was bound to come sooner or later. He knew David had his own life and had to make his own plans. But it was happening too fast.

"I get it," he said carefully. "You need to be on your own. That's a good sign. But what's the rush? Why not stay a few more weeks until you feel really strong?"

"No, Dad. I can't," David said. "I'm ready now. I'm strong enough now. I know you mean well but—"

"I just don't want you to go so quickly, David. Or move far away again," Jack told him honestly. "Where are you going? What are you running to? You tried that once, son. I just don't see that it was a very good solution for you."

Jack saw David's face get that tight expression. He hadn't meant to criticize, but he knew David had taken his words that way.

"Is this about Christine?" Jack asked quietly. "I know she's engaged, but maybe you should still tell her how you feel. People break off engagements every day," he added. "If you don't put yourself on the line, she'll never know. And you won't either."

"It's not about Christine, not entirely," David answered. "I need to wipe the slate clean, Dad. I don't think I can do it here. And Christine . . . I can't do it if I'm still seeing her every time I turn around. It's not the main thing, but it doesn't help."

Jack nodded. It was complicated. He understood that. He

knew David wanted to have something to offer Christine, a solid future. Right now, he didn't have much to show. Jack could understand why he wouldn't fight for her. It was just too bad. Jack had always thought that the two of them were perfect for each other, even more so now that they were older.

He rested his hand on David's shoulder as they headed back to the truck. "I'm not telling you what to do, David. You're a grown man now. I have no right. All I'm saying is to slow down. Think things through. Don't just . . . take off. Get what I mean?"

David sighed as he pulled himself onto the front seat. He was relieved his father had not started some big argument. Maybe Jack really had changed. Maybe they both had.

"Yeah, I get what you mean, Dad. I have been thinking about this. I've thought about it a lot."

Jack didn't answer him right away. He stared out his window. "So when will you go?" he asked sadly.

"I'm not sure. Probably in a day or so. Don't worry. I'll let you know where I am this time," he promised.

Jack wondered if he really would. He had to trust him, though, and not nag about it. He had to trust that David would figure out the tangled knots in his life, that the boy knew what he needed to do.

Even if it did seem to Jack like he was running in circles.

EVERY HOUR AFTER THAT, JACK WONDERED WHEN DAVID would go. He wanted to tell Julie, but somehow he couldn't find the words. Two days after their visit to Angel Island, Jack woke up in the middle of the night. Or he thought it was. He checked the clock. It was still pitch-black out, five a.m. He wasn't sure what had roused him.

He listened, wondering if David had been having a bad dream and had been calling out. But the house was silent. Just the usual night sounds, the heating pipes rattling and clocks ticking. Julie slept soundly beside him, her breath slow and even.

He finally rolled over and went back to sleep. But the next morning, he was not surprised to find a note on the kitchen table, written in David's bold, square hand:

Dear Jack, Julie, & Kate,

I'm sorry I didn't say good-bye this morning. I wanted to get an early start (and you know how I hate a big good-bye scene, Dad). Thank you for all you've done for me these past weeks. I couldn't have made it this far without you. Especially not without my dear little Katie.

Don't worry about me, Dad. I'll be okay. I'll call or send an e-mail soon to let you know where I am and what I'm up to.

You all take care. Happy New Year.

Love,
David

Jack sat down hard on a kitchen chair, reading the note again and again. He would have rushed out the door, jumped in his truck, and chased David down, but he knew that his son was long gone.

Tears filled his eyes. He wiped them away with the back of his hand. He wanted to run back to David's room, to see if this was all some big mistake. He imagined seeing David's long, lanky form under the twisted blankets, his mop of dirty blond hair on the pillow.

But he knew David would not be there. The room would be empty now of his possessions, all packed in the big green army duffel.

They'd had some time together, some good talks. Jack

knew he had to count himself fortunate for that much. David had to make his own way now. That was all there was to it.

He bowed his head and said a quick prayer. "Dear heavenly Father above, please guide and protect my son wherever he goes, whatever he does. If he ever needs us, please help him remember we're still here and we love him."

DAVID HAD FORGOTTEN ALL ABOUT NEW YEAR'S EVE. The past few days, since he had left his father's house, he had pretty much lost track of time. Easy to do on Angel Island. In fact, it was almost expected, the reason a lot of people came here.

There was little sign of the holiday at the Angel Inn. But in the early afternoon, just as he was leaving for a walk, he passed a young couple, about his age or a few years older, walking in. So that made three guests staying here, including him. The place was getting crowded.

The couple looked happy together and he envied them. He thought about Christine, wondering where she would be tonight, what she'd be doing. Ringing in the New Year with her fiancé, he guessed, kissing him at midnight.

He pulled himself back from picturing that scene. He wasn't here to think about her, to wallow in his hopeless, pointless feelings. He was here to sort things out in his head. When he left the tree farm, he knew for certain he had to go. There was no question. He had felt so relieved leaving there, as if a giant weight had been lifted off his back, as if he could finally take a good, deep breath.

He had hitched a ride to town and stopped at the Clam Box for breakfast. It wasn't even light out yet, and the place was just opening up. There was only one other customer, a truck driver who sat nearby at the counter. Noticing the army duffel and David's jacket, the trucker struck up a conversation then ended up offering David a lift. He was driving north, making deliveries all the way to Toronto.

David quickly accepted. He had expected to hitch up to the turnpike before finding a good ride like this one.

"I just need to stop on Angel Island, then we'll get on the highway," the trucker explained as David climbed into the cab. "I have a delivery to make at the General Store."

"Sure, no problem." David clipped his seat belt, thinking the island would look interesting this early in the day, with the sun just rising and flocks of sea birds feeding on the shoreline.

It did look interesting. Beautiful and mysterious. David felt some static sensation in his mind clearing instantly as they drove over the land bridge and up the same road he had been on a few days ago with his father. They passed the inn and eventually arrived at the little cluster of shops.

The driver parked in front of the General Store and hopped out. David hopped out, too. He offered to help the driver unload his delivery, but the man waved him off. "That's okay. I just have to settle this bill. I'll be right out."

David wasn't really sure how it happened, what impulse had taken hold of him. Some people said the island held mysterious powers. Spiritual powers. Healing energy. There was some legend, too, but he couldn't really remember it.

Didn't matter. He wouldn't go that far, but the place always got to him, touched him deep down inside. He breathed in the sea air and instantly felt calmer. He stared around at the deserted road and past the few shops, all shut tight. He spied the beach and ocean in the distance, past an open stretch of land.

There was no sound but his own breath and some gulls, calling out on the beach. There was not a soul in sight. The silence and solitude, the early morning light illuminating the blue sky, it all seemed almost—sacred.

This was a good place, he thought. As good a place as any—maybe better than most—to stop and think. To sort out the questions that plagued him. To figure out some sort of plan.

The trucker had been confused when David told him he was staying on the island, but he drove David back up the road to the Angel Inn and David grabbed his gear.

"Good luck, soldier," the trucker said as David hopped out of the cab again.

"Thanks. I need it," David admitted.

He needed more than luck. He needed . . . a revelation.

The past few days, he had been hanging out, walking the beach, thinking things through. So far, he'd only come to one conclusion: Running away solved nothing.

Now, he walked along the water's edge, long enough so that the inn disappeared from view and the high bluffs came into sight. David knew it would be a challenge to climb the steep path up to the top, but something compelled him to try. He had been away from the PT sessions for almost a week. He didn't want to get soft, did he?

He struggled up the path, slipping back and even falling to his knees at one point. He used his cane like a pick, steadying his balance and levering himself up, step-by-step.

The climb was arduous, but for some reason, the effort felt like it meant something. Maybe it just helped him feel he had accomplished something today besides wading around in his own confusion.

The view from the top was astounding, an ample reward for his hard work. Dizzying. Amazing. Well worth the aches in his legs and hip. David took deep, gasping breaths as he turned his head to take it all in. The beach was far below, the waves moving in slow motion at this distance. Far off, he spotted the rooftop of the inn, a tiny white building, nestled in a clump of trees.

The very edge of the bluff was rocky but soon stretched out to a large flat meadow, covered this time of year with brown and yellow beach grass and large boulders.

Hadn't his father brought him up here once? David made his way across the field, toward a large flat rock, a good place to sit and rest. He seemed to remember sitting on the big rock once with Jack after they climbed the bluff. His mother had not come. She wasn't very athletic and liked to let Jack have his little adventures alone with his son.

David reached the boulder, sat down, and took a long drink from the water bottle in his pack. Yes, he had come here with Jack once, in the summer, during one of their family camping trips. He was sure of it now. He suddenly remembered something else about this place, something strange and interesting. Was it still here? Could he find it?

He stood up and began to search the ground.

Not too far away from the boulder, David spotted what he had been looking for. A path of rocks, laid in the ground in a spiraling pattern. He expected to find it hidden by the weeds by now, but it looked well used and carefully tended.

David remembered how, as a boy, he thought the pattern of stones was so strange. "Did aliens leave them here?" he had asked his father.

Jack had a good laugh at that one. "No, Dave. I'm positive they did not. Some people who lived here a long time ago laid the stones down."

David had been disappointed to hear that. But he still had more questions. Like what was the point of this place? What were you supposed to do here?

It was odd how clearly he remembered it now. "This place is called a labyrinth," Jack said. A labyrinth is not a maze or a puzzle. It's a circular path that winds to its center. "Some people come here just to slow down and find a peaceful moment," Jack had explained. "They come when they feel sad or troubled or have a question.

"There's no right way to do it," his father told him. "You can follow the path all the way around and walk in slowly. Or go right to the center. On the way in, you let go of all the stuff bothering you and try to open your heart. When you get to the center, you can stand there as long as you like. Think things over. Pray maybe. Some people like to trace the same path going out that they used going in. But I can never remember," Jack admitted.

"I do remember I was told that going out, you're joining God. Feeling healed from whatever is hurting. Going out to do good work in the world."

David recalled his father's words and also remembered that, at eight or nine years old, he hadn't understood very well. What did he know about pain and confusion at that age? About yearning for healing. For peace in his heart and mind.

Now he did.

He stared at the path of stones, noticing some visitors had left little souvenirs at the center, dried flowers held down by small rocks and even a few coins and bits of folded paper.

He did not believe that walking the path would instantly heal him or solve all his problems. But he had made it this far. Might as well give it a try, David thought. He used his cane to steady himself on the bumpy ground as he chose a place to start.

He paused and took a breath. He looked down at the flat gray stone at his feet and then out at the rolling waves and the wide stretch of slate-blue sky, where the afternoon sun was just starting to sink toward the sea.

Alone on the bluff, in the middle of the meadow, David felt close to something larger than himself, some power greater than he could imagine.

He began to walk the path, very slowly, putting one foot in front of the other.

NEW YEAR'S EVE WAS A HOLIDAY LILLIAN DISLIKED MORE than any other. So puffed-up and prefabricated. So superficial. The media pressure to be happy, to be gay. It positively turned her stomach. It was a holiday she ignored on principle. That was *her* New Year's Eve tradition.

Of course, she would spend New Year's Eve with Ezra. They were together nearly every year on that night, and this one would be little different.

Lillian had been spending almost every day at Ezra's and practically every night, too, since his return from the hospital. During the Christmas week, Mrs. Fallon was often visiting relatives in the evening, and Lillian thought it best for Ezra to have some company, just in case there were any emergencies.

They would get involved playing cards or watching a television show, and it would grow late before she realized. Too late to go home. So she had come into the habit of spending the nights staying over in the guest room.

Some people might gossip about the situation, she realized, but what did she care? At her age, being gossiped about was quite a feather in her cap. The live-in housekeeper made it all appropriate, Lillian believed, especially someone like Mrs. Fallon.

Lillian had never believed she could abide live-in help in her own house. But Martha Fallon was not like all the silly women—and a few silly men—Emily had sent her way. Mrs. Fallon was able and unobtrusive, and she had a wealth of common sense. You hardly knew she was there, yet she took care of everything so smoothly, so perfectly.

Mrs. Fallon was a jewel. Period.

For instance, she had left them a wonderful cold supper of steamed lobster before she left for her own New Year's Eve celebration. The table was set with real linen napkins and candles. Everything was taken care of, even the lemon slices for their water glasses, cut very thin.

Lillian had dressed for the evening in a blue crepe dress with her pearl and diamond earrings. She walked into the living room to find Ezra dressed up as well, in a dark gray suit, with a yellow vest and his red bow tie.

"Well, look at us," he said, handing her a glass of sherry. "Don't we look fine tonight, Lily."

"Not bad. You look very fit, Ezra. You have much better color than you did even a few days ago."

"Due to your excellent nursing care, no doubt."

"I've done nothing," she said, sitting on the couch. "Just hung around and beat you at Scrabble."

He laughed. "Can I help it if you know more words that contain Zs and Qs than the fellow who wrote the dictionary?"

"That's how you get the high score. You must learn to use your high-point letters." She took a sip of her sherry. "You're recovered now. You don't need me around anymore. I should be spending more time back at my own house."

"You sound unhappy about that, about the prospect of returning to Providence Street," he said with genuine surprise. "I thought you loved that old hulk of a house, and you prized your sovereign solitude. How does the poem by Dickinson go? 'The soul selects her own society, then shuts the door. On her divine majority, obtrude no more . . .'"

"Lovely recitation, Ezra. You must have won all the prizes at school. But let's not go dragging Emily Dickinson into it."

"Oh . . . why not?" he asked curiously. "I'd expect you would enjoy the comparison."

Ordinarily, she would have. In the past. The recent past even, Lillian realized. But since Ezra's heart attack, she'd had a change of heart. She didn't know what else to call it.

Lillian sighed and shifted in her seat. "I do love my drafty old house. But I must admit, I was feeling a bit lonely after my granddaughter left, and it seems a very dismal prospect to me now to go back, after being here with you all week."

Lillian was not one who confessed her deepest feelings easily. She was a very private person. But it was different with Ezra. She trusted him completely, more than anyone she had ever known. Even her late husband.

"My, my. Where is all this coming from?" Ezra asked, sitting down next to her on the couch.

Lillian shrugged. "I don't know. I'm not looking forward to being alone. I wish . . . I wish I could find someone like Mrs. Fallon."

"Oh." He sat back and put his hands on his knees. "Mrs. Fallon, I see. Is that what this is all about?"

Lillian nodded. "My life would be so much easier with the proper person around. I can see that now, what my daughters keep harping on. I wouldn't have to bother them all the time. I wouldn't have to move out of my house to an old-age home . . . if I could find someone like Mrs. Fallon."

"Mrs. Fallon is one in a million," Ezra replied evenly. "It's highly unlikely you'll ever find another like her."

"Yes, I know," Lillian said sadly.

"But take heart, Lily. I do see a way to solve your problem."

"You do? How, Ezra?"

"It's very simple. You can come live with me—and Mrs. Fallon."

Lillian sat back. "That's quite a proposition. What will people say? They'll be scandalized. Even at our age."

"Not if we marry," he pointed out.

Now she was shocked. Had she really understood him correctly? "Marry? You and me?"

"Yes, you and I. Don't you think it's time? I've waited for you for over fifty years. That must be some sort of record."

Lily pressed her hand to her chest. "Yes . . . it must be."

"You must know how I feel about you. How I've always felt. Why, I loved you from the first moment we met—"

"Ezra, please." She put her hand on his, hoping he would immediately cease this silly . . . nonsensical talk.

"Don't shush me, Lily. I've had a wake-up call. I've had a brush with mortality. I've bided enough time, don't you think? I must tell you how I feel, it's now or never."

She looked down at her lap. "Go on, if you must."

"I love you with all my heart and soul. I love you hopelessly. Helplessly. I know the best of you and the worst. I have no illusions. I love and accept it all. It would be the greatest honor and joy of my life if you would, at this late date, become my wife."

Lillian felt stunned speechless. She knew Ezra could be eloquent at times. But this heartfelt proposal was pure poetry. She was quite moved, unexpectedly moved.

"I don't know what to say," she began.

She had never considered it before . . . this wild idea. But these last few days, she had to acknowledge, something had changed between them. Something ineffable. Indefinable perhaps. After his heart attack and the long hours she had sat by his bed, keeping him company, watching over his recovery, they had crossed some sort of line, one she had not even been aware existed. But a line nonetheless, a line of . . . intimacy. For the first time she recognized feelings that had, until that point, been unacknowledged. Even unconscious.

Ezra's proposal had come as a complete surprise, but now that the words were spoken out loud . . . Well, it was not that much of a surprise really, Lillian knew.

Deep down in her heart she also knew she did indeed love Ezra. Had always loved him, too. Not the same way she had loved her husband, Oliver. But it was a type of love that at this stage of their long lives seemed even deeper, even more precious, and even more rare.

As for her sovereign solitude, Ezra was the one person who might share that sovereign space without intruding on her peace of mind. She had come to see that clearly these past few days. At this point, diminished by age as they both were, two made a whole, didn't it?

"Well . . . say something," he urged her. "What are you thinking? For a woman who is rarely without comment, you are most frustratingly silent."

"I did realize, or at least suspected, that you had feelings for me, Ezra," she began slowly. "But at this late date, I never expected to hear you reveal yourself . . . unless one of us was breathing our last."

"Good God, is that what you're waiting for? I certainly hope not."

"I didn't mean that the way it sounded," she clarified. "I'm taken by surprise, that's all." She took a breath then a sip of sherry. "If you must have an answer now—"

"Yes?" he cut in. "Go on."

"Then I would have to say . . . yes." She turned to him, her chin up, her lips slanted in a small smile.

Ezra clapped his hands together. "Saints be praised," he said. Then he cupped her thin face in his hands and kissed her squarely on the mouth.

Lillian sat back, gasping with astonishment. "Ezra . . . your heart condition. Let's not get carried away, shall we?"

"We shall, my dear. We certainly shall." He grinned from ear to ear. "We can live in your house if you like. I don't care. Whatever you please."

"What about Mrs. Fallon?" she asked carefully.

"Oh, she'll come with us. She's part of the package," he promised. He lifted his glass and toasted to her. "To us," he said, touching his glass to hers. "Happy New Year, Lily."

"Happy New Year to you, Ezra." She touched her glass to his with a contented smile. "You never know in life what's going to happen, do you?"

"No, we don't. But they say, good things happen to those who wait. I've certainly spent my fair share waiting for you."

"Well, it appears that you've finally got me," Lillian replied tartly. "I hope it turns out to be worth your wait."

"I'm sure it will be, all that and more, Lily. All that and more." He squeezed her hand and laughed. "What is the rest of that poem? Wait, I think I've got it. . . ."

He sat up straight and began to recite again, "'Unmoved,

she notes the chariot's pausing at her low gate; Unmoved, an emperor is kneeling upon her mat. I've known her from an ample nation choose one . . . Then close the valves of her attention like stone.'"

"Well done. I'm impressed." Lillian applauded him.

"Thank you, madam."

"And I have chosen you, Ezra. You are the one."

Ezra did not reply. He lifted her hand to his lips then kissed her palm.

REVEREND BEN HAD NEVER BEEN A VERY ENTHUSIASTIC New Year's Eve reveler. He had spent the holiday with his wife and some close friends. The husband of the couple was another minister, at a church in Essex. They had enjoyed some good food and drink, watching the festivities broadcast from around the world, then toasted in the new year in a very thoughtful, thankful manner.

Which was why he was able to get up early on New Year's Day and take a quick ride out to Angel Island. He had plans to see a member of his congregation who had been housebound this winter with a bad bout of bronchitis, Elizabeth Dunne, who ran the Angel Island bed-and-breakfast. A loyal church member, she had missed all the Christmas services this year, and Ben knew she felt bad. He had spoken to her on the phone but promised to visit her soon, and this seemed as good a day as any.

His other purpose for coming out to the island so early was not nearly so altruistic or pastorly. He was dying to try out the new rod and reel set his son, Mark, had given him for Christmas. Surf casting was still one of his passions, though he rarely caught anything worth bringing home. But he did love the rhythm of it, the challenge of bringing his mind and body in sync with the ocean waves. It was a kind of meditative exercise for him. Maybe that was why the fish didn't matter so much.

Once out on the island, Ben headed for his favorite fly-casting spot, on a stretch of beach not far from Elizabeth Dunne's inn. Low clouds hung over the island and shoreline, a bit of foggy mist in the air.

He parked his car, took out his fishing equipment, and pulled on a pair of long rubber boots made for wading into the surf that he kept in his trunk. Then he headed out toward the beach, taking his time as he walked through the sand down to the shoreline.

New Year's Day, in Ben's estimation, was the perfect day for complete rest and reflection, setting goals, seeing where you might have strayed off course, and making some corrections.

Ben felt optimistic about the year ahead. He had many plans for the church. Though his church was centered in its own wonderful traditions, it was important to keep a steady stream of new ideas and approaches to worship, to keep encouraging spiritual growth in his congregation. Most of all, it was important for him to keep in touch with them all, to understand what they were thinking and experiencing.

Sometimes he thought of this earthly adventure as an amazing lens. If you slanted it right and had some idea of what you were looking for, you could be graced with just a tiny glimpse of the other side, the divine.

You could see signs of it all around if you looked closely enough. In our joys and suffering. Hidden in the veins of the material world, in a tree leaf, or in a tiny white shell. He bent over and plucked up one that he spotted at his feet then studied it awhile.

Then he looked up at the long empty stretch of the shoreline and rolling blue ocean, the gray-blue sky above. Surely, this very spot could be a postcard from heaven, he thought.

But he wasn't alone on the beach, Ben noticed suddenly. There was someone else, sitting near the shoreline not too far away now. It looked like a young man, his arms loosely circling his knees that were drawn to his chest. Ben squinted into the sunlight, shielding his eyes with his hand. Yes, he recognized this boy. Even at a distance, he was unmistakable in that army-issue camouflage jacket.

Ben waved at David Sawyer and received a wave back. Then David rose, picked up his cane, and started making his way down the shoreline.

"Happy New Year, David," Ben said, stretching out his hand. David shook it and returned the greeting.

"Did you come all this way to go fishing, Reverend?" David looked amused, glancing at the rod and reel.

"Actually, I came out to visit a member of the congregation. She's been ill and I wanted to look in on her. She runs a bed-and-breakfast on this side of the island."

"Yes, I know, the Angel Inn. I've been staying there the last few days." David gave Ben a rueful smile. "I thought I was leaving town. I didn't get very far, did I?"

"No, you didn't. But maybe that's a good thing. What made you change your mind about leaving?"

"I'm not sure. Maybe I just needed to go someplace where I could think and get my head clear. It's hard to do in the house where you grew up. Too many ghosts or something. Sometimes I felt like I was a time traveler going backward, acting like I did when I was in high school. I almost couldn't help it."

"I understand." Ben nodded.

"I did figure out something important, I think."

"Really? What was that?"

"Oh, just about where I've been and where I'm going. And what happened to me in between."

Ben wasn't sure if he should reply. He sensed that David wanted to say more, and Ben didn't want to fill in the silence with a lot of meaningless chatter.

David picked up a stone and tossed it at the waves. Ben watched it skip twice before it sunk out of view.

"Where are you going, David? Any idea of that now?"

David glanced at him, then selected another stone from the sand. "Well, Reverend, here's the situation. When I left home the first time, after a few years of knocking around, I just wanted to know who I was in the world. I didn't have any handle on it. So I joined the army. I put on the uniform, I went through my training, I learned to take orders and do what I was told, to be a soldier. And I was a soldier. I was a pretty good one."

David took a breath. Ben could tell it was hard for him to explain this insight.

"Then my squad was hit and I had to come back. Once I took off the uniform, what was left? Not much. I thought I had figured out who I was, but it was just from the outside in, see?"

Ben nodded quickly. "I do see. I understand completely."

"I know now, finally, what I have to do. What I should have done years ago. I need to work from the inside out. Not just put on a uniform—a cop, a firefighter. Maybe it's even better I won't end up in a job like that. I don't want to just playact at something. It's got to be real. It's got to come from here," David said, tapping his chest.

Ben touched his arm. "You did figure out something important."

"I'm trying. I have a ways to go. There are things that happened to me, in country," he said, meaning in Iraq, Ben knew. "Things that I'll never forgive myself for, things I'll never forget. It's hard to put that behind you. I mean, I've seen guys come back fine. I wish I could be that way. I don't know what they do, how they manage to find that peace of mind, Reverend. How they can just shove it all in a box and put a lid on it."

Ben knew what David was trying to say. It was hard to live with himself after being a solider, after fulfilling a soldier's duties, doing what a soldier had to do just to survive.

David was turning to him for answers to some of the

most challenging moral questions a person might ever ask. Was there any forgivable, acceptable circumstance for taking another human life? Even in self-defense? Even in defense of his country?

"Do you pray at all, David?" Ben asked.

"You don't find a lot of atheists out on the battlefield, Reverend," he answered with a harsh laugh.

"I've heard that before," Ben said with a nod. "David, there's not much I can say to help you. Only that I believe God's love is truly without limits. If we truly repent and ask in sincere prayer, He will bless us with His mercy and forgiveness." Ben paused, wondering if the little wisdom he offered was getting through.

"The challenge in this life, David, is to forgive ourselves. Not excuse ourselves," he went on. "Not brush things aside and deny our actions. But to repent and accept . . . and then forgive."

David looked at Ben a moment, then back out toward the long, smooth waves rolling into the shoreline.

"We can't hold ourselves above God," Ben added quietly. "If in His wisdom He forgives, who are we to put ourselves above Him and say we know better?"

David didn't answer for a moment. He dug his hands into the pockets of his jacket and let out a long, slow breath. "You won't tell my father I'm out here, will you?"

"Not if you don't want me to," Ben promised. "Are you going back to the inn now?"

David nodded. "I was headed that way. It's getting cold out here, and I didn't bring any gloves."

"I'll walk with you. I can try my fishing rod out later, after I visit with Elizabeth. It looks as though the clouds are burning off a bit," he said, taking in the patch of blue sky that was beginning to open up ahead. "It might even be nice out here later."

"Yes, it looks like it's going to be a good day after all," David agreed. "A good first day of the new year."

* * *

ON MONDAY JACK KNEW IT WAS FINALLY TIME TO
clean up the tree stand and start the new year. Julie and
Kate had both gone back to school. The holiday and their
long vacation were over. He started the day feeding Feathers, cleaning out her stall, and giving her fresh hay. Despite
his explanation to Julie, a pony was more work than having
a dog—though he would be hard-pressed to ever admit it.
Besides, Kate was so thrilled by her new pet, it was worth
all the work and then some.

But even Feathers could not make up for Kate's sadness
over David. Jack hoped that once she started school again
and was distracted by her friends, she would start to accept
that her stepbrother was gone from her life, as quickly as
he had appeared. It was hard for a little girl. It had to be. It
was hard for him, too.

On New Year's Eve and even on New Year's Day, Jack
had waited and watched for some word from his son. It
seemed an appropriate time for David to get in touch and let
them know he was all right and where he had ended up this
time.

But there was no word, which had started Jack's year on
a sour note. Julie had tried to comfort him, but she hadn't
said too much. He had a feeling she was wondering how
David's disappearance would impact the baby question.
Jack didn't know, and he wasn't ready to talk about it.

Jack worked hard all day, clearing off the tables and pil-
ing up the leftover trees and greenery. It would take him a
day or more to toss all this stuff in the grinder and make
mulch and wood chips out of it. He would keep it on hand
for the spring and use it for his landscaping projects.

By the time Julie and Kate returned home that afternoon, he was beat. Hard work was always his cure-all for
emotional troubles. If he exhausted himself, it was hard to
feel anything.

They sat down to an early dinner of leftovers from Christmas Day, the feast David had prepared for them. There had been so much, Julie had put away a full extra dinner in the freezer. It still tasted great, but Jack soon lost his appetite. Another sad reminder, though nobody at the table mentioned it.

Jack was cleaning up the kitchen and Julie was upstairs giving Kate a bath, when Jack heard a knock on the back door. Before he had time to dry his hands, the door opened.

"Anybody home?"

Jack thought he had to be dreaming. He stepped toward the door, as if in a daze. "David . . . for crying out loud. You nearly gave me a heart attack."

"Sorry, Dad." David walked in and shut the door. He came into the kitchen and rested a hand on his father's shoulder. "I didn't mean to scare you. I didn't get very far," he confessed. "Not if you're counting mileage."

David quickly told him how he hitched a ride into the village, had some breakfast at the Clam Box, met the trucker, and wound up on Angel Island.

"So I rode out there with him and decided to stay. I'm not sure why. But it turned out to be a good idea."

Julie and Kate suddenly rushed into the kitchen. "David, where did you come from?" Julie asked, laughing. Jack could tell from her expression how pleased she was to see her stepson.

She quickly hugged David as Kate claimed the other side of the prodigal son. She climbed on a kitchen chair and practically choked him, slinging her arms around his neck. "David, I love you. If you stay with us, you can have Feathers, okay?"

David put his arm around Kate and held her close. Jack couldn't tell if he was crying or laughing. "That's okay, Kate. You keep Feathers. I'm not going anywhere for a while."

* * *

EVERY DAY AFTER HE MOVED BACK HOME, DAVID THOUGHT about calling Christine, but he was sure that her boyfriend was still in town, on his winter break between semesters. David wasn't entirely ready to face her again. He wanted to take care of a few more things, get some more ducks in a row, so he would have something substantial to tell her. Some proof that he was on the right track now, and it wouldn't be an act of utter, blind trust to expect him to amount to something in the world.

But on Friday morning, just after his father had dropped him off in town, there she was. Her totally real, completely beautiful self stood on the sidewalk staring at him. All he could do was stare back. Then she smiled at him and he thought it might be all right.

"Hello, David. You didn't leave town yet?"

"Yeah, I did. But I came back," he explained simply. He could relate the Angel Island adventure another time. "How was your holiday? Did you have a good vacation . . . with your boyfriend?"

Christine's smile faded. She looked out at Main Street, watching a bright blue car park in front of the diner.

"Oh, it's been all right. Alex and I decided to break up. That made Christmas sort of weird for me, I guess."

David's heart jumped in his chest. "What happened? Did you have a fight or something?"

"No, nothing like that. We just had some talks and decided things weren't, you know, right between us. We're going in different directions or something." She lifted her chin, finally looking at him again. "It's all for the best. I know I did the right thing."

David nodded. His head was bursting with all the things he wanted to say to her. He swallowed hard, not sure where to begin.

"So, what's going on with you?" she asked. "Why did you change your mind about leaving town—or did you just put that off awhile?"

"I got a new plan. I'm going to stay in town and start school," he told her. "I met with some counselors at the VA, and I still have time to register for next semester."

Christine looked surprised and impressed. "Wow, that's great. What are you going to study?"

"I'm not sure yet. I have to take a lot of prereqs to start. I know I like cooking. Maybe I can figure out some way to work that into the plan."

She smiled at him, her warm gaze making him feel good all over. "I'm sure you can."

There was an awkward pause. David realized if he didn't speak up, she was going to make some excuse and disappear on him. "Listen, you want to grab some coffee and take a walk or something?"

She looked surprised at the invitation but nodded. "Okay, sure. I'm not doing anything special today. I just have to return some books to the library."

"I have an appointment later to look at some apartments," he told her. "I'm going to move out of my dad's house as soon as I find one. They've been great, but I need to get out on my own."

"I think that would be good for you" she said.

"Maybe you could look with me? I mean, if you want. It's always good to have another opinion."

"Sure, I'll come. It would be fun."

It would certainly be more fun checking out apartments with her than without her, David was sure of that.

David bought two cups of coffee for them at the Beanery, which was on the corner of Main Street across from the village green and harbor. They walked across the street and entered the green. Reverend Ben's church was on the other side of the green, and the sight of it made David think of him and their talk on the island.

They sat on a bench facing the harbor. There weren't many boats in the water now. David liked sailing and thought he might get a little day-sailer and keep it here this summer. Christine liked to sail, too. She was a good sailor, he recalled.

"I have more news, too," he began. "There's this operation a doctor told me about, for my leg. They take scar tissue off the muscles where the nerves aren't working right. It might help, but it might not."

"Is it very complicated?"

"No, they don't even keep you overnight. But you don't know right away if it's helped or not. It takes time."

"Oh, I see." He wondered what she was thinking. He didn't like reminding her of his disability, but it was important to be honest with her, especially now.

"Do you think it's worth a try?" she asked.

"Yeah, I do. I'm going to do it, probably at the end of the month. Either way, I'm going to start school and get on with my life," he told her. "It's funny, it seems like just when I accepted that I wouldn't be able to walk normally again, I find out about this operation."

"Maybe that's a good thing," she said. "I mean, now you can deal with it, whether it works out or not."

"Yes, I think I can." He turned to her. "Could you?"

He waited a breathless moment for her answer, his gaze locked on her expression.

"David . . . I didn't care how you came home. As long as you came back. Don't you get it?"

David sat back, almost afraid to believe what she had said. "No, I guess I didn't," he admitted. "I was thinking too much about how I love you. And how I wasn't right—I mean with my injuries and all—so how could you want to be with me?" He could see his words had surprised her, too. "I love you more now than I ever did, more than when we were in school. I know I've been a mess, but I'm trying to straighten myself out. I just want to be with you. You're the only one I ever wanted. Do you think you could try again with me, Christine?"

Christine didn't answer him. She leaned forward and kissed him instead, her soft hand cradling his cheek.

"I never stopped trying, David," she whispered. "I know you have a lot to figure out, a lot to deal with. But I want to be there for you. I want to help you. You're the reason I broke up with Alex," she admitted. "I knew I could never marry him. Because I love you."

Those were the only words David needed to hear. He wrapped his arms around her and hugged her tight, burying his face in her long hair. Was he crying or laughing? He wasn't sure. A little of each maybe. He did know that the road ahead was long and would be rough for both of them.

But now that he had Christine, he could do it. He could do anything.

EPILOGUE

∼

$\mathcal{I}$T WAS EZRA'S IDEA TO MARRY ON VALENTINE'S DAY. Lillian was initially surprised by the notion. Then appalled.

"Ezra, you can't be serious. Oh bother, I think you are." She appraised his expression across the table. They were in the sunroom at Ezra's house, where Mrs. Fallon had just served lunch. They had decided that morning to start planning their wedding.

"We want to be married quickly," Ezra reminded her. "No need to wait at our age. February fourteenth falls on a weekend and is about a month from now, enough time to get our ducks in a row without dragging it out. A very romantic choice, I might add."

"I'll say. Positively sappy," Lillian replied. "It might be a dandy choice for a pair of swooning twentysomethings. But people our age?" She shook her head. "Most inappropriate and utterly embarrassing. I won't be made a laughingstock. People are already talking about us."

"When did you ever give a hoot what anyone in this town said about you? No sense starting now," he advised. "As for the date being inappropriate, I think romance is even more touching and sincere at our age. And rare."

Lillian sighed and tried to stare him down. It was no use.

So this was how it was going to be. Ezra was no pushover. Never had been and in the passing years, he had developed into an even stronger adversary. She could not cow him or win her way that easily. Which was probably why she had always respected him and at least part of the reason she was willing, at this late date, to marry him.

"Valentine's Day is the anniversary of a Christian martyr's burial, you know. The unhappy event was totally misrepresented and commercialized by some silly woman in the 1800s," she continued, getting in one last shot.

"I know all about it, another clever hoax of the greeting card companies."

He was making fun of her dislike for what she called "trumped-up" holidays.

"Exactly. National Turnip Day will be next," she insisted. When he didn't respond, she added, "I don't know why we're debating, Ezra. The church is probably already booked with a wedding on Valentine's Day. Why, people shallow enough to want it probably reserve the date years ahead."

"Very true. Quite likely." Obviously, it had not occurred to him. Lillian sensed the tide turning her way.

"More than likely, I'd say. I can almost guarantee it."

"Would you? All right, here's a proposition. If the church is free, we tie the knot on the misrepresented anniversary of the Christian martyr. If it's booked, you get to choose any date you like."

"I accept that offer," Lillian answered.

She felt certain of victory, but when she called the church a short time later, she discovered that she had celebrated too soon. The date of Saturday, February fourteenth was free, and Reverend Ben was happy to perform the ceremony.

Lillian related the news to Ezra with a glum expression.

"Valentine's Day, in all its silly, treacle-laden glory, it is," he said gleefully.

"So it seems. I hope you're pleased," she snapped. "Let's move on to the rest of the list, shall we?"

He had won, fair and square. No use arguing about it any longer. Even she could see that. Perhaps this was an omen of things to come, Lillian realized. Perhaps in Ezra she had finally met her match.

ON THE DAY OF HER WEDDING, LILLIAN SAT AT HER dressing table, wondering how she had ended up with a holiday for both of her marriages. Her first marriage, to Oliver Warwick, had taken place on Christmas Eve, 1955. Her family had forbid her to have anything to do with Oliver but he was so charming and determined, he had won her over anyway and persuaded her to elope. They were married in secret, in Boston's City Hall.

It seemed odd to Lillian, but on the day of her second marriage, she was thinking quite a bit about the first. She was pleased this time to be married in a church, a simple affair with her family in attendance. Ezra didn't have many relatives in the area anymore, though he did invite a younger sister, who was a widow now, and some nieces and nephews. He also had a few friends, mainly other retired doctors and their wives, who were happy to attend.

Lillian did not have any close friends, or even acquaintances, whom she wished to invite. The fact was, she realized, she was marrying her only good friend. The most loyal friend of her life.

Although she had been shocked by the idea at first, in the days after their engagement, marrying Ezra made more and more sense to her. She was completely resigned to the idea now, even pleased about it. She did love him. Why hadn't she ever noticed before? What a clever notion for them to be married. Why hadn't they thought of it sooner?

Though it seemed awkward and even frightening to make a new start at this stage of her life, it was also a great relief. The long shadows of age had been creeping up on her. So many times lately, alone in this big old house, she had felt herself staring into a dark wood, a wilderness that was strange and frightening. And there was no choice but to follow the path into that dark place. But with Ezra by her side, neither of them had to face the inevitable adventure alone. That was a great comfort, come what may.

She was thankful for this marriage, this second chance. At the time of her first marriage, she had felt swept off her feet, ruled by her passions and terribly unsure if she was doing the right thing. But today she felt not a single doubt. And in her heart, she felt blessed.

After she married Oliver, her parents had banished her from the family, disowned her. She had been able to keep in touch with her younger sister, Beth, seeing her from time to time. But Beth had died when she was a relatively young woman. That loss had been a great blow to Lillian. With Beth's passing, Lillian lost her only family tie.

When her parents were both gone and their grand house on Beacon Hill was sold, her brother Lawrence had sent her a few items. Among them, a set of pearls that had been passed down in the family for generations. Every bride wore the pearls, and her mother had often shown them to her but never let her try them on. "You'll wear these the day you get married, Lillian," she promised. "But not a moment sooner."

Well, she had never gotten the chance to wear them, though her two daughters had enjoyed the privilege. The blue velvet box now sat on Lillian's dressing table unopened. Lillian wasn't sure if she was going to put them on, after all.

What was the point? She was an old woman. What would it prove? That she was finally going to get it right this time?

Her parents had warned her that if she married Oliver Warwick, she would be sorry. Well, they had been right, in a way. But she had loved him truly, and most of the time, she felt no regrets. Nothing was as simple as it seemed from the outside, was it?

A knock sounded on the bedroom door. "Mother? It's me, Emily. May I come in?"

"It's open," Lillian answered. She patted some powder on her face, not really looking at what she was doing. She rarely wore makeup now and was having trouble remembering how it was applied. The foundation first? Oh, dear. She had forgotten that step.

"You're not ready yet?" Emily looked very elegant in a dark blue satin dress that crisscrossed over the bodice and had a banded waist.

"Here, let me help you with that—" Without waiting for an answer, Emily took the powder puff from Lillian's hand and dabbed on the powder in a way that made Lillian think she was about to have a coughing fit. Before she could protest, Jessica walked in. "Mother, we're all waiting downstairs. The cars are here. We thought you were dressed."

Jessica looked very lovely, too, she noticed. Also in a satin dress similar to Emily's but not exactly the same. They were both in the wedding party, but everyone agreed matching dresses would look silly at their age. This seemed a good, tasteful compromise.

"Calm down," Lillian told her daughters, who were now both swarming around her like satin-covered bumblebees. "I'm almost ready. They can't start without the bride, you know."

"Of course not, but let us help you," Emily said. For once, Lillian did not protest. Maybe she did need a little help. It was a big day, and her thoughts were wandering.

A short time later, her hair was pinned in place and her makeup done properly. She stood up, put her arms over her head, and her daughters slipped on the dress she had chosen—a champagne-colored silk slip covered with a layer of lace, decorated with tiny iridescent beads across the bodice, with long illusion sleeves. The dress was a simple princess style and fell just below her knees. Silk pumps and a fringed lace shawl completed the ensemble. Lillian had also had a small headpiece made from a bit of lace that matched the dress. Not a real veil of course, just something to indicate she was indeed the bride. When the side zipper was fastened, she stood up straight and appraised herself in the mirror.

"You look stunning, Mother," Emily said. "That dress really suits you."

"I knew it was the one the moment I spotted it in the window of that shop in Newburyport," Lillian replied. She had always had a good eye for style.

"All you need is some lipstick." Jessica chose a tube, and Lillian let her apply it. Her hands were shaking today; she couldn't risk messing it.

"And jewelry," Emily said, gazing down at the dressing table. "The pearls will be perfect with that dress."

She picked up the velvet box and opened it.

Lillian glanced at the pearls but made no motion toward her daughter. "I'm not sure about that," she said quietly.

Emily and Jessica stared at her. "Why not? I thought you were dying to wear these someday," Emily said.

"Here's your chance, Mother," Jessica prodded her.

"Oh, I don't know. I think I missed my moment with that necklace," she confessed.

The truth was, she had secretly believed her first marriage had been cast in an unlucky light because she had not worn the pearls, and it was too late now to make that right.

"But maybe this is the moment, Grandma. Ever think of it that way?" Sara stood in the bedroom doorway.

They all turned to look at her. Sara wore an ice-blue silk

dress that set off her dark hair and did wonders for her blue eyes. *I had eyes like that once,* Lillian thought. *I looked a lot like she does now, didn't I?*

"I'm sorry, what were you saying?" Lillian asked her. "So many people in here, talking to me all at once . . ."

"Maybe you're supposed to wear the pearls for *this* wedding," Sara said slowly. "That it was always meant to be this way, not for the day you married Oliver Warwick."

Lillian stared at her a moment, then turned back to the dressing table. "I never thought of it that way, I must admit." She gazed down at the necklace. Was she meant to wear the pearls with Ezra?

Well, anything was possible. Didn't this wedding day prove that? Lillian knew too well about unexpected turns in the road. But if there was one thing she had learned these past weeks, it was that no matter how we envision our life, no matter what we hope for, God often has plans so wonderful for us, they're beyond our wildest imaginings.

"All right. In for a penny, in for a pound. Go ahead, put them on," she urged Emily.

The pearls did look beautiful, resting just below her collarbone on the champagne-colored lace. Just the right touch, she thought, admiring her reflection in the mirror.

"Mother, you always said a bride is not a bride without pearls," Jessica reminded her.

"Very true," Lillian agreed. "And now, for the earrings."

She scanned her dressing table and finally chose a pair of pearl drop earrings with small diamonds on the studs. A gift from Oliver, on some big occasion, she couldn't remember now. She was sure Ezra wouldn't mind. It seemed fitting to take a piece of her old life along to start her new one.

A few moments later, she was led downstairs and then out to the cars. The ride to church went by so quickly, Lillian was surprised when she looked out the window of the limousine and saw the village green.

As the limo pulled up beside the church, her son-in-law

Dan ran out and pulled open the car door. "Finally," he said. "Everyone's waiting."

As they should be, Lillian thought. She sniffed and tilted her chin, then allowed him to help her from the car.

They regrouped in the narthex. Her daughters checked her hair and lipstick once more, and someone handed her a bouquet of white flowers. Gardenias, of course. The flowers Ezra had chosen for her so long ago.

Lillian had asked her two daughters to walk her down the aisle and give her away. Untraditional, but it did seem fitting. Emily and Jessica were, in fact, handing her over to Ezra's care, as much as any paternal figure might. Being flanked by her daughters as she walked down the aisle also allowed her to walk without her cane, another advantage to the role reversal.

The church was quite crowded, Lillian noticed, though they had only invited a handful of guests to the reception at her house later. Far more people had come to watch her and Ezra get married than she ever expected. So many of the church members—Sophie Potter and Vera Plante, Lucy Bates and the Hegmans, Molly Willoughby and her husband, Dr. Harding. Up toward the front, she saw Carolyn Lewis, the reverend's wife, and their daughter, Rachel. Even Dan Forbes's daughter, Lindsay, was there, taking time off from running the newspaper. And there were Jessica's two boys and her husband, Sam. Sam was holding her newest grandchild, a little girl named Lily Rose. Lillian had been surprised and even flattered when they had named the child after her, but she still wondered why they couldn't find a sitter for the day. She hoped the infant would not start squalling and disrupt everything.

My, my, she and Ezra seemed to be the hot ticket in town today. She smiled slightly and nodded at the familiar faces. She felt unexpectedly grateful to see them all here, though she suspected that most had not come on her account. After years of being the town's only doctor, Ezra was well liked. She was sure that he was pleased by the turnout.

When they reached the altar, her daughters each kissed her on the cheek, Emily on the right, Jessica on the left. Ezra met her and held out his arm. His blue eyes twinkled behind his spectacles. He looked very happy, she thought. As happy as she had ever seen him.

And as handsome as she'd ever seen him, too, dressed in a three-piece suit he bought for the occasion, a fine pin-striped navy blue with a vest, a stark white shirt underneath, and a burgundy bow tie. His silver gray hair—he still had a lot of it—was freshly cut and smoothed back flat.

The church had been decorated with thick white ribbons and more white flowers and greenery. Just the right amount, Lillian thought, festive but not too showy.

Reverend Ben stepped toward them, and smiled. "Ready?" he asked.

"I've been ready for over fifty years, Reverend," Ezra answered. "Please proceed with the ceremony."

Lillian saw the minister hide a smile as he opened his prayer book and began.

It all went by in a blur. Lillian soon heard Ezra speak his vows in a clear, strong voice and she repeated her own. He slipped a beautiful gold band on her finger, and she gave one to him as well.

"I pronounce you man and wife," Reverend Ben said. "You may kiss the bride," he told Ezra.

Her new husband leaned closer and gave her a heartfelt kiss. Lillian heard applause and even a few low whistles— her onerous grandson-in-law, Luke McAllister, she suspected. She felt herself blush. The nerve of that young man.

They received a final blessing from Reverend Ben, and music burst from the pipe organ in the balcony, a joyful piece by Bach that they had selected.

Everyone stood to watch them walk down the aisle. Lillian felt breathless. She pressed her hand to her chest.

"Are you all right, Lily?" Ezra asked quietly.

"Just getting my bearings. Perhaps I need my cane, after all," she whispered as she started down the long walk to the back of the church.

Ezra wound her arm in his own. "You have me to lean on now, dear. We'll do just fine."

Lillian glanced at him, surprised for a moment by his answer. He was right. She had forgotten. She had grown so used to managing on her own.

She tenderly pressed her hand over his. "We will do just fine. I'm sure of it," she said.

And she was, too.